BY KIM HARRISON

TROUBLE WITH THE CURSED

KIM HARRISON

ACE
New York

ACE
Published by Berkley
An imprint of Penguin Random House LLC
penguinrandomhouse.com

Copyright © 2022 by Kim Harrison
Penguin Random House supports copyright. Copyright fuels creativity, encourages
diverse voices, promotes free speech, and creates a vibrant culture. Thank you for buying
an authorized edition of this book and for complying with copyright laws by not
reproducing, scanning, or distributing any part of it in any form without permission.
You are supporting writers and allowing Penguin Random House to continue to
publish books for every reader.

ACE is a registered trademark and the A colophon is a trademark of
Penguin Random House LLC.

ISBN: 9780593437520

Ace hardcover edition / June 2022
Ace mass-market edition / May 2023

Printed in the United States of America

For Tim

CHAPTER

1

IT WASN'T EVEN TEN YET, AND THE CICADAS WERE ALREADY screaming in the hot, muggy air. Uncomfortable, I fidgeted, my sandals scraping the time-warped porch boards as I impatiently waited for Pike to pick the lock of the dilapidated Victorian he'd tagged as an unregistered blood house. It was stifling under the overhang and scraggly street trees. My camisole and shorts seemed woefully inappropriate to be kicking vampire ass in, but Pike had promised it was a five-minute thing. In, out, iced coffee and Band-Aids before noon.

Traffic was a distant hum, the bars and restaurants a comfortable two blocks away. It was a perfect location for a blood house where consenting vamps could finish out their evening or, more often, where others could hide from unwanted attention. Working on all levels, blood houses gave the highly charged, highly dangerous vampires a secure place to indulge and find refuge—often at the same time.

The age-old dichotomy didn't make sense until you saw it in action, but vamps, both living and dead, had an unfailing need to protect the distressed even as they endangered those they professed to love. When it went bad, the abuse went bone-deep, fueled by the trust these houses engendered. Why it was up to me, a witch-born demon, to ferret out and "gently" correct the problem was a long story with a short motive. I didn't like bullies.

Tired, I tucked a strand of hair behind an ear. The humidity was breaking through my anti-curl charm and the red mass was frizzing right out of my braid. "I thought you had a key," I muttered, and Pike, crouched at the lock, softly swore.

"Yeah. Me too." Pike's low, intent voice pulled an unexpected pulse of libido from me, and I shifted to put more space between us in the hopes he wouldn't notice. It was the pheromones he was unconsciously kicking out, not a real attraction. It didn't help that Pike wasn't your usual living vampire, his unerring, classic beauty still showing under a disturbing number of scars. There was a hint of gray in his short-cut hair, evidence of his early-thirties maturity. His light shirt and slacks were cut for ease of movement, his languid grace held a definite pull, and when his eyes went black? Da-a-amn.

But it was Pike's confidence that elevated him beyond the usual living vampire, and I was secure enough in my relationship with Trent to admit that he was . . . well . . . mmmm. Most vamps were confident on the outside, but Pike was truly comfortable in his skin. It set him apart, as did his numerous scars, most of which had been gained from his brothers trying to kill him as opposed to bedroom fun. Working under my protection was safer than him being on his own, but that's not why he had agreed to do it.

In contrast, my few scars were recent, almost hidden behind what passed as a tan for me. I missed my old ones—scars, that is—the ones that had real meaning. My almost-dormant vampire bite hidden under the curse-virgin skin tended to drive the undead wild, something that wasn't actually advantageous in my line of work.

"I got up early for this," I grumbled, tucking my sunglasses into my bag before gingerly sitting on the edge of the dusty porch chair. The residential street wasn't busy, and my eyes narrowed as I tracked the passing car, frowning as the black Crown Victoria parked at the curb.

Doyle.

Pike glanced up, his incredible senses attuned to my sudden unease. Doyle worked for Inderland Security, an I.S. detective now if I remembered right. That the living vampire was watching us break into an unregistered, and therefore illegal, blood house didn't bode well.

"So . . . did you ask me to help this morning because Doyle is following you?" I said.

Frowning, Pike returned to picking the lock. "He's not following me. He's watching the house. Same as I am." Pike's weight shifted as he tried a new angle. "He's probably waiting for us to do the hard part, then swing in and take credit for it. The I.S. wants this place shut down as much as we do."

True. I stood, hands on my hips as I stared provocatively at Doyle. Vampires were weird contrasts. The undead ones did ugly things thinking it was love, the living ones endured ugly things thinking it was love, but they both had a protective streak a mile wide. True, it was a little warped in the long undead, but *no one* liked underage predation, and that's why we were here.

Unlike the I.S., I didn't need three days on a missing person's report before I opened up a can of ass-kickery. So when Kip, Pike's number one, had failed to report in after tracking three missing teens here, Pike had called me. I didn't know the small woman well, but Pike both trusted and relied on her.

"You think Doyle will give us trouble?" I said as Doyle grinned, showing me his short but sharp canines as he took a picture of us. "We have probable cause."

"No." Pike frowned. His eyes lost their rims of brown as his pupils dilated, and the delicious scent of vampire incense rose in the stifling air, reminding me of when I had been younger and stupid. *Still smells good, though,* I thought,

a pheromone-induced quiver of angst and desire rising before I stifled it. Sensing it, Pike smirked. I liked working
with Pike, even if resisting his vampiric charms was often
a challenge. I loved Trent, but finding someone to kick
ass with was difficult, and Ivy had been stuck in DC for
months.

"Maybe I should have brought Jenks," I muttered, and
his smile vanished. But truth be told, I didn't need my usual
backup for this. It was part rescue, part reminder to a few
uppity vamps that the law was there for the living *and* dead.
Still, I was beginning to regret telling Jenks to stay home.
Standing outside a door this long looked unprofessional.

"You need some grease?" I said as I checked my phone
for the time.

"I've got this." Frustrated, Pike angled the pick another
way.

"I can check to see if there's a back door," I offered,
wanting a coffee.

"There's no back door," he said flatly. "Will you shut up
so I can concentrate?"

Well, excu-u-u-uuse me. I stood, going to the dirty window to put a hand to my face to peer in at the front room.
Jenks could have been in and out by now, verifying the
floor plan that Ivy would have dug up online somewhere.
But this was Pike's run, not mine. I was here to help. *If we
ever got in.* Frustrated, I checked my phone again, attention
returning to Doyle as I tucked it in my pocket. Damn it, he
was laughing. "Maybe Doyle has a key," I said sourly.

Pike exhaled heavily. "Yes. Why don't you go and ask
Doyle if he has a key."

Ooh, sarcasm! I'd had enough, and as the cicadas sang
in an irritating whine, I strengthened my grip on the nearest
ley line and mulled over which "find" spell would work
best. Nearly all worked on auras, and the undead didn't have
much of one unless they had just fed—and then it wasn't
even theirs. Most finding charms didn't work well underground, either, which was where this was going to end up.

I knew it. Many of Cincinnati's original homes had sub-basement floors, and this was one of Cincy's older "ladies."

The ley line slipped into me like sunshine, warm and tingling to my toes. I let the unfocused energy pool up in my chi, then spindled a wad of it in my thoughts before I let the energy find a path back into the ground and make me part of a circuit. *"Invenio,"* I whispered, feeling the energy take direction and the charm invoke. With the force of creation running through me, I opened my second sight.

Distorted as if by flame, the image of an open field in the ever-after wavered into existence, overlaying reality in a disjointed double vision. The front room became indistinct, almost like colored chalk lines. I wasn't exactly seeing through walls, but they didn't exist in the ever-after, and the effect was the same. Pike's aura was obvious beside me, but nothing else. The upstairs was clear as well. If Kip or the kids she was trying to find were here, they were downstairs.

"We're clear aboveground," I said as I let my second sight drop—and the image of an open field vanished and reality returned. I held on to the line, though, letting it continue to run through me like a second sun. "Excuse me," I said as I picked up the porch chair. Gut tight, I slammed it into the big front window. Glass shattered inward in a satisfying feeling of give, and then the chair rolled across the faded, crushed carpet to thump into the wall. Smirking, I reached in to unlock the door from the inside.

Pike slowly got to his feet, his dark eyes going from the broken window to me. "You are no fun when you're in a hurry, you know that?"

"I have things to do today." My gaze went to the black Crown Victoria, my brow high in challenge. "Maybe Doyle will get off his bear-claw-fat ass and either help or arrest us now."

But the vampire didn't move, watching us as he talked to someone on his phone. A faint but insistent tingling in my fingers became stronger. It had been growing since the chair smashed the window. *Charmed?* I wondered as I made a fist to drive away the uncomfortable sensation. It would explain why Pike had been trying to finagle the lock.

"Dual electronic- and magic-based alarms," Pike said as he dabbed the sweat off his forehead with a patterned, silk handkerchief. "They know we're here."

My attention flicked to the camera tucked under the porch overhang. They'd known the instant our feet had hit the worn floorboards. His "lock picking" had been a psychological ploy. As had been me smashing in the front window.

"At least we know it won't be ringing at the I.S." I turned to Doyle. "Hey!" I shouted, and his phone conversation hesitated. "You coming?"

Smirking, Doyle ended his call and settled back, pretending to sleep.

"My tax dollars at work." Pike ran a hand over his short, styled hair, smoothing it.

"Just as long as they don't cite me for destruction of private property and illegal entry and revoke my runner's license." It was the one thing I paid on time every year, ensuring I stayed a certified, independent runner. I'd been one now for over four years, one of a handful in Cincinnati, and certainly the most well-known. With that, probable cause, and a filed complaint, I had a reason to be here— though the busted window might be questionable.

"There's usually a door downstairs in the kitchen." His mood suddenly closed, Pike ghosted past me into the house.

I followed, my steps short to avoid the glass. Immediately I stepped to the side, pausing to get a feel for the place. I didn't like that there'd been a magical alarm, and even less that I'd tripped it. Jenks would have warned me.

Pike's shoes were silent as he vanished into what was obviously the kitchen with its faded linoleum floor and bland yellow cupboards. It was air-conditioned cool in here, but I left the door open for Doyle, scanning the faded wallpaper and scratched floorboards. What little furniture there was was old and mismatched, giving it the look of Early American College Student. There were no obvious cameras, but I knew we were being watched. Feeling sassy, I pulled my splat gun and checked the hopper in a show of defiance. The cherry-red, Glock-size, air-powered paintball gun was my go-to, but instead of paint, mine shot sleepy-time potions.

Oh, I had plenty of spells at my fingertips, but some whiny baby always claimed they were dark magic, which meant paperwork proving they weren't and possibly a visit before a judge for a show-and-tell. Besides, the potion-based spells in my gun were easy to break with salt water. Even the human-run Federal Inderland Bureau, or FIB, knew how. My spoken, ley line–based charms were harder to undo, and I was anything but accommodating. *Yeah. Right.*

My head came up at the sliding thump from the kitchen. "You good, Pike?"

"Yeah . . ." he said, voice strained, and I started over, my sandals clinking on the broken glass.

Nose wrinkled against the faint smell of vampire, I halted in the open archway. Everything in the kitchen, apart from Pike, was old and small—clean, though, as if just wiped down. The only window was shut and too small to easily wiggle out of. "Do you think they left?" I asked as Pike tapped the floor and walls of the broom closet.

"Perhaps." Pike paused, listening for an echo. "Kip tracked the vamp who'd been seen talking to the teens here. Either they caught her and she's being held, or she simply needs help getting them out. Either way, Kip wouldn't leave them. Not even to make a call." Frowning at the closet, Pike exhaled. "Hence me asking for help."

Head down, he put his shoulder against the fridge and pushed it from the wall to study the strip of grimy linoleum he uncovered. *No door.* I wasn't going to feel guilty for ogling his muscular shoulders as they bunched and moved in the effort. "Besides, Doyle is out there," he said as he easily moved the oversize fridge back in a hiccuping sound of plastic and linoleum.

"Bedroom closet?" I offered. "They know we're here, but they will ignore us unless we find the way down."

"Bedroom closet," he agreed. His pace slipping into an eerie, overly fast glide, Pike went for the bedrooms. Again I followed, my steps crunching on the broken glass.

Doyle was still at the curb when I glanced out the broken window, making me wonder if we might have stumbled on one of Constance's kickback moneymakers that the I.S. would just as soon ignore. But even the I.S. had to admit that me taking Cincinnati over from Constance was already showing benefits. The streets had been pleasantly quiet the last few months, like a held breath as you look across the room to someone you love or hate. Cincinnati's vampires were waiting—not to see if I had the chops to keep them in line, but if I would make good on my promise of a spell that would allow them to keep their souls when they died their first death.

Unfortunately the complex curse was currently stuck in FSCA hell. Apparently the Federal Spell and Charm Administration wasn't yet convinced undead vampires having access to their original souls was a good idea. Neither were the long undead in DC. And so we waited.

"Good God," Pike said, balking at the door of the overdone, black and pink bedroom with bleeding hearts, lightning bolts, and heartthrob posters, but I strode in, sure this was where the stairs had to be, at the heart of badass girldom. We only had to find them.

At his nod, I tossed my bag to the bed and stood eight feet back before the closed closet door, my feet spread for balance and splat gun pointed. His eyes shifting to a pupil-wide blackness, Pike flicked the closet door open with a vampire quickness. I tensed, but it was only a standard, empty four-by-six. Slowly my braced arm drooped.

"Thump it," I said, and he made a fist, smacking it into the walls and stomping on the floor until an echoing boom rose. His scarred, broken-nosed, tanned face turned to me in a smile, and I stifled a desire-born shudder at his small but very sharp canines.

"Fire in the hole," I mouthed, and he lurched out of the way.

"Corrumpo!" I exclaimed, funneling the ley line energy running through me out my fingertips. The curse-harnessed power left me with a delicious, inside-out feeling, the gold and red ball of magic slamming into the wall with an attention-getting *boom!*

I ducked, invoking a protection circle as the wallboard exploded out to send dust and chunks of wall everywhere. The haze flowed up and over me with only the faintest scent of plaster, and Pike waved his hand, squinting as he tried to see what we'd found.

But all we'd done was expose the metallic fire door behind it.

"That's not the main door, it's an escape hatch," I said, and he nodded, squinting as he ran a finger, lumpy from past breaks, over the inlaid control panel blinking a faint green. Again I wished for Jenks, making me wonder if I had gotten soft, or if I had ever been capable on my own. I relied on the skills of others too much . . . maybe.

"We should have brought Jenks," Pike said, and I spun, intuition and a soft shoe scrape turning me to the five really big men suddenly staring at us from the door. They were clearly living vampires, dressed in jeans and logo-emblazoned tees. Their fangs were small but sharp, and their eyes were pupil black. Each one was a marvel of muscle, each one built for hurt.

"Found 'em," Pike said as he dropped back and undid his belt. It pulled from the loops with an ominous hissing sound, running through me like ice.

"Gentlemen?" I offered as they filed in, each one barely making it through the door without having to step sideways.

"We've had some complaints," Pike said, half the belt now wrapped around his knuckles, the tail hanging like a makeshift whip. "You should have returned my calls."

But they said nothing, arraying themselves between us and the door. The window had bars on it. *No wonder Doyle didn't come in. . . .*

"Okay. We can do this one of two ways," I said as I leveled my splat gun. "One—"

They moved, liquidly fast.

I gasped, arm rising instinctively to ward off a blow. It struck with a shocking pain, startling me alive. Three went for Pike, and then I saw little else as I retreated, arm numb as I struggled to evade another hit. "Son of a pup!" I exclaimed as I brought my splat pistol to bear, but the two coming for me were too close. They'd simply dodge it.

Crap on toast, I miss Jenks. He never would have let me get cornered. My splat balls broke against the wall, useless. The potion only acted on bare skin, and I shot six more, making a nice dripping cluster but not hitting anyone.

I winced at the dull snap of a bone and low bellow, emboldened when two of Pike's guys rolled across the floor, tumbling into the wall, where they shook their heads and tried to get up.

Black eyes found mine, and then they came at me again. "Off!" I shouted when thick arms encircled me, and then I gasped when the air was suddenly squished from my lungs.

His teeth were way too close. I fought him, my splat gun hitting the floor as I kicked out at the second man, using the one holding me as leverage. The first wouldn't let go, but he'd eased his grip when my feet thumped into the second, and I got a breath of air as he stumbled from me.

"This is Rachel Morgan?" the vamp holding me said as his buddy got up and touched his lip to find it bleeding. "The demon subrosa? She's smaller than I thought she'd be."

"And you," I panted as I readied a massive amount of ley line energy, "are dumber than evolution allows. Let *go*!"

Twisting, I jabbed my elbow and stomped on his foot— just for fun—and when his weight shifted, my feet planted themselves solidly and I wrenched his arm, sending him over my crouched back to slam into the wall and my still-dripping smears of potion.

The man let out a yelp of surprise, and then the spell soaked through his shirt. As Pike howled exuberantly and snapped more bones, my attacker collapsed, out cold. Chest hurting, I limped to get my splat gun.

I never made it, yelping as the other guy dragged me

away. I was caught from behind in a bear hug again. *Crap on toast, how many times does a girl have to say no?*

"You want some help?" Pike said, and I grimaced, blowing the hair out of my face as the guy lifted me up, squeezing the breath out of me again. Pike had his three men cornered and bleeding, cautious now that they had bones breaking the skin, their blood making the floor slick. They had to be hopped up on something, as they gathered themselves and rushed him together. Pike moved in a blur, belt smacking bare skin to make them jump and his knuckles doing damage. He spun like a dancer, sending them crashing into the walls before turning to me.

"I got this," I gasped, then funneled the ley line into the man holding me.

The vampire screamed in shock. My crushed ribs rebounded. Gasping, I flailed my arms as I found myself hurling through the air until I hit the floor with a pained grunt.

"Ow . . ." I whispered, arm throbbing. The man I'd just jolted was hunched, staring at me as if I had broken a rule. There was no rule here, and I stood, pulling more ley line energy into me until my hands glowed and the tips of my hair began to float.

"You. Settle down!" I shouted. "What's the code for downstairs?"

His black eyes suddenly wide in fear, he launched himself at me again. He was more afraid of his master than us. *I can fix that. . . .*

I dove for my splat gun, arm warming with a floor burn as I grabbed it, spinning to plug him dead in the face.

He howled and pawed at his eyes . . . and then he fell on me, out cold.

His weight hit me hard, pinning me. *Damn it all to the Turn and back!* I thought, struggling to push him off. One of Pike's guys tripped over him and fell, and I downed him, too, before wiggling out and standing up.

"Put 'em down!" I shouted, my good mood spoiled. "I'm not here so you can play!"

Pike grinned at me from across the broken room. He

was hunched and in pain, but clearly getting the better of the last two facing him. I'd once seen him flat out kill five assassins in as many minutes, but it was hot, and I had things to do. "I lost my gym membership last week," he said, attacking with his belt before grabbing the vanity's chair and brandishing it like a lion tamer. We had three of the five down, and if they hadn't sent anyone else up, they probably didn't have anyone.

My phone, I realized, was humming, and as Pike gleefully snapped his belt and busted the frilly chair over the arm of one of his attackers, I dropped back to glance at it.

Ivy! I thought in pleasure, wanting to take the call. "Do your cardio on your own time," I said, gathering myself to wrap this up fast. My phone hummed again as I pulled on the line and focused on first one, then the other. *"Stabils! Stabils!"* I exclaimed, shuddering at the twin bursts of line energy flowing through me as it hit first one, then the other. Hodin claimed there was a way for the curse to act on them at the same time, but I hadn't found the knack.

"Hey!" Pike exclaimed as they fell in turn, the one still in Pike's grip almost dragging him down. "How am I supposed to beat the door code out of them when they're out cold?"

"They can still talk. Beat away," I said as the two vampires began swearing. One was facedown on the floor, the other now staring at the ceiling with his leg awkwardly pinned under him.

Rubbing my bruised ribs, I hit accept and Ivy's low voice rose in greeting.

Immediately I felt my body relax. "Hey, Ivy. How you doing?" I said as Pike stood domineeringly over the two downed men. My breath was fast, and I flexed my sore arm, glad it wasn't broken.

"Good," she said, her voice like living dust, silky and gray. "You sound busy. Is this a bad time?"

I glanced at Pike manhandling the thugs upright, none too gentle as he slammed their heads into the walls to get them to pay attention. "No, you're good. I'm helping Pike with some underage predation. He's done playing." My voice rose. "Right?" I said loudly, and Pike made a "maybe" gesture.

"Door code!" he shouted, and the two spat empty threats.

"I can call back," Ivy said. "But it won't take long if you have a sec."

Sore, I rested my butt on the windowsill and reclined against the bars, careful to stay out of the sleepy-time potion. The room was in shambles, and I nudged the torn canopy off the air duct in the hopes of some cool air. There were pillow feathers everywhere, looking like falling snow as they settled. "What's up? Everything okay with you and Nina?"

Pike smacked one of the vampires hard enough to split his lip. "Where's Kip?" he demanded, eyes black. "Little thing. Short blond hair. Likes the color red."

"Never saw her." The vampire sneered. "Go bleed yourself."

"We're fine," Ivy said. "She's wreaking havoc with the old undead, but it's a good thing. I'm going to be in Cincy tomorrow night. I'm hoping more than a visit, but that depends on what the master vampire I'm escorting thinks."

She's coming home? But my elation hesitated. "Master vampire?" I asked.

I could almost see her wince, her pale, oval face scrunching. "The DC undead know that Constance isn't running Cincy," she said, and I slumped. Pike's gaze rose, finding mine as he paused his interrogations. "They think she's twice dead and that you are responsible for it."

"Imagine that," I muttered. The distasteful, psychotic, narcissistic vampire *was* alive. She was a mouse, but she was alive, kept in a very nice cage in Piscary's old quarters where the light couldn't reach her. "Would it help if Hodin put in an appearance as her again?"

I wasn't exactly thrilled about asking him. The first time, I'd had to give him six months rent free in the church in exchange for ten minutes of his time. He'd been an okay roomie, but I didn't like the vibe I was getting between him and my other roommate Stef. I was already counting the days until our deal was up and he was gone. *Al might talk to me again, too. . . .*

"Probably not," Ivy said. "This guy knows her. An old undead named Finnis. He's the reason for half her hang-ups, and he'll be able to tell if it's not her. Rachel, if you can't produce Constance, they'll assume she's twice dead and press charges. Body or no."

I ran a hand over my snarled hair and sighed, startled when I found a pillow feather. "I don't know what their problem is," I said, ogling Pike's shoulders as he resumed harassing the vampires. "Pike and I are maintaining order just fine."

"Maybe that's it," Ivy said, and Pike began a rhythmic punching, his fist thumping into one, then the other in a cringeworthy assault set to his hummed tune of "Frog Went A-Courting." *Weird.* "They're not happy you can do the job. It makes them look bad and opens the door for other powers to oversee their own people."

My head bobbed in understanding. Pike was probably making progress, but it was hard to tell. Until he managed to best the pheromones turning their pain into pleasure, they wouldn't care how much he beat them.

"Hey, tell Pike to threaten to break a fang," Ivy said suddenly, clearly overhearing Pike. "That usually brings good results when they are hopped up on Brimstone and phero-mones."

I glanced at Pike, and as he straightened with a shrug of shoulders, I stretched for the broken chair leg, tossing it to land in his grip with a solid *thump*.

Without hesitation, Pike jabbed it into the larger man's face. The vampire howled, blood gushing as the other stared in horror. Pike had done the unthinkable by damag-ing the one thing his undead master valued above all else.

"Ooh, Pike," I said, cringing as the blood flowed.

"I said threaten, not do," Ivy said, clearly guessing what had happened by the sudden burbling babble rising from both vampires.

"Three kids. Downstairs," the intact vampire said, his voice loud and panicked. "One chaperone and two clients. The code is 55512."

Eyebrows high, Pike pulled the torn canopy off the four-poster bed in a sound of ripping fabric. Motions rough, he wiped the vampire's face and let the bloodied rag drop to his lap. My shoulders eased. The thug's fang was still intact. It was the right front tooth that Pike had knocked out. I might have felt sorry for him, but there were three kids downstairs, three kids who were the tip of an ugly iceberg. He deserved far worse, and once he hit prison, he'd get it.

"Thanks, Ivy," I said. "I'll call you tonight after I talk with everyone."

"Sounds good," she said, and my head rose at a tinkling of broken glass from the front room. "I'll let you go. I wanted you to hear it from me, not Edden or the I.S. Love you."

The seldom-spoken words shocked through me, followed by a warm understanding. Ivy was deeply committed to Nina, but there was all kinds of love, and we'd been through a lot. "Love you, too," I said, glad I could say the words as well, and the phone clicked off. I did love Ivy, not the way she had wanted, but we both understood each other and were happy with our relationship now.

I knew Pike had heard us over their continued babbling, but that was okay. He'd never met Ivy, but I was sure he knew our history. Hell, everyone in Cincy knew our history.

"Thank you, gentlemen," I said as I tossed Pike my splat gun to do the honors. "You should have gone with option number one."

His lips quirked in an ugly smile, Pike shot them both and tossed my gun back to me. Motions fast, he all but danced through the broken room, his eyes black as he entered the code. The door lock thumped as it released, and a wave of warm, incense-heavy air flowed up and out.

Suddenly, my mood crashed. The scent was betrayal and violence made real, and it struck me to my core, bringing uncomfortable memories of being trapped underground with an undead. They were soulless, their power born in our need to see them as they were, not as they are. Dead.

Pike took a deep breath, almost shuddering as the pheromones hit him. The young wouldn't have the ability to say no. Hell, I wasn't sure Pike could, or even wanted to, because even though there was nothing but lies down there, the pleasure was still real.

"Hey, uh, you mind if I stay here to keep your way open?" I said, and Pike nodded, his expression grim.

"Stay," Pike said, voice husky, and in a dark flash of movement, he was gone.

Silence echoed up, and then a scream and thump. "Pike! You good?" I shouted down the black stairs. *Please be okay. Please be okay. Don't make me go down that hole. . . .*

"Just a sec!" his voice echoed faintly, then, "Kip! Focus! Where are the kids?"

Relieved, I inched away as more swearing, more screaming rose up. None of it was Pike's, and I tightened my grip on both my gun and the ley line at the sudden thumping on the stairs. The steps were fast, and light, and I lifted my hands high in reassurance when three kids boiled up from the darkness, their eyes wide and vacant as they slid to a frightened halt and took their first untainted breath for what might have been days. They were still in their school uniforms, and I had a hope that they were in the same condition as when their parents had last seen them.

"You're safe," I said, trying to smile as I lowered my gun and shifted to stand between them and the door. *Wild horses, skittish and scared.* "Hang tight until Pike and Kip come up. We've got a car, and we'll get you home."

They were young, well into their teens, clean limbed and soft. Fifteen, maybe. I didn't dare touch them lest I spook them into running, and as they gathered in a frightened huddle by the bed, my anger grew at whoever had tried to steal their youth. They were living vampires and therefore doomed to a life that wasn't their own choosing. But to take what little chance they had to fight it . . . That was unforgivable.

"Please. No. He'll kill me!" came a high-pitched, terrified voice from the stairwell, and then Pike shoved a tall woman up into the light before him, propelling the well-dressed brunette across the blood-slicked floor and into the broken bedframe. "I want I.S. custody. I need a safe house!" she babbled, clinging to the bed as if it might save her.

"I'll get you a safe house," Pike growled, and the woman cowered as he stood over her. She held her arm close. One of her heels was missing and her bare foot was starting to swell.

"I don't know who those kids are!" she shrieked, then dissolved into a sobbing babble.

"Where's Kip?" I said, and his angry frown quirked into a grin to tell me the small woman was okay.

"Following two undead." Leaning, he looked down the stairway. "There's a secondary tunnel. If she can identify them—"

"She can't best the undead!" I interrupted. "Hell, I can hardly best the undead!"

"Nice you know your limits," came a low voice from the door, and I spun, my rising splat gun falling. It was Doyle. His focus was on the kids, and I could tell he was as angry as we were.

Seeing him, the woman at the bed made a sudden dive for freedom, shrieking as Doyle snagged her with an impossibly fast hand. Slamming her face-first into the wall, he held her there as he shouted the Miranda and Pike zip-stripped her hands behind her back. They released her together, and she fell into a despondent, sobbing pile of expensive linen and silk.

Annoyed, I dragged my purse from the bed and slung it over my shoulder before Doyle claimed it was evidence and took it. "Nice of you to show up," I muttered, and his neck went red.

Yes, we had our differences, but they seemed to vanish

when he turned to the kids, his badge and low, calming voice making a comforting presence as he tried to verify their names.

"They've been spelled," Pike said softly as one of the girls took a breath, confusion clouding her when she realized she couldn't remember who she was.

"That's okay." Doyle reached for his phone. "We know who you are. Your parents have been looking for you," he added, and the three collectively seemed to relax as the whoop of a siren came from the front. The I.S. had finally arrived in force—now that it was over.

Doyle was right. They'd be okay, but their next twenty-four hours would be hell as they were poked and prodded. I could try to take the befuddlement charm off, but they were relatively calm right now, and I wasn't up to dealing with three hysterical teenagers.

None of this would make the evening news, not because they were minors, but because it might scare the humans. Sometimes, I thought the only reason we got along was because the mundanes didn't know the truth—how dangerous we were and that it was only law-enforced tradition that kept them safe. And we did keep them safe.

Radio chatter filtered in from the front living room, and feeling the pinch of past misunderstandings between me and the I.S., I leaned against a dented, blood-splattered wall, fighting to keep my arms from rising up about my middle. A uniformed woman came in for the kids, and Doyle began cuffing the downed men with a wad of zip strips, being careful to stay out of the still-dripping potion. "This was our run," I said, seeing even the street cred for this vanishing, and Pike sighed.

"You owe me, Morgan." Doyle turned his sharp-canine smile to me. "I lost my job because of you."

"Detective is a promotion," I said, but he clearly hated having no one to boss around.

"I take them in," he said, trying to get all dark and angsty, but it was hard at ten in the morning in the sweltering heat. "Or I take you and Pike in for trespassing, assault, and perhaps underage predation. Walk away, Morgan. It's easier that way."

"Got this all figured out, eh?" I said, my gaze going to the officer ready to back him up standing in the doorway. A flash of anger rose and fell. Doyle taking credit for my work was not the message I wanted to convey. Pike and I were keeping the vampires in line. Not the I.S.

Pike leaned close. "Let it go, witch," he muttered. "This is not necessarily a bad thing."

Sullen, I nodded, still not liking it. The subrosa was a hidden position. Anonymous. Like the Mob or Batman. Pike didn't seem to care, but I wasn't about to have this become a pattern.

There were people in the front room now, and the kids drew together at the new faces peeking in. I could see the headlines tomorrow, and my name was nowhere in them. Not getting credit for it was one thing, Doyle taking it from me was another. "Is there anything else we can do for you, Detective? Maybe wipe your ass?" I said sourly, and Doyle snickered.

"Nope. We're good." He smiled at the kids and gestured for the officer to escort them out. She was a witch or warlock, judging by the charms around her neck, far easier for the kids to handle after their ordeal. Their onetime chaperone sobbed as she was dragged out behind them. She might not have touched them, but she was complicit in their betrayal and would be charged the same.

"Not even a thank-you," I muttered as three more uniforms came in, the living vampires discussing the unconscious thugs before calling for an agent with ley line skills to de-spell them.

Pike sidled next to me, his eyes on the self-centered man. "Don't take too long," he said, chin lifting to indicate Doyle. "I'll be in the car. I want to show you a couple of logos I worked up over that iced coffee I promised you."

"Logos, right," I said, and Pike sauntered out, limping and covered in blood, clearly pleased to be able to pound people into submission and then walk out between the cops with impunity. My car was a block down, and a sudden urge to talk to Trent made me itchy. Ivy was coming, dragging trouble along with her. But I had one thing to do, first.

"Doyle?" I said sweetly, and he put up a finger for me to wait as he gave someone instruction. Jaw tight, I stood, weight on one foot, arms over my middle. Burning.

Finally the last of the men were dragged out, the witches in uniform glancing nervously at me as they discussed how to break the magic keeping them unmoving. The sleepy-time potions they could handle, but the spoken curses were out of their league. They knew I'd cast them, but since Doyle was going to take the credit, they couldn't ask. "I have no idea," I heard faintly, and in a moment of sympathy, I tweaked the spoken curses, and they broke.

"Doyle," I called again, seeing as he had conveniently forgotten me and was following the last of the officers out.

"What do you want?" he said caustically, and I pivoted, slamming my foot into his chin.

He hit the wall with a thump, his sudden outcry bringing an officer to the door. The man took one look at Doyle on the floor, then fled.

"Morgan, what the hell!" Doyle sputtered, and I sauntered closer, tossing the torn coverlet to him to clean up his face before I extended a hand to help him up.

"You're welcome," I said dryly, giving a heave, and the man lurched to his feet.

"You're going to rot for that," he said, face red as he hunched in a pupil-black-eyed frustration, but he didn't dare make a move against me. Not when I was pissed. Not when I had a ley line burning through me, itching for direction. It was just him, and me, and whispers from the front room. I could smell the old blood on him, the danger, but after living with Ivy, I could tell he was small potatoes. And now, he knew I knew.

"Rot? Maybe someday, but not because of you," I said softly, and he knocked my hand away before I could smooth his shirt. "If you don't have a little blood on you, your bosses will know all you did was sit in the car. I'm the demon subrosa, and I will not have my I.S. contact under suspicion of misconduct because he took credit when credit was clearly not due. Now you look like you did something. You're welcome."

Doyle sputtered, his pupil-black eyes showing an increasing rim of brown as he glanced at the front room. "*Your* I.S. contact?"

Beaming, I rocked back a step. "Isn't that what you're doing? Covering my ass? Keeping my actions secret?" Sighing, I checked my phone. "Good of you to anticipate my needs, but call first next time. Now, if you will excuse me, Ivy is coming in tomorrow with a representative from DC. If you want in on this, I'll be at the church in an hour for a meeting with my team to discuss how to deal with it. Hope to see you there."

"What the fuck," he whispered as I strode out, not sure if he would show or not.

Keeping Cincinnati's paranormals in line was not an easy task. Despite the massive offices of the FIB and I.S. doing the day-to-day, I was where the buck stopped and no I.S. flunky was going to jeopardize that. Taking control from Constance had cost too much to let it slide. I needed him, or someone like him, in the I.S. Badly.

I just hope he never figured it out.

CHAPTER

2

"THANK YOU," I SAID TO THE MAN HOLDING THE DOOR TO Junior's for me, leaving as I was going in. The charmed door chimes clunked dully, and I hesitated on the threshold, appreciating the dry cold Mark kept the place in as I waited for Pike. The mixed-population coffeehouse was a few streets off the waterfront, near enough to the stadiums that you couldn't use it on game day, and far enough from Fountain Square that it didn't become crammed with tourists. Even so, it was always busy. The air-conditioning was a heavy roar, and still it smelled faintly of sweaty Were and vampire. *No, that's Pike. . . .*

"Ah, I got this," I said as Pike shuffled in behind me, the man still holding a silk handkerchief to his nose. "Why don't you snag us a table."

"'Kay," he muttered. Between his torn shirt, scraped knuckles, and swollen face, he was getting noticed. Watching the expressions shift as he wove through the tables was almost worth the price of admission to my weird life. Smiling, I headed for the long line.

The decor in Junior's was . . . unique. Painted circles adorned the floor, the wall, the counter, in what might be art deco but I knew was in case there was trouble and a secure protection bubble needed to be set. The ornately painted circle in the back was a designated place for demons to pop in and out without fear of landing too close to someone, but the ropes had gotten dusty. Where there had once been dozens of pictures of babies dressed like fruit, there was now only one, and someone had painted the huge front windows with roller coasters and the needle at Kings Island.

I *needed* coffee. My arm was sore from hitting something stupid, and my chest hurt when I tried to take a deep breath. Tired, I settled in at the end of the line by the cold shelves. It might be a while. The man before the register was putting in an order for what could have been an entire office floor. Worse, the three young Weres in front of me were giggling, trying to flirt with Mark's latest hire: a Were with tattoos from three different packs. His long hair was in a man-bun and yet he somehow managed an attractive scruffy behind his green apron and tidy slacks. I couldn't help my sigh as the guy asked if he could get the oat milk caramel latte mocha with fat-free whip and peppermint sprinkles.

Slumping, I glanced at Pike scribbling on a napkin so stiff it wasn't much good for anything else. "Logos, right," I whispered. My arm was really hurting, and as the guy moved to the pickup counter and the three Were pups began to place their orders, I swung my big canvas bag around to find a pain amulet. The finger stick to draw the blood to invoke it was in a side pocket, and I hardly felt the prick as I snapped it open and jabbed my pinky.

Immediately the living vamps enjoying the sun at the front of the shop turned, their heads swiveling to find me. The mixed group coming in noticed, too, and Pike, who looked up from his logos to give me a thin smile.

And Dali, I thought as I quickly smeared a drop of blood on the wooden amulet and dropped it around my neck. The surly demon often lurked in the back until it got busy, whereupon he'd come out for twenty minutes, use his magic to burn through the line, and then go hide again. Today, though, he was working the drive-through with the help of a pixy. Mark took being an equal-opportunity employer seriously. Or maybe it was because getting anyone to work with the demon was hard. His HELP WANTED sign was in neon.

"My apologies," I mouthed to the vamps in the sun as the ache in my arm vanished and my shoulders drooped in relief. Brows furrowed, they returned to their conversations. The scent of my blood was a minor irritant, especially compared to Pike. After working with him for several months, I was beginning to suspect that he liked wearing someone else's blood as a badge of honor. I thought it totally unfair that it made him more attractive. I just looked a mess covered in blood.

The line was hardly moving, and taking the opportunity, I twisted to find my phone to call Jenks. He picked up immediately, his hail loud over Attenborough's voice narrating a nature documentary in the background. "Hi," I said, tapping my phone's volume down when one of the girls turned to me, her eyes widening at the blood splatters on my shorts. "Did Ivy call you?"

"Yep." Jenks's voice was clear; the four-inch man was probably standing on top of his phone. "I got her flight info. She knew you were busy. I told her there's a demon in her room, but she was planning on staying at the Cincinnatian, anyway. The master vampire she's bringing has her on a short leash."

"Oh." Disappointment slumped my shoulders, but work was work. "Hey, could you do me a favor?" I asked, reconsidering my initial thought to bring everyone in on this. "Could you make sure David knows what's up and that I'll call him if I need him? Keep watch for trouble. I don't expect anything, but I don't know what this guy wants yet."

"Sure," he said, and then louder, yelling, "Oh, for Tink's little pink rosebuds, Brandy, out! Do a perimeter like I asked! I'm recording it."

"Never mind. I'll call him." I inched forward in line. "You're busy."

"No, I got it," Jenks said, voice heavy with ire at his pixy tenants. "Are you at Junior's?"

"Yep." I stepped forward when one of the girls finally moved to the pickup counter. "You want something?"

"A short latte with honey. And one of those lemon scones. Maybe I can bribe Baribas into taking the church's security seriously. All he cares about is the garden."

"Can do." I knew he was starting to regret letting a pod of displaced pixies rent out the graveyard in return for policing it, but any pixy presence was better than none, and he couldn't patrol the entire block-wide plot alone. "Short latte and a scone. Whole milk, no foam, honey," I said, and the speaker crackled when his dust hit it. "Be there in twenty."

"Wait!" he called, and my hovering finger hesitated. "How did the run go?"

"Pike had fun," I said, glancing at the vampire still busy scribbling. "It would have been easier if you had been there."

Jenks huffed, his dragonfly-like wings rasping. "Never send a vamp to do a pixy's job. Hey, before I forget, the library called. Some guy named Lenny wants to talk to you. Someone has been permanently checking out books from the ancient book locker."

Nick . . . I thought, brow furrowing, but Nick was dead, starved to death in Newt's oubliette. And then the original ever-after collapsed and took even his bones. Slowly my expression lifted. Missing books? It was a real job, maybe one where I could show off my spelling skills instead of my head-busting ones. "Really?" I said as I flexed my sore elbow. "Can you text me his number?"

"Oh, for Tink's contractual hell," he grumbled. "Yeah, let me get right on that. I'll just punch it out for you with my feet. For ever-loving moss wipe, the phone is bigger than me."

"Great. Thanks, Jenks. I appreciate it. See you in a few," I said, right as Jenks ended the call. I held the phone for a moment, then scrolled for Trent's number. Ivy coming in

with a master vampire was going to mess up our weekend.
He'd appreciate a heads-up.

I hit connect, and the picture I'd taken of him asleep
under an apple tree with his horse nosing his wispy blond
hair vanished when he picked up.

"Rachel," he said in obvious surprise, and then in worry,
"Are you okay? Pike—"

There was soft conversation in the background, quickly
muffled as he moved somewhere more private. "All fine," I
said, glancing at the vamp. "Kip is doing some wrap-up,
but the kids are okay. Don't look for it on the news."

"Always a good sign," he said, but I could hear his
worry, and a flash of guilt rose and fell, guilt that I was
working with Pike and not him. It was quickly followed by
annoyance that Doyle was taking credit for our work. *Am I
really that vain?*

"Ah, Ivy called," I said as two of the girls in front of me
texted their phone numbers to the barista, giggling like
mad things. "She's coming in tomorrow with a DC rep."
My voice softened. "He's checking on Constance. I could
use your input on this. I know you're busy . . ."

"I can be at the church in fifteen," he said, and I blinked
in surprise.

"You're in town?" It was my turn at the register, but I
gestured for the guy behind me to go ahead. It would be a
half-hour drive from his estate.

Trent was silent for three heartbeats. It was an eternity
for the quick-thinking man, and my suspicion deepened.
"Ah, yes," he said faintly. "I'm taking care of some business, but I can step out for a moment."

I waited for more, but there was only silence. He usually
tried to arrange lunch or dinner together when he was in
town. But then again, he had known I was on a run. "Oh.
Well. I'm at Junior's, actually . . ." I said.

"I can be *there* in five," he said, almost interrupting in
his haste to reassure me.

He is downtown? My focus went to the big plate-glass
windows. "Cool. I'm next in line. You want your usual?"

Mark was smiling at me from behind the register, and I stepped in front of him. He'd sent Sexy Were Pup to fill the girls' drink order, and that was fine with me.

"Sounds good. See you in a few," Trent said.

"You got it." Eyes on Mark, I ended the call. The first time I'd met Mark had been about four years ago when Ivy and I had walked into this place having decided to quit the I.S. and make our own runner firm. He'd been brave but sort of stupid back then with misunderstandings and bad data. But so had I. Now he was the owner, having gotten it cheap after I'd trashed the place while trying to catch a banshee. We'd both grown, and it felt good to know that change, real change, did happen when people paid attention and tried to learn.

"Hey, Rachel. Your usual? Tall latte, no fat, no foam, pump of raspberry. And cinnamon on top. You want that on ice today?"

I dropped my bag on the counter, feeling as if I was home. "Perish the thought. Hot, please," I said, eager for the sweet drink.

"One tall, hot, skinny demon," Mark said as he punched it in.

"I need a grande iced black for Pike. And a short latte, whole milk, no foam, with a shot of honey," I added. "One of those lemon scones, three baseball cookies, and a tall caramel latte, skim, no foam. Hot."

"Jenks and Mr. Kalamack coming?" Mark asked as he reached for the tongs and put *four* iced cookies into a bag. "Should I turn the CLOSED sign on?"

I grinned at his half-earnest sarcasm. "No fight this time. Promise," I said, tapping my card as the total flashed. My lips curved up at the names on it. Tamwood, Jenks, and Morgan, LLC. But slowly my smile faded. Ivy hadn't worked with us since Nina died and she became Nina's scion, but I wouldn't take Ivy off the card or the sign out in front of the church for anything.

"Hey, do you know anyone looking for a job?" Mark asked as I put my card away. "Dali's given me his notice." He leaned forward, whispering, "Just as well, I think he's stealing the napkins. We're going through them way too fast."

Dali is quitting? I thought, surprised as I glanced over the counter to the somewhat portly demon handing someone their drink order through the drive-through window. "No, but I'll keep an ear out," I said as I stuffed a couple of bills into the tip jar.

Mark smiled as he saw the extra. "Thanks. Go sit down. Dali or I will bring it out."

"You got it," I said, beaming as he gave me a second bag with Jenks's scone.

"Dali? One tall, hot, skinny demon!" Mark shouted, and I smirked as the demon actually shuddered. Why he wanted to appear as an out-of-work civil servant in slacks and a starched white shirt when he could be anything was beyond me. But I suppose slinging coffee in his spelling robes with bells and embroidered stars would feel even worse. No wonder he was quitting. I'd always thought he'd taken the job as a way to sell illegal curses under the table. Maybe that hadn't worked out.

A flash of guilt took me, not because he was working a minimum-wage job, but because I still had to return the books that Al, my demon teacher, had stolen from him. I knew he wanted them, but honestly, Dali's student couldn't even talk yet.

"Hey, ah, Rachel?" Mark said before I could walk away, and I turned to see him holding out an invoked amulet. "For Pike. If he wants it. I jammed my finger last week, but the amulet is still good, and he looks as if he could use it."

"Thanks," I said as I took it, feeling a fluid moment of dizzy overmedication until I dropped it to hang by the lanyard. Unlike ley line amulets that simply needed to be in your auratic sphere, wooden potion amulets had to be touching your skin to work. "I'm sure he will appreciate it."

Mark ducked his head, clearly pleased. Satisfaction gave my hips an extra sway as I made my way through the coffee-house, eager to give Pike something to make his life easier.

The place was busy, but there was an obvious ring of empty tables around Pike, his attention down as he scribbled. *Able to bust heads and still look studious,* I mused as I smiled, the honest-to-God pleasure of having beaten the bad guys with him racing through me—and then I jerked to a halt, almost breathless at an unexpected pulse of desire-born heat. Swallowing, I paused at a rack of mugs, refusing to get closer until I caught hold of myself. I wasn't so naïve as to think it was real. No, it was from our fight, the frightened kids, the relief of saving them.

And yet, the memory of him trying to seduce me several months ago made my pulse fast as I pretended to consider a mug emblazoned with Carew Tower. It had been all business ever since, so there was no lingering awkwardness. Much. But the residual adrenaline combined with seeing him confidently bruised and physically satiated brought it all back.

Damn vampire pheromones, I thought as I set the mug down. The pearl ring Trent had given me caught the light, and I exhaled, forcing the chemical-born ardor away. I loved Trent. This thing with Pike wasn't real. Hell, it wasn't even a thing.

Still, he looked more than good sitting there as I crossed the coffeehouse, my calm restored. He'd been sipping on Ivy's undead mother to keep his scion abilities of heightened hearing and strength and maintain the illusion that Constance was still his master. But it was becoming obvious that he wasn't satisfied. It wasn't just blood that a living vampire craved, but the highly charged sex that often went along with it. I knew he was finding himself increasingly frustrated and randy. *That's not why he asked for your help.*

"For you," I said as I stood before him, and he blinked in wonder at the pain amulet dangling in my grip. "Courtesy of the management."

Pike's gaze went to Mark behind the counter. "You know I don't need that."

"Take it anyway." I beamed, refusing to let my thoughts linger on how attractive his slight annoyance was with his faint stubble. "Thank the man."

Sighing, Pike hung the amulet around his neck and gave Mark a somewhat sarcastic, toothy smile. Mark's pleased expression paled, and then he turned to help the next person in line.

"The things I do for you," Pike grumped, and I eased myself down on the long bench beside Pike where I could see the door. A long finger went out to shift the bag. "Cookies?"

My phone dinged, and I glanced to see Jenks's text with the library's phone number. *Thanks, Jenks.* "Trent's coming."

"Of course he is." Pike eased back, clearly annoyed. "This does not concern the elves."

"It never hurts to have an outside opinion." *See, I can sit here and not think about how dark his hair is, or how tall he stands, or his lean, hungry quickness.*

"Oh, my effing God," Pike swore softly, and my attention flicked up, breath catching at the sultry confidence that had blossomed in his suddenly pupil-black eyes. "Jenks was right. You really do get off on kicking ass."

My lips parted, and I slid two feet down the bench away from him. "I do *not!*"

"You do!" he insisted, his lips quirking as if it was funny. "You're as randy as a goat."

"Shut it!" I all but hissed, lips pressing as I shot a glance at the nearest tables, praying that no one was listening. "I do not . . ." Words catching, I lowered my voice. "I do not get off on kicking ass."

A smile played about his lips. "I think it's sweet," he said. "A strong, capable enforcer who gets excited at a little tussle."

"Stop," I said, voice cold, and he sighed, almost in regret.

"Sorry." My foul mood hesitated at the sincerity in that one word, but he ruined it, his lips curving up in half a smirk as he leaned into the hard cushion. "I think it's great that you enjoy your work," he said, deadpan. "Not everyone does. Find something you love to do, and you never work another day in your life."

"You really need to stop," I warned him, and, chuckling, he drew his scribbles close.

I was sullenly silent as I glanced around the shop to see if anyone had caught that, but my good mood began to trickle back as I realized all the angst and pheromone-induced attraction was gone. Pike had intentionally nullified it by bringing it out, showing me how foolish it would have been to act on it. *He's a good man,* I thought as he flicked another drawing into the growing pile.

"Fangs?" I guessed as I pulled it to me. "You getting a tattoo?" I asked, sure he wasn't. Vampires didn't get them. Weres did as a way to show pack affiliation and establish who was senior alpha without a growl or ill look. But since pain was part of the experience and vampires could turn pain into pleasure, no self-respecting tattoo artist would ink anyone with fangs.

"Not exactly." His smile returned, pride having utterly replaced any sexual charge. "We need something we can tag a building with when we do something to keep the city safe."

My eyebrows rose. "So the I.S. can take credit for it, but the people on the streets know it was us?" I pulled the five sketches closer. "Nice." Leafing through them, I slowed at four Xs. "Four strikes and you're out?" I guessed, and his expression took on a hint of embarrassment.

"It's actually a *W* and an *M* intertwined. Morgan and Welroe."

"Oh!" I squinted, seeing it now. "I like it." Jenks wouldn't, but Jenks hadn't been policing Cincy's vamps for the last four months. Pike and Kip had been doing most of it, with me providing extra muscle when needed. It was working, and everyone seemed content. For now.

Pike took the sketch and dropped it on the pile. "Why are you bringing Trent into this? We work better without him."

My gaze shot to my pinky ring, not entirely comfortable that Pike had noticed that, too. *Where is my coffee?* "Because

Finnis wants to see Constance," I said. "And if I need some help from the Weres or the elves or even the witches, I want them prepared." *Vivian,* I thought, brow furrowing. It was not coincidence that the leader of the witches' coven of moral and ethical standards had temporarily moved from San Francisco to Cincinnati to teach a couple of classes at the university. Vivian was here assessing the threat I was, a friendly eye or not.

"Hodin?" Pike offered, and I shook my head, watching the door.

"Finnis knows her. That won't work." *Not to mention I don't trust him.* Hodin was starting to feel easy like a wish, and wishes always came back to bite you on the ass.

"You're overthinking this." Pike sketched another twined *M* and *W* to look like a diamond hanging between two parallel lines. "All we need to do is pay the dead clot off. He goes home. Life goes on."

"Buy his silence?" I said, all thoughts of how good Pike smelled vanishing as a real worry took me. "I don't have that kind of money, and we are not going to extort it from the people we protect. So unless you are sitting on a money tree or a silver mine . . ."

He leaned away, the rims of brown around his pupils shrinking. "There is Piscary's. I've almost got the MPL pushed through, and with that, we can open."

My eyebrows rose. A mixed-population license was harder to get than a liquor license.

"New money stream—" he added, his words cutting off as his attention jerked up.

I followed his gaze, blinking at Dali's ample middle unexpectedly fronting us, the demon looking rather surreal in his red and white apron. He had our drink order in one of those paperboard trays, and he set it down, his expression empty. "Ah, thanks, Dali," I all but stammered. "I could have gotten it. You shouldn't be bringing me stuff." The iced coffee was cold in my hands as I worked it free and handed it to Pike.

"Not at all," he drawled sarcastically. "It's what I live for." Lips pressed, he watched Pike take a sip.

"'S good. Thank you," the vampire said, but Dali didn't move, arms over his middle in an obvious annoyance. *His books . . .* I thought suddenly.

"Hey, uh, I promise I'll bring your books the next time I come out," I said, forcing myself to not cringe when he squinted malevolently at me. "Or you can pick them up," I added, voice rising. "Jenks knows where they are if I'm not there."

His lips pressed together. "Are you still harboring Hodin?"

Hiding behind a sip of hot coffee, I nodded.

"Then I will not be coming over. Lest I forget myself and wring his treacherous neck for his appalling lack of consideration in clinging to life when those who trusted him lost theirs. Excuse me." He turned on a heel, people leaning to get out of his way as he strode behind the counter.

"Stop it," I hissed when Pike snickered. "Don't discount him because he's in an apron and working as a barista. He could bring down Carew Tower with a word if he wanted."

"I don't discount him," Pike said as he tidied his scribbles to leave the bracketed diamond on top. "But I do think it's funny he's eavesdropping on us."

My shoulders slumped. "Yeah. I noticed that, too." But my coffee was perfect, and I let the hot, creamy, raspberry-flavored yumminess slip into me as I watched the door for Trent. "Pike, I don't like the idea of opening up Piscary's, especially if it's to pay off the vampires."

Pike slumped into the bench, his long legs stretched under the table as he dabbed a bloodied knuckle with a stiff napkin. "Rachel, you know a lot about vampires, but you aren't one. The undead will take care of themselves, but the living need a place to cut loose. Somewhere without an undead mucking it up. Somewhere they can forget about the hellhole they're in."

My thoughts went to Kisten. He'd run Piscary's when

the master vampire had been in jail, turning it from a vampire pickup joint to exactly what Pike was talking about, and as I thought of him, my focus blurred. Even now, I missed Kisten, the way he had made me feel, both alive and on the edge.

"It's been a bitch working past your reputation," Pike added. "It's taking twice the bribe money to move things along, but I should have the MPL by the end of the month."

"I thought it was going to be a vamp-only establishment."

"You serve alcohol, you need an MPL," he said. "But yes, it would cater to vamps."

"What if a human walked in? On a dare?" I stifled a shiver as I remembered getting blood-sugared, basically drunk on vampire pheromones. I'd been at their mercy. That they took it as a compliment and their compassion had been all-encompassing was not the point.

Pike grinned to show his chipped fang. "So I make tomatoes the motif. On the walls, on the menu. Everything. No human will dare show his or her face." He balled up the napkin and tossed it to the table. "You and I have been where the buck stops since March. The honeymoon is over. They need somewhere to go and blow off steam. Think of it as a safe place to bring their concerns without their master vampire knowing."

Oh. I pressed my lips together, not liking that he was right. "Okay, but Piscary's isn't neutral. It's me. It's you." *It's Kisten.* "Isn't there somewhere else we can do this? Somewhere with better air replacement?"

"Like your church?" he said doubtfully, and I shook my head, horrified. The surrounding conversations suddenly went whispery and I glanced up, not surprised that Trent was coming in, the chimes on the door glowing a faint red at whatever security spells he had going in the background. Somehow he managed to appear cool even in his lightweight, pale gray suit. His shoes were new, his fair hair wispy, and his chin clean-shaven. A smile lit his entire face, going all the way to his eyes when he saw me, and damn it if I didn't feel a trill of excitement.

This, I thought as Pike stifled a groan. *This is real.*

"Oh, good God. Get a room," Pike muttered.

"Jealous?" I said, ignoring that I'd been daydreaming over him not five minutes ago.

"Rachel," Trent said as he nodded to Pike and slid in beside me, all three of us with our backs to the door. "You look good."

I flushed as he slipped an arm around my waist and tugged me into him. There were too many people with cameras for a kiss, but it was in his touch. A trickle of ley line energy warmed me as our internal balances equalized, and I felt myself relax. *Yes. Real . . .*

"Trent," Pike said flatly, and Trent flashed him a professional, media-worthy smile. Clearly there was still some unresolved friction between them. I wasn't going to feel guilty anymore that it was easier to work a run with Pike than Trent. I'd do ugly things if anyone seriously hurt Pike, but if the same happened to Trent, I'd take unforgivable action.

"Mr. Welroe," Trent said amicably. "The run went well?" he asked, noticing the pain amulet.

Pike grimaced and took it off. "She made me wear it," he muttered, and Trent chuckled, tugging me closer again before teasing another pillow feather out of my hair.

"I didn't know you were in town," I said. "What brings you in?"

Trent pulled his coffee closer, eyeing the bag as if knowing it held cookies. "Just some business," he said lightly. "Nothing certain yet."

Pike stuffed the scribbles into his pocket. "Isn't your birthday coming up, Rachel?"

It was, but Trent seemed to freeze as if only now realizing it, making me even more curious as to what he was doing downtown.

"Cookie?" I said sweetly as I held out the bag, and Trent hesitated a telling instant before taking one. "Pike?" I said next, and Pike shook his head as if sensing danger.

"Pike wants to buy Finnis off," I said, snapping a cookie

in two and nibbling the smaller half. "Which I'm against. He knows Constance, so Hodin impersonating her is out. Even if he is the demon's best doppelganger spell slinger according to Al."

"Paying him off is easy. Safe." Pike inched down the bench away from me, his coffee in hand. "Life goes on. We'll have a steady stream once Piscary's opens."

"You're reopening Piscary's?" Trent said, and I lifted one shoulder and let it fall.

"We're talking about it," I said, and a smile flitted about Pike's lips.

Trent took a second cookie, silent in thought as he removed the lid from his coffee and dunked it. "I'm with Rachel. Bribing a master vampire might work in a closed vampire system, but in Cincinnati?" Trent gazed out the windows, his focus distant. "Word will get around, and every wannabe alpha and upstart undead will want the same deal. Controlling a city by paying citizens to follow the law only gives them money to buy the muscle to bring you down. Better to settle it and have the fallout be a warning to others."

I couldn't keep magicking every vampire they sent to run Cincinnati into a mouse, though. Killing them twice would put me in jail.

Trent leaned an elbow on the table. "Do you think Constance will play nice if you turn her back?"

"No." Pike went distant in memory. "She's . . . No," he finished, tone resolute.

"Then I suggest you find out what Finnis wants." Trent pointed a half-eaten, coffee-soaked cookie at Pike. "They know Constance hasn't been calling the shots or they wouldn't be checking on her. Clearly the city is running smoothly. They probably don't like that they have zero control over you. Makes them nervous. Maybe he simply wants to talk. Find the rope to hang you with if you do something they don't like."

Other than hurting Ivy? I thought, worried.

"Yeah, okay," Pike scoffed. "He wants a kickback. I can have that in twenty-four hours with the right bet."

"No," I said softly. "Trent's right. If you start paying powers off, pretty soon, you don't control the city, the city is controlling you." I winced as my birthday got sidelined. "I'm giving David and Vivian the heads-up. If there's going to be trouble, they need to know."

Pike gestured in exasperation. "This is such a waste of time."

"Talking is never a waste of time." Trent sighed, twisting to reach his phone when it dinged. "Ah, Rachel . . ." he said as he read the incoming text. "If you have this . . ."

"Go." Smiling, I rolled down the cookie bag and handed it to him with a little kiss. "Will you be done by tonight?"

"Absolutely." Standing, Trent texted someone. "You. Me. Date night."

"Oh, goodie . . ." Pike grumped, and I "accidentally" kicked his foot under the table. Date night would become date weekend if Finnis didn't drag his dead ass into the party.

Trent tucked his phone away, his smile widening as he looked into the bag. "What's your afternoon like in case I wrap this up early?"

"Spelling." I relaxed comfortably where I sat, content that between Pike, Trent, Jenks, and Ivy, we could settle this without anyone dying or turning into a mouse—or both. Behind him, Mark convinced someone to delete the video they were taking of us for a month of free coffee. *Thanks, Mark.* "I need to make up a couple batches of splat balls," I added. "Maybe go shopping for something that says city ruler." Ivy was coming in. I wanted to look nice.

"Shopping?" Trent hesitated. "You're, ah, taking Jenks, right?"

I made a face at Pike's confusion. Jenks wouldn't be backup but shopping consultant, making sure I didn't come home with something totally inappropriate. I could pick out something nice on my own . . . even if I was a sucker for sequins and mismatched glitz. "Jenks, right," I said sourly, and Trent's eyes crinkled in amusement. "Oh, and I've got to call the university library. Someone broke into their ancient book locker, but I won't be doing anything there until Monday, the earliest."

Trent's brow furrowed. "Really? I thought they upped their game after you and Nick—"

"They did," I said, interrupting before Pike got interested and asked. "It would take a demon to get in there now," I said flippantly, but then I thought about it. If it *was* a demon, I had a big problem, and my gaze went to Dali behind the counter, his supercilious attitude firmly in place as he slung drinks in his apron uniform. They'd promised to behave, but that was nearly a year ago—and demons were extremely high-risk when they got bored.

"University work. Nice. I'll see you later, then." Trent's fond attitude vanished as he turned to Pike. "Pike," he added flatly.

"Trent," Pike said, just as blandly, and then Trent started for the door, head down over that bag.

"I should go, too." Pike downed the last of his coffee and slid to the edge of the table. "Kip is probably out of the tunnels by now."

"You need a ride?" I asked, and he stood, the motion slow and languorous, like a big tomcat as he tested his range through the bruises.

"No. Thanks, though." His attention went out the window to a black, four-door truck. The windows were illegally tinted, and Trent was watching it in passing. "My ride is here. Hey, do you want to take these?" he added, holding out the napkins he had been scribbling on. "Give them a look. Tell me which one you like the best."

"Sure." I took them with a thin smile, stuffing them in my bag. "Pike, I know you want to pay Finnis off, and I agree, it sounds easy, but easy always comes back to bite me on the ass. Let's see what he wants before we start writing checks." I'd finally paid off the bill to repair the church, and the last thing I wanted was to dip into the red again, and not for a vampire.

"I hear you," Pike said, but he was walking away, his mood distant.

Sighing, I sipped at my cinnamon raspberry coffee and scrolled through my phone to see how long it had been since I'd talked to Vivian. Teaching night classes meant her schedule was as wonky as mine, and chances were good that I could snag some advice, not only for Finnis, but a dress as well. It would do my stinging pride good to prove to Jenks that I could pick out something nice to wear without his help.

But my motion to call and find out if she was available faltered as I noticed Dali staring at me as he made someone's high-priced, high-calorie caffeine monstrosity complete with whip and sprinkles. Though across the room, I knew he had heard everything, and my vague feeling of nervousness grew as he turned away, eyes narrowed and holding a knowledge he wasn't going to share.

If the demons had decided it would be more fun to watch me try to make them play by our rules than it would be to exploit every loophole within them, I was in deep troll doo.

CHAPTER

3

THE DRIVE FROM JUNIOR'S ACROSS THE RIVER AND TO MY church was short in terms of distance, but long in attitude, and the shift from busy metropolis to shady streets and abandoned bikes on green lawns was welcome. Even so, it wasn't until I pulled into my carport that the worry Dali had instilled in me began to ease. The church was in a pleasant neighborhood made up of middle- to low-income families, mostly Inderlanders. They were quiet about it, though. The Turn, where all of us apart from the elves had come out of the closet to save humanity, had been over forty years ago. Regardless, no one was eager to stand out, even if some of the basketball hoops were twice regulation height and most of the basement windows were boarded up. Flowers were planted in friendly hexes, and the chalk on the sidewalk was as likely to be runes as ABCs.

Jenks's coffee was a yucky cold when I took it out of my car's cup holder, and I warmed it up with a quick thought and burst of ley line energy as I got out. The thump of my door was loud, and a flash of pixy dust high over the grave-yard showed that I'd been seen by the sentry.

The church itself was small, with stained glass on two sides and a respectable steeple. Worn concrete steps led up to twin wooden doors that opened into a foyer that *still* didn't have any electricity in it. The empty sanctuary was a mix of living room and dojo at the moment, with Ivy's baby grand on the raised stage and Kisten's pool table by the entrance. The hallway led to the original two bathrooms and small clergy offices turned bedrooms, but the large kitchen/spelling area and covered porch were new, having just been rebuilt after a misunderstanding with Cincy's vampires.

Coffee in hand and bag over my shoulder, I scuffed my way up the worn steps. My leg hurt even with the pain am-ulet, and I wondered how much grief I'd get from Jenks if I added a second. "Jenks?" I shouted as I came in, then halted, blinking at the chaos beyond the foyer.

Pixies and fairies darted in the bands of hazy light, dust sifting like living sunbeams as they shrilled at each other to make my ears hurt. In a calliope of color and noise, they flowed from one side of the sanctuary to the other, the rasp-ing of pixy wings lost under the piercing calls and almost subliminal screeching of fairies.

"What the Turn?" I whispered, breath catching when I noticed the hapless bumblebee caught in the mix. The pix-ies were trying to drive it away as the fairies fought to push it deeper into them. At least, that's what I thought was go-ing on until they all cheered and the bee rose up, fleeing to bump against a window.

"Point to pixies!" Jenks shouted, wings chirping as he rose high.

It's a game? Bemused and ears hurting, I came in, wav-ing at the spent pixy dust. "Jenks?" I called hesitantly, and immediately he arrowed down, his gaze never leaving the game. Everyone seemed to be involved, and there didn't seem to be any rules.

"No fair!" one shouted from the open rafters when three fairies rose up with a tissue box, dropping it on the pixies' line to scatter them.

"No penalty!" Jenks exclaimed. "You don't like it, keep your Tink-blasted eyes open!"

Wincing, I leaned against the pool table, watching the chaos. "Don't come crying to me if someone gets stung and dies." I glanced at the injured pixy. "Where are Rex and Boots?"

"Hiding." Jenks hovered beside me, hands on his hips. "Way too much stimulation."

No doubt. The noise was atrocious. "But a bee?" I said, remembering Jenks telling me he had once nearly died from a sting.

"Relax." Lips twisted into a smirk, he showed me a nasty-looking needle about the length of his hand before hiding it. "It's safe."

"Damn, Jenks," I whispered, wincing when the excited flow of pixies and fairies knocked a lamp to the floor. "How did you . . . that's like defanging a snake."

He shrugged, his focus shifting from the game. His devilish smile made me feel good. I hadn't seen it enough since his wife died. "It's the first time I've been able to get them to cooperate," he said, and then his attention dropped to the cup in my hand. "Is that my coffee?"

"And scone," I said as I took it out of my shoulder bag.

"Great. Thanks," he said, then darted straight up into the open rafters, his dust an unusual gray. "Time!" he shouted. "I'm calling it! Game over!"

An ear-hurting protest rose up as the watching pixies dropped from the ceiling. The fairies were in a tight group congratulating themselves, looking like little grim reapers with butterfly wings, their spiderweb clothes giving them a goth mien. Their wicked long fangs used to kill spiders were enough to leave me with nightmares, even if they were only six inches tall.

"Winners divide the scone," Jenks said as he handed the

oldest fairy a wooden garden sword. "And the loser picks who gets what half."

I smiled as a lisping, hissing groan rose up from the gathered fairies. Jenks had been a great dad. Never would I have believed that fairies and pixies could do anything together but fight, and I watched, smirking, as the fairy cut the scone in two, sharing it with hardly more than a grimace as the pixies darted down and absconded with their half.

"Have I told you recently that you are amazing?" I said as I headed for the kitchen, Jenks flying backward to keep them in sight even as he followed.

"Yep. Every day and twice on Sunday," he said as we passed the his-and-her bathrooms, long since converted into something a little less industrial and more functional. The old church offices were to either side, now Hodin's room on the left, Stef's on the right, though I had a suspicion that they might be sharing a bed.

I was bunking in the belfry. It was hot up there despite the windows and insulation, and I suspected it would be cold in the winter, but my agreement with Hodin would be up in October and he'd be obliged to find new lodgings. I was already looking forward to it.

I checked my phone as I entered the kitchen, disappointed to see that Vivian hadn't returned my text yet. "No news is good news," I whispered, and Jenks's wings clattered as he darted to the top of the fridge, where he kept his food stash.

"Hi, Stef," I said as I noticed the young woman at the center counter in the middle of the large room, her strong shoulders moving evenly as she grated something.

"Oh, hey. Hi!" the average-height, early-thirties woman said as she glanced up from what seemed to be spell prep. She wore a faint flush, either from her work or surprise, and her hazel eyes darted away as if embarrassed. Her auburn hair was darker than mine, but enviably straighter, the short cut professionally styled to frame her long face. She'd lost some of her chair weight in the last few months, and whereas

I wouldn't say she was athletic, her curves showed more. She'd always been strong. Most nurses were. A good half-dozen ear piercings shifted with her movement, the silver rings all in a row along the arch of her ear. She'd been paying Jenks rent for a good five months after having been kicked out of her apartment in Constance's grief-and-annoyance campaign. That Stef had stayed when her apartment had become available again gave me hope that she was beginning to loosen up. I felt as if I didn't know her; I was always busy, and she kept to herself when she wasn't at the hospital.

"I thought you were working today," I added as I set my bag on the counter and leaned against the long eat-at bar between the kitchen and the open-aired porch. The half-wall, half-glass partition looked out onto the garden, and I loved it. The porch itself was even better with a full roof, fireplace on one wall, and open to the garden and graveyard on another. I was already studying up on how to make a ward so as to close the huge opening come winter. Sitting in front of the fire with a book and hot cocoa to watch it snow sounded divine. Lee had made the ward at Trent's estate, and if worse came to worst, I'd ask him.

My contractor, Finley, rebuilt the back to create space that had multiple uses in case the church ever became a paranormal shelter again, meaning the kitchen could function as a soup kitchen and my winter reading area could double as a dining area. With only me, Stef, Hodin, and Jenks in the church, much of the space was going to waste, but I appreciated that Hodin and I had multiple areas to spell in without stepping on each other's robes.

The double-size lot with both a formal garden and the wild meadow among the tombstones was a welcome relief in the city. Pixies zipped about like hummingbirds, and fairies flew like giant butterflies to make a singularly pleasant sight, and I felt my shoulders ease. Even the soft sounds of Stephanie working at the island counter were soothing. Boots, Stef's cat, watched Jenks from his cat tower, set where he could see the garden, only the tip of his tail moving. He was missing three whiskers and a chunk off his right ear, all of which had been intact when he moved in. Pixies took no prisoners.

"So . . . no work?" I asked again. I'd been finding her home unexpectedly lately, making me wonder if she'd lost her job, as unlikely as that seemed. Stef was nothing if not conscientious.

"Ah, I wanted to work on something today, so I switched schedules with Hank," she said, but she looked up, and I wondered if she was stretching the truth.

"Oh." I glanced at Jenks atop the enormous, twin-door fridge for his opinion, and he shook his head. The pixy could often see it when people lied. Apparently our auras flared. "You're . . . making lunch?" I said, seeing the piles of carefully pulped and mashed garden.

"It's a spell, actually," she admitted, voice breathless.

My lips pressed together. There was no recipe on the counter. "By heart?" I questioned, and Jenks flew down to land on my shoulder.

Her flush deepened, and finally her hazel eyes met mine. "Hodin is helping me get my witch degree. I need it to move into a managerial position," she blurted, and my lips parted.

"Oh!" I said in understanding. "That's great!" Witch was a designation of ability, not sex, and once you proved you were able to stir a spell by heart, you moved up from warlock. My smile faltered. "I didn't know you were going for certification," I added, feeling bad that I'd been so busy that she hadn't come to me first. But then again, I wasn't tall, dark, and broody. "So, what are you making?" I asked as Jenks darted out of the room, drawn by a sudden, ear-piercing complaint and nearly ultrasonic uproar.

Stef watched Jenks leave, her shoulders relaxing as she began to grate a white root. "A charm to clear acne?" she said, almost questioning herself, and I nodded even as I chided myself for thinking she should have come to me first. I was the last person who should assume that Hodin was up to no good simply because he was a demon.

And yet, it wasn't because he was a demon that I was concerned. In the last few months, Stef had lost all her fear of him, which was both gratifying and worrying. True, Hodin had been nothing but grudgingly helpful, but Al never gave his hate lightly, and it seemed more than sibling rivalry or the fact that Hodin mixed elven and demon magic that had set my estranged teacher off. Dali's continued disapproval, too, was telling.

But what I disliked the most was that their relationship wasn't equal, and I wasn't sure Hodin had any respect for that.

"Good place to start," I said, instead of what I wanted, as my gaze traveled over the prepped ingredients.

Stef carefully gathered the grated root, weighing out an ounce on a set of unfamiliar scales. "Hodin has been a big help," she said as if trying to convince herself.

Suspicious, I tightened my grip on the nearest ley line and opened my second sight. Again, the world became overlaid with a second image of field and sun, but it was Stef's aura I was concerned with. When we had met, her aura had been a spotless green apart from a healthy yellow around her hands and heart to show her giving nature. Now, a faint hint of smut darkened it. There was only one place she could have gotten it. Worried, I dropped my second sight and bit my lip. *Going for her witch degree?* "You know . . . if you ever need anything or want to talk—"

My words cut off as the big bell in the steeple gave a faint bong, and I stiffened when a faint gray mist seemed to rise from the tiled floor between me and Stef. I backed up as Boots jumped to the floor, slinking out as the fog began to condense. It had to be Hodin, though it was hard to tell from just the demon's red, goat-slitted eyes staring from a thickening haze.

Frantic, Stef began to tidy her work area as the mist solidified into a tall, sinewy man with a dark complexion and thick wavy hair held at his nape in an ornate metal clip. His chin tended to narrow, but his jaw was strong and his body was trim, looking good in both a spelling robe and his more typical bad-boy black jeans and cotton shirt.

This time, he chose to come in casual, and I eyed his biker boots in envy, even if it was pushing eighty in here.

The demon liked his jewelry, and his hands glinted with old rings. I had a feeling his belt buckle was an amulet, and maybe the earring, too.

"Stephanie has been more than an apt pupil," the demon said, clearly having been eavesdropping.

I flushed, hearing in his softly accented words a hint of jealousy that I might be trying to poach her from him. Far from it. The last thing I wanted was an apprentice. And I didn't like the demon's proclivity for lurking, either. That's why the bell, though it lacked a little something when Hodin rarely left the grounds.

"Hi, Hodin," I said, glancing up as Boots tore back in, a chorus of pixy cheers loud behind him. Jenks followed, dusting heavily as the cat slid to a halt, stared at Hodin with a black-eyed stare, then slunk behind the stools at the eat-at counter.

"It's okay, Boots," Stef cooed, and Jenks chuckled as he landed on my shoulder.

"Awww, it's just Hodin." Jenks jammed his wood-handled sword into its scabbard with a *snick*. "Ya know," he added as he rose up to front the stoic man, hands on his hips, "the bell wouldn't ring if you didn't translocate in the house."

Hodin frowned to ruin his youthful, slightly stubbled expression with a deep wrinkle. I knew it bothered him that I hadn't removed the charm that rang the steeple bell when a demon showed up. I *had* dampened it, but clearly that wasn't enough, and I pressed forward, wanting to change the subject before Hodin turned Jenks into a little lead soldier with wings. "Hodin, I'm glad you're here. Did Jenks tell you that Ivy—"

"Yes." Hodin studied Stef's preparations. "Do you wish for me to pretend to be Constance again?"

"Ah, no," I said, adding, "Thank you, though," when Stef stared at me as if I was being rude. "I appreciate the offer, but Finnis knows Constance, and I'd rather come to an understanding without looking stupid by trying to trick him."

"Mmmm." Hodin picked a discolored juniper berry from the pile Stef had weighed out, flicking it away and making Stef wince. Boots's ears pricked, his attention drawn by the soft sound. Jenks, too, tracked its path until it rolled to a stop.

"Pike wants to buy his silence," I said, focus going distant in thought. "But that's a short-term solution having a high risk of becoming a long-term problem. Not to mention we don't have the money. I should probably find out what he wants before I start mortgaging the church." Okay, my words sounded bitter even to me, but I had a feeling that money, even lots of it, wouldn't change things. They wanted a vampire in charge, and if Constance didn't put in an appearance, I'd be in jail for wrongful death.

Wings rasping, Jenks swooped to get the berry before Boots could. "I don't know why the soul-searching, Rache," he said when I took it to the top of the fridge. "He's coming into your garden. Kill the bloodsucker and send his fangs back to DC as a warning."

I smiled at my warrior-poet, wishing it was that easy. But I'd never killed anyone—at least, no one who hadn't wanted to be dead—and I wasn't going to start now. "And end up in Alcatraz?" Pulling out a stool, I sat, elbows on the eat-at counter. "No, thanks."

Stef had begun to work again, Hodin murmuring a suggestion before turning to me. "Have you considered a fulfillment curse? One that would send Finnis home with feelings of everything being settled but no concrete idea of how?"

My head came up and I met Jenks's eyes as he flew to me. "Is it white?" I asked.

Hodin shrugged. "There is no death involved. I could teach you . . . for a price."

Stef cleared her throat in a soft rebuke.

"Or for free," he amended, clearly pained. "As a gesture for the common good, seeing as we share living arrangements."

Jenks snickered from my shoulder and Stef went back to her work, content. *How many practitioners does it take to make a spell? Three. One to do the work, and two to talk about it.*

"Free, eh?" I said, and his expression stiffened. "I don't want you to feel as if you're being taken advantage of."

"No," Hodin said, somewhat breathless. "Stephanie is right. I have witnessed much unequal give-and-take between you and your pixy backup. If I'm to live in a communal setting, I need to contribute to the well-being of it."

Jenks dusted an angry red. "Unequal give-and-take?" he muttered, but I'd always felt as if I was getting the better end of our friendship.

"Aid without thought of future compensation creates a continued smooth function," Hodin finished sourly, and Stef bobbed her head.

"Which is a long-winded way of saying that you help your friends when you can," I said, wondering at Hodin's sudden interest to fit in. Maybe he was working for an extension. *Maybe he's learning how to function in our society since the demons won't have him.* "What's in it?"

A rare smile curved his lips up, and he snapped his fingers. "Stephanie. Attend," he said as he handed her the paper and pen that had appeared in his grip.

Immediately Stef wiped her fingers on an ion-free cloth tucked into her waistband, moved from her spell prep, and stood ready. Her face was studiously blank, making me think this wasn't the first time she'd made Hodin's list. Jenks noticed, too, and we exchanged a concerned look.

"To promote carelessness, we need elderberries, skullcap, chickweed flowers, licorice seeds, and spikenard leaves," Hodin said, a hint of frown on him.

All of which are female oriented and lend themselves to water invocation, I thought as Stef wrote that down, but elder, licorice, and spikenard generally promoted fidelity, not careless thought, and I wondered how he was going to make this work.

"To stimulate mental fog, we require rue, celery, mustard seeds, rosemary, green walnut leaves, and a bowl made of walnut, preferably a hollowed shell," he added.

Masculine, I mused. All tending toward fire release and mental clarity, not fog. "Is it earth magic?" I asked, thinking

if he put all that together it was going to result in the op-
posite of what we wanted.

"It is demon," Hodin said, and Stef's brow creased with
a hint of concern. "And therefore it will require an invocation as well as your blood to invoke it. Reflection will twist
the properties of fidelity and higher alacrity into their mirror selves of distraction and dull wit. Which reminds me.
We also need a stick of mercury chalk and a blemish-free
mirror."

I nodded, getting it. It was like tarot cards, where something considered bad was actually good when the card appeared upside down. And the blood thing was not a big
deal. All earth magic required a drop or two of blood. The
magic was in the witchy enzymes.

"I've got a mirror, but elderberries won't be in season
until mid-August, earliest," I said. "Jenks, do you have any
in your long-term stores?" I asked, and he shook his head.
"I don't have spikenard in the garden, either," I mused
softly. "The mercury chalk will be difficult."

"Findlay Market will have it. And the elderberries and
spikenard, too," Stef said brightly, and Jenks and I turned
to her.

How does she know? I thought in worry.

"Findlay Market?" Jenks said, voice high in concern.
"Rache, didn't you spend six months down there hunting
dark magic practitioners when you worked for the I.S.?"

Annoyance pinched Hodin's expression, vanishing under a practiced smile.

"For all the good it did," I said, remembering the head-
aches I'd come home with from trying to see past the
don't-notice charms hovering over the more illicit products.
Findlay Market sold more than tomatoes—especially after
sunset. "I'll do some calling around. Maybe we can find a
local source. We're going to have to go to the university's
bookstore for the mercury chalk, anyway." I reached for my
phone, worried. I wanted to avoid going online for supplies.
You never knew what you were going to get.

"Findlay Market will have everything you need," Hodin

said with a sniff. "How lucky that they're open today. Otherwise, you might have to wait an entire week or go out of state." He held out his hand and Stef put the list in it. "Stef will shop for you if you are afraid."

"I'm not afraid." My gaze rose from my phone, now showing the local spelling shops. "Seriously, Hodin? I'm a little old for reverse psychology."

Unperturbed, Stef leaned to see what Hodin was adding to the list. "It's not a problem. I was going anyway."

Jenks went to see as well, and Hodin blew him halfway across the kitchen with a little flick of yellow-and-green-tinted magic. "I need three virgin-metal rings, and that's the only place I've been able to find them," he said. "Other than a renaissance faire."

"Yeah?" Belligerent, Jenks hovered out of Hodin's easy reach as Stef read the list and stuffed it in a pocket. "Why is *Stef* doing *your* shopping at Findlay Market?"

Silent, I turned to Stef, curious as well.

"I'm going for my witch license," she said, the lie coming from her far too easily for my liking. "It's good practice."

I couldn't very well talk to her with Hodin looming over us, and I flicked my fingers, telling Jenks to stand down. "I'm going," I said, and Hodin seemed to start.

"There's no need," he said, his sharp tone cutting Stef's words off.

"I need some virgin rings, too." I slid from the stool. "You good with that, Stef?"

My sarcasm failed to reach her, and Stef beamed. "Sure! I'd love the company."

Smiling my most prettiest, I turned to Hodin. "Great. It's a date."

"I'll get my purse," Stef said brightly, but her quick step to the door hesitated as she remembered her spell prep, disappointment settling into soft lines in her forehead.

"Go," Hodin said immediately. "I'll finish here. A fulfillment curse takes some time to twist, and Rachel will want it ready before Finnis arrives."

"I thought you were practicing for your witch's exam," I said, and Stef paused as Hodin smoothly stepped forward.

"I meant that I'd clean it up is all," Hodin said, waving an extravagant hand. A glowing fog of yellow and green sifted down over the counter and everything vanished. "Easily done."

"I'll be right back," Stef said softly, eyes returning to the counter as she hustled out. I could understand her reticence. There'd been a lot of prep work there, now gone. *Or is it?*

Jenks's rasping wings were obvious as he rose up and down in indecision before following her. I was alone with Hodin, and for the first time in months, I felt unsure.

Something was off, pinging my witchy-sense. If I didn't know better, I'd say that Stef was making charms for Hodin, not practicing for an exam—as if she was his familiar. Harmless enough on the surface, but if she truly became his familiar, he'd control her, body and soul.

Most witches had familiars. They enabled the practitioner to reach ley lines over water and when too far under the ground. They also helped even out the flow of ley line energy, sort of like a surge suppressor. When things went bad, it was the familiar who suffered, not the witch, but there were countless cases of familiars surviving a misaligned spell when the witch took the brunt instead out of love. It was an age-old symbiosis that served both the witch and familiar.

The stronger the practitioner, the smarter the familiar had to be—which was why demons preferred keeping witches or elves instead of cats, bats, and, in the case of elves, horses. Perhaps it was because they saw themselves in those they subjugated, but demons were cruel, forcing their familiars into extensions of themselves with no will of their own, trading them between each other as their mood changed. Al had been one of the best at luring skilled elves and witches into servitude, breaking them into obedient vessels who made all but the most dangerous curses that demons used to appear all-powerful.

The demons had released their human familiars in an

effort to rejoin the rest of society, but I'd always felt their enjoyment in dominating another was too much to let go. Maybe I needed to have a talk with Hodin. Make sure there was an equal amount of give-and-take in their relationship and that his goal was teaching, not enslavement.

"This is a white curse, right?" I asked again, seeing as Hodin hadn't moved, making me doubly curious as to if that spell prep was still there, just hidden.

"The smut is minimal," he said, as if that was all that was needed to be labeled white.

Sandals scuffing, I checked my phone to see if Vivian had called before I tucked it in a pocket. If not for Hodin's rings, we could blow off Findlay Market and try to find everything in downtown Cincinnati. We were a metropolis. There were options. Expensive, but options.

"Well, I appreciate the help. Thank you," I said, and he smiled, turning himself from a demon into a biker dude. "Finnis is going to be a bear."

"Of course. Stephanie is trying to teach me modern social skills."

"Great," I said as Stef came in with a black gathering scarf around her neck and an enormous market bag. Jenks was with her, but he flew to Hodin, wings snapping aggressively.

"Hodin, since we're going to Findlay Market, you got any more ideas on how to separate Bis's aura from the baku?" he asked, and my gaze flicked to Hodin in guilt. Jenks and Bis had been best buds, and I'd found nothing but dead ends in my limited research.

Smirking, Hodin crossed his arms over his chest. "Nothing that Rachel Morgan, the white magic demon, will consider," he mocked.

So much for his new social skills. "I am not going to steal someone's soul and give it to Bis in the hopes that it will bring him awake," I said, feeling torn. "You don't even know if it will work. Al says—"

"Al says," Hodin scoffed.

"Al says," I continued, "that he won't be himself or even

remember why he's living in a church with a pixy and demon-born witch." Depressed, I slumped. "It won't be Bis."

"How about that aura-solidifying curse?" Jenks bobbed up and down, clearly not ready to give this up. "It's not dark. Rache's got the materials upstairs. Solidify his aura, separate it from the baku. Or are you just going to help on the easy stuff?"

"Jenks . . ." I said softly when Hodin's confidence vanished. "Solidifying Bis's aura will make it harder to separate it from the baku, not easier." It was a dead end—and it hurt. "Stef, you ready?" I added, wanting to get out of here.

"As always," she said with an overdone cheerfulness, and I pushed into motion, depressed. Okay. Hodin was being helpful, but maybe it was that very helpfulness that had me on edge. No one ever got anything free from a demon, even when it looked as if they did. Even me. There was always a price to pay.

CHAPTER

4

ON THE SURFACE, FINDLAY MARKET LOOKED LIKE ANY OUT-
door market, having longtime vendors with semipermanent
open-air kiosks as well as one-shot wonders at the family
card table with bewildered, sometimes desperate expressions. Up until last fall it had been a square of walkable,
trendy storefronts, but the area had burned down when
Landon broke the ley lines. Some said rioters caused the
fire to cover their theft, but I suspected a more sinister reason; Findlay Market was where you went to find your dark
magic supplies, and something ugly probably got loose
when magic was suddenly not there anymore.

I knew a lot of people still faulted me for that—which might
account for the occasional malevolent stare from the more
permanent vendors as Stef, Jenks, and I wandered the rows.

Yeah, we bad, I thought as I gathered my wildly frizzing
hair in a ponytail and let it go. The sun was past its zenith,
but it was still hot, especially here among the winding turns
and ever-changing paths that ran through the noisy chaos
of Findlay Market.

"I haven't been here since it burned down," I said, and Stef, who was clearly being recognized for a completely different reason, nodded.

"It's something, isn't it?" she said. "I love knowing who makes or grows the food I eat and that I'm a part of their noncorporate success. Mmmm, Rose is here. Do you like rye? I'm going to get some. Rose makes a great rye bread."

Without waiting for an answer, she cut a sharp right, her enviable straight hair swinging as she gave the ample woman behind the table a cheerful, familiar hello.

Jenks's wings brushed my neck, pulling a shiver from me despite the heat. "She knows her by name?" he said, and I winced.

"I'll talk to her." I wasn't sure I liked Stef's level of familiarity with the vendors of Findlay Market, her being a part of their noncorporate success aside. The freshening wind was a scant relief as I eased in beside Stef. The bread smelled fantastic, but I couldn't very well interrupt as Stef and Rose talked about how the garlic brought out additional flavors of the rye.

"It freezes?" Stef said, clearly pleased. "Oh, I'll buy two, then."

I took a breath as Stef searched for her wallet, my words hesitating as my phone began to buzz. *Trent?* I thought, stifling a little quiver as I saw the picture of him sleeping in the shade.

"Oh, for Tink's little pink dildo," Jenks muttered.

"Just stick with her, okay? And watch what she puts in that bag," I whispered. Dropping into the iffy shade of a sapling tree, I hit connect. "Hi, Trent."

"Rachel." His voice came smoothly, but I could detect a hint of irritation. There was a loud commotion in the background. It was either a party, or ducks. It was hard to tell the difference. "Is this a bad time?"

My attention dropped to the ring Trent gave me. The elven magic made it almost glow in the humidity. "No, I'm shopping with Stef. I have a minute, though. What's up?"

"Ah, I hate to do this, but do you mind pushing our dinner plans out? I've run into a snag and I can't walk away without compromising the situation."

It was unusually vague, but I didn't think whatever he was doing in downtown Cincinnati was about my birthday—not with the hint of worry in his voice. Still, Kisten had taught me that though family and friends come first, sometimes business intruded and not to get bent up about it. "Actually, that would work better with my day," I said, only now realizing it. "Hodin offered to show me how to make a fulfillment curse for Finnis."

"Fulfillment?" he questioned. "How does that convince him that Constance is alive and running Cincinnati?"

"Not sure," I mused as Stef and Jenks ogled the homemade soap. Sure, the bars on the table were lavender and pine, but soap was made from fat. So were a lot of dark charms. Usually the fat for dark charms came from unborn pigs that never made it to a high school dissection class, but it could be worse. "The ingredients look okay. He said it works by instilling a sense that everything is as it should be. Fulfillment." I hesitated. "He's showing me for free."

"Free?" His obvious surprise bolstered my own suspicion.

"Stef is coaching him on the niceties of give-and-take when you're sharing space," I said, not believing it even as I said it. "He didn't say, but it probably has to be done after sunset. Add in time to clean up . . . I might be done by midnight?" I winced. Midnight was an awkward time for him, seeing as elves preferred to sleep in four-hour blocks, once around noon, and again around midnight. "Do you want to make it breakfast instead?" I offered, voice small.

"No," he said immediately, but I could tell he was distracted. "I can swing midnight. Would you excuse me for a sec? I'll be right back."

The wind had freshened under the shade of the cloud, and though muffled through the speaker, Trent's voice was a sudden, surprisingly firm shout. My lips parted as I realized he was talking money, and I hoped it was incoming, not outgoing. Jenks and Stef had moved, and I followed them to a kiosk of hand-spun, hand-dyed gathering scarves, settling myself beside a produce vendor and out of the way. Jenks was on Stef's shoulder, and I smiled as he told her about his late wife's prowess at the loom.

The tomatoes looked fantastic, and I picked out a couple as I waited for Trent. I loved my BLTs, and having tomatoes in my bag would make a great excuse if anyone I knew saw me here. Most places wouldn't sell them except around Halloween. Oh, they weren't illegal, but when half of humanity dies from eating a genetically modified tomato, consuming or buying it publicly gets you ugly stares and maybe your car keyed. That the T-4 Angel tomato had long since been eradicated didn't seem to matter.

My attention went to the new clouds as the wind picked up, but my gaze returned to my phone at a muffled burst of outrage and Trent's calm answer. "Sorry about that," he said, and in the background, the fighting resumed without him.

"Not a problem." I eyed Jenks, now giving me a pixy version of "thumbs-up," and I stiffened, wondering if I smelled Brimstone. *God, I hate this place.* "Do you need to go?"

"Ah, not yet," he said, voice hesitant. "Unless you need to. They think I'm on the phone with an advisor."

"You are," I said, and he chuckled.

"Financial advisor," he amended, and I could hear the smile in his voice. "The battle is won in the mind, not the battlefield."

"And elves know about the battle of the mind," I said, feeling good. Our lives seemed to have drifted lately, and to be able to help him, even if it was just pretending to be his financial advisor, was reassuring.

"Let me know if you decide against Hodin's curse," he said, reminding me he had an entire library of spell books, some of them demon. "I asked Quen to go through my mother's spell lexicon. He knows it better than me, and elven magic is harder to trace than demon. I'd like to know when you and Pike are going to meet with him, too. If you don't mind. So I can come with you. To observe."

"I'll let you know what time Pike and I settle on," I said cagily. Observe, he said, but if it got ugly he'd be throwing the odd spell. It wasn't a bad idea, but I was always nervous when we worked together. Not like when I worked with Pike. Working with Pike was . . . fun.

"Ah, I should get back to it," Trent said as the argument in the background became obvious. "Thanks. I needed the break."

"Anytime," I said, waving Jenks's dust away when he flew too close. He seemed agitated, worrying me.

"Midnight," Trent continued. "Your church? Call if you need more time."

"Okay." I frowned at Jenks, hands on his hips now as he listened. "Love you."

"Love you, too. Desperately."

"Oh, for Tink's contractual hell. Find a hole in the ground," Jenks muttered as Trent ended the call, but I could tell he was pleased for us both. "You were right," he added as I tucked my phone in a pocket. "She's buying stuff not on the list. Some kind of dust and a busted bone. Finger, maybe?"

"Thanks, Jenks." I stiffened when a gust blew through the market, leaving a cry of dismay in its wake as canopies threatened to lift and vendors tried to hold everything down. "I'll talk to her."

"Good, because I like her," Jenks said, and I nodded. I liked her, too, which made the thought of possibly having to beat some sense into her all the harder. We weren't good enough friends that my word would carry much weight, and if I got aggressive, she'd probably leave and make things worse on herself.

"Oh, and Vivian has been watching you since we left the parking lot," Jenks added.

"What?" Face warming, I followed his gaze to a nearby produce stand. Sure enough, the head of the coven of moral and ethical standards was calmly eating a homemade sweet, watching me across a crate of tomatoes. Small, petite really, the slim West Coast blonde would not be my first pick for being one of the premier spell slingers in North America.

With her short, styled hair and wispy, elegantly cut green and tan summer dress bumping about her calves, Vivian gave off all-the-powerful-vibes without sacrificing her femininity. She'd been the junior coven member until Brooke, the previous head of it, tried to make me the broodmare of her private army. Vivian had not only survived being my friend, but prospered. So far.

"I didn't tell her we were going to be here," I said as I gave the smart woman a wave.

Smirking, Vivian pushed off the stand and came over, the crowd simply . . . parting around her despite her diminutive height. "Hi, Rachel," the woman said as she reached me, and I gave her a hug, feeling our internal energies try to equalize before I rocked away. Her blue eyes held the question as to why I was down here, and I smiled, envying her tan. It was deep for Cincinnati, but she'd only been here a few months. "I got your text. I was trying to get a block of time free before I answered."

"Hiya, Strawberry Shortcake," Jenks smart-mouthed, and I smirked, having forgotten the moniker.

"Jenks," the woman said, nodding. The gems on her dangly earrings caught the light, glimmering to make me think there was a charm attached somewhere. Her Möbius pin was proudly displayed on her lapel, subtle but telling. It was the only sign of her office other than her unshakable confidence. It had been a simple band of twisted silver the first time we met. Now it was encrusted with diamonds, more evidence of her promotion.

"Ah, I haven't done anything, have I?" I said, wondering if she'd followed me from the church. She'd shown up in Cincinnati right about the time I got out of jail for that petty conviction of Brimstone distribution.

She laughed, the sound of it rising into the new gust of wind as if it had caused it. "No. Not that I know of. What brings you to Findlay Market?" she asked, knowing my history more than most. "There are no ridiculously wonderful dress shops down here."

Jenks snickered, and I rattled my bag. "Tomatoes. It's BLT season."

"Wow." Vivian grinned, our internal balances rubbing against each other as she linked her arm in mine and pushed us into a companionable stroll. "That's exactly what I'm doing."

But then her chin lifted, indicating a patron three stalls down. "Check out that guy. I don't like his aura," she whispered. "What do you think?"

My eyebrow rose. *She's working?* The man had one of those fifteen-pound, shaggy, waggy-tail mutts, and I briefly brought up my second sight, making a soft, knowing sound at the coat of gray dulling his aura. You'd never guess it from the way he was baby talking to his dog about which gluten-free, organic dog treat to buy. "Yikes," I said, then started, my second sight vanishing and my arm slipping from Vivian as Stef stepped up, suddenly between him and us.

"Hi," she said brightly, shrugging her heavy market bag higher on her shoulder and sticking her hand out. "I'm Stef. You must be one of Rachel's friends."

"When I'm not putting her in Alcatraz," Vivian said brightly as they shook, and Stef's smile froze.

I cleared my throat nervously. "Ah, Vivian, this is Stephanie. She got caught up in Constance's evictions and decided to stay at the church. Stef, this is Vivian." I hesitated. "She heads the coven of moral and ethical standards."

Stef's lips parted. "Y-You're Vivian Smith?" she stammered, and Vivian practically beamed.

"Guilty," she said, holding a hand up. "How do you like living in the church?"

Stef retreated a step, one hand possessively on her market bag. "It's great."

Jenks snickered. "When she can keep the pixies out of her underwear drawer."

A tiny warning flag went up as Stef continued to rock back in tiny, minuscule steps. "It's nice to meet you, but do you mind?" She took another step away. "I need to get some spikenard, and Harry usually closes his stall by three."

And you know that how? I mused darkly, but Vivian only smiled wider.

"Go," she said pleasantly. "Rachel will keep me company."

"Thanks." Clearly nervous, Stef spun, her pace fast as she darted into the crowd.

"Spikenard?" Vivian said, her tone wary. "That's for memory. What is she doing that needs spikenard?"

"Jenks, follow her," I said instead of answering, and the pixy hummed off, his dust torn apart by the rising gusts. *It's going to rain,* I thought, feeling the pressure shift.

"So." Vivian took a daisy from a nearby stall and gave the man a dollar. "What are you really doing down here, Rachel Morgan?" she said, watching me over it as she took a deep sniff.

"Making a white curse. I hope," I said, wondering if she'd give me her opinion if I showed her the list of ingredients. "Hodin—you remember him?"

The tips of Vivian's hair began to float as she tapped the nearest ley line. I could feel her aura tingling, and I put a few more inches between us as we slowly followed Stef. "Red eyes," she said, pulling the petals off, one by one. "Cosmic powers. Living in your church. Looks like a skinny biker dude poet."

"That's him." I took a breath, exhaling slowly. "He's helping me twist a curse to convince some old dead guy coming in from DC tomorrow night that Constance is still calling the shots. It uses elderberries, and the ones in my garden aren't ripe." I squinted at the darkening clouds. People were leaving, and the pinch of time began to prick at me. "Vivian, will you look at this?" Head down, I rummaged in my bag for a copy of the list I'd made while Stef had chatted up a flower vendor. "I'd like your opinion."

"Sure." Vivian's brow furrowed as she quickly read it. "Mercury chalk? That's old-school. The ingredients are okay, but you're dealing with memory, which makes this a gray curse, sliding one way or the other depending on what you do with it." She held the paper out. "What are you doing with it?" she asked pointedly.

I shoved the list deep into my pocket, glancing at Stef as she paid some woman for a bind of metal rings. "It's to convince the DC rep that Constance is well and in charge."

Vivian's eyebrows rose. "Is she?"

I shrugged. "She's well. And in charge of everything she sees."

Immediately the small woman relaxed, a wicked, shared-mischief smile rising to blot out the worry pinching her brow. "I'm so glad we had this chat," she said, her shoulder knocking into mine as we followed Stef. "Everyone appreciates stability except those who thrive on chaos. One person-specific gray charm to prevent a whole lot of misery? I can look the other way."

"Thanks," I said, and she nodded, twirling what was left of her daisy between her thumb and fingers until it was a blur.

"Summum malum," she whispered, but it was a spell, not in response to anything I had said, and the flower in her hand suddenly fell apart, the petals rising up in a soft glow.

"A DC representative, eh?" she said as she watched the swirling flower petals drift away. "I didn't know that. Thanks for the advance notice." Her attention flicked to me. "Hence you needing something nice to wear."

I shrugged. "Ivy is escorting him."

Vivian chuckled, but she was focused on the petals, not me, the tiny bits of glowing white now swirling about the man with the dog, plastering themselves on his back. "I bet Nina is happy about that."

It's a charm, I realized. *Responding to the smut on his aura.* "Pike and Trent are working with me. David is on standby." I jumped as a gust of wind knocked down a temporary sign. "I don't think the witches will be involved, but now you know. His name is Finnis."

Vivian looked up from rummaging in her purse. "How much is this curse costing you?" she said as she put on a pair of wire-rimmed glasses, grimacing at whatever she saw in the petal-coated man.

"Nothing."

She turned from the guy in disbelief, and I shrugged. "He has a vested interest in me staying this side of the ley lines," I said, and she frowned, clearly not liking that any better. But in all honesty, Hodin did have a reason to help me, seeing as I had promised to help him if his kin tried to put him in a bottle for practicing elven magic. I was starting to think elven magic wasn't the real reason they wanted him locked up, though. I did the occasional elven magic, and they weren't trying to lock me up.

"Thank you," Vivian said, now eyeing Stef. "Your new roommate. She's . . ."

I winced at the three petals on Stef's shoulder, then brushed one off my arm. "She's worrisome," I said with a sigh as the first patters of rain began to fall and the vendors hustled to cover their tables. "I'm glad she and Hodin are getting along, but . . ." I met Vivian's gaze, worried. "I think she's spelling for him."

"That's not a crime."

"No," I agreed. "But I think she's skipping work to do it. She didn't get that layer of smut from hospital work."

Vivian gave me a sidelong glance through those glasses. They didn't have any lenses, and they probably showed long-term aura damage. "Yours used to be heavier," she said.

"Yeah, but I know how I got mine."

"And you get along with demons, too," she said as we paused under one of the more substantial stalls. Stef had found the spikenard and some early elderberries trucked in from downstate, and I wanted to leave.

"Hey." Vivian turned to me, her eyes alight. "You know demons."

I wasn't sure I liked her excitement. "I am one," I reminded her, and the owner of the stall we were in chuckled, eavesdropping and thinking I was joking.

"Even better." Vivian glanced at the man with the dog. He was vanishing around a corner, petals and all, but she was clearly not concerned. "How would you like to teach a couple classes in demonology?"

"What?" I almost yelped, and the head of the stall's owner snapped up, his face ashen.

"Just until we find the instructor," she said, oblivious to the man slowly retreating to the other side of his stall. "It would be good for your PR and help me out."

"Ah . . ." I looked through the increasing rain for Jenks, but he was hiding in Stef's hair if the green dust sifting down her shoulder meant anything.

"Temporary," Vivian wheedled. "I'm sure Professor Sikes is only taking a few sick days and forgot to call in."

The scent of hot, wet concrete grew thick, pleasant almost, as the world darkened and people ran for their cars. "Vivian, I don't know," I said, trapped by the pouring rain. "I'm not good at teaching." Teaching? I wasn't good at being a student. The last time I'd taken a class, I'd accidentally made my boyfriend into my familiar—then drove him halfway around the world as he tried to get away from me.

"Sure you are," Vivian insisted. "The kids would love it, and you'd be doing me a huge favor. Classes are Monday, Wednesday, Friday, one to three."

Stef shook a mass of elderberries deeper into her market bag. The rain pelted down between us, and she squinted up at the skies, clearly not wanting to venture out. "Three times a week?" I said, feeling myself weakening. "I've *got* a job. And an aggressive undead coming in tomorrow."

"Please?" Vivian begged. "A couple of hours in the afternoon. That's it. Even if you could do one class it would help."

I didn't have the time for this. But the thought of teaching a class in the same university that I'd once been kicked out of had a definite appeal. "Let me check my schedule," I said, knowing it was a mistake the instant it came out of my mouth.

"Oh, thank you!" Vivian almost clapped her hands, sounding nothing like the badass magic practitioner she was. "I really appreciate this. I'll text you the building and room number."

Across the aisle, Stef had noticed the charmed petals on

her shirt. Brow furrowed, she began plucking them off. "I haven't said yes yet," I warned Vivian.

"But you will," Vivian said confidently. "Thank you *so* much. This is great." Clearly pleased, Vivian squinted up at the rain beginning to ease. "I'm going to take a rain check on dress shopping," she said as the petals Stef was shaking off her fingers floated purposefully through the air, clearly tracking the man with the dog. "That's a nice ring Trent gave you," she said, smirking as she half turned, her eyes on my pinky ring. "It's on the wrong finger, though."

I grinned, waggling it at her, and then she took off, pace fast, focus intent. "Glad she's not tailing me," I whispered, starting when Jenks landed on my shoulder and shook the damp off his wings. "Think I should have offered to help?"

Jenks sneezed, a veritable explosion of silver dust coming from him. "Nah, she's got it," he said, gaze on Stef crossing the aisle to join us. "She's as badass as you."

I smiled as I remembered the two of us destroying a produce section the first time we met—hence the nickname, Strawberry Shortcake. She'd been sent to follow me, and I thought she was a dark witch trying to buy a curse off me, not taking no for an answer. Apparently they still had my picture behind the help desk. Banned. The story of my life.

"Got everything?" I said as Stef rocked to a halt. "I wasn't much help shopping, was I," I added, surreptitiously taking the last petal off her. It fell to the ground, its magic spent.

"No worries." Stef scanned the market, rain spotting her. "Which way is the car? I got turned around."

"West lot," I said, feeling a new mugginess rising up from the damp concrete as the rain ended and the lowering sun peeked out from under the clouds. The market had emptied apart from the vendors, and our way was clear. "Did we get everything?" I asked, trying to look into her shoulder bag.

"Yep."

It was rather short, and Jenks and I exchanged concerned looks. "Ah, Vivian wants me to teach a class on demons," I said as the pixy gestured for me to get on with it. "Hey, if there's anything you want to know about demons but don't want to ask Hodin, stuff that won't be in any textbook—"

"No. Not that I can think of."

It had been too fast, and Jenks's eyebrows rose. We'd left the stalls behind, and the usually packed lot was only half full. "Stef," I said softly. "I haven't been spying on you and Hodin, but I can't help but be concerned."

Her eyes were fixed on my little red MINI. "We're fine. I'm fine."

"I know you're smart," I said as Jenks's wings rasped. "And I know you can take care of yourself, but I also know the attraction to the dangerous. How easy it is to give a little for something you think you can't get on your own. I just want to know that you're okay. That you feel comfortable."

Her steps slowed as we neared the car. "I'm okay." It was almost a whisper, and she wouldn't look up from the steaming pavement.

"Would you tell me if you weren't?" I said, not wanting to get in the car until we found some sort of closure to this conversation. "Because I can help. I brought you into the church. I brought him into the church. I'm somewhat responsible for whatever happens to you."

Her head came up, blinking fast to ward off tears. "I appreciate that."

Jenks hummed off my shoulder, his dust a brilliant silver. "Are you two bumping uglies or not?"

"Jenks!" I exclaimed. "Don't answer that, Stef," I said, then glared at him. "God, Jenks."

"What?" The pixy darted up and down in the humid air. "It's a fair question. If she's going to give up her room and move in with him, I want two weeks' notice so I can rent it out." His wings glittered in the low light, and behind him, a rainbow blossomed in the dark sky.

Stef evaded me, her gathering scarf held close. "I'm not giving up my room."

My God, they're sleeping together. Or they had, and my focus blurred as I wondered what that had been like: Hodin's confident power, the chance he might overstep, the risk she'd taken, and the probable ways the former sex slave knew how to use ley line energy. That she wasn't giving up her room hinted that she wasn't entirely comfortable, and I took her arm.

She jumped, startled. "I'm okay," she said. "I . . ." Her voice trailed off. "I'm not sure," she said faintly. "Sometimes I feel as if I know him down to his core, and then he says something and I don't know him at all. I'm trying to be open-minded." She looked at me, pleading. "I know nothing of his past apart from what he tells me. Rachel, am I making a mistake?"

I felt cold, and as Jenks hummed protectively closer, I forced her to meet my eyes. "I don't know. Has he hurt you? Accidentally, I mean?"

"No." She turned to the car as if wanting to end the conversation, and I unlocked it from the fob. "But sometimes I can't tell what he's thinking, or I can and it's not good."

The market bag went on the tiny rear seat, and then the back door thumped shut. The gathering scarf was still in her grip, and my suspicions tightened. "What does your gut say?" I asked as I moved to the driver's side.

"That I could make a mistake and not even know it." Stef eyed me over the low hood of my car. "I can't tell if it's my gut instinct or my preconceived impressions. They're hell to live with, you know?"

I did know, and I nodded as I lingered outside the car. She seemed as if she was wound too tight, and I grimaced, remembering feeling that way myself when I was dancing with the bones of my buried past. "Tell me if you are ever afraid, okay?" I said. "And if you can't tell me, put a flower on the sill in the kitchen."

Lips pressed, she nodded and got in.

Jenks was right there, and we exchanged a weary, concerned look. "I'll watch her," he said, and I shook my head.

"She doesn't need watching," I whispered. "Hodin does."

Jenks nodded, his altitude dropping as a glum gray dust slipped from him.

Breath held, I swung myself in, marveling aloud at the twin rainbow arching over the Hollows, the smaller appearing to end right at my church.

Omen? I wondered as I started the car. *Or promise.*

CHAPTER
5

THE RAIN ON THE ROOF OF THE BELFRY WAS MORE THAN pleasant as I knelt on the floor, shuffling through a box my mom had sent me months ago. The three leeward windows were open, and the hush of leaves mixed pleasantly with the soft sounds of my spelling robe and the come-and-go of Jenks's wings. We weren't working with auras so I didn't need the wide-sleeved, belled-sash spelling robe that eliminated auratic contamination, but Hodin was wearing his, and I had felt like a slob in my shorts and lightweight tee. Besides, the silken loveliness graduating from a bright gold at my neck to a deep red at the hem made me feel as if I knew what I was doing.

"I've never heard of mercury chalk," Jenks said, his voice almost too faint to be heard as he tugged a light-weight blanket over Bis. The young gargoyle was high at the conical ceiling on his shelf next to the bell. Beside him was the bottle that held his soul and the baku both, looking innocuous next to my jewelry box and the empty cricket cage that Hodin had loaned me to practice dividing a spo-

ken curse between two people. I hadn't found the knack
before the crickets had died, and I had shoved it up there to
get it out of the way. I probably should have returned it, but
it was too high to reach without standing on a box, and he
hadn't asked for it.

"Magnetic chalk is cheaper and nontoxic, so no one uses
it much," I said, depressed at not having found a way to free
Bis's soul from the baku. "I think I've got a stick of it in my
pencil case. God knows how it got there." I sat back on my
heels, blowing a strand of hair from my eyes and smiling as
I thought of my mom starting her life over on the West
Coast with a man who desperately loved her. She was safer
there with Takata than with me.

But I froze, startled when my shuffling fingers went
numb and every ounce of ley line energy drained from me
with the suddenness of a cracked whip. I yanked my hand
from the box, pulse fast as I stared at the lead-lined bag my
fingers had grazed, but it was only that no-magic-zone
amulet that I'd taken from Constance last spring. The bag
was supposed to block its effects since I'd lost the invocation pin and couldn't turn it off, but clearly the charm's in-
fluence had been only muted, and I wrung my fingers, still
feeling the sting of disconnection.

"Jenks, will you bury this in the garden somewhere?" I
said as I took the ley line amulet from the supple but heavy
bag, holding the metallic amulet from a thick strand of
black gold as if it was a dead rat.

"No prob." Jenks's wing pitch rose as he slung the lanyard over his shoulder and laboriously flew out the screenless window, his path dropping fast from its weight.

Immediately I renewed my hold on the ley line, eyes
closing as it rushed in with a satisfying ease. Sitting on the
floor, I sent my senses out to find Hodin and Stef on the
porch. The pixies made bright spots of thought flitting in
the garden in the rain. Much more somber were the fairies,
hunkered down in the dry areas. That they were able to
share the same garden was both unexpected and a miracle.

What is that? I mused, sensing an odd, faint hum of

power in the floorboards. I hadn't noticed it before, but I didn't do a mental search of the grounds very often.

Eyes still closed, I narrowed my search, a frown finding me as I traced a silvery network of energy ribbons running through the floor and walls and up over my head like a net, culminating in the iron bell that hung from my peaked ceiling. It encased the belfry in a snug, protective net, unseen until now. Maybe the no-magic-zone amulet had been interfering. *WTF?*

"I like this one," Jenks said, and my eyes flew open to find he had returned, standing on the dresser to look very Peter Pan–ish as he stared down at Pike's sketches. "Four strikes and you're out," he added, poking his sword at the napkin with the four *X*s on it.

"It's an *M* and a *W* intertwined," I said, deciding the protective net must be something the gargoyles put in to protect Bis and his displaced soul. They were guardians, after all. "Morgan and Welroe. Where's the amulet?"

"In my storehouse under Pierce's tombstone," he said, studying the doodles. I still hadn't picked out my favorite, and I wasn't even sure I liked the idea. "I thought it was four *X*s. One for you, Pike, me, and . . . Trent?" Jenks's angular face pinched. "I don't think Ivy is coming back to the firm even if she comes back to Cincy."

"Me either," I said around a sigh. Ivy was good at busting heads, but she was even better at the ugly niceties of politics—which were just as bloody.

"Four strikes and you're out," Jenks said. "I like it."

"Yeah, but the subrosa is supposed to be hidden. Won't leaving a tag every time we do something give it away?" I scooted up onto the fainting couch as I found the dented pencil box with love-worn She-Ra stickers. The low couch had been my bed now for months.

"You can be hidden and still have a logo." Jenks held up another sketch in consideration, the rough napkin as tall as he was. "Make a statement without identifying yourself. Like Batman." He turned, grinning. "This would be stellar as graffiti," he said, eyeing the sketch of a diamond between two parallel lines.

The top of the case stuck—as usual—but it finally popped open to leave me blinking at the worn nubbed ends of a couple dozen colored pencils. *And one mercury chalk,* I thought in satisfaction. *Still in its wrapper.* "Found it." I held up the shiny, crackly package. "My dad must have put it in here before he died. I don't remember buying it."

Jenks dropped the logos and flew closer. "It's not opened."

I frowned as I read the toxic warnings on the packaging. "It's probably been in there for nearly fifteen years. No expiration date, though."

A spike of angst flashed through me, and I stood. My dad. Not my birth father, who my mom was currently shacked up with, but my dad, the wickedly clever human who had taught me my pentagrams and successfully pretended to be a witch until he died from complications of a vampire bite, gained while looking for a sample of untainted elven DNA so Trent's dad could break the curse sending them into extinction. I was sure my dad had known I was a witch-born demon, and I was still finding things he had put away for me: demon tomes, rare ley line equipment, and now, a mercury pencil.

"How come Hodin doesn't have one of those?" Jenks asked, and I frowned.

"Hodin doesn't have a job and they're expensive," I said sourly. The protective covering crackled as I dropped it into a pocket. "Coming?" I asked, and Jenks hummed into the air, checking on Bis one last time before following me out.

Steps slow, I felt my way down the cramped dark staircase to the foyer, wondering if I imagined a soft snap of protection falling away as I left my high haven. My shoulders slumped at the reminder of Bis, comatose and pale, but somehow alive without his soul. Hodin had promised to help me find a way to bring him back. It was part of the reason I'd vowed to help keep him out of a bottle if the other demons tried anything. That I mixed elf and demon

magic never seemed to bother them as much as Hodin doing it, and I seriously wanted to know what they were refusing to tell me. I was sure it involved Celfnnah, Al's late
wife.

Jenks landed on my shoulder, the glow from his dust
lighting my fingers trailing along the old wood. "Could we
at least try the aura-solidifying curse on the baku?" he
asked, and I shook my head, the bells on my sash jingling
as I found the foyer and shut the stairway door behind me.

"Until we know how to reliably hold the baku, we can't
let it out of the bottle," I said, just as disappointed as he
was. The sanctuary was blessedly quiet with the pixies outside, a single light beside Ivy's baby grand dimly lighting
the large space. Jenks flew ahead, and I followed him to the
kitchen and out into the three-season porch.

*If I can get Lee to help me with a ward, it could be a
four-season,* I thought, smiling at Stef and Hodin clustered
beside the low slate coffee table before the black emptiness
of the unlit fireplace. Even with the humidity, it was a
pleasant place to spell with the enclosing three walls and
roof, the last wall completely open to the wet garden. The
flashes of pixy dust in the rain made it rather surreal, and I
honestly thought the porch was the best part of the church,
cool now in the softly pattering rain.

A soft anticipation born in learning a complex magic
lifted through me. Hodin's fancifully embroidered black
robe made him into the picture of the studious demon, and
I jumped when he snapped the book in his hand closed
against Jenks's dust, a spiderweb of energy crawling over
the bound leather before vanishing. Stef looked up, her subdued green and yellow robe mirroring her aura. *As does
mine,* I thought as I touched the gold and red silk.

It was obvious that they worked well together, making
me wonder how many spelling classes I'd missed, busy
with my own life. Seeing them at the table with the curse's
ingredients arrayed before them, I felt as if I was witnessing
the distant past, or maybe the future: quiet study, steady
progress, charm after spell after curse through the ages.

"Did you find it?" Stef asked as she continued to pulp the elderberries into a black, ugly juice. Her fingers were purple, and I felt a flash of guilt. She was prepping the spell for me, like a familiar.

"Still in the package." I brought the stick out of my pocket, waggling it before setting it on the table. "I should be doing that," I said as she strained the juice through a copper sieve and dumped the waste into the trash. Crap on toast, even the herbs were prepped and measured.

"I didn't have work tonight." Stef wiped her hands on a cloth Hodin handed her, and the purple stains vanished. "I could use the practice."

Hodin tugged his robe to make the bells on his sash chime. "Stephanie is an apt student," he said, and she beamed. "Besides, if I instructed you, you might accuse me of teaching you something."

He'd said the last rather dryly. I flicked my gaze to Jenks, the pixy hovering almost sideways as he looked for a title on the book tucked under Hodin's arm. There wouldn't be one. Demon books never had titles.

I sank down in the indoor-outdoor couch across from them, the low table between us, the empty fireplace behind them. "So is there a recipe, or are we making it up as we go?"

Expression sour, Hodin dropped the book on the table. Bells jingling, he flicked out his robes and ceremoniously took the chair kitty-corner to me, his long face drawn into speculation. "Stephanie, make up the smudge stick while Rachel and I go over this, will you?"

"I can make the smudge stick," I said, but Stef only gave me a smile and drew the rue, mustard seed, rosemary, and walnut leaves closer.

Jenks hovered annoyingly close as Hodin leafed to the proper page. "This is legal, right?" the pixy asked, and my eyes darted to Hodin's. "I mean, Rachel, you freaked when Trent removed the memories of those two assassins in your kitchen."

Assassins in my kitchen? I mused, then remembered. That was when I had escorted Trent to the coast to steal his daughter in an arranged elven tradition. He'd been somewhat loose in his adherence to the law at that point. Still was. Kinda.

"That was an elven memory curse," I said. It wasn't dark, but yes, illegal. "Fulfillment is different. Right? Vivian says the intent is the tipping point since the ingredients are balanced toward neutral."

"Vivian Smith?" Hodin's long fingers shifting the pages slowed. "You asked the leader of the coven of moral and ethical standards if a curse was *legal*?"

He looked aghast, and I pushed deeper into the cushions to cross a knee over the other. "Yes," I said, chin high. "I cleared this with my friend Vivian."

Hodin stared at me. "Why?"

Jenks snickered, his dust a cheerful yellow as he went to sit on Stef's shoulder as she rolled the rue, mustard seeds, and rosemary into a cigar, wrapping them in the green walnut leaves. "I ran into her at the market," I said. "I'm not going to twist dark magic, Hodin. You said it wasn't illegal. If it's not dark, and it's not illegal, what's the harm in showing what goes into it?"

Eyebrows high, Hodin turned to Stef, who shrugged, her brow pinched as she tied a Gordian knot with the celery string. "I don't want to go to jail when this is done," I said softly.

Hodin still seemed at a loss. "The entire point is that no one knows you did this. That's why they call the position the subrosa."

"Trust me, Hodin. Everyone will know it was me," I said sourly. "Besides, all I did was ask her about the ingredients. Thinking I gave her the know-how to stir a curse by telling her the ingredients is like saying someone can write Shakespeare because they know all the words."

Hodin's fingers held a place in the closed book. "You gaining this spell for your library is not my intent."

I sucked on my teeth, foot bobbing. Did he really think I wouldn't know how to stir this after doing it once? Besides, clearing the ingredients and getting Vivian's advice ahead of time was going to be my ace in the hole should this go sideways.

Stef was done with the smudge stick, and she set it aside, quiet as Hodin tried to decide if he was going to continue or not. I arched my eyebrows in challenge, and he frowned, setting the book on the table and flipping it open to the right page.

I looked down, breath catching as I saw the ingredients listed on the left, the corresponding instructions on the right, and the occasional illustration sandwiched between wherever there was room. It was a messy but efficient way to put down a curse, and no one but Newt wrote them down quite this way.

"This is Newt's book," I said as I studied the circled, six-pointed star with runes at the tips.

"Not anymore," Hodin said.

"Where did you get this?" I said, reaching for it. "I mean, when?" I amended when he drew the book out of my reach, his thin lips pressed together.

"As you can see," he said, ignoring my question, "the smudge stick is made of rue, stolen; mustard seed, gathered before dawn and after the equinox; rosemary from your own garden—all bound by walnut leaves and celery twine."

"Fire herbs," Stef said as she began pulping the spikenard, skullcap, chickweed flowers, and licorice seeds in a stained mortar. Her very nonchalance made me think she had been grinding up herbs for Hodin for a while.

"That's five," I said, looking at the six-sided star. "What's the sixth ingredient?"

Hodin stiffened. "The sixth is the fire itself, born from your thoughts, not your hearth." His eyes narrowed. "Can you make a flame with your thoughts?"

He knew I could, and I nodded. The curse was a mix of earth and ley line magic, but most demon magic was.

"You will use the decoction of chickweed, spikenard, skullcap, licorice seeds, and elderberry juice to make the ash into a slurry that will then be drawn to the runes and create the curse," he said, and I studied the six-pointed star.

It was old-school, but I'd found that Hodin generally used
outdated methods, probably because he didn't have access
to the demon collective where all the shorthand spells were.

"Two invocations . . ." I mused, finger tingling as I
traced it down the page to the Latin at the bottom. *Damnatio memoriae* was the damnation of memory, and *in statu
nascendi* roughly translated to the state of being born.
There was no *"ta na shay"* to attract the Goddess's attention, but it felt elven even if it was Newt's curse.

"The quencher herbs are all feminine," I said, gaze lifting to the ingredients. "That balances out the masculine.
But I see only five again."

Hodin's fingers tightened, nearly pulling the book away,
and Stef, who was adding the pulped herbs to the juice,
seemed to stiffen. "The blood used to kindle the reaction is
the sixth," Hodin said coldly, and Jenks snickered from the
mantel.

"Look, I'm not poking fun at your curse," I said, remembering having a problem with his methods being too loose
for me before. "But if you have a six-pointed star, and six
runes, and six herbs in the ash, you probably have six herbs
in the quencher, too. I'm just asking questions."

He glared at me, his thought to walk away obvious.

"But if you say the sixth is the blood to kindle it, that's
okay with me," I added, and he sniffed, pulling the book
protectively on his lap. "How many drops?"

He was silent, and a roll of thunder echoed softly between the hills surrounding Cincinnati. "Six," he finally
said, and I stifled a smile. "One drop for each time you
want to invoke it."

"It's repeatable?" I said, pleased. "Fantastic!"

Hodin's eyebrows rose mockingly. "Wands usually are."

"Wait. What?" I sat up, shocked. "This makes a wand?
Wands have to be redwood."

Hodin stood, and I followed the book in his hand with
my eyes. "This is not witch magic. It is demon. Hence the
elderberries," he said as if that meant something.

"Oh." I licked my lips, then eased back into the cushions

to hide that I was so excited I could sweat gummy bears. I'd always wanted to make a wand. They were so flashy. "Do you use the mercury chalk to draw the star? The recipe doesn't say." Actually, the recipe seemed to lack a lot of information. But that was standard for Newt.

"Obviously," he drawled, and I reached for the mercury pencil, carefully opening it to find the toxic lead was encased in a neutral, hard wax. *Cool . . .*

"So." Hodin used a black silk cloth to wipe the stray ions from the mirror. "The smudge stick is prepared. Thank you, Stephanie. It goes down and the star drawn around it. Runes first."

Stephanie set the smudge stick dead center of the mirror, and I pulled myself up to the very edge of the couch. Dragging the mirror closer, I studied the book still in Hodin's jealous hand, my pulse fast as I read Newt's cramped handwriting and what few instructions there were. The star wasn't drawn the usual way, but was rather three sets of parallel lines sketched from rune to rune.

"Runes first," I said softly, deciding to start at the top and move deasil around.

"Widdershins," Hodin directed, and I stifled a grimace.

Change, I mused as I wrote the first on the mirror, then will, and death, followed by kindle at the bottom, growth, and finally harvest. They were powerful symbols, and old, so old.

With the runes to guide me, I began to draw the lines of the star. Harvest to will, growth to death, change to growth, will to kindle, harvest to kindle, and finally, change to death. The mercury pencil laid down a thick, heavy line, and though I usually maintained a light connection to the ley lines, I felt it strengthen, becoming almost dizzyingly surreal.

Hodin's shoulders slumped, frowning as if something should have happened, and I studied the sketch. Newt was notorious for leaving things out of the printed text if there was an illustration. "It needs a circle," I said, and starting at the rune for change, I drew a circle from point to point, again naming the runes as I went, feeling my connection to the lines become stronger as I reached the end.

"Change," I whispered as the circle was complete, and with a startling whoosh, the smudge stick ignited.

"Wow." Stef looked up from the prepped quencher. Hodin, too, seemed impressed, and he scooted closer, making a notation under Newt's script to add the circle. A muttered word of Latin cemented the scribble into place.

"Good." Hodin eased away in satisfaction as the honest odor of rosemary turned bitter as it burned. The acidic smell of walnut joined it, and the electrifying scent of something I couldn't identify. "Quench it," he said, eyes alight. "Six drops, and douse it."

Now? I thought, beginning to wonder if Hodin had ever done this charm in his life. Stef quietly pushed forward the quenching solution and I took it in hand, hesitating. The smudge stick was still burning like a Christmas tree in July. Hodin fidgeted, clearly wanting me to douse it, but I waited, rolling the finger stick between my thumb and index finger until the smudge stick was nothing but ash, the rising smoke seeming to hum through me like electricity.

"Six," I said softly, the jab of the tiny blade on my Jupiter finger almost unnoticed. Six drops of crimson went plinking in, and the scent of redwood rose high. The quencher was activated. I was doing this right, and a smile curved my lips up.

Hodin inched closer, the bells on his hem chiming. "Recite the invocation."

The faintest hint of burnt amber brought me up short, and I paused. He was a little too eager, and I didn't like it. "Hodin, what's the smut payment on this?"

Hodin's expression blanked. "It's a little late to be asking that."

I glanced at Jenks, and his wings blurred to invisibility though he didn't move from the mantel. "No, it isn't. How much?"

Hodin grimaced, eyeing the glowing lines and fading embers. "It will be what you make of it, obviously. There will be more cost to cloud a strong will than a weak. A small change from reality is less than a large lie."

It was what I expected, and reassured, I carefully quenched the ashes.

"Invoke it," Hodin said. "Now."

I didn't like him barking orders, and not sure I trusted his eager hunch, I took a steadying breath. *"Damnatio memoriae,"* I said, starting as a ping of sensation darted through me, thrilling as it tingled to my extremities and backwashed into my chi, warm and scintillating. My lips parted as the muddy ash crawled to the drawn lines of the star like a slime mold.

"Holy cats!" Stef said. "That is creepy as all hell," she added, and Hodin gave her an annoyed look.

Clearly he had tried this curse before and failed, and I couldn't help feeling a little smug as the mercury lines made a glowing hexagon through the coating of ash and elderberry juice.

"Seal it," he said, but I was already reaching for the clean sand, pouring it over the six-sided star until the soft lumps of the glyph's lines were hidden under a smooth layer. When you got down to it, magic was really variations on similar themes.

"In statu nascendi," I said, jumping at the abrupt snap of disconnection. Suddenly the world seemed a dimmer place, the pixy lights in the garden subdued, and the shine on the leaves duller. I'd lost my connection to the universe, and I shuddered at the lack.

"That's it?" Stef said, and Hodin nodded, his tension almost palpable as he carefully blew the sand aside. But his hand jerked away when the tube of black sand he had exposed crumbled to nothing.

"Mother pus bucket!" he swore, and in an unusual show of temper, he shoved the book sliding across the table to crash into the stained sieve. Stef scrambled to keep it from tipping, and Jenks dropped down, his wings rasping in warning as he landed on my shoulder.

"It worked," I insisted, my own hands going to brush the

sand and collapse three more tubes. "I know it did. I felt it!" But there was nothing there but disintegrating brown sand, and I sat back, flummoxed. "Have you ever done this charm?" I accused, and he glowered, sullenly slumping into the chair. "Oh, so you thought you'd give it to me to figure out? Maybe blowing myself to the ever-after in the process?"

"You and Newt think alike," he muttered, broody.

I glanced at Stef, peeved that she hadn't told me this was a spell in progress. Maybe she didn't know. "Do you have any idea how dangerous it is to try to duplicate one of Newt's charms?" I said. "No one even pulls them from the collective anymore."

Hodin gave me a shrug. "I thought you could do it."

Which was both gratifying and infuriating; gratifying because he thought I was skilled, and infuriating because now I had no fulfillment curse.

"This is why there are no mercury pencils in Cincinnati," Stef said as she began to tidy. Everything she put into the woven basket vanished, probably reappearing in the kitchen sink. "He used up his entire stash. Gone."

Hodin glowered at her, and she grinned at him.

"But I felt it work," I said as I brushed the stained sand from the mirror to see that the mercury lines were gone. Only the runes were left. Even the circle was gone.

"So did I," Hodin all but growled. "I see no wands, though."

My eyes flicked from the book to the runes. The lines had vanished. Where had the power gone?

I stiffened with a sudden idea, searching the table for the mercury pencil. "Where is it?" I said, not seeing it.

"Where is what?" Hodin stared at the ceiling, clearly put out.

"The mercury rod!" I said, and Jenks darted from my shoulder, the pixy's wings a harsh rasp as he dropped to the table.

"Careful!" Hodin shouted, scrambling up as I followed Jenks to where it was hidden under a wad of unused walnut leaves. My fingertips tingled as I grasped the smooth finish of the wand, because that's what it was now. The power in the ash had soaked into the lines with the quencher, and then the invocation had centered it into the rod. *All six charms of it,* I thought in satisfaction. I could feel it, simmering within the protective wax coating.

"It's in here," I said as I brandished it, and Hodin lurched forward, grabbing my wrist and lifting my hand so I wouldn't accidentally invoke it.

"Let her go!" Jenks shrilled, and I yanked my wrist free.

"Relax!" I shouted at both of them. "Jeez, Hodin. I'm not going to spell you," I said, but he wouldn't take his eyes off it, and I shook my sleeve to cover it. "Look. It takes a gesture and invocation word both."

I pointed with my free hand to the book that Stef had opened, and Hodin's lips pressed, his expression shifting from worry to . . . relief? "Amazing," he said softly, and I smiled at Stef's fading alarm. "You have the potential to be one of the ever-after's most powerful practitioners if you leave that unimaginative hack of a spell slinger."

Immediately my good mood soured. "You mean leave Al to work with you?" I shook my head, gaze traveling over my new wand. "No. This was luck. You press it too many times, and you end up a dark smear on the ceiling." Wand held behind my back, I got into his face. "And if you ever bring one of your experiments to me under the guise of a well-spelled curse again, I will kick your ass to the ever-after and you will be on your own. Got it?"

Stef was quietly cleaning up, reminding me of Ceri. I'd been used by demons before so this wasn't altogether unexpected, but I was disappointed that Stef hadn't said anything. She had known that Hodin was having trouble with it.

"This is mine," I said as I used my phone to take a picture of the spell. "All of it," I added as I turned the page for the countercurse, frowning when I realized there wasn't one. *Swell.*

Hodin jerked his sash tighter, bells ringing. "I did not intend to give you the how of this."

"No, you intended for me to figure it out and leave you

with a functioning curse while all I got was a measly wand." I closed the book and shoved it across the table. "You have a lot to learn about friendship, Hodin."

Stef seemed to shrink in on herself, clearly feeling the sting as well.

"And you have much to learn about the origins of power." Hodin's eyes narrowed. "Teaching an entire class of witches because a *friend* asked you?"

My lips parted as I turned to Stef. The woman wouldn't look at me, but it was obvious that she had told Hodin about my teaching gig.

"It's called giving back, Hodin," I said, standing up to leave. "Once you reach a certain level, you begin to give back. Dali is teaching a student for free. Al taught me for free." But it wasn't free. He had required my trust. And here I was, working with the demon he warned would use me, a demon who had apparently betrayed them all when they were at their most vulnerable. *Crap on toast, how badly did I screw this up?* "Hodin, what did you do to Celfnnah?"

A flicker of anger passed over Hodin. "Could you excuse us, Stephanie?" he said softly, but I could hear his frustration, and my thoughts went to the wand. *A rise up and flick, and he won't remember me asking.*

"Um, sure." Head down, Stef gathered the last of what was on the table and left, shutting the French doors between us and the kitchen as she went.

I stood waiting. Hodin's gaze shifted between Jenks and me. Tugging his robes free, he sat down. "Celfnnah died trying to escape the elves," he said shortly. "Gally blames me."

"Was it your fault?" He was silent. My jaw clenched, and I forced it to relax. "You like living here?" I added.

"I was to be the demon's mole," he said, his voice light and bitter. "My own brother sent me to be caught so I could help him get the rest out. Three hundred years I worked with a slave collar on my ankle, learning there was no escape. Not even death was allowed. I learned how to please them. How to get warm clothes and a soft place to sleep.

How to amuse them until I got myself sold to the very elf who held the keys to our freedom."

"And?" I questioned, and his eyes came to me. "Al seems to think that you had more to do with her death than that," I said, and Hodin made an ugly sound. "That you had a chance to free them and you turned them in. For your benefit."

"Turned them in to dine on raspberries and sleep on silk," he said bitterly. "That's what he told you, yes? *I* was the one tortured as they developed the baku, stripped down to almost nothing again and again as it ate my soul. *I* was the one they practiced their foul spells and curses on, perfecting them. They kept me alive because I *entertained* them, becoming skilled at impersonating beasts so well even they couldn't tell the difference. My own brother sent me in," Hodin practically spat. "He begged me to go, and he never lifted one finger, said one spell to get me out when it was obvious that I was as trapped as those he thought I could free. He blames me for her death? Well, I blame him for what they did to me, over a thousand years of torture. A thousand years, Morgan, and he left me there to rot when he could have brought me back with one word."

I felt cold, frozen where I stood.

Hodin stood, and I jerked, startled. "I'd appreciate knowing if the wand works." Expression grim, he picked up the book, vanishing even as the binding left the slate table.

Jenks's wings were cold against my neck, and I shuddered. "I gotta check something in the garden," he said, then hummed up and away.

I was alone, not knowing if Hodin had told me everything, or just what left him looking good. Fatigued, I sank down before the empty fireplace, the bells of my sash jingling. I really needed to talk to Al and hear the other side of this story. Too bad he wouldn't speak to me.

CHAPTER

6

"WHAT TIME IS IT?" I WHISPERED, THE SOFT GRAY OF PULLED curtains giving me no clue.

Warm air smelling of cinnamon puffed as Trent rolled over, his arm curving about me in a delicious feeling of belonging. "Go back to sleep," he whispered, and a shiver iced through me.

My grip on him tightened as he began to pull away, and a sleepy smile spread itself across my face. "It's Sunday. No way," I whispered. His green eyes traced my curves, and I tugged him down, finding his lips with my own.

Desire woke from my core, shocking in its suddenness, but oh, so welcome. His arm about me became more certain and his weight was a pleasant warmth. Stubble was a rough sensation on my fingertips, and I sent my hand across his shoulders, drawing him closer. The sheets were tangled, and I kicked them off . . . everything coming to a screeching halt as his phone vibrated.

Trent's lips parted from mine. Head rising, he stared at it on the bedside table, then sighed. "That's the girls. I thought you were asleep and I texted them," he said, and I let go, knowing he would take it. It wasn't that the two toddlers being raised as sisters were spoiled—which they were—but because they were, by birth, pawns in a very dangerous game. It would be years before they made their theoretical way across the chessboard and back to be queens. Until they found their strength, he was their knight.

Crap on toast. It's too early for metaphors, I thought as I rolled over and put my feet on the floor. Toes digging into the soft rug, I reached for my own phone. *Eight thirty?* I thought in disgust as I let it drop. But if it was early for me, it was late for Trent, and I appreciated him lingering in bed as long as he had. Elves were crepuscular, meaning they napped at noon and midnight. His natural sleep rhythm didn't mesh as badly as one might think with a witch's wont to sleep to nearly noon and crash well after midnight. He seemed annoyingly bright and awake at the moment, but he'd be nodding come noon, ready for his four-hour nap.

I felt good as Trent said hello, his musical voice taking on that firm and loving tone he probably didn't know he used with the girls and only the girls. His trim silhouette showed in the dimness, making me wish that whatever calamity had befallen Ray or Lucy had waited for just thirty minutes longer.

"Lucy? Lucy," he said patiently, trying to get a word in as the little girl prattled on about cereal and jelly. "Let me talk to your mother. Lucy, I hear you, and I know what you want. But your mother is the deciding factor when you are at her house. If you let me talk to her, I might be able to intervene on your behalf."

I smiled. Lucy was only two, but Trent's habit of talking up to them rather than down seemed to work—most times.

"Lucy, give the phone to your mother," he added as he headed out into the main common room, and I stood and shuffled to the bathroom, grinning. I loved both girls, but man, I was glad I was not involved in deciding if jelly was an acceptable cereal condiment.

Nothing less than the scent of coffee could have pulled

me from Trent's excessively indulgent shower, and twenty minutes later, I padded out into the common room in my robe and slippers on permanent relocation to Trent's estate. I was still not awake, but at least my hair had been tamed by product and charm. Trent was puttering about in the small efficiency kitchen, and I flopped onto the couch, content to watch him as I tried to wake up.

Four stories down, Trent's estate sprawled in countless rooms to entertain and work, often at the same time. The ground floor with its adjoining underground garage was mostly party, with an eight-person-staff kitchen, enormous bar, and the great room opening to the extravagant pool. His mother's newly discovered spelling lab was to the right, and the hallway to his father's public offices, now mostly unused, to the left. Above and overlooking the great room were the live-in apartments for the staff once needed to run the place. Most of them were empty, especially on the weekend. The medical and administrative floor was above that, again, open to the great room. It, too, was mostly vacant, abandoned when Trent was accused of manufacturing and selling illegal medicines—which he did. Does. Whatever.

Trent still sprawled his living from one end of his estate to the other, but it was here, high above the great room, where he began and ended his day in four large suites opening to a common living area and a small eat-in kitchen. *This* was where Trent conscientiously tried to be a normal single parent, and I smiled fondly as he took a tray of cookie-like morning biscuits from the toaster oven.

I loved Trent when he was spelling, his fair hair staticky and his green eyes glinting with discovering how much power he could wield. I loved Trent when he was putting unicorn Band-Aids on scrapes and kissing little-girl tears into giggles. I loved Trent in the boardroom, his icy control striking doubt in those facing him as he outwitted them with lifelong relationships and cunning foresight. But I think I loved him best when he was in the kitchen, content and happy as he was free to be . . . what he wanted to be.

His eyes met mine, and I felt a delicious pang of love.

"The Goddess help me, you are beautiful in the morning," he said as the toaster oven shut.

"So are you," I shot back. "Did Lucy get jelly on her Cheerios?"

Trent laughed, the warm sound going right to my center. "One measured spoon, yes, but we agreed that it was inappropriate for Buddy."

I nodded, glad the little dog had joined the weekend migration to Ellasbeth's penthouse on the Hollows side of the river.

"They miss you," he said as he came out balancing two oversize mugs of straight black coffee and a tray of tiny pastries. "Do you have time next week to go to the zoo with us?"

He sat down, and I carefully snugged in as the tray and coffee went on the low table. I would have said the iced pastries were store-bought, but Trent had someone come in once a week from one of the culinary schools and do most of his meals. "Us being you and the girls, and Ellasbeth, and Quen, and Jon?" I said glumly. Being Cincinnati's most prominent elven citizen meant security atop security, and though that was my job most times, Trent liked a few more pairs of eyes when the girls were involved. Not to mention that Quen would appreciate a day at the zoo with his daughter, Ray. It was an odd sort of family, but the girls were loved, and that's all that mattered.

Trent settled deeper into the couch with a mug and sighed around a sip. "You, me, and the girls," he said. "Quen has been taking Ray out on her rides. It's their alone time, and he thinks she needs more time with you."

"Me?" I looked at him over my mug. "Why me?"

His smile went loving, and a spike of fear hit me for what might come out of his mouth next. "She sees you as a mother figure more than Ellasbeth," he whispered. "Hey-y-y, don't freak out," he said, setting his coffee down when I began doing just that. "I'm not saying you should move in with me and start making her lunches. Ray simply likes what you do more than what Ellasbeth does. Quen thinks she would benefit from spending more time with you. That's all." He took a slow breath. "And I agree."

Holy crap on toast, how did this happen? I thought, but then I frowned. Quen. He'd been the Kalamacks' head of security since before Trent was even born. Ellasbeth was nice, in a prickly way, but Quen's daughter, Ray, was showing all the signs of being a sneaky, powerful elf who worked best in the shadows. Ellasbeth had both girls dressing in pinks and sundresses, eating their peanut butter sandwiches at five-star restaurants, and where Lucy took to it like a duck to water, a day at the zoo in pullovers and sneakers was far more Ray's speed. Ellasbeth would ruin it by trying to get the girls on the front page of Cincinnati's society pages.

"Let me get this thing with Finnis settled first," I said, and Trent tugged me closer, a happy sigh slipping from him.

"It never ceases to amaze me how someone can possess the world or nothing at all, and still have their happiness hinge on the small moments between them and the ones they love." Trent nuzzled the damp hair from my neck, making me shiver as he breathed in my scent, content.

I set my coffee down, a new stirring bringing me all the way awake. "Where's Jenks?" I said as I eyed the pastries and wondered if we really had the entire four-story monstrosity of Trent's estate to ourselves. More or less.

Trent's lips brushed my neck, little kisses sending jolts through me. "With his son and grandkids in the solarium," he whispered, and I shivered, turning to face him more fully. "He's teaching them a new security measure. Should be busy for hours." He smiled, his love showing. "I have to thank you for convincing Quen to allow them and the fairies into his security plan. Together they have caught three incursions in the grounds before Quen's systems just this year. Oh, and Izzy is pregnant again, so we should have an even better coverage by fall."

"That happens with pixies." But my good mood tarnished as I thought of Jenks, and seeing it, Trent used a finger to shift my chin so he could search my expression.

"Izzy being pregnant makes you sad?" he guessed, misreading my mood. Elves and witches, even one who was a demon, could not have children together. But it was Jenks whom I was worried about.

"It's Jenks," I admitted, and Trent nodded, clearly not convinced. "He's doing okay, but the memories of Matalina are bringing him down, and he won't allow himself to make any new ones with anyone else. He misses Bis, too."

"Hodin hasn't come up with any new ideas for separating his soul from the baku?" Trent asked, and I shook my head.

"None I like. And Al won't talk to me as long as Hodin is in the church," I said. "Jenks is frustrated with the pixies he's renting the garden to in exchange for security. They police it for pixy threats okay, but not my security and he's at his wit's end." My eyebrows lifted in amusement. "Though he has gotten them to work with the fairies, somewhat. He had them playing a game, yesterday."

Trent's arm slipped from around me. "You never told me how twisting that curse went."

I reached for my coffee and took a sip, my thoughts on where we might go dress shopping. Unlike my past boyfriends, Trent liked to shop—as long as we included a shoe outlet along the way. "Good and bad," I said, focus distant in memory as my arches found the edge of the coffee table. "I made a wand," I said, thinking of it tucked in my pencil case, where it would stay until I needed it. "It's got six fulfillment curses in it."

"And the bad?" Trent said cautiously.

"Bad news is that I thought he was giving me something he knew how to do, not one of Newt's forgotten curses that he dug up and had never done before. They can be dangerous. She tends to leave things out." I sat up, reaching into my robe pocket for my phone. "Want to see it?"

"You brought it with you?" he said, relaxing when I began scrolling.

"I took a picture of it," I said as I found it, shifting the phone so we could both see. "I cleared it with Vivian. I'm good."

"But you don't want to get caught using it, regardless," he said as he read it over, frowning at the two distinctive handwritings. "Mercury chalk, eh? That's old. And it's a white curse?"

"Ah, not exactly. Vivian says that since the base ingredients are benign, it depends upon what I'm doing with it. Since I'm convincing someone that Constance is alive and safe—which she is—the curse is technically white. If I used it to convince someone that Constance is alive and safe and she wasn't . . ." I glanced at Trent, seeing his understanding. "Then not so much. What bugs me is that it doesn't have a countercurse."

"Drastic situations require drastic measures," Trent said grimly, and we knocked our coffees together before sipping them. Drastic measures. That might be okay if he was your average Joe, but Trent had done some really nasty things in the name of saving his species from extinction. And so had I.

"I've about had it with Hodin," I said, taking a tiny pastry when Trent lifted his phone to check his email. I'd be ticked, but the man did supply the entire eastern U.S.'s Brimstone and ran a good portion of the train system. "I'm counting the days until he's out of the church," I said around a bite. "Actually, I'm surprised he didn't ask for an extension in return for the curse. But then again, he wasn't sure I could do it. I want to give him the benefit of the doubt, but when he's not asking for stuff, he feels easy like a wish, and wishes always come back to bite you."

Trent chuckled as he set his phone down and took a pastry.

"So." I ran a finger down his neck and he froze as goose bumps rose in its wake. "Do you have the entire day free, or will you be incorporating an hour or two of business downtown?"

Trent looked at the pastry he was holding, then me. "All done. I'm yours today."

"Good." I snuggled in deeper, breathing him in. "Do you want to . . . go shopping?"

He chuckled as he ate the sweet pastry, the sound rising through me as more of a feeling than sound. "That's right. Ivy's coming home."

"I'm not dressing for Ivy," I said, but we both knew that wasn't true. "I need something that says smart and demonic for a class I'm teaching on Monday for Vivian." I frowned. "Maybe Wednesday if they can't find the regular professor. He just skipped out. No notice. Nothing."

"At the university?" Trent's eyes widened as he reached for another pastry. "That's fantastic! Check out Ellasbeth's old closet. She left lots of demonic power outfits in there." Slowly his smile faded into annoyance.

"No, thanks." I laced my fingers in his and gave them a squeeze. "I'll find my own power dress."

"Probably a better idea." Trent sipped his coffee, and my tension rose. He was thinking. "I'm, ah, glad that you found a curse for Finnis," he said, a faint flush rising up his pointed ears. "I have apparently misplaced some of the books I was going to show you."

I hesitated, quashing a sudden worry. "Er, were they demon?"

Trent's brow furrowed as he read my concern. "They were. Why?"

"The library is missing some, too," I said. "I was going to wait until this thing with Finnis is settled, but maybe I should check it out."

A worried sound slipped from him. "You think the demons . . ."

I shrugged. "Missing books, missing ley line professors." Son of a bastard. The demons testing what I would do if they broke the law was not what I needed right now.

"I'm sure it's not them." Trent eased into the couch and tugged me closer. "Chances are the missing professor stole them and lit out of town."

Which wouldn't explain Trent's missing books, but it wasn't hard to mis-shelve a book with no title. "I hope so."

"Ah, I know you don't want me there when you talk to Finnis, but—"

"Stop." I clasped his hand between both of mine. "I do, but if you're with me, I'll be more concerned about you than what's going on."

"But you can work with Pike," he said. Jealousy colored his voice, and I beamed.

"I don't love Pike, you goose!" I said, adding, "You're jealous," when Trent made a frustrated sound.

"Damn straight I am," he muttered, tugging me closer. I relaxed into him, feeling the masculine taste of the ley line energy in him mixing with my own.

Until someone's phone hummed.

"Oh, for Goddess's sake, now what?" Trent frowned as he took his phone up. "It's not me."

"It's David," I said as I glanced at my screen and stretched for my phone.

Scowling, Trent put an inch or two of space between us and pulled the tray of pastries closer. "You and your men," he grumbled as I beamed and hit the accept key.

"Hi, David," I said brightly as Trent hunched over the tray, clearly frustrated. "This better be important. I'm still in my robe."

"It's almost nine—oh. Sorry," he said, remembering my sleep schedule. "Ah, I'm out at the wharf. Hollows side. You might want to come out here. Pike's got himself into some trouble."

I could hear the wind against the speaker, and I slumped, startled when Trent held out a pastry, popping it into my mouth when I opened it to speak. "'Rap on 'oast," I mumbled around my full mouth. "'Ike's a big boy. Can it wait?"

"No," David said sourly. "We're lucky I was sent out to

adjust the claim, or you might not have found out until it's too late."

I swallowed, almost choking. "Claim?" I echoed. "What did he do?"

"Ah, he sunk a casino boat," David said, his voice distant, making me wonder if he was at the docks, looking at it. "Seems he made a large bet last night, and when he couldn't cover it, he cried foul, tried to leave, and sunk it before they pinned him down."

"Is he okay?" I said, suddenly concerned. *Bad bet?* My eyes narrowed as I figured it out. Pike had been trying to win the funds to pay off Finnis. "Damn it, I told him we were going to talk to Finnis and find out what he wanted, first."

"Yeah, well, word is the casino owner has Pike. He's probably still alive," David said, chilling me. "It's only been a couple of hours and they know he belongs to you. Do you want Mr. Castle's number?" There was a hesitation. "I probably have his direct line."

"Yes," I said, thankful when Trent pushed a paper and pen in front of me. "I'm set. What is it?" I didn't own Pike, but everyone knew he was important to me.

David rattled off an out-of-state number, and I wrote it down. I didn't know Castle personally, but everyone had heard of the werefox who Lee had sold his casino license to. "I need to get dressed," I said faintly, mind whirling. *What the hell was Pike thinking?* But he hadn't, and now he was in trouble. "Thanks, David," I said, then hesitated. "Do you think Castle might be willing to settle this without filing charges?"

"Seeing as he hasn't filed a police report yet, I would think he would, yes," he said with a light chuckle, but he quickly sobered. "I'm sorry, Rachel. If Castle was a regular Were, I might have some pull, but werefoxes don't look to anyone."

"As long as he's not dead. I can't work with him if he's undead. Thanks, David."

I ended the call, surprised to see Trent dressed and standing before the dull reflection in his big-ass TV, his shirt tucked and his long hands gracefully tying his tie. "Son of a bastard," I muttered as I punched in Castle's number, then pulled myself straighter, trying to find my cool. "Jenks!" I shouted as it rang, wanting him with me when I went to talk to the werefox. He might not hear me, but someone would and would relay my call.

The plate of pastries silently slid out from before me. "What happened?" Trent said as he took it to the kitchen, his sock feet padding softly.

"Pike made a bet to get the money to bribe Finnis. He lost. Destroyed a boat. Castle has him. So far, he hasn't called the I.S."

The phone was ringing, but no one was answering, and I stood, frustrated.

"Mmmm." Trent dumped the pastries into a colorful paper bag. I'd seen the girls take snacks to the stables in them before. "I'll come with you," he said.

I slumped, my arm around my middle as the phone continued to ring. "Yes on you coming, no on your checkbook joining us. You can't keep buying me out of my scrapes."

Trent rolled the bag down and set it beside two small thermoses. *Our coffee? To go?* "I'm not getting you out of a scrape," he said, his faint smile devious. "I'm getting Pike out of jail. He's going to owe me. I like that."

I took a breath to protest, words catching when someone finally answered.

"Rachel Morgan," a light, satisfied voice said. "As expected."

I had the right person, and I exhaled, hoping he wouldn't hear the stress in it. "Mr. Castle? How much?" I said flatly.

Castle chuckled, low and deep in his throat. I hadn't had much to do with the werefox who had taken over the gambling cartel when Lee had retired and left Cincinnati. His establishments were organized and up-front. He was a model citizen. *Yeah. Right.*

"Let me see," Castle said, and I put the phone on speaker

so Trent could hear. "He owes me five hundred thousand to cover the bet, two hundred thousand for the boat, and maybe another five hundred thousand for the downtime while I repair the boat itself."

"A million two?!" I exclaimed, warming when I realized I'd shouted it. "Hold up, Castle. Don't jerk me around because you think you've got me over a barrel. I know for a *fact* that your insurance will be taking care of the boat and double-dipping makes you greedy and wreaks havoc with your taxes. You've got three other boats in dry dock you can put out, so don't give me any crap about downtime."

"You don't have a million two?" he mocked, and I unclenched my jaw. "No? I'd wager even your rich boyfriend doesn't have that much in liquid assets," he added, and I felt myself go cold. "That's okay. I've got a gentleman standing in my office who has agreed to meet my price for Pike, and since he doesn't care if he's alive, twice dead, or somewhere in between, I am going to have a very pleasant afternoon before I give Pike to him."

"Castle, wait." *One of Pike's brothers,* I thought, panicking. They wanted him twice dead so they could inherit the family fortune. They'd probably collectively spent twice his debt on assassins over the years. "I've got the money," I said, feeling like a failure when I looked at Trent and he nodded, flashing me two fingers followed by four. "All of it." I took a breath. "I need twenty-four hours."

"You have six." Castle laughed patronizingly. "You'd have less than that if I didn't want to play with him a little before I scrape him off my floor and sell him."

"I want to talk to Pike," I said, but Castle had already disconnected.

Six hours? Fear and failure twisted my gut as I pocketed the phone. "I am so sorry, Trent," I said in a small voice, and he pulled me into a hug.

"Get dressed. I'll have the car waiting in the garage in ten minutes," he said, and I turned to the clatter of pixy wings. It was Jenks, his bright sparkles rising up from the lower levels of Trent's estate. "Quick stop downtown for the cash, and we can be there before Castle does anything permanent."

"Tink's tampons, I was right in the middle of a tea party," Jenks complained as he brushed dandelion seeds off his sleeves. "What's up?"

My gut hurt as I felt my choices spiral down to nothing. "We've got a problem."

CHAPTER
7

TRENT'S FAVORITE CAR WAS TWO-DOOR, LOW TO THE ground, gray in color, fast, and had more gadgets on it than an entire 007 movie. The pretend back seat was good for nothing but keeping the insurance down or maybe seating a leprechaun. But it didn't matter how luxurious the leather was or how far I sank down into it, I was upset, and I couldn't stop my foot from tapping the door with an irritating rhythm that made Jenks roll his eyes and Trent wince.

I grabbed my bag as we pulled onto my street, anxious to jump out. There were a few things I wanted before we talked to Mr. Castle. A denuding curse, maybe. Harassment without any lasting harm—my specialty. The finding charm sensitized to Pike that I had made three weeks ago would be useful. A change of clothes, certainly, because I wasn't going to lean on Cincy's gambling cartel in jeans and a green T-shirt.

"Hey, I want to talk to Baribas about upping the church's security," Jenks said, his wings rasping when Trent eased the car to a halt in front of the church. "How long we got?"

"Ten minutes?" I said, and he darted out the window, rising high with a sharp whistle as he entered the grave-yard.

My seat belt recoiled with an aggressive sound of sliding fabric and I reached for the door—only to hesitate when everything seemed to crash down on me. Lip between my teeth, I sat there with my bag on my lap, fingers pressing into my temples. I had a headache starting.

Trent silently put the car in park. "Pike is going to be okay."

"That's not . . . I mean, I'm worried to death about him, but . . ." Hand dropping, I looked across the small car. "I don't like taking advantage of you. I mean, over a million dollars. I will never have that much mone—"

"Shhh." There wasn't a hint of smile on him as he leaned across the car, taking my hand and giving it first a squeeze, and then a kiss. "You aren't taking advantage of me," he said, and I cringed. "If anything, I'm taking advantage of the situation. Pike is going to owe me one hell of a favor, not you." Now he smiled, a hint of evil elf lord showing. "Maybe it will be enough to convince him to stop trying to seduce you."

"Pike is not trying to seduce me," I said, flushing.

He gave my hand another squeeze and let go. His car was a bastion of safety, somewhere I knew what was real and could make good decisions. Beyond was the church, and lately . . .

I didn't like thinking I couldn't make it on my own.

"Rachel, I understand," Trent said. "Remember how you saved my life?"

I found a small smile. "At the boat?" Kisten had blown it up not knowing I was on it at the time. I had saved Trent from drowning. And he had done the same for me.

"No." He lifted my hand and kissed it again, his eyes fixed on mine. "Not that time."

I thought for a moment. "When you were a slave in the ever-after about to be auctioned off?"

His grin widened and he ducked his head, embarrassed.

"No. It was when you agreed to go out on a date with me. A real one, not all those times when I asked you to be my security to a function I didn't want to go to except that you'd be with me."

The band about my chest seemed to ease, and I took a clean breath. "Okay, I see where you're going with this." My hand slipped from his as I opened my door and got out. I wouldn't make the promise that I would repay him, because I couldn't.

Leaning in through the window, I stretched awkwardly across the seats and gave him a kiss. "Thank you," I whispered, one foot on the ground, the other in the air as I hung half out of his car. "You want to come in while I change?"

Trent shook his head. "No. Do what you need to do while I go to the bank. I've got a hot date tonight, and I need some extra cash."

"I can't believe you can liquidate that much in an hour," I muttered, half envious, half dismayed as I began wiggling out of the car.

"I'm not." Trent fixed his hair in the rearview mirror to cover his pointy ears. "Lucky for us I had it already pulled for something else, but this is more important."

His business downtown, I thought, and a flash of guilt hit me. "Love you," I said instead, and he leaned across the car toward me.

"I love you, too. Desperately," he whispered, his hand leaving tingles as it slipped from my jawline.

I'm going to spell Pike into next week for this, I thought as I disentangled myself from Trent's car and gave him a stupid little wave before going up the stone steps and to the heavy oak doors. The sun peeping through the heavy leaf cover was inordinately hot, and I hesitated just inside, relishing the blast of cooler air coming up through new floor vents. Behind me, Trent's car idled softly away.

Solemn, I shut the door. "Thank you, Finley," I whispered in the dark chill of the foyer. The contractor who had renovated the church had put the air conditioner in to help alleviate the vampire pheromones if we ever found ourselves a paranormal shelter again, but that wasn't going to stop me from appreciating it when it was only me, Stef, Jenks, and Hodin.

My headache was promising to evolve into something worse, and I left my bag by the door to go up to my room for a change and some charms. I would've blamed Trent's pastries since anything with prepared lemon juice gave me a raging migraine from the sulfate preservative, but I knew it was stress.

Six hours, my ass, I mused as I threw on my lightest leather pants, a lined black camisole, and a lightweight leather jacket. It was too hot for leather, but animal hide was a layer of protection from spells and, er, teeth.

"Charms," I muttered as I checked my splat gun and tucked it in a pocket. The finding amulet sensitized to Pike was next. My key ring had a zip-strip snipper on it, but I quickly wound my hair into a bun, hiding a second clipper at the center of it. *Live and learn.*

"Boots . . ." I mused, not seeing them.

My gaze landed on the pencil case. Sure, I could use the fulfillment curse on Castle, but it would make linking Finnis's sudden contentment to me a lot easier.

Frowning, I pulled one of my demon tomes to check a curse I'd found while looking for a spell to capture the baku. If I had it right, it would have the same effect as a denuding charm. All I had to do was tap a ley line and say the words to pull it from the demon collective. Some other demon, probably long dead, had made and stored the curse, but I could buy it in exchange for taking on the smut it created. The imbalance would be minimal. Well worth the result.

The trick to getting my way and staying out of jail was to be powerful without being threatening, keeping my magic annoying but not so much anyone would complain. And whereas removing Castle's hair could very well be considered assault, embarrassment would likely keep him from filing a report.

Quod periit, periit, I thought in satisfaction as I read the short curse, then I shelved it between the *56 Ultimate Cookie Recipes* and *Betty Bob's Cookbook for One.* I was feeling good in my working leathers, and my gaze again slid to the pencil case.

"No, Rachel," I said. What if they took it from me? *What if Pike's brothers kill him?*

Frustrated, I opened the box, stared at the wand, picked it up. *Last resort,* I thought as I tucked the pencil-length spot of coolness between me and my sock. I'd feel really stupid if I needed it and it was in the belfry. Unlike my splat gun, the curse couldn't be used against me as it needed both a word and a gesture. For all Castle's men would know, it was a piece of chalk to draw a circle with.

Which isn't a bad idea, I thought, my sock feet thumping lightly on the steps as I headed downstairs to find my boots. The barest hint of burnt amber was a half second of warning, and I gasped, jerking to a halt before running into the tall, dark shadow at the bottom of it. "Hodin!" I exclaimed, and he smirked, backing into the light spilling in from the sanctuary.

"My apologies. I was checking to see if it was you," he said, decidedly attractive in his lightweight slacks, white shirt, and colorful vest. It was a new look, and I wondered if it was for Stef. "Weren't you spending the day with Trenton Aloysius Kalamack?"

I pushed past him, breathing in the scent of Brimstone, the bump of that wand feeling obvious in my sock. "Pick a name," I said, not turning around. "Saying all three like that together makes you sound like a demon."

"I am a demon."

I dropped to my hands and knees to peer under the couch for my boots. *Got you. . . .*

"Kalamack," he said at my continued silence, the demon still lingering in the archway to the foyer. "I thought you were spending the day with Kalamack."

"Something came up." Stretching, I pulled one boot, then

the other out from under the couch. Scooting up onto the cushions, I shoved a foot in, heel thumping. "I'm changing my clothes and picking up a few charms," I added, wondering why he was standing there like a flustered roommate who had a hot date in his bedroom.

"Oh." He moved, his pointy-toed shoes making a soft scuff. "Is there a problem? You appear stressed."

"Pike did something stupid last night," I said, bent over as I tied my boot. "Trent and I are going to bail him out before he gets sold to one of his brothers for the bounty on his head."

"Mmmm."

I looked up, my second foot thumping into place. "They will kill him. Twice."

A flicker of something passed over the demon, and then Hodin nodded in concern. "Is there anything I can do?" he asked as if remembering it was the polite thing to say. Stef was beginning to have an effect, but I was sure Hodin would put a price tag on his help.

"No." I laced up my other boot. "Jenks and I have it." I hesitated. "Unless . . ." Guilt swam up, and I stifled it. *Al, if you want to be my teacher, you need to be present, not moping about in the middle of an ever-after forest in a trailer.* "Um, hey. I know I said I wouldn't take instruction from you, but I spent six weeks in jail trying to get an immobilization charm to work on those crickets you gave me. I give up. How do you do it?"

Hodin hesitated, a hint of suspicion finding him. "Crickets?"

"You know. The crickets," I said, too embarrassed to tell him they had starved. "In the cage. I tried focusing on their auras, their physical state, I even tried using two ley lines. I give up. How do you make one curse act on many at the same time?"

"I never gave you a cricket cage," Hodin said, and I felt my expression blank. "And I certainly did not instruct you to try to do something that was impossible."

"Then who did?" I said, lips parting when I figured it out. *Al.*

"Gally!" Hodin barked, his face a mix of anger and what might be fear as he eyed the ceiling. "You talked to Gally thinking it was me? How long ago?"

"March," I said, my brow furrowed as I slumped on the couch over my knees. "Right after I put in that elven bell charm." I glanced up, blanching at Hodin's white-faced anger. "He looked like you," I said, remembering the crow. *A crow with shiny, tidy feathers,* I thought. Hodin always made a scraggly bird. His robe at the time had been a featureless black, too, very unusual for the typically flamboyant dresser. And the flat-topped hat? *Son of a bastard, it was Al.* "But now that I think about it, his choice of words was more like Al's than yours," I whispered.

I pushed deeper into the couch as Hodin fumed, clearly angry, but having no outlet for it. I wasn't happy, either. "He was probably trying to suss out if I was taking instruction from you," I said, and Hodin's malevolent gaze landed on me.

"And were you?" Hodin asked sarcastically.

"No." My distant focus sharpened as I thought of Stef, who *was* taking instruction from him. "Is Stef here?"

Distracted, Hodin waved an expansive, ring-decked hand. "Work," he said shortly.

"Good." I stood, feeling capable in my leathers and boots. If Al had been checking if I was taking instruction from Hodin, then I'd passed his *little test.* "I want to talk to you about her. I'm glad you're making friends, but friends don't ask friends to skip work to spell for them."

He pulled himself up short, his thoughts almost visibly shifting. "You should keep your thoughts out of Stephanie's life. We're more than friends, and therefore the give-and-take is greater."

Oh, really. . . . My eyes narrowed, and I wondered if he truly liked her or if he was using sex to expand how much energy Stef could handle to make her more useful. "There are laws that span both sides of the ley lines." I took a step closer, arms loose. He was far older and had a larger magic lexicon, but I was used to fighting for my life. "One is that it's illegal to use a sentient being as a familiar. Come on, Hodin. Let me hear you say it."

Hodin's smile expanded, his need to dominate chilling me. "Nothing is illegal when there's consent. Seems to me you're using her as your familiar more than me."

"You mean the fulfillment curse?" I said, glad the wand was hidden in my boot. "She's not going for her witch degree, is she," I accused. "You've got her prepping your curses. Hodin, I will not let you make her your familiar. Got it?"

He took a breath, brow furrowed and expression cross. "Why do you even care? It's not as if you are her friend. You don't do anything with her outside of arranging who will clean the toilets and run the dishwasher."

"Hey!" I shouted, flushing at a tinge of guilt, then jumped as the woman in question blew in, trailing a haze of pixy dust and a multitude of shrill voices. Jenks was hot behind her, his dust an ugly red as Baribas followed him, his sword brandished as Stef rushed closer, clearly upset.

"Hodin?" she shouted, a near sob of relief coming from her as she saw us in the sanctuary. "Oh, God. Rachel. I'm so glad you're here." Then her mood shifted. "Back off!" she exclaimed to the surrounding pixies, all of them shrilling to make my ears hurt. "I said back off! She needs help."

She? I wondered, seeing Stef's hands cupped protectively as she glared at the angry pixies wreathing her, all of them shedding a bright red dust.

"Leave!" Stef shouted, and Jenks made a sharp whistle. Like fish fleeing, the pixies darted to the rafters. All except for Baribas hanging before her in a clear threat. "Let her die," the small pixy said, words so fast they were hard to understand. "She was poaching!"

Poaching? Is it a pixy?

Stef came closer, hunched over her cupped hands. "I didn't mean to hit her," the woman said, tears showing on her face screwed up in fear. "She flew right in front of the car. I didn't have time to stop. She was just suddenly there!"

Jenks's wings hit a higher pitch as Stef opened her hands and a small gray and black puddle of fabric quivered in her palms. It *was* a pixy, her clothes mismatched but well sewn, one brilliant dragonfly-like wing gray where it had snapped and was leaking dust.

"She needs help," Stef said, almost whispering. "I hit her with the car. Can you fix her, Hodin?" she said, tear-wet eyes fixed on him in hope.

My gaze flicked up. He seemed sad, but I wasn't sure I believed it.

"She was poaching!" Baribas said again, and from the rafters came a resounding agreement. "She dies. Give her to us, lunker!"

The pixy in question trembled violently, and Stef drew her close to her middle.

"She's still breathing," I said.

Baribas dropped down, expression ugly and sword bared. "Drop her. I'll make it fast."

My God, I thought, horrified, but when I looked at Jenks for support, he shrugged. "Jenks," I protested. "Tell them to leave her alone. They will listen to you. It's your church."

Jenks winced. "Well, if she was poaching . . ."

"Jenks!" I exclaimed, and he sighed. Okay, I knew it was pixy law, and that upholding it was often the difference between surviving the winter and watching your children die, but Jenks owned the church. He was renting out the property. He had resources that no pixy ever had before, and with that stability should come a new benevolence.

"Interesting," Hodin said, and I spun, thinking he was commenting on the bloodthirsty nature of pixies, but he was bent over Stef's hand, one finger forcing the pixy woman to uncurl.

"I'm no poacher," the pixy breathed, hardly conscious as she pushed at Hodin's finger, stabbing it with a wooden dagger.

Jenks turned. Blinked. Dropped six inches. I took a breath, my words remaining unsaid. She was like Jumoke, all dark hair and dusky eyes. They struck me speechless as she vacantly blinked at us, clearly suffering. Her clothes showed wear but were clean apart from the dust from a busted wing. And she was scared, leaking dust and blood fast. Too fast.

"How come no one killed you yet?" Baribas said, and she focused on him, her hand trembling as she threatened him with her wickedly sharp wooden dagger.

"I'm not saying they didn't try," she said, her high voice musical even as she sounded ill. "I wasn't poaching. I had on my red hat. It's gone. Where's my hat?"

Jenks choked back a cough as the pixy woman sat up in Stef's palm, tugging her skirt straight as she looked for her missing hat. She appeared to be eighteen, full-figured and with what might be a henna tattoo peeping from behind a new rip in her sleeve. No shoes. Dirty feet, but clean hands. Clearly she was a loner, rare at her age. But everything about her was rare.

"You should have been left to die of exposure when a newling. Crush it, demon Hodin, or I will run it through," Baribas said, and I stiffened.

"Whoa, whoa, whoa!" I exclaimed as Jenks rose up, clearly distressed.

"She was poaching!" Baribas said, mystified.

"She said she lost her hat, and I believe her," Jenks said, and the ragged pixy stiffened, her shoulders rising higher in fear, not hope. "This," he said as he hovered before Baribas, wings clattering, "is my land. Or do you want to fight me for it, Baribas?"

Baribas dropped away, wing pitch lowering in fright. "Pixies don't fight over land."

"Then there's no problem. Is there." Jenks's dust sparkled an almost unreal silver. His thoughts were the same as mine. Had Baribas taken her hat so he could kill her with impunity? Dark pixies were not allowed to survive birth.

Usually, I thought. Jumoke was one of Jenks's children,

a rare, dark-haired, black-eyed son who would have normally been left to die of exposure. Instead, he'd been lovingly raised and given the chance to defend a garden. The pixy in Stef's hand had somehow survived as well, but no pixy could hold land alone, and no one would marry her. She had no recourse but to find food where she could. And to have survived this long? She had to be one hell of a pixy.

"No one is going to kill her," Stef said. "I believe her, too." Her tear-wet face lifted to Hodin. "Please. Help her."

My shoulders slumped and I glanced at Jenks. Hodin was a demon, but he'd been trapped in a bottle for at least two thousand years. He might know elven lore, but the newer, more complex curses that could save a life were beyond him—beyond both of us.

"I don't know a healing curse," he admitted, and tears began to well in Stef's eyes.

Jenks's wings rasped as he rose up. "I'll get the kit."

My gaze went to the belfry as if I could see through the ceiling. "I've got a pixy-size pain amulet," I said, pushing into motion. "Stef, keep her in your hands," I added over my shoulder as I jogged for the belfry stairway.

Jenks darted for the door, his path making a quick arc U-turn when a high-pitched complaint rose from the rafters. "If even one of you says a cross word to her, you will all be on the curb. Got it?" he shouted at the renting pixies, and a tiny gasp rose.

"She doesn't look right! This isn't done!" Baribas protested, and I slid to a halt inside the dark foyer. Jenks was facing the smaller pixy, his hand on the hilt of his garden sword.

"Neither is allowing another clan freely into a cultivated garden," Jenks said, his dust a clear, brilliant silver in comparison to Baribas's dull, sickly orange. "Should we adhere to all the traditions now? Or can we keep bending them so your children have somewhere to park their asses and nectar to put in their bellies?"

The pixy glanced at his kids in the rafters, chirped his wings, and darted out, all of them flying close behind.

Stef shivered as their dust sifted down on her. Clearly relieved, she opened her cupped hands, and both she and Hodin peered down at the small woman curled in a ball, that dagger still in her grip. "Is she breathing?" Stef whispered in agony. "I can't tell."

"She's not gone yet," Jenks said. "Be right back."

"Get her under a warm light," I said as I ran for the belfry. "Watch for the cats!" I shouted over my shoulder, and then I was thundering up the dark, cramped stairs.

I blew into my room, squinting at the brighter light as I teased free one of the tiny amulets I'd made for Jenks. "Why am I not carrying these in my bag?" I muttered as I pricked my finger and invoked it even as I headed downstairs.

The honest scent of redwood blossomed in the tight confines of the stairway. I held a pinky-size amulet in one hand, the other running along the wall for balance. And then I jerked to a halt as a wave of ley line energy seemed to rise up from the sanctuary to pulse over me. One hand to my chest, the other pressing into the wall, I hesitated, feeling the net of glowing lines the gargoyles had put around the belfry flash into a brilliant gold and red glow, as visible as if I was using my second sight as the surge of energy raced over and around the net . . . and was repelled.

If I'd had any doubts that the glowing lines were there to protect, they were now gone. Someone had put a substantial protection grid over the belfry, but why? And perhaps more importantly, who? My initial thought that it had been Bis's dad, Etude, seemed unlikely after seeing it in action. Gargoyles' magic was far more subtle, and my stomach tightened into a queasy knot as I paced into the sanctuary to see Hodin, Stef, and Jenks at Ivy's baby grand, the intense page light swiveled to make a spot of heat on the dark wood. Seeing Hodin's affected concern, I stopped short. *Hodin wouldn't have done it.*

My pulse quickened, and I put a hand to the archway. It had to have been Al. Probably when he had dropped off that cricket cage. He had been protecting me even as I had refused to listen. And here I was, ready to walk away and give up on ever finding what we had once had. After all that we had done and been through. *Am I really that stubborn?* I thought, and guilt slithered out from the dark places where truth hid.

"You're going to be okay," I heard Stef say weepily, and I pushed forward. The pixy woman was up and awake, clutching a pixy-size pillow to her middle as dust leaked dangerously from her snapped wing. Jenks stood before her, his wing-repair kit in hand, stymied as she threatened to stab him with her dagger.

"Stay away!" she demanded, and Jenks turned to me, his desire to help pinching his face.

"I felt a spell," I said, deciding to keep quiet about how it had been repelled by the protective net around the room where I slept. "What did you do?" Though not healed, the pixy was clearly not at death's door. "Stef?" I prompted warily.

"You're going to be okay now," Stef said to the tiny woman, practically sobbing the words. "I'm so sorry I hit you. You're going to be okay."

My eyes went to her wrist, and I slumped. "Oh, Stef," I whispered as I saw the demon mark. There were two slashes across it, one of them red rimmed and brand-new. Two. I hadn't even known she'd had the one. It used to be a veritable death warrant. What it meant now . . . I had no idea. *Why?* I thought as I stared at Hodin. It was obvious the spell I'd felt had come from him and that Stef had bought it with a third of her soul. One more, and he'd own her. Maybe.

"Ah, Rache?" Jenks's wings snapped as he darted out of the tiny woman's reach, her dagger swinging. "She's still leaking dust pretty bad. Tell her I'm not trying to kill her."

"You think she'll listen to me?" I said as I set the invoked amulet down.

Jenks bobbed up and down, distressed. "You're the demon."

Yes, I was the demon, and I glanced at Hodin. This wasn't over, and we would talk. "You're going to be okay,"

I said, and the small woman got to her feet, wobbling. "Jenks raised a son with hair as dark as yours."

The tiny woman looked at Jenks . . . then ran for the edge of the piano, trailing a sickly green dust.

"No!" Jenks shouted as he darted into the air after her.

"You're still hurt!" Stef cried as she reached out, but the pixy woman was faster, and busted wing leaking dust, she flung herself into the air.

Shrieking, she dropped.

Jenks was there, snagging her wrist and flipping her into a skirt-flailing arc before catching her in his arms. There was a tiny clatter as her dagger hit the floor, and then he was struggling, trying to keep her from falling as she fought him. "Knock it off, woman!" he shouted as she reached behind him, pulling his wing out of alignment and sending them crashing down.

They hit the floor with a thump and rolled apart. Scrambling, the woman went for her dagger.

"Jenks! Cat on the floor!" I shouted, and Stef gasped, falling to her knees, arms spread to keep the pixy from running. It was Rex, the orange tabby having been drawn by the sound of wings under stress.

"I'm not trying to kill you!" Jenks exclaimed, clearly annoyed as he stood with his back to the approaching cat. "What the Tink-blasted hell is wrong with you! I could have busted a wing with you bringing me down like that."

But the woman wasn't listening, fixated on the large tom pacing forward.

"No, wait," I said, grabbing Stef's elbow as she went to intercept Rex.

Jenks's head was down, spinning in a slow circle as he tried to reach the base of his wing. She'd pinched a nerve, and it hung wrong. The pixy woman watched the cat, a wicked smile on her tiny face. "Fool pixy," she said, clearly expecting Jenks to be cat chow.

Jenks looked up as Rex batted a velvet paw at him, sending his tiny master sliding four inches before Jenks caught his balance.

"Knock it off, Rex," he muttered, rising up as he finally got his wing in line. Smug, he flew a bare inch off the floor to where the pixy woman stood, stunned, her mouth open and her eyes wide. "Are you okay?" he said as Rex flopped onto the floor behind him, his white belly showing. "Can I fly you up? Rex is a good cat, but he *is* a cat, and you can't fly."

I felt good as he held out his hand for her, even if she watched in near terror as his cat cleaned his ear with one white paw.

"I'm Jenks," Jenks said, hand still outstretched. "Ah, Rex probably won't hurt you, but Boots is still around and he might take a potshot at you."

The small woman seemed to start. "You live with two cats? I mean, I heard stories, but I thought . . ." Her high voice faltered. "Spring frost take it, I . . ."

Jenks beamed, his dust a cheerful gold. "Rex was my kid's cat, but he couldn't take him when he moved out. Boots is Stef's familiar. I'd watch out for him. He's only been here a few months and still thinks pixies are food."

Frightened, she backed up three steps, then almost fell when her knees buckled.

I reached out, but Jenks was there, scooping her up and flying her to the piano. He set her down with a sudden thump when she smacked his face, and there she sat, wings leaking, dress hiked up to her knees to show her patchwork tights, staring at us staring at her.

Stef inched in closer to Hodin. "I'm so sorry for hitting you. You can stay with me until you can fly."

The small woman's wings drooped, and her dust went gray as she hung her head.

"I think she's going into shock," I said, not liking the faint rise to Hodin's lips. "She could probably use some pollen. Jenks, wasn't there some goldenrod in the far corner of the graveyard that was flowering early?"

Stef's frightened gaze went from me to Hodin. "You stay. I'll go see," she said, and I stifled a frown at how much that had sounded like a request to leave his presence.

Hodin didn't move as she inched away, then turned and paced quickly out.

Jenks was at his wing-repair kit, carefully unpacking it where the woman could see. The imprint of her hand was a bright red on his cheek, and she stared at his metal, wood-handled garden sword with envy.

She'll be okay if we can stop that wing leak and get her to eat, I decided, then faced Hodin. "What did you do?" I asked belligerently, and the demon's attention flicked up to me.

"An elven charm that negates the body's ability to feel pain," Hodin said, smugly, I thought. "She's running on adrenaline and will need continual care." His brow furrowed in what I thought was a mocking concern, and I rounded on him.

"I meant, what did you do to Stef?" I almost hissed. "You sold her a curse she didn't need, didn't you?"

A chill dropped down my spine when he took my right hand, shifting it over to where Al's mark once lay.

"I gave her what she wanted," he said, and I yanked my wrist from his grip. "I have things to attend to."

"Hold it, Hodin," I said, and he jerked to a halt, his goat-slitted eyes narrowing. "I don't know what you're playing at, but don't make an enemy of me," I added, the tips of my hair beginning to float as I tugged on the ley line.

"Enemy?" he mocked, and Jenks turned from trying to convince the pixy woman to let him cauterize her dust leak. "You promised to stand by me."

Son of a pup . . . "I promised to not let the demons put you in a bottle for practicing elven magic. But if you break the law, I'm all over you. Stef is not your familiar. I don't care how many favors she owes you. Got it? You pull a ley line through her without her permission, and I'll be on you like icing on a cake."

A frown crossed him, but as I took a breath to really let him have it, he vanished.

My exhale was long and worried. *Stef, what are you do-*

ing? I thought as I looked through the walls to the unseen garden. She had two demon marks. It used to mean you were about to make a mistake and be dragged to the ever-after for a lifetime of servitude, but things had changed. Hadn't they?

Maybe I was overreacting. It was just a promise to repay a favor. Until you got three.

"How is she doing, Jenks?" I said, worried as I focused on the hot spotlight. That pixy-size amulet lay forgotten and unneeded on the piano, and my shoulders slumped.

Jenks rose up on a column of gold sparkles. Behind him, the pixy woman sniffed at the acorn cap full of a yellow ointment before gingerly applying it to her coming bruises.

"She says her name is Get," he said softly as he hovered by my ear, both of us watching her. "I'm not calling her that."

I nodded. A get was an unwanted animal. "Getty?" I suggested, and he nodded, his wing hum lowering.

"I told her she can stay until her wing heals, but she's rightly terrified Baribas will try to kill her. Rache, Stef can't keep her safe if Baribas decides to off her while I'm on a run. It has nothing to do with her maybe poaching," he finished bitterly.

My brow furrowed. I'd been counting on him being with me this afternoon to recover Pike, but I could do this with only Trent. "Then you should stay here," I said, and his wing pitch rose in protest. "Stef's room isn't safe. Do you think Getty would let me carry her to the belfry? Baribas already knows to stay out."

"I could defend her alone there," he said, green eyes pinched. "But I'm coming with you."

"No, you should stay with her." I smiled at Getty, wishing she'd stop staring at me with mistrust. "Keep her safe. Stef can't do it. She's too slow."

"You need me to rescue Pike," he said, and I shook my head, missing his presence already.

"Trent is coming. He can watch my back. Jenks, it's not

that big of a deal. We pay the man and walk out with Pike. Done and done."

Jenks frowned at Getty. Her tousled black hair was down to her waist, and she sighed at a new hole in her stocking before tugging her dress to cover it. "She doesn't trust me," he said, his dust taking on a blue tint.

"She doesn't trust me, either. Why don't you see what's keeping Stef. I'll get her upstairs. Talk some."

Jenks nodded, his dust still that depressed blue as he went to hover before Getty. "Getty," he said, voice unsure as he glanced between us. "This here is my partner Rachel. She saved my life more times than I have dandelions in my garden and is wickedly good with her circles and spells. Baribas won't dare take a potshot at you while I'm out finding where that pollen Stef went to get is. She's going to take you upstairs where you will be safe, but if you so much as scratch her, I will dump your lily-white ass on the curb, busted wing or not. Got it?"

Getty's narrow chin lifted. "How do you know if my ass is lily-white or not, city boy?"

Jenks blinked, his altitude dropping when his wings cut out for a bare instant. "I'll be right back," he muttered, then darted out into the hall and presumably the garden.

I exhaled, using a pinky to pull that pixy-size amulet off the piano and cup it in my hand. Outside, there was a sudden burst of pixy noise, and both Getty and I turned to the stained-glass windows.

"Getty?" I said, and the woman paled, that wooden dagger again in her grip. "Jenks is trying to help you. Ah, I'd usually take you up in my hand, but I could find a cup . . ." I scanned the living room, but I wasn't confident that she wouldn't try to leave the instant I was distracted.

Getty squinted at me. "I'm not a poacher."

"Even if you were, I think Jenks would want to help," I said, a feeling of satisfaction growing when she wobbled to her feet, her patchwork, faded gray dress moving about her like silk. "Jenks and I are known for helping lost causes," I said, even more pleased when she cautiously, and painfully, climbed into my hand. Her grip on my upraised thumb was tight as she eyed the small amulet in distrust, and I again wondered how she had managed to survive on her own for so long.

"Why would he help me?" she said, and I slowly headed for the stairwell.

"One of his sons has dark hair. His name is Jumoke, and he lives about an hour outside the city at a private garden with his wife, four fall-born kids, and newlings on the way. I've known Jenks for over four years and wouldn't be alive if not for him."

Getty was silent. She was beautiful, and dark, and dangerous. And if she was a pixy, she'd be courageous, and truthful, and honest to a fault. I couldn't tell where her thoughts were as I rose up the belfry stairs.

"If he has kids, where is his wife?" she said as I pushed the door to my room open with my foot, and sunlight spilled over us.

I could understand her question. Pixies died of heartache when their spouse passed. "Under the bluebells," I said softly in case Jenks was lurking about. "She died protecting the garden and her children. They had no newlings, and their children scattered except for Jumoke. Jenks would have joined her, but I shrank down to his size and begged him not to. I needed him in order to survive. So he lived. It's not been easy for him."

I stood in the center of the room, wondering if I had been selfish asking him to let his wife go like that. Getty's gaze traveled over the room, out the windows to the pixy- and fairy-filled garden, and finally up to the bell, where it lingered on Bis's gray shadow.

"He kept me alive," I said as I rested my hand on the marble-top dresser and she slid off, taking that amulet with her. "He owns the church. Baribas is merely renting the graveyard in exchange for security. As slack as that's been," I finished sourly.

Getty put the amulet on, eyeing Pike's logos as she went to sit on the edge of one of my books. Her wings were a dangerous gray, but at least they weren't leaking dust. "I've heard of you." She fingered the amulet. "You're a demon witch."

I nodded and went to shut the screenless window. "On my good days." I sighed at my spelling supplies still out on the dresser and thoughts of Pike returned. "Hey, ah, I've got to go, so as soon as Jenks gets here I'll leave you with him." I hesitated, thinking the marble top was a cold place to be. "Um, that wing snap of yours is bad. Where would you like to be?"

Her attention immediately went to the small, very defensible shelf above the bell.

"With Bis?" I said, not surprised as I searched for something to stand on. "Sure. He's asleep, but you could always put your back against him. Or duck into that cricket cage and stab at everyone through the bars."

"The gargoyle is alive?" Getty's eyes were wide. "I thought he was a decoration."

"Yeah, you aren't the first," I said, mood souring. "He's sleeping while we find a way to separate his soul from the baku. They are both in that bottle there, so don't open it." All my packing boxes were gone, and I didn't even have a chair to stand on. "Mmmm," I muttered, at a loss until Jenks tapped at the window.

Getty jerked, that wicked dagger suddenly in her hand as she stared at him. But wonder of wonders, she tucked it away, giving me a nod as I went to open the window. His dust was an odd blue-gold, and I smiled at the smears of pollen on his front. It had been a while since I'd seen him like that. He wore gardener very well, and I shut the window after him.

"I brought you some pollen," he said as he set the wad as big as his two fists down. "If you sit on that vial of lavender, I can tape your wing so it heals right."

"You will, huh? How come, pixy buck?"

"Because you can't work off the food you're going to eat if your wing doesn't work," he said, and her tight features eased. "This here church is a paranormal shelter. You can't come in and take what you want. But you can work for it." He took a step closer. "Please, Getty? Baribas is utterly useless in keeping the grounds clear." Jenks made a sour face. "You'd be doing me a favor if you'd stay while your wing healed."

"I'd be doing *you* a favor, eh?" Getty said, and he nodded, his wings hitting a higher pitch even though his feet never left the dresser. Pixies were proud to the point of death, and it might be the difference between accepting help and starving.

I stiffened at the low thrum of Trent's car at the curb, audible even through the closed windows. *Crap on toast, I have to go.* "Hey, Jenks, you got this okay?"

Jenks stood in front of Getty, hands on his hips. "I don't know. Do I, Ms. Getty?"

She flushed, nodding, and Jenks's shoulders slumped as he held out the pollen. Getty took it, gingerly settling herself on the vial, her back to him. "Thank you," she said softly as she began to eat.

Finally, I thought, but my smile faded as Jenks began to tape up her wing, sparkling tears slipping from him, tears he wouldn't let her see. His dust was that uncomfortable blue that meant he was missing Matalina.

"You okay, Jenks?" I said softly, one hand on the door. Trent could wait a few moments.

"Fine," he said, voice short and stilted.

Torn, I shut the door behind me and headed down, my steps slow. Jenks wasn't fine—unless we were using Ivy's definition of the word. Even so, this was where he needed to be. I was glad he was staying with Getty, but I felt his absence from my shoulder keenly. I didn't like that Stef was getting herself tied up with Hodin so deeply, and if Pike wasn't in danger of being given to his brothers for the bounty, I would have insisted the quiet demon and I have a talk right here and now.

"Thank God Trent is here," I whispered as I found the

dark foyer and went to get my bag, still by the couch where I left it. I wasn't happy that it was his money that was going to keep Pike's ass above the grass, but when I looked into my bag to make sure everything was still there, I decided using money to balance the scales was better than magic any day.

Wasn't it?

CHAPTER

8

"THE CHARM WOULD WORK FOR AT LEAST A DAY EVEN IF HE was undead," I said, looking up from the finding amulet as Trent eased his small sports car to a stop. "His aura would last that long. I don't think he's here."

Here being the waterfront. A half-sunk, brightly colored casino boat was tied to the dock, the water lapping sadly about the upper windows and roof. A smaller casino boat needing a coat of paint was tied up beside it. Two mechanics were working on the decorative paddle wheel, but it was the three men in security black at the foot of the gangplank who caught and held my attention.

"Castle probably has him off-site." Trent's low, musical voice went well with the smooth jazz on the radio, and I took a slow breath when he snapped it off and silence filled the car. "If I was going to meet with a witch-born demon with hell in her pocket, I'd have my ace stuck in a hole somewhere so she wouldn't tear up my other boat to get him."

I squinted at the amulet, not liking its ambiguous reading. "Either he's halfway out of the Hollows aboveground, or across the street below it." Worried, I tossed the amulet in my bag with my splat gun. "It's a finding amulet, not a GPS."

"But he's alive." Trent was eyeing Castle's waiting security, and I bit my lip.

"Probably." It had only been an hour since I'd talked to Castle. Seeing his security there and waiting, I decided there was no way I'd get in to talk to him without a search. Reluctantly I worked the wand out from between my sock and boot, tucking it into a pocket inside my bag that was designed for pens and a pad of paper but had only ever held snack bars.

"I'd feel better if Jenks was here to do a quick recon," I said as I clenched my bag shut and held it on my lap. The pixy could have zipped in, gotten a security count, and zipped out before we even said our first hellos. "He's busy with an injured pixy," I added, still not believing it. Perhaps Getty was so different from Matalina that it didn't hurt as much, but remembering his tears as he tended Getty, I doubted it.

"Mmmm." Motions slow, Trent took a heavy satchel from the back seat. Exhaling, he leaned across the car, opening the glove box in front of me and stuffing it inside. I breathed him in as he drew close and away, the scent of tense elf almost electrifying. "He has a soft spot for the downtrodden," Trent added, his thoughts clearly on other things.

I nodded, biting my knuckle in worry. Castle's security had noticed us, and one of them was now trudging up the gangplank. "It's amazing she survived this long without a garden or spouse," I said as Trent checked his phone and dropped it into a jacket pocket. "She's at least sixteen. Maybe eighteen?" I hesitated, wondering if I should put my phone on airplane mode. "Did you know that Jenks used a wish to make himself sterile to prolong Matalina's life? If she's single, Getty might not be that old, biologically."

"She must be very sneaky." A soft frown pinched Trent's brow as he gazed at the two people in security black now coming down the ramp. One was a woman. *And baby makes four* . . . I thought, thinking she was really small. If

Castle was a werefox, it wouldn't surprise me if his head of security was, too. "Ready?" he said, and I nodded, bag in hand as I got out.

Trent's door thumped shut, then mine, and I stood, feeling the heat and humidity curl my hair through the straightening charm as Trent's car beeped and locked. I gave Castle's security a bland smile, my shoulder bag held tight as Trent joined me and we started over. Cicadas screamed, and I pulled a strand of escaped hair from my mouth, missing Trent's air-conditioned car already.

Trent's pace met mine perfectly, his steps silent as his feet seemed to hardly touch the ground. He looked good in his jacket and tie, not hot at all, which I thought unfair. His eyes were on the sunken boat, and he made a low, musical whistle. "Pike did that? With no magic?"

"Apparently." Seeing the paddle steamer resting on the bottom of the river, my thoughts went to Kisten. Even now, I missed him, and I shivered when an unexpected thought of Pike's teeth raced through me and was gone.

"You okay?" Trent asked, clearly noticing, and I felt myself redden.

"Fine." My gaze went to the woman standing front and center. *Large and in charge,* I mused, knowing she'd be formidable despite her small size. Her reddish-black hair was short and curly, close to her skull to give her a trendy appearance. She had a slim build designed for running, not fisticuffs, and the three men with her seemed bulky by comparison. Even from here, I could tell her dark skin was absolutely perfect, without a wrinkle or blemish.

A man in a suit waited at the boat's railing, flanked by three more security men in black. He also had reddish-black hair, a glass of something in his hand as he gestured at us, talking with his security.

"Castle?" I said as our pace slowed.

"He matches the photo Quen texted me." Trent frowned. "He's from Australia. Half his ancestry is from Ireland, brought over when it was a penal colony, the other half is Aboriginal."

I nodded, halting as the confident woman raised a hand. Her nose was broad and her jawline was sharply angled. The woman's strong features would make her stand out anywhere, but her silver-gray eyes were utterly captivating. I had met a few werefoxes before, and though they all held a feral, dangerous beauty, she was unique among them, beautiful with heritage drawing from all sides of the planet.

"That's close enough. Ms. Morgan?" she said, her high voice cutting through the wind with an unfamiliar accent. *Must be Aboriginal?* I wondered, never having heard its like.

"Yes," I said, wanting to be nice even if they had taken advantage of a desperate vampire. "And this is Trent Kalamack. Castle is expecting me."

"You're early. I'm Cassie," she said, but I didn't extend my hand, seeing as there was ten feet between us. "Could you put your purse on the ground and step away, please? Both of you?"

Some mistrust was to be expected, but she was really tense. Trent's laughing scoff vanished when two of the men beside her took mundane, bullet-shooting pistols from their belts and pointed them at us.

"Kind of jumpy, aren't they," I said as I dropped my bag and moved closer to Trent. Its loss was expected. I could do far more damage with a spoken spell or charm anyway. I was already tapping into a ley line, but I strengthened my hold, feeling it tingle down to my toes. One man went to my bag, the remaining two making a beeline to Trent and me.

Trent grimaced when one of them took a spell detector from a back pocket, and we both raised our arms so he could wand us. "Is there a problem?" I said as her security did a scan.

"No, and I want to keep it that way." Still standing at the gangplank, Cassie watched us with her silver eyes as they took my phone. "The new boat's security system isn't up yet," she said. "You can't blame Mr. Castle for taking a minimum of precaution. You have a reputation for blowing up casinos, Ms. Morgan."

I couldn't help my flash of a grin, but it faded when her man took my bag to her. It was thought that werefoxes were witches once, cursed as the Weres had been. Their blood has lost the enzymes to kindle magic, but they could still tap a line well enough to dump off and take on mass, allowing them to shift size as well as shape. Their population had never been high in the U.S. Most lived in what was left of Russia. *And Australia's outback, apparently.*

"A wand?" Cassie's expression was tight in question as she peered into my bag but wisely didn't reach for it. "That's new for you, isn't it?"

Crap, she did her homework. "It's not lethal," I said, not knowing why I was telling her other than I didn't want her to drop my bag into the water. "It takes a word and gesture to invoke it, and I'm not telling you what that is. You can't use it."

"And now neither can you," she said, handing the bag with all my charms and splat gun back to the man, who had moved to stand behind her.

Whatever, I thought, knowing they would've been really stupid to let me on board with it. "Where's Pike?" I said, and the man searching Trent returned his wallet to him. "I know he's not here, and I've got a class to prep for and another meeting tonight."

Cassie faced the man who had searched us. "Well?"

He shrugged. "Just what you see, ma'am."

The woman's smile widened to show her somewhat large teeth. "No money? No Pike."

Trent's face became almost bloodless. "You're not getting it until we see Pike."

"Then we have a problem," Cassie said, pouting dramatically.

My shoulders shifted in a tired sigh. "Give it to them," I said to Trent, my voice rising as I squinted at Cassie and her crew. "If they screw us over, I'll sink every single boat they ever put on the river, because taking a wand from me does not take away what I can do . . . Cassie."

Trent's lip twitched. I knew this was hard for him, but I

was willing to show them mine first. "The money is in the car. Glove box," he said as he tossed the man the key.

Cassie's face went slack. Eyes wide, she looked at Castle standing at the railing, then motioned for her security to check it out. Behind her, Castle started for the gangplank, his three security men with him.

Something had shifted, and adrenaline trilled through me, intoxicating. *Eight on two?* I mused, liking the odds when magic put them in my favor. Forcing a pleasant expression, I planted my feet and pulled on the line until my hair began to snarl. *Go ahead. Make my lousy week better.*

Behind us, I heard Trent's car unlock and begin dinging. "Ma'am, it's all here," the security man said, and I broke my gaze from Cassie as he came forward with Trent's satchel.

Cassie glanced inside. "Does it wand as real?"

"Yes, ma'am," her security man said, and I swear, I saw the woman begin to sweat.

"I didn't have time to get a money order," Trent said dryly. "Pike, please."

"Shit," the woman whispered, and I tensed, that wrong feeling growing. Emotions sifted over her: anger, annoyance. *Fear?* "I told you Kalamack could pull together that much scratch," she muttered, then turned to the boat, her anger swelling. "Castle?" she all but barked.

It was more directive than I would have expected from his head of security, and I squinted, watching the man come down the gangplank, his dress shoes clicking. The amulet said Pike was alive, but where? "Where is Pike?" I said again, not liking her flash of fear, and Castle huffed to a halt, his security in tow.

"Ms. Morgan." Castle's toothy smile was wide and, I thought, a little . . . oily. "Pleasure to meet you. Mr. Kalamack? Delighted."

I ignored his extended hand. *Siblings?* I wondered, seeing the same angular face, same silver eyes, same accent. His complexion was rougher, though, showing the mileage of a vigorous nightlife. More telling, Cassie was acting as if she was a long-suffering sister, not an employee. *Not just siblings. Twins,* I decided.

Grim faced, Trent didn't take Castle's hand, either, and the man pulled back, his forehead creased in anger. Security had arrayed themselves around us. All their guns were out now, and I didn't like Trent's expression, hard and unforgiving, as Castle began to sweat, the odd, musky scent of werefox rising.

"Mr. Castle," Trent said, his tone deceptively soft. "I have paid Pike's mark. I want him."

My eyes narrowed on the sweating man as he took a breath to speak. "That's not Castle," I interrupted, and he started. "She is," I added, my chin flicking to Cassie.

"Now wait a moment . . ." Mr. Castle began, but his words cut off with a surprised grunt when Cassie lightly backhanded him in the gut.

"Perceptive," she said, shocking not only Trent but the woman's own security. *They didn't know,* I mused, thinking it would be funny if I wasn't so worried about Pike.

"Ahh . . ." The man everyone thought was Castle began to protest.

"This is Ken. My brother," Cassie said sourly. "I found out fast that a woman running a casino has to break heads twice as often as a man, but the casino is mine. I trust both of you will keep this to yourself." She looked at her security, one of whom was now a bright red in embarrassment. "All of you."

"That depends." I put a hand on my hip. "Where is Pike? We agreed that we pay off his debt, and we all go home. You have it. Right there." I hesitated, grimacing at my bag and Trent's satchel in her security's possession. "Where is he?" *Crap on toast. Did they give him to his brother?*

"Yes. About that . . ." Ken murmured, and my entire side tingled as Trent tapped a line, gold and red energy hazing his fingers.

"I told you she'd get it," Cassie muttered. "I don't know why I listen to you."

"Shut up, Cassie!" Ken shouted, clearly ticked as their

security began to fidget. "I have this under control!" His dark face spotted with sweat, Ken smiled at us. "He slipped our security," he said, but I didn't need Jenks to tell me he was lying. It was only my amulet saying Pike was alive that kept me from blowing their second boat clean out of the water.

"He's already sold him to his brother," Trent said, his voice hard.

"No," Cassie said, her bewilderment obvious. "When Ken told him we'd already made a deal with you, we were attacked. They cursed my security and . . . took Pike. . . ." She finished flatly, her expression shifting as understanding crashed over her and she turned to Ken. "You little cur! You sold him to his brother, then staged the assault so you could pocket the money and leave me hanging?"

Nervous smile wide, Ken backed away. Trent stiffened when the small man took the satchel from their security, and my gut tightened. *Don't do it, Castle.* . . .

Trent extended his hand, his lips pressed to near white. "If you sold him, Pike's mark has been paid. My money, please."

"You son of a bitch!" Cassie shouted, lurching forward to shove her brother to a scuffing halt. Their security seemed at a loss, but I thought it interesting that they were watching Cassie and Ken, not us. The woman's brow furrowed as she glared at Castle in a growing fury. "Where's the money, Ken?"

"You gave us six hours!" I exclaimed. "Pike lost a bet, and I'm here to cover it."

"It's been covered." Trent's voice held an icy hardness I seldom heard. "His brother paid for it. That satchel is mine, Ms. Castle. Give it to me, and we will walk away."

"You lied to me *again*!" Cassie said, oblivious to the glowing magic dripping from Trent's clenched hand to hiss against the pavement. "Damn it all to hell, those were *my* people those assassins downed. You made a deal with that bloodsucking vampire, didn't you!" she shouted, her small form shaking. "My people get hit, you take the money, and I lap up your lies that you knew nothing about it!"

Assassins took him? I glanced at Trent, wishing he had been wrong. I took a step forward, jerking to a halt when Cassie lunged at her brother, howling in anger. Ken retreated with a comical yelp as Cassie was yanked away by her own security.

"Knock it off, Cassie!" Ken bellowed, Trent's satchel hidden behind his back. "How was I to know they would be able to dig up that much money?"

"Get your hands off. Get off of me!" Cassie shouted as she tugged free, furious as she stood before Ken. "How much did those assassins give you to open the door and let them in? All of it?" she said, then softer, knowingly, "All of it. A million two. You are a total ass, Ken. This is my casino, not yours."

"I was going to tell you," Ken said, but he was almost whining.

"The hell you were. Those are my people in the hospital!" she exclaimed, telling me she was more concerned about her people than the money. "It's not a witch spell, Ken. It's a demon curse. They don't know how to break it."

My interest took a sudden right turn. Demon curse? Where had Pike's brother gotten a demon curse?

Trent made a soft, knowing noise. "I didn't realize Al was so angry at you."

"It wasn't Al," I said, remembering the net of safety he'd put about my bedroom. "Dali, maybe?" But why? Demons didn't do anything unless there was profit in it.

"And you still think I'm playing you?" Ken said. "You said it yourself. It was a curse, Cassie. *Morgan* downed your people," he added, and my lips parted in outrage. "She was the one who stole Pike, which is why she's here saying he's dead so she doesn't have to pay off his mark. Wise up. This money probably isn't even real."

"It's real," Trent said.

"Ah . . . Pike isn't dead," I said.

Cassie, though, didn't hear, the woman having shrugged off her security again. "No," she said, and the man who had restrained her swore under his breath at the fury in the tense word. "I'm done believing you. You are a liar, Ken, and I won't look past it anymore because you're family. Dad left the business to me, and you've lied your way out of even a piece of it. Have a good life. Don't call me." She hesitated as Ken stared at her. "That means *get out!*"

"Ah, my money?" Trent said, clearly torn as Ken walked away, but there were still three men holding guns, and we didn't follow Ken with anything other than our eyes.

Damn it, Dali, I thought in frustration, wondering what the demon was getting out of this other than making my life hell. Pike was the one who made this subrosa thing work, and without him, I'd have a devil of a time convincing Finnis that Constance was still in charge. Maybe I should return his spell books.

"You got nothing but a boat and some dice, Cassie!" Castle shouted over his shoulder, his stilted, quick pace never shifting. Behind him, their security personnel looked at each other, a decision clearly being weighed. "You won't make it without me. One week, and you'll be begging me to come back! You stupid dog-whore!"

Pissed, Cassie gave him a one-fingered salute. Their security wobbled for a moment, then half of them jogged after him.

"I'd appreciate my money, please," Trent said, voice so cold it was scary. "Clearly Pike's mark has been paid by his brothers, Ken lying to you aside."

Money. Yes. That was the deal. But I wanted Pike, not a million two. "Go get your money," I said, gesturing to Ken's retreating figure. "If she doesn't give me a name or number to find Pike, she's going to be out another boat."

Frustrated, Trent shifted from foot to foot, his expression becoming murderously ugly as he shook his head and turned to Cassie. "It can wait," he almost growled, but his gaze was fixed on Ken as he got into the back of a big-ass SUV and yelled for his security to hurry up.

My bag sat forgotten on the pavement, and giving her three remaining men a glare, I stomped over and picked it up. "Who and where?" I said. I wasn't making sense, but everything was confused.

"I don't know," Cassie said, twitchy and distracted. "I only saw the security footage." She grimaced. "There were three. Witches, I think. They walked in, said some Latin, twisted a ring, and everyone in the room except them went down. If I didn't know better, I'd think they wanted us to see them." Her silver eyes narrowed. "They walked right out the door with him," she said bitterly. "My people still aren't conscious."

A ring knocked them out? I thought. *All at once?* It sounded like an elven charm, and my thoughts went to Landon. But Landon was in isolation at the monastery. Ring magic wasn't unheard-of, but a ley line amulet with a pin was the usual method.

"Excuse me a moment," Trent said suddenly, and with a fierce yell, he overhanded a wad of unfocused energy at the car. Wincing, I held my breath as it arced over the empty parking lot. Ken's security saw it coming and scattered, but Ken was too slow, and it hit the car just as he got his door open to flee.

With a thunderous woof of air, the SUV rose up a good five feet, the outgoing wave of force shoving the fleeing men down and rolling them across the pavement like fallen leaves. Groaning, the vehicle hit the ground with a crack of broken plastic and twisted metal. Steam poured from the radiator and the car's alarm began hooting. Ken had been thrown clear, and he looked up from the pavement, clearly stunned.

"I, ah, am sorry about this," Cassie said as one of the men beside her pointed a fob and the alarm cut off. "Get Mr. Kalamack his money," she whispered, and the man smirked before jogging away. "I should have known Ken was playing us off on each other. He is such an ass. I don't know why I believed him. I'm truly sorry."

"That doesn't fix this." I felt better now that Trent wasn't out a million two, but Pike was still missing. His brothers had been trying to kill him since he was eight, and now they had him.

"Give me the amulet," Trent said, and my head went down over my bag, the charm flaring as my fingers found it. "I'm going to triangulate," he added, and after an irate glance at Cassie's man walking to the downed SUV, he jogged to the far end of the lot, jacket flapping.

Cassie followed Trent with her eyes, clearly worried. "Odds are he's still breathing," she said. "I heard them say on the security tape that he's worth twice as much alive."

Behind her, Cassie's man pulled Trent's bag from the car. Ignoring the groans of his downed peers, he made a comment to Ken before returning, his pace slow and confident. At the far end of the lot, Trent hesitated for a moment, then jogged to another corner. Frustrated, I rubbed my forehead. "Why didn't you tell me when it happened?"

"I, ah, Ken convinced me you wouldn't have that much liquidated cash," she said, lips pressing in a thought she didn't share. "I mean, who does that? If you couldn't find it, I wouldn't have to admit that my own security had been taken down. My people would have been able to keep him safe if Ken hadn't sold them out. Ms. Morgan, I'm willing to accept some of the blame for this, seeing as my brother is a total ass, but I don't know how to help."

His head down, Trent jogged to a third corner. Cassie's security scuffed to a halt, smiling as he handed her the bag, and with a little sigh, Cassie handed it to me in turn. "How long has it been?" I asked, relieved.

"Twenty minutes?" Cassie said, and my shoulders slumped. They could be anywhere in twenty minutes. "Ms. Morgan. This is not how I do business," she said as I spun on a heel and walked to Trent's car. "I'm not a brave person," Cassie added as she followed. "Which is probably why I looked the other way so long about Ken. I know dice and cards and percentages, and the chances were ninety to one against that you would be able to get that much liquid cash in six hours. That's why I didn't tell you. I thought the problem would go away, no one the wiser."

I had reached Trent's car, and I hesitated as I opened the door. Trent was already inside, and the car started up in a satisfying rumble of ancient-Detroit muscle. I extended his satchel, tossing it into the back seat when Trent didn't take it.

"I think he's at the airport," Trent said over the roar of the car's air-conditioning, and I felt my pocket for my phone. Edden. He could shut down the terminals for a few hours.

"Morgan?" Cassie prompted, and I hesitated before getting in. "I really did try to stop them," she said, her silvery gray eyes shocking against her dark skin. "If I could, I would have. I didn't know . . . well . . . I guess I didn't want to know that my brother was trying to cheat both of us."

It would have been nice to have Jenks tell me if she was lying or not, but I nodded, my lips pressed together. "If Pike is not alive when I find him, I'll be back," I said, then I got in and slammed the door shut.

Trent's grip was white-knuckled on the wheel, and his jaw tense. Exhaling, I tried to relax if only to get Trent to calm down. Pissing off a witch-born demon was one thing. Trying to swindle money from an elf was a veritable death sentence.

"We need to shut down the airport," Trent said as he hit the gas and I started, a hand going to the dash as the acceleration pushed me into the seat. "Edden?" he suggested, and nodding, I dropped my bag on my lap and opened it to find my phone.

If anyone could do it, it would be Edden.

CHAPTER 9

THE BITING SCENT OF EXHAUST AND THE ECHO OF IDLING engines were an uncomfortable assault as Trent and I hustled into Hollows International, or the Big HI, as most everyone called it. His grip was on my elbow, surreptitiously guiding me since I was head-down focused on the finding amulet. Pike hadn't moved for a long time—but he was here. Tense, I looked up when the sliding glass doors shut behind us and the tinny announcements over the airport's sound system became obvious.

"Wow. What a mess," I said as Trent led me to the side and we stopped. Long queues ran from the counters. Luggage and despondent people sat against the big windows. Another line stretched from the coffee kiosk to the stairway leading to baggage claim and car rentals.

"Watch it!" Trent exclaimed, jerking me out of the way of an angry man followed by a frustrated woman and their three bored kids, oblivious with their phones and dragging luggage. I rose up on my toes, seeing a bigger mess past the nearly empty spell-check lanes.

"You owe Edden big," Trent said, a worried slant to his brow as he studied the board.

Delayed. Delayed. Delayed, I mused, wincing when a flight clicked over to canceled. "I hope they have this cleared before Ivy's flight tonight."

"If she's traveling with someone with light restrictions, she'll get through." Trent stood beside me, reminding me of Jenks in a suit as he studied the board. "The smaller carriers are still running."

Worried, I glanced at the tracking amulet. "TSA usually lets you through if you're waiting for an incoming passenger, but probably not with this hot mess."

Trent's smile became confident, pleased almost, as he glanced at the long lines at the counters. "I hear Alaska is nice this time of year."

"Alaska?"

His hand touched the small of my back, turning me. "Smallest line," he whispered, his breath against my ear making me shiver. "The ticket will get us past TSA."

"Oh! Sure." I smirked up at him, but it slowly faded. Vanity and medicinal charms were allowed past the gate, but my splat gun would be a problem. The wand, even more so. Wands never did anything nice. We could put them in a locker, but I might need them. That was kind of the point.

"Relax," Trent said, having felt me tense. "You're on camera."

My gaze flicked to the security cameras. *God, I miss Jenks.* "Sorry about this," I said as we settled in behind the two people talking over their outgoing flight with the counter attendant.

"About what?" Head down, Trent shot a message off to Quen.

Everyone else had luggage. All we had was my shoulder bag. It wouldn't be my lack of a smile that pinged security. "This isn't your fight."

Thumbs moving fast, Trent focused on his clicking phone. "How do you figure that?"

"Pike is important to me, not you."

Trent's green eyes held a breathtaking intensity as he put his phone down. "It's not a matter of importance. It's a matter of what's right and wrong. This is what you are doing. I'm not going to walk away."

I slipped an arm around him, giving a little tug. "So it's not about Ken trying to con you?"

Grimacing, he studied the departure board. "Oh, it's about that, too," he said, a hard promise reminding me of who he was. "But money can be made as well as lost. It's a variable that can be replaced. Pike? Not so much. You need him to keep your subrosa position."

"He's one of a kind, huh," I said, wondering when the two people ahead of us would move so we could buy a freaking ticket and get on with our life. "And here I thought you didn't like him." My arm around him slipped away as the relief trickled in. At least, until my attention dropped to the tracking amulet. *I'm coming, Pike. Hang on.*

I jumped when my phone hummed, worried when I saw it was Jenks. "Hey, could you hold this for me?" I said, handing the amulet to Trent before hitting the accept icon.

"Hey, Rache." Jenks's high voice was unusually loud through the phone's speaker. "You got Pike yet?"

"Working on it," I said, giving Trent a mirthless smile. "We're at the airport."

"She called you?" Jenks blurted. "I told her you were busy."

"Her, who?" I asked, then my lips parted. "Ivy? Is she coming in early?"

Trent's eyebrows rose.

"My fault," Jenks said merrily. "I told her you were having trouble and that I was taking a sick day. Let me guess. You're why the airport is stickier than Tink's—uh . . . Never mind. What did you do?"

I went on tiptoe again to see over the crowd as if I might spot her, which was silly. She'd come through baggage even if she didn't have any luggage. "We haven't done anything yet," I said as I dropped back down to my heels. "Castle made a boo-boo giving Pike to his brother. The amulet says he's here, and Edden shut down all outgoing flights so he stays here. I think flights are still coming in, though."

"Sounds about right," Jenks said, his voice glum. "I'll have Ivy text you when she lands. She's going to need a ride. Her rental won't be ready until midnight."

I looked up at the board as another outgoing flight popped up as canceled. "Okay, thanks," I said. "Hey, Pike's probably going to be a mess. Would you try to get ahold of Stef and ask her if she could bring home a care package to stitch him up?"

"Sure, but she didn't go in today." He hesitated. "Rache, be careful. It feels weird not being there with you."

I glanced at Trent frowning at Pike's amulet. "Me too. How's Getty?"

There was a long hesitation. "Okay, I guess. Gotta go."

The call ended with an unusual abruptness, and I tucked my phone away, disconcerted.

"Mmmm, I'm no expert on these," Trent said, squinting at the amulet. "But aren't we almost on top of him?"

"He moved?" Alarmed, I cupped my hands around Trent's to pull the amulet closer. "He moved," I whispered, my gaze rising to find the doors. Frustrated people moved in and out, the mass of cars dropping off and moving on a constant motion, but no Pike. "He's like right here."

"Perhaps they put him under a don't-notice charm to get him past security." Concerned, Trent stretched to see over the milling people.

"Maybe." Wincing, I pulled Trent out of line when the people ahead of us finally went to TSA, their luggage rolling along behind them. I bit my lip, missing Jenks again. "Do you think they know we're here?"

"I don't see anyone who looks as if they don't belong. Maybe downstairs?" Trent eyed the signs hanging from the ceiling. "Car rental . . . baggage claim . . ."

I stiffened. "Their flight was canceled. They're trying to get a rental car."

"Stairs." Trent's hand went to the small of my back again, this time so he wouldn't lose me as we wove through the clusters of stymied people. A zing of energy stretched between us, feeling like a rubber band and tantalizing as it made a stray strand of my hair float.

Distracted, I put the amulet in my bag, fingering my splat gun a bare moment before quickly tucking it into my pocket. Trent's internal energy balance began to shift as he slowly pulled energy into his chi. You could do ley line magic at the Big HI, but a heavy draw always brought in the airport police. This slow trickle would remain unnoticed and still give him a big pop.

Breath quickening, I pulled on the line as well, feeling my hair grow staticky even in its bun concealing the zip-strip clipper. I filled my chi and then spindled even more in my head. My heels thumped quickly down the stairs, slowing as I hit a veritable wall of noise.

"The Goddess help us," Trent whispered as we reached the floor and stepped aside.

"We'll never find him in this," I said, feeling claustrophobic despite the large space. At a loss, I began to work us through the crowd to the carousels. The moving bands with their sporadic luggage were relatively open, but people lined the edges of the static ones, sitting on the raised belts. The tiny kiosks for rental cars were a mess with jaded, patient businesspeople and angry, red-faced elitists, all talking to the frazzled desk clerks trying to explain that they had only so many cars, and would they like to be put on a list for no-shows?

Trent smirked as a woman in white began shouting, demanding a car. "That's not how you get a vehicle when there are only three left," he said. "You want to split up?"

My head hurt. I did not want to split up; I was afraid I might never find him again. "No," I said as I scanned the edges for beaten and bruised faces. "Assassins always work in threes. They wouldn't draw attention to Pike when they could stick him in a corner under guard while the third gets a car. Let's walk the perimeter."

A phone camera clicked, and Trent gave the woman who

had recognized him a neutral smile. "This place isn't that big. He must be disguised."

Again my head throbbed as my eyes found a patch of sun that had made it down here, feeling better as I looked away. *Looked away* . . . I mused, forcing my gaze to the glow of light only to have my head begin to pound again. The aversion reminded me of the ward on Trent's spelling hut, and I gave Trent's hand a squeeze.

"Can you see what's in that corner?" I said. "Blue chairs?" I guessed, unable to focus.

He was silent, brow furrowing as a woman with three dogs breezed by, self-important and absorbed in her own-little-world concerns. "Huh," he finally said, rubbing his forehead to leave worry lines. "No. It's charmed."

"Then that's where he is. No, wait," I added, pulling Trent to a halt before I took out my phone and snapped a picture, my head almost exploding. The agony was worth it, though, even if my feeling of victory faltered as we looked at the image of Pike sitting in a wheelchair, wrapped in a blanket with his chin slumped to his chest. His dark hair was matted with what was probably blood, and he was missing a shoe. Two men in security black sat several chairs away, their backs to the window, watching him. They were the only two people in the area other than Pike, a ring of empty chairs between them and the surrounding chaos.

"We could wheel him right to the car," Trent said, and I peered at the sunny corner, my head throbbing as I tried to see what my phone had captured.

"Sure, if we can distract his babysitters long enough," I said, and Trent's lips curved up in a wicked smile.

"One hell of a distraction, coming up," Trent said. "How much time do you need?"

"As much as you can give me. That charm would have to be on him, not the chairs. I have to break it or I'll be working blind and with a migraine."

"Got it," he said, leaning to give me a kiss. "You want a full-size luxury sedan, right?"

I grinned, feeling lost as he stepped away and his hand slipped from mine. *I need a disguise,* I thought, envying Al's ability to become anyone. I didn't have much, but when Trent grabbed a ball cap from a passing display, then dropped his sport coat on a stack of luggage, I took my bun down and fluffed my hair. It predictably haloed under the combined heat, humidity, and magic, and I grimaced as I took a sun hat from another pile of luggage and fixed the sunglasses it came with atop my nose. It looked ridiculous with my leather, so I took my jacket off, leaving me in my black tee and long pants.

Jacket over my arm, I worked my way through the crowd to the corner, my eyes on the ground, not the dizzying chairs. Trent had gone right for the busiest counter, ignoring the line and pushing his way to the front. But the closer I got to Pike, the worse I felt until I finally stopped before I threw up.

Eyes squeezed shut, I felt for a chair and sat down, willing the nausea to leave. *I can smell him* . . . I realized, and my heart gave a thump.

"What do you mean you have no record of my reservation?" Trent's voice rang out, and I smiled through my spell-induced migraine. I didn't see it often, but no one could do obnoxious privilege like Trent. "I missed my reservation because we circled for an hour. You knew my landing had been delayed. And don't tell me I could have texted you. I couldn't use my phone!"

"Pike?" I whispered, choking down a rising gore when the matted carpet at my feet seemed to move. *Crap on toast, I think he's right next to me!* "Pike, I can't see you, but I know you're here. You're under an avoidance charm, and I need you to touch me to break it."

I waited, breath held as Trent's harangue rose higher.

"My assistant made the reservations a month ago! Where is my car? You. Back up. Back up and give me space. I have a reservation. Black car. Four-door, luxury model."

Heads were turning, and I managed a smile even though I felt as if I'd slammed a glass of red wine with a sulfate-laced lemon cookie chaser. "Pike," I whispered, straining for any sound from him. "You have to wake up. Trent and I can wheel you out, but you have to touch me to break the curse."

"If I had wanted a two-door, I would have reserved a two-door!" Trent shouted. "I wish to speak to your manager. You're joking. I'm not waiting. All I have done today is wait. You will deal with me now. There is a key behind that desk. Find it."

Good God, I thought, wondering if Trent was channeling Ellasbeth or his father. Trent was always more inclined to buy his way to the front of the line than scream for it. He knew a bad temper didn't work nearly as well as a pleasant demeanor and a vote of confidence. Smiling, though, wouldn't be much of a distraction.

"Pike!" I whispered, doubling over as my head throbbed. "I know you're here. Touch my foot or something." I blinked, nauseous as I tried to break through the charm. It had been witch-cast on the spot, not made elsewhere and invoked. *Cassie said his assassins were witches. Swell.* "Pike," I pleaded. "I don't think I can move without throwing up."

And then I jerked as a thrill of line energy darted through me, pulling the agony away with the sharpness of a flag snapping in the wind. My head rose, and I took a clean breath, almost shocked at the lack of pain.

Pike was beside me, his foot having touched mine when it slipped off the support. "Oh, Pike," I whispered, gut clenching. One eye was swollen shut. His lip was busted and bruised, and his lumpy nose was broken again. His hands lay in his lap like dead things, swollen and scraped, and one side of his face was beginning to turn black-and-blue. *Damn it, Ken, this is on you.* No wonder they put him under an avoidance charm. Even TSA would question this.

"What are you doing here?" he rasped.

Standing, I nervously glanced at his two babysitters. As expected, they were watching Trent's tantrum, confident that nothing could break through their charm.

That is, until one of them felt me watching. His expression of surprise vanished fast and, rising, he tapped the arm of the other. My pulse jackhammered. I reached for my splat pistol out of habit, but they were far enough away that they'd just dodge it.

"*Stabils,*" I whispered, feeling like a demon as the curse hit the one standing, and he fell into the chair. "*Stabils,*" I said again, my face cold as I backed up a step, downing the second even as a wad of unfocused energy flickered in his hand and went out. *Crap on toast, this could have been bad,* I thought as Trent's demands became louder.

The avoidance curse had been broken, though, and people were already hustling to the now-visible cluster of chairs. Unfortunately the two downed assassins could still talk, and as one of them began yelling into the flat carpet to stop me, I put Pike's foot on the footrest, unlocked the brake, and pushed him to the nearest door. *Please don't let me run into the third man . . .* I silently begged. Assassins always worked in threes, especially if they were witches.

"You look like cold troll turds, Pike," I said as I tossed my borrowed hat to a pile of luggage. "Where is the third man?"

"There are two left," he choked out, voice raw. "Female assassin, and my brother Brad. They're trying to get a car." He gasped as I bumped him over the lip and out into the pickup lanes, headed for the parking garage. "Good God, your hair is . . . Wow," he said as the wind caught it. "Castle said you were letting me swing because I made that bet," he croaked out.

"Which one? Ken or Cassie?" I asked, and he blinked up at me.

"They're family?" he rasped. "Ken. He's the sadistic bastard who beat me. Rachel, I can't believe you came for me."

My jaw clenched. I was glad Cassie wasn't lying to us. Better, I now had proof that her brother was.

"Ken played us and his sister both," I said, grim faced as I pushed him to the crosswalk and strode out into traffic. If the drivers didn't stop, I'd sue them so hard they'd be paying for my adult education until the day I died. "Tried to con Trent out of a million two."

"Trent paid my mark?" he said as I reached the other side, then slowed, backing us both into a shadow to wait. "Fuck that," he said, the scab on his lip cracking open as he tried to smile. "I thought he didn't like me."

"Seems he does," I said, distracted. *Hurry up, Trent,* I thought, then stiffened when I spotted him striding from the building. Somehow I stopped myself from waving like an idiot, instead making a sharp whistle. It was the one Jenks and I used, and recognizing it, he shifted his angle and jogged across all the lanes, nothing but his confidence and an extended hand to stop traffic.

"Hey, thanks, Trent. I owe you one," Pike said, his swollen hands fluttering as Trent reached us.

"Me? No. Your brother paid your mark," Trent said flatly, steps fast as I pushed Pike into the garage. "How many are there? There have to be more than the two Rachel downed."

Trent was staring at my hair, and I grimaced, unable to flatten it as I was pushing Pike.

"Total of three witches," Pike said, the cool dark of the parking garage seeming to revive him. "One brother," he added, spitting a wad of blood at a pylon.

The pavement seemed to rumble up through my hands, and I took off my borrowed glasses so I could see better. We were on the ground floor and had to go up two levels. "We're down to one witch and your brother," I said. "Maybe we'll get lucky."

"Keep going," Trent said when we came to the parking ticket kiosk. "I'll catch you up."

But I shook my head, spinning Pike around so we could watch the terminal while Trent had his back to it as he paid for his ticket. Our exit would be another long line, otherwise. "Trent?" I called when three people bolted from the entrance, their sudden hesitation at the curb drawing my attention. "Pike, is that them?" I asked even as I recognized two. *Crap on my daisies.* . . . But at least we were away from the crowd, and I glanced at the security cameras, missing Jenks.

"Yep," Pike said with a sigh. "Either of you magic users have a gun?"

I eyed his swollen, bleeding hands, deciding I'd keep my weapon.

"You didn't use a sleepy-time charm?" Trent asked, and I grimaced at his tone.

"Everyone knows how to break a potion," I said as I wheeled Pike between two cars to hide him. "I thought a curse would give us more time."

But I'd been wrong, and even though we had Pike, we were now going to have to fight for him. Jaw clenched, I squeezed out between Pike and a car to stand beside Trent.

"You got the ticket?" I said, and Trent stared at me as if I'd asked him if he wanted to fly to the moon. "I'll hold it," I added, taking it from him and stuffing it in my pocket.

"Sure."

My side tingled as Trent pulled on the ley line, and I settled into a wide-footed stance between Pike and the three silhouettes coming to a cautious halt under the low ceiling. "Sit tight, Pike," I said softly, knowing he could hear me. *Witches,* I thought as I pulled on the line to balance my energy with Trent's. Why did it have to be witches?

"Can't you just zap them and be done with it?" Pike said, and I flicked a burst of raw energy at the nearest camera.

"No," I said, dismissing the few lethal spells I knew. "We have to keep it legal." Unfortunately, they didn't. Oh, if they got caught, they'd be tried, but somehow, assassins never did. I looked askance at Trent, his hands glowing an eager red-streaked gold. "Right, Trent? Keep it legal?"

His smooth features bunched into annoyance as he watched the slowly advancing trio. "Fine. Legal," he muttered, and I stared at him, a little uneasy. He had changed, become different. The businessman was gone. The loving father was swamped. He stood beside me as if oblivious to everything that could be or had been between us, his power as yet unshackled by charm or spell dripping from his fingers in little hisses. His shadow was long behind him, his face hard in a way that promised hurt. He'd become the elven warlord, and I stifled a shudder, feeling it go all the way to my groin.

"Oh, for God's sake," Pike muttered from behind us, the vampire having clearly sensed it, and I pulled my eyes from Trent and shoved my libido away.

The lead assassin stopped, her feminine curves obvious from the bright light behind her. She must have been at the rental counter. "Circle. Squeeze," she said simply, and the other two turned, one going right, the other left. If they got behind us, we were done for.

I took a breath, pulling the line in until my blood nearly sang with it.

"I got this," Trent said, his hand moving in a complicated gesture. *"Entrono voulden,"* he shouted, and my breath hissed out in surprise when a visible thread of line energy sped from his palm-thrust hands, circling the trio. I'd seen this before in the belly of the monastery, but instead of binding them into a cluster and knocking them out with one spell, it broke, little trills of energy snaking about until it touched one of the assassins.

Like a whipcrack, the entire spell snapped to the hapless man, downing him alone until the woman shot a little blue ball of force at him and Trent's spell disintegrated.

I took a step, alarmed as the once-downed man bounded to his feet, an ugly expression on his face.

"She's good," Trent said grimly.

"Not good enough." I looked at the woman, pointing at her, then me in invitation. *You're mine, witchy witch.* "Someday, you're going to have to teach me that spell." My smile widened as the woman nodded her agreement, an ugly blue dripping from her hands as she headed right for me. "Incoming!"

I sprang one way, Trent dove the other. Pain throbbed as my shoulder hit the pavement and rolled. The assassins scattered, their intent obvious.

"Don't let them circle us!" I shouted, then rolled again to evade the glowing blue balls that woman was throwing at me, pure energy right off the line. Even without being modified by a spell, it would fry my synapses like toast on the sun.

"*Rhombus!*" I shouted, jerking when three individual spells hit my invoked circle. A whoosh of energy flamed through me, and I stared. She had modified her raw, thrown energy to match my aura and fry me from within. But I was a demon, and all it did was make me stronger.

Ticked, I got to my feet, static shooting from my unbound hair. "Nice try," I said, my hands coming together in a sharp clap to gather her energy . . . then shove it back at her.

Yelping, she dove to the right. My gold-tinged ball of power struck a parked car, lifting it three inches. It hit the ground and the alarm went off.

"You good, Trent?" I shouted, spinning to the man behind me. "*Rhombus!*" I exclaimed again, seeing as I'd hit my circle and it had fallen. My circle rose up anew, and then the man's black goo coated it, becoming hard, trapping me.

Adaperire, I thought smugly, and his binding spell flaked off in shiny sparkles of gold. I inhaled, drawing energy into me like water. A thread of my thought reached out to find the demon collective. Stored curses sifting past my awareness like snow—until one fell lovingly into my hand. "*Implicare!*" I shouted, shoving it through my hands and hitting the startled man square in the chest. He went down, tangled in a glowing net of gold and red. *That one is legal, right?*

And then I was falling, my balance gone as the ground shook.

Gasping, I rolled. It had been Trent. I looked up from the cold pavement to see he was okay, half kneeling under whatever force he'd just unleashed. The lead assassin was picking herself up, but another cowered under an orange bubble.

"You okay?" I shouted, and Trent grinned, a new spell already forming in his hands. My man had gotten up. It was our two on their three, and I smiled back.

"Someone give me a fucking gun!" Pike demanded, and I spun, lips parting when I saw that he'd wheeled himself out, one eye swollen shut, the other utterly black in rage.

That's right. I have a gun, I thought. Lips rising in a wicked smile, I drew it, running at the woman while shooting at the man circling behind me.

The man deflected it, the little blue splat ball busting to make a wet smear. But that was okay. I was really after the woman.

"Arrrrrgh!" I shouted, launching myself feetfirst at her. The solid impact of hitting her gut sang through me, and then I hit the ground in a controlled fall. "Take a nap, sunshine," I said as the woman gasped, my unexpected physical attack reaching her whereas everything magical had been deflected. Satisfied, I shot her with my splat gun, and she was out.

"One down!" I shouted, then cowered at the boom of electricity that shook the ceiling. Little patters of concrete rained down, and I squinted, scrambling up as more car alarms began hooting. The lights, such as they were, flickered and died. *Jeez, Trent. I thought elves are supposed to be stealthy and quiet.*

"Pike, stay out of this," I demanded as the man wheeled himself to a halt beside me.

Trent had blown the electric grid, and it was twice as dark. His opponent was still up, and I cried out a warning, cowering as Trent deflected a glowing mass to hit a pillar, cracking it.

But with one of them down, they couldn't circle us, and I shot little bolts of energy at the man facing me, driving him back and preventing him from retaliating until I was again between him and Pike.

"Gun," I said as I tossed it to the beaten vampire, and Pike caught it, swollen hands fumbling. "If you get hit with magic, throw it before the splat balls burst and knock you out."

"Fire in the hole!" Trent shouted, and I lurched to Pike, snapping a circle of protection around us as flames billowed up and over. For an instant, I thought I'd made a mistake as the air flashed hot and my hair lifted in a wave of heat, and then it was gone and Trent was rising tall amid the stench of charred paint and melting rubber. His man was down. *This is going to be expensive. . . .*

"I'm not paying for that," I said, jumping when a tire exploded, a veritable cannon under the low ceiling.

"There!" Pike called, and I turned to the remaining assassin, my hips swaying and line energy crackling from my wild hair as I let my protection bubble fall.

"Too late to walk away," I said as the man dropped to his knees, his hands scribing a glyph before him. I frowned, not having seen this before, halting when he rose to stand on it, the energy in his hands flashing a brilliant orange.

"Rachel, down!" Trent shouted, and I set a circle. "No!" he exclaimed, and then the assassin's energy hit me, going right through my circle as if it didn't exist.

And as the man before me smiled, I found I couldn't breathe.

Son of a bastard, I thought, staring at the glyph. Okay, my lungs weren't working, but I could still hit him, and I ran forward, a surge of energy a flash on my skin as I broke my circle.

The man's eyes widened. His hand shifted to make a new curse, and then I was there, a roundhouse kick sending him flying off the glyph.

My chest was on fire. I dropped, fingers scrabbling to erase the glyph, but my breath wouldn't come in.

"Rachel!" Trent cried, and then he plowed into the man to send them both scraping across the pavement. I. Couldn't. Breathe. I dropped to a knee, my vision graying. "Circle it! Make it yours!" Trent exclaimed, throwing me the stick of chalk he'd taken from the assassin.

It hit my palm with a firm and certain thump.

Circle it, I thought, little bumps of sensation rising through me as I scribed a line around the glowing glyph. *You are mine.*

And when the beginning and end of the line met, the suffocation charm broke with a ping.

I sucked in my air with a gasp, hand shaking as I looked up past my hair. The assassin had forced Trent to retreat, the close-magic hissing and popping between them. Pike's hand was steady, but he didn't shoot, afraid of hitting Trent.

Curse me with a suffocation charm, eh? I thought, still gasping as I struggled to my feet. I was still on the glyph. *"Pacta sunt servanda,"* I intoned to bounce the curse back to him, and the assassin jerked, spinning from Trent to me in horror. Immediately Trent downed him with a spell, and the man lay on the cement, clawing at his neck.

I stood taller, feeling filthy and sore. "If you're going to use a glyph to kill someone, make sure it stays yours," I rasped.

"Always coming in light," Pike said, then plugged him with a sleepy-time pellet.

Still clutching his neck for air, the man slumped, out cold.

CHAPTER

10

THE THOUGHT TO LEAVE THE LAST ASSASSIN TO SUFFO-
cate under my sleep charm was hard to best, but I sullenly
drew a tail on the glyph, breaking the curse completely.
The assassin was still unconscious, but his chest rose and
fell, and color returned to his face.

"Son of a bitch," Pike muttered. He was still in the chair,
but his kick sent the man sliding all the way to the woman
out cold by the cracked pylon.

Back hunched, Trent dragged the last man to them both.
He looked marvelous, even if he was limping and had a dirt
smear running the entire length of his side. Thankfully the
car alarms had stopped, but the biting scent of burnt rubber
was chokingly thick and people coming from the terminal
had noticed, gathered in small knots to watch from a distance.

"Everyone alive?" I said, wishing I had a hair scrunchy
in my bag.

"For the moment." Trent's voice was low as he tried to
smack the dirt off himself.

"I don't have enough salt water to break a sleep potion," I said, and Trent nodded, a brief glow of magic wreathing his hand before a visible haze coated the assassin he had downed.

The man came to with a jolt as Trent's counterspell soaked in. Pike grinned a cracked-lip smile at him as he struggled . . . then he went still, a resigned expression on his face.

Dirty and sore, I ambled over, collecting my bag and jacket as I went. The cameras were busted, but there were people watching. Whatever I did would be online in thirty seconds.

What would I give for some privacy. I handed Pike my jacket and bag to hold, then bent over the assassin glaring up at me, helpless with his partners sprawled around him. "Everyone here is alive," I said. "Think about that. Come after Pike, and you are coming after me. I thought that would have been obvious. Spread the word."

He looked at his partners, then me. "Sure," he croaked out.

"Okay, put him back under," I said, and Trent made a satisfied sound.

Pike, though, wheeled himself closer, the spicy, sour scent of angry vampire rising even through the smell of melted tires and singed paint. "Kill them," he demanded, and Trent shook his head, aware of the phone cameras on us as well.

"No," I said as magic wreathed Trent's hands. "They did this for money, and money isn't worth dying an excruciating death. Right?"

"Right," the assassin rasped, and then he was out, downed by a whispered elven word.

"Son of a bitch, I don't believe you!" Pike raged, shaking as he sat in his chair. "They were going to kill me twice, and you're letting them live so they can try again?"

"They won't try again. You can hit them if you want," I suggested as I fingered my sore knee, and his lip curled. Damn it, I'd scraped a hole in my best pair of lightweight leather pants.

Smelling of green trees and grass, Trent sidled up beside me. "Are you okay?"

I frowned, not liking how he was staring at my wild hair. "We need to get out of here."

Still in his chair, Pike kicked the woman, the ugly thump making me wince as she groaned under the sleep charm. "That's for the crack about my mother," Pike said, his voice thready with pain.

"Okay. You avenged your mom. We need to leave," I said as I swung his chair around.

A low chuckle echoed in the underground garage, and I jerked to a halt, focusing on it.

"Little brother, you must be a cat. How many times do I have to try to kill you?" a tall man in slacks and a lightweight shirt said, phone in hand as he stood beside a pylon.

Crap on toast, it was Pike's brother.

"Took you long enough." Pike spit a wad of blood, and it hit the cold cement with an ugly sound. "Brad." He handed me my bag and jacket, but I wouldn't let him stand up, and he dropped heavily into his wheeled chair as I shoved him down. "You look sucked out."

"Are you sure you're not dead? You look dead." The man pushed from the pylon but didn't come any closer. "Why should I get my hands dirty when I can pay someone to do it?" A wide, long-toothed grin crossed his face. "Well, that didn't work. I thought witches might get through. I'll try something else next time."

"You talk too much," I said, splat gun raised. He'd only dodge it, but it would get him to shut up.

"Wait!" Trent shouted, and I jerked, my splat ball bursting against the low ceiling when a gray, slim shadow darted out, aiming right for Brad.

"Ivy!" I cried, recognizing her as she slammed into Pike's brother, knocking him into the pylon before swinging him to thump into a car. The car alarm went off, and she bitch-smacked his head into it again to make the alarm warble and turn off. Three hits in two seconds—and he was done.

"My God, you look great!" I said, pacing forward as Pike's brother slid to the pavement at her feet. "Jenks said you were coming in early. This is lucky!"

Ivy took a slow breath, beaming one of her rare, beautiful smiles. "I see nothing changed while I was gone," she said, and I gave her a hug, eyes closed as I felt her arms wrap around me. Her quick squeeze and even quicker release were a reminder of how rare and fleeting any touch was for her, and I smiled, feeling the tears threaten. It had been months, and I'd been worried.

"Damn," Pike swore as I beamed at her. I knew I was flushed. I didn't care. The scent of happy vampire coming from her was hitting me as if I'd been sipping tequila all day.

Trent limped forward, relief and welcome on his face. "Impeccable timing, Tamwood," he said, and the two nodded warily at each other. It was the best he'd get. Ivy was not free with her trust, but when she gave it, it was absolute.

"You're Ivy Tamwood?" Pike said as he wheeled himself forward, and Ivy nodded before reaching to slam Brad's head into the car again to keep him out. "Damn, girl, you're . . ."

"I'm what?" she said, her low voice like living dust, swirling through and around us, hissing into the corners of the dark garage.

Pike's gaze ran down her skintight, black knit traveling outfit. "Worth dying twice for," he said, and I smiled all the wider.

It was obviously over, and the people at the outskirts were coming closer, a few daring to walk quickly past us one aisle over. Her flight, perhaps. We needed to leave before the airport police showed up. "Ivy, this is Pike Welroe. He's been keeping the Cincy vamps in line. I've hardly had to do anything."

"So I see." But Ivy was smiling as she sauntered over, her vamp-made boots silent on the cold cement. "Pleasure," she said, showing her teeth as she carefully shook his swollen hand. "Any friend of Rachel's stays off my shit list until they prove me wrong."

"Nice to meet you." He held her hand for an instant too long, one eye narrowed in thought as she smirked at him. "Who have you been sipping on, tall, dark, and deadly? And can I join you?"

She laughed at that, my lips parting in surprise when she bared her long, pale throat in what might be invitation. "You're sweet," she said, then sort of shoved me out of the way to get behind his chair and push him into motion. "Where's your car?"

"Trent is parked two flights up," I said, jumping when Pike's brother made a soft groan, and Trent slammed Brad's head into the car again.

"He can hardly stand up, and he's flirting?" Trent whispered, but I thought it was more than that. Ivy had two souls in her—her own and Nina's. The incongruity created an almost visceral attraction, whether the vampire was alive or dead, apparently. And where allure settled, so did the power to persuade. Not that Ivy had *ever* had any problem in that area.

"Seriously," Pike said as she wheeled him closer. "How long are you in Cincinnati?"

"Maybe when you're up to it," she said. Ivy liked scars, and I flushed, a hand running over my perfect skin. It hadn't always been like that.

"Ladies, what do you want to do with, ah, Brad?" Trent asked, voice tired. "I can't keep slamming him into cars."

Pike snickered. "Why not?"

"They confiscated my knives," Ivy said. "I wasn't expecting having to go through TSA."

"I've got one," Pike said, and Ivy almost purred, wrestling it out of his hand when it glittered in the faint light. "Hey!"

"Don't pull it if you aren't going to use it," she said, which made no sense to me, but I think she was flirting.

"Whoa, whoa, whoa!" I said when Trent pulled Brad's

TROUBLE WITH THE CURSED

head up by his hair and Ivy took a step closer. "Come on, guys. We're probably still on a camera."

"I know a basement with a dirt floor," Pike said, and Trent glanced at me hopefully.

"Good Lord, no," I said firmly as I swung my bag around. "I have an idea. One that might serve us twice."

"Still the fun-sponge," Ivy said with a sigh, and Trent eased his grip on Brad's hair. Yep, all my friends were savages. Sometimes I wondered what that made me.

"He's *my* brother," Pike said as I searched my bag to find that wand right where I left it. "I say he dies. One less idiot gunning for me."

There it is. . . . "You screwed up, so I decide who lives and dies today." Wand in hand, I dropped my bag at my feet and took a wide-footed stance on the humid-wet pavement. "Pike, how many brothers do you have?"

"One less by sunset tonight," he muttered, and Ivy grimaced suspiciously at the wand. She never did like the witchier aspects of me, probably because I'd used them on more than one occasion to remind her that no means no. *We all have our pasts to overcome.*

"Okay." I stood before Brad, wand tapping my palm to send little jolts flickering through my aura. "You kill him, and more come. I have an idea to maybe stop it all."

"Yeah? What does it do?" Pike asked as Trent made a worried *mmmm* of sound.

"Buys you some freedom?" I suggested.

"You need that for Finnis," Trent said, and a flicker of worry pinched my brow.

"It holds six curses." I paused, nudging Pike's brother with my toe. I was betting that he was awake and faking it so he wouldn't get his head thunked again. Jenks could have told me just by looking. "Ivy, smack him awake, will you?"

Ivy drew her hand back, and Brad opened his eyes. "Hit me again. Thrill me," he growled as he pulled his feet under him and sat against the pylon. Her perfect face placid, Ivy cracked her knuckles, considering it.

"Don't move," I threatened, feeling the balance of something shift. "I'm the only one here who doesn't want you dead. Understand?"

Brad scowled, and I strengthened my hold on the line. The wand felt slippery in my grip, and I took a firm stance, the stench of melted tires sticking in my nose. *What are the words?* Oh yeah. At the hour of sleep. *"Hora somni,"* I intoned, waving the wand to make the "as is" glyph.

Yelping, I dropped the wand as it flashed warm and a black and gold haze settled over Pike's brother. He stiffened, lips parting.

And then I doubled over, shocked as the smut slammed into me.

Groaning, I waved everyone off as Trent called my name in alarm. Oh, God, it was bad, and the feeling of wrong slithered over my aura, refusing to settle in even as it burned like ice. *I accept this,* I thought, but it was heavy, and it didn't matter how I tried to take it, it seemed to slither of its own accord into my outer aura, where it hung as if waiting for direction.

"Rachel?" Trent's hand landed on my shoulder, and I gasped, pulling the dark ugliness deep inside me as it tried to shift from me to him.

I accept this. This is mine, I thought again, and the smut grudgingly settled into my chi. *This is mine!*

"Is she okay?" Pike's voice sounded as if I was at the bottom of a well.

"I'm fine," I said as I opened my eyes, panting.

"He looks overmedicated," Ivy said, and my attention flicked to Pike's brother. My lips pressed together and I glanced at Trent, taking a step back so the smut wouldn't try to jump to him again. That wand was still on the pavement, and I gingerly took it, stuffing it into a pocket, where it lay like a heavy lump. *Hodin, we need to talk.*

"I'm fine," I said again as I frowned at Brad's slack expression. "I didn't expect that much smut." My hands were shaking, and I clenched them to try to hide it. What the devil kind of curse did Hodin teach me? It felt dark, but the ingredients had been okay. I hadn't even set the parameters of what I wanted it to do yet.

"Rachel?" Trent shifted my face to his, his finger warm on my cold chin. "That's a lot of smut."

I swallowed hard, shuddering as I felt it try to leave me again and I yanked it back. "The amount of smut doesn't mean it's a dark curse," I said, feeling ill. "It only means I changed reality more than usual. Give it a sec to soak in. It will get better." Damn it to the Turn, if Hodin had lied to me, I was going to be pissed.

Pike jabbed his foot at his brother, and the slack-eyed man didn't move. "How is this better than dead?" he said, and I fisted my hands, not liking that they were still trembling. I could feel the curse still linking Brad and me, and it felt wrong.

But wrong or not, I had to continue, and I scrunched down to put my face beside Brad's and finish the thing. "You remember Ken Castle?" I said, and he blinked at me. "Ken," I said firmly. "At the casino. A werefox. You gave him money, and he gave you Pike."

Brad nodded, glancing up at Trent and Ivy as if never having seen them before, but his gaze hardened as he spotted Pike, bloodied and beaten in the wheelchair.

"Well, Ken cheated you," I said. "He took your money and gave you a fake Pike thinking you would kill him right away and never discover it."

Pike's brother's jaw clenched in anger. "Son of a bitch," he whispered.

"That's right," I said. "This is the wrong man." I turned to Pike, who had begun to smile. It wasn't a nice look on him at the moment, seeing as his eye was swollen shut, his lip was busted open, and his nose was broken. "He's not Pike," I added, and Brad's confusion returned. "Pike is in the Bahamas. That's why you are at the airport, but you should get your money back from Ken first."

Trent hid a smirk behind a hand, and even Ivy chuckled.

"Right." I stood, and Brad followed me with his eyes. "Ivy, I think he can stand up now."

Ivy extended a hand. "Up you go, sunshine," she said, hauling him stumbling to his feet.

Groaning, Brad put a hand to his head. "Why am I at the airport?"

"You were going to take Pike to your grandfather," I said, confused, and Pike's ugly smile blanked. "But Ken cheated you. Soon as you get your money from Ken, you're going to track Pike down in the Bahamas."

"Oh yeah. Right." Brad squinted at the bright wash of sun outside the parking tower. "That must have been some party. My head is exploding." He blinked at us blankly. "Did someone mug me? Where am I?"

I glanced at Trent, a sick feeling winding its way around my heart. "Ah, the airport."

"Son of a bitch," he muttered, feeling his ribs. "What the fuck am I doing here?"

Pike's frown deepened. "You need to get your money back from Ken Castle."

"Pike." Brad scrambled up, confusion flickering over him as he slowed, just now noticing his new bruises. "God-damned witches!" he swore as he noticed the three downed assassins.

"That's not Pike," I said quickly, but that cold feeling was becoming heavier. "That's the man Ken Castle spelled to look like Pike to get your money. You were on your way to recover it, remember?"

Still eyeing Pike, Brad reached for his phone. "I don't remember Castle. Is he the one who mugged me? Who are you, anyway?"

Trent touched my elbow. "Could you excuse us for a moment? Ivy, maybe your boyfriend can call someone to get him on a bus home or something."

"Boyfriend?" Ivy said, and Pike cleared his throat, drawing her attention.

"That would be me," Pike said as Brad frowned at his phone.

"What am I doing in Cincinnati?" he whispered, his confusion growing, and Trent pulled me a few steps away.

"This doesn't seem like fulfillment," I said, not at all happy. "That feels like a memory curse." He remembered Pike, but not me and what I'd told him thirty seconds ago.

"Let's get Pike out of here before it wears off," Trent said, and I nodded. *If it wears off. . . .*

"Hey," Brad said loudly as he looked at the paint-peeling cars and flat tires. "Do any of you know where my car is?"

"The east lot," I said as I motioned for Ivy to get Pike. There were amber lights flashing outside in the sun, and we needed to go. "Thanks for everything. See you around."

"Right." Brad rubbed his head, glancing at the three assassins before limping to the blue and amber lights like a moth to a flame. "See you around."

Trent looped an arm in mine, and we angled to the elevator. I was still queasy from the smut. Something was seriously wrong. I had to talk to Hodin. Now.

"I would have rather killed him," Pike muttered sullenly, and Ivy, pushing him like an especially svelte, exceptional day nurse, huffed her agreement.

"No, this is good." I exhaled, feeling a little better. No one died. That had to count for something. The assassins would be revived, and in time, word would go out. My reputation was intact. And at the end of the day, that was all I really had.

A call went up behind us, and we didn't turn, focused on the elevator as we slowed before it and Trent hit the up button. Slowly Pike's anger shifted, and he flexed his hands, staring at them. "Thank you," he said softly. "No one has ever risked their life for me before."

I felt odd, and I wished the elevator would get here. "You're worth saving," I said, and Trent's shoulders slumped. "Even if you did screw up by placing that bet," I added, glancing at Ivy. "We need to find out what Finnis wants."

Ivy reached past Trent and tapped the up key so fast it seemed to hum. "To see Constance."

But it had to be more than that, and I sighed, relieved when the doors opened and there was no one inside. Trent

held the door, and Ivy trundled a silent, thoughtful Pike in.
I was last, giving the small crowd around Brad and the
downed assassins a final glance as the doors slid shut. *Halfway home.*

"Hodin said it was a sure bet," Pike muttered, and my
gaze shot to him.

"Hodin?" I questioned, and Pike shrugged, then winced,
a hand going to his ribs.

"We are not all going to fit in your car," I said as the
doors slid open and a fresher brand of parking-garage air
flowed over us. "Pike, we might have to leave your chair
behind."

Trent grinned. "No problem. I have an accessible van
waiting for us. We just have to get to the car rental."

"Seriously?" I said, remembering his distraction. "You're
amazing."

"And don't you forget it," he said, tugging me into him
for a sideways hug.

Ahead of us, both Ivy and Pike sighed, probably for the
same reason. My head thumped onto Trent's shoulder, and I
felt the ugly knot of unease begin to untwist. Pike was
going to be okay. I might even be able to patch him up
enough so he could come with me to talk to Finnis.

But as Pike's light, raspy chatter mixed with Ivy's snappy,
on-point comebacks, I began to wonder.

Cassie had said the assassins had used a ring-based
curse to down her people. My assumption that only a skilled
practitioner such as Landon or Dali could have made it
could be widened to include Hodin. He used ring magic
extensively. But it couldn't have been Hodin who helped the
assassins walk out with Pike. Hodin needed me.

Didn't he?

CHAPTER
11

THE TURN TAKE IT, I'VE GOT TO MAKE SOME CHANGES, I thought as I shuffled into the church. Fatigue and the ache of coming bruises made me slow, but my shoulders slumped in relief when the blessedly dry, cool air bathed my face. The sun would set in a few hours, but it was going to be a hot and muggy night, and the windows would likely stay shut. "Jenks?" I called as Ivy pushed past me, her shoulder under Pike's as she helped him in. "We're home!"

I drew aside, waiting for Trent before shutting the door and leaning back against it. "Hodin?" I said, tone wary, but there was no answer. Trent was on his phone with his banker, and I dropped my bag and jacket by the stairs and headed for the couch.

"No. I've got it," Trent said as I passed him. "In hand, actually," he added, a hint of deviltry in him. "Cash?" He hesitated. "You know me better than that. Okay, you got me there. Would it help if my lawyers talked to your lawyers to keep everything in the open?"

Ivy's beeline for the bathrooms slowed as she took in the

changes, her gaze going from her baby grand on the raised stage to the elegantly repaired hole in the floor to the furniture around the coffee table. "Are those new?" she asked, eyeing the stained-glass windows.

"Yep, and unlike the old ones, they open when it's not eighty-five degrees and a hundred percent humidity outside." I flopped onto the couch, feeling as if I might never get up. "Finley found them in the abandoned stretches in Tennessee. Don't you love what she did to the floor?"

Ivy nodded, easily supporting Pike's weight as the man stifled a groan.

Why does this seem so familiar? I mused sourly as Ivy told Pike to suck it up and that she'd have him in a tub of warm water before he could get his remaining shoe untied.

"I don't need help," Pike protested, his expression pinched as he tried to pull from her.

Ivy's grip on his elbow tightened. "Not everything is about you, Welroe."

Both Trent and Pike looked up, and Pike blinked, suddenly unresisting in her grip. "Oh!"

Oh, indeed. "At least the pixies are outside," I said, scanning the rafters to find them utterly absent. Getty's presence was already showing benefits. "Jenks?" I called again as the bathroom door clicked shut, and almost immediately his wings sounded in the hallway. The pixy was decidedly frazzled, a weird, blue-gold dust lighting his path.

"Damn, girl!" Jenks said as he circled me once before alighting on the arm of the couch. "What did you do to your hair? Stick your tongue in a light socket?"

I reached to touch it, appalled to find it had snarled into a mat. Trent, who had sat down across from me, stifled a chuckle as he waited on hold. "It's humid," I said, and Jenks laughed, his voice like wind chimes.

"You could lose a faire of fairies in that thing," he said. "Where's Ivy? She with Pike in the shower?"

He hadn't landed on my shoulder. It might have been because of my hair, but I had a feeling it was my new layer of smut that he was studying. "How did you know she was . . ." I started, then nodded. The pixy had better hearing than a pack of Chihuahuas. "Ah, yeah. She's helping him get cleaned up."

"Good." He finally took his eyes off my aura, and I slowly exhaled, glad he hadn't said anything. "If anyone can get Pike upright in time for tonight, it's her. She's good at getting men upright."

Trent pointedly cleared his throat, never looking from his phone as the pixy giggled like a sixth-grader. But Jenks's mirth vanished at Pike's startled yelp from the bathroom. "I knew I should have gone with you," Jenks said. "What the Tink-blasted hell did you do to your aura?"

"I'm wondering that myself," I said, relieved when the shower started and drowned out Pike and Ivy's muffled conversation. "Is Hodin around?" My feet hurt, and I pulled up one leg to work my boot off. "I need to talk to him. He egged Pike into making that bet." *And maybe sold the curse to the assassins that downed Castle's security.*

"Yeah? He wanted to help watch Getty, so I took her down to the kitchen," Jenks said. "Baribas has been sulking in the garden since you left."

"You think he's going to leave her alone?" I asked, and the pixy shrugged.

Trent stood from the couch, his phone in hand. "Rachel, do you mind if I use your porch for a moment? I need to take this."

"Sure. Bring me something cold on your way back?"

"You got it." His voice taking on a professional lilt, he headed for the hallway to the back of the church, his hand trailing across my shoulder to leave tingles.

Jenks rose up and down, clearly impatient to see Ivy but knowing better than to interrupt whatever was going on in the bathroom. "What does Ivy think about the new addition?" he asked.

"Don't know yet." I puffed in relief as a boot came off. *Blood and Brimstone, Brimstone and blood.*

"Cool. Dibs on giving her the tour." He snickered at the

empty hallway, probably hearing stuff I was glad to be missing. "So . . . how did it go besides you rolling your aura in filth?"

My second boot came off, and I hesitated, trying to decide what to say as I arranged them. "Between you and me, I think we could have done it twice as fast and with half as much pain if you had been there," I said softly, which, while not entirely true, wouldn't hurt his pixy pride. "How is Getty?" I asked as I fingered the new hole at my knee.

"Okay." He frowned in stark contrast to a sudden brightening of his dust. "She doesn't trust me, which I get. Baribas insists that she was poaching. No one is happy. She keeps trying to . . . She's fine."

"So, business as usual." I put my arches on the edge of the table, listening to the sound of running water and glad Finley had put in an on-demand water heater. I wanted to take a shower and tame my hair, but not until I found out what Trent was doing for the next few hours. "Will her wing mend?"

"Oh, sure." He sat down, wings blurring to invisibility until he settled. "But she won't be flying for a few days. She was lucky it wasn't a main vein that snapped. I don't know who is going to kill her first, Baribas, or me. *He* says a passing pixy told him she was poaching, but she insists she got caught in a downdraft and was just doing a flyover on the garden."

I didn't dare smile. "Jenks, what would you say if I asked you to stay with Getty when I go talk to Finnis tonight?"

"I'd say your cheese is about to slip off your cracker." Brow furrowed, Jenks glanced up from smoothing a wing tear. "You asked me to sit out paying off Pike's marker, and you come back with your aura looking like troll shit and a scraped knee. I don't even want to talk about your hair. Hodin can watch Getty."

"Hodin makes mistakes," I said, not sure I trusted him anymore. Actually, I never had. "You don't."

"That's what I mean," he complained. "Pike—"

"Will be fine," I finished, my feet thumping to the floor.

"Ivy will be there, and Trent," I said. "I'm only seeing what Finnis wants. I threaten him. . . . He threatens me. . . . I come home and make some charms. We all go out together later and convince Finnis he'll live longer if he ignores me. Getty needs you more than I do right now."

"Getty doesn't need me," Jenks said. "She's made that perfectly clear. With lots of big words. I swear, she must have spent all eighteen years of her life in a library. I know what Finnis wants. He wants to off you. He wants to off you and take your place."

My hand cupped around Jenks and I wished, not for the first time, that we were the same size. "Ivy wouldn't be here if that was his goal," I said, and Jenks continued to scowl in disbelief. "There are easier ways to take a potshot at me than traveling five hundred miles and doing it in person. He's here confirming that Constance isn't running Cincinnati so they can send in the big guns. All we have to do is convince him she is."

But not with that "fulfillment" wand, I mused as I pulled my hand from Jenks. My smutty aura was tingling as if the damage was trying to jump to him, and I didn't like it.

Jenks's wings drooped. Damn it back to the Turn, I'd known something like this was going to happen when I agreed to take on the subrosa position. I did *not* want to run Cincinnati as its grand pooh-bah, strutting around with a wand in my hand, a pixy on my shoulder, and a billionaire in my pocket. Every wannabe ruler would challenge me.

Jenks's angular features eased in sympathy. He knew this was not what I had wanted, but he also knew that becoming the subrosa had been my only choice—easy, hard, or otherwise. "He wants to see Constance? Show him the mouse," he muttered.

"I doubt that would help." Focus distant, I curled my feet up, cold in the air-conditioned chill. "She's not running Cincinnati, and that's all the DC undead care about. That she's a mouse and they can't incarcerate me for killing her twice will make them even more angry."

My hand felt slick, almost greasy from that wand, and I curled my fingers into a fist, not liking that half the world's population could see my new smut. Vivian's curse wouldn't have even noticed that man at Findlay Market. "I don't think that curse Hodin gave me was white," I whispered, genuinely afraid to use it again.

"Ya think?"

But then Jenks rose up, turning as the bell made a soft bong and Hodin appeared, materializing dead center of the new inlaid floor as if it were a designated jump-in/out spot. "You used it?" the demon exclaimed, his features pinched in both alarm and disbelief as he stood in his biker's best. "You used the wand to rescue Pike? What are you going to use on Finnis? That was the whole point!"

"You left Getty alone?" Jenks shouted, his wings an aggressive clatter, and Hodin opened his palm to show a disgruntled, disheveled, and very annoyed pixy.

"You green-slimed, degenerate freak of a fatheaded, feathered fairy whore!" Getty swore, and Jenks's wing hum went silent in what I thought was admiration. "What the Tink-blasted hell is wrong with you! I'm a person, not a gummy bear you can stuff in your pocket!"

I stood, reaching for her. "Getty, I'm so sorry," I said, but Jenks was faster, and he swooped down, grabbing the woman and rising up, his sparkles a bright silver. Getty wiggled, and I gasped when he dropped her only to dart down to snag the woman by her foot a narrow six inches from the floor.

"Put me down!" she shouted, her skirts over her head to show her elaborately embroidered underthings, and he swung her up into the air, catching her by the waist and rising to set her on a rafter. There was a smart smack and he retreated, but not before she put a bright red handprint on his cheek.

"I swear," Jenks said as he hovered, shaking before her and shedding a bright red dust. "If you bend my wing again, I will snap your other wing, woman! I'm not trying to kill you. Why by Tink's contractual hell do you think I want to hurt you?"

"Everyone else does!" she shouted. "The only time anyone touches me is to hurt me!"

Jenks's wing hum vanished as his flight evened out. "I'm not everyone else," he said, and she flushed.

Hodin's hard-soled boots thumped as he came to stand before me. "You used the wand on Castle?" he prompted, and my attention fell from the rafters, my brow furrowing at Hodin's shocked expression. "Fulfillment will not balance books. Pike's debt is not paid and they will be back for him. It was a poor use of resources."

"The debt is paid," I said sourly. "I used the wand on Pike's brother to convince him Pike is in the Bahamas," I said, wondering why he was upset. "Pike's brother paid off Pike's mark when he bought him from Castle."

A long-fingered hand going over his hair, Hodin looked at the bathroom. "Kalamack didn't pay his debt? So everything is returned the way it was," he said, sounding doubtful.

"More or less." My gaze went past Jenks—hovering before me with his hands on his hips. "Even better now that Ivy's here." I carefully arranged my boots beside the couch so Ivy wouldn't raise her eyebrows at me for leaving them in the middle of the floor. "All that's left is convincing Finnis that Constance is in control so he'll go away." Which might be hard now.

"Good." Hodin's smile was stiff, and his hands were hidden in his sleeves. "Very resourceful. Seems you have this subrosa position under control."

I sat on the arm of the couch, eyes narrowed. Had that been annoyance in his congratulations? "Pike says *you* put him up to making that bet. That it was a sure thing."

Hodin's long face went empty of emotion. "It was a sure thing," he said, his low voice holding a hint of anger that I would question him. "Something went wrong. You worked around it. No harm done."

"No harm done!" I exclaimed, then swallowed my anger. Sure, the shower was on, but vampires had very good hearing. "Pike is beat up and I'm covered in smut."

Hodin snickered as he practically flopped into the chair across from me, his long arms and legs angling everywhere. "Don't you think it's odd Trent won't tell you what he's doing with that much money?"

I stared at him, wondering what his game was. He hadn't asked after Pike. Hadn't offered to help. Hadn't explained about the smut. And now he was trying to change the subject. "No. You said there wouldn't be that much smut. What do you call this?" I said, gesturing at myself.

Hodin frowned, one knee going across the other. "You were supposed to put it on the one you cursed. Why, by the Goddess's halo, did you keep it?"

"Because I'm the one who made it," I said, feeling foolish, though I'd do the same thing if given a choice again. "It's a lot of smut for a white curse. What gives, Hodin?"

My question hung in the uncomfortable silence as Trent scuffed to a halt at the top of the hall, his phone in one hand, a glass of iced tea in the other. Jenks's wings hummed from the rafters, and Hodin's gaze shifted between the three of us. "You saw what went in it. You said yourself that Vivian Smith agreed that its rank hinged upon what you were doing with it. You must have tried to convince someone of a horrendous lie."

That was exactly what I had done, well, not horrendous, but a lie nevertheless. Even so, I still thought the error was in the curse itself, not how I used it. The smut had hit me way before I told Brad to believe a lie. Besides, Brad had seemed more confused than content, unable to remember even what I'd told him. If Hodin hadn't known how to work the curse, then maybe he had misunderstood what it was supposed to do. Newt was crazy. Who knew what her version of fulfillment was? I should have stopped the moment I'd realized the curse was one of hers.

But I hadn't, willing to risk it in the hopes it would make my life easier. Easy like a wish.

I slid off the arm of the couch, angry at him, myself, and

everything. "You have no idea what Newt's curse does or how it works. What time does Stef get off work?"

Hodin's focus sharpened as he tracked Trent coming in and setting the dripping glass of tea on a coaster. "Why?"

"I want to know what went into that wand that wasn't on that list," I said, and Jenks's wings rasped a warning. The smut had been horrendous, and it wasn't as if I could slough it off, making a new ever-after as I had before.

"You created it," Hodin said stiffly, and Trent's hand touched my shoulder in support.

"I saw Stef make a smudge stick and the quencher," I said, still not liking that he practically ordered her around. "What did she put in it that wasn't on the list?" Blood and flame were not ingredients. They were catalysts and accelerators.

Hodin's gaze sharpened on me, a flicker of anger lighting his red, goat-slitted eyes. "This is what I get for trying to be helpful," he said, his outline growing misty.

"Hey!" I barked, but he was gone in an inrushing sound and the scent of burnt amber.

"The Turn take it," I muttered, frowning as my bad mood worsened. Lips pressed, I stifled a jerk as Pike's muffled yelp from the bathroom cut through the sound of the shower. "At least we got Pike back."

"Do you think he will be okay for tonight?" Trent asked, and I shrugged.

"If Ivy can jam enough Brimstone cookies into him."

"Then it was a good decision. He's key to your power structure," Trent said, but I still felt as if I'd made a mistake.

"Everyone here is key," I said as I sat down, feeling strong with Trent at my side and Jenks hovering over my shoulder. *Everyone here except Hodin.*

I couldn't tell what was going on in Hodin's thoughts, and I stifled a shiver when Trent's hand slipped from me. Hodin and I weren't done yet, but following him was out of the question—worse than following a vampire.

"You okay?" Trent whispered as he leaned over me, and

when I nodded, his focus went distant. "Ah, would you mind if I take off for about an hour? If I get the funds in the bank before close of business, they have agreed that the money never left. I'll be back in time to meet with Finnis."

My distracted mood sharpened on him. "Absolutely! Take Jenks with you. He could use some time out of the church."

"Rache . . ." the pixy complained, rising up with an annoyed expression. "Trent needs me like a hole in his head."

"Getty?" I peered up into the rafters. "You want to take a steam bath and get warm?"

"Rache." Jenks bobbed up and down, way too close to see clearly. "Trent doesn't need me to go to the bank."

An ugly gray dust was spilling from the rafters. *What did Ivy just say? Oh yeah.* "It's not always about you, Jenks," I whispered, and his wing hum eased as he followed my gaze into the rafters. "No, you should go," I insisted, louder now as I stood and stretched, feeling every ache that hitting the hard cement had put in me. "I'll watch Getty. The heat and humidity will do her wing some good." Jenks took a breath to protest, and I added, "It's a million two, Jenks. Cash. He needs a wingman. Besides, I have to do something with my hair before I set foot out of this church."

Silent, I pleaded with my eyes, and torn, Jenks spilled a sickly green dust. "Tink loves a duck. Fine," he finally said, his wings a harsh rasp as he rose straight up, hands on his hips. "You going to be nice when I help you down, or do you want to smack my face again?" he said loudly.

A tiny, pale face peeked over the edge. "Why don't you go tickle Tink's rosebuds."

Jenks's lips parted in shock, and then his wings rose in pitch. "Fine. Fall for all I care. Maybe you could land in Rachel's hair. It's big enough to catch a hawk in."

Trent shifted from foot to foot, clearly eager to be gone. "Great. Thanks, Jenks." He leaned close and gave me a quick kiss and sideways hug. "Bye, Rachel. See you in about an hour. Plenty of time before meeting Finnis."

"My hair isn't that big," I muttered, and his smile widened. But he pulled away, as I knew he would, looking as good as rain in the desert as he headed for the door, Jenks at his shoulder. The pixy turned when Trent opened it, making the "I'm watching you" gesture to Getty before he darted out and the door thumped shut.

What is he doing with all that money? I wondered, frowning at the empty rafters. "Getty? I can't take a shower unless you come with me. I'm a good catch. Really."

Again her tiny face showed, sparkles on her cheeks from her leaking wing. "I'm fine."

My neck was getting a crick, and I sighed. "Until Baribas shows," I said. "Please? Jenks will stab my ear if he comes back and you're dead. The steam will do you a world of good, and isn't that what you want? To get out of here?"

"I suppose," she said, and then she shifted, hanging her feet over the edge until she pushed off.

My breath caught as she dropped . . . and then I had her in my cupped hands. I jerked as that smut seemed to rise up, wanting to swamp her, but I caught it before it reached my aura, and I shoved it back into my chi, leaving me to wonder if Getty had sensed it when she nervously tugged her skirt to cover her dirty feet. Pixies saw auras all the time, no second sight needed as for everyone else. "Do you want to be on my shoulder? Jenks likes to sit on my earrings."

"This is okay," she said, and I nodded, taking my iced tea in hand and going into the hall. We'd always had twin bathrooms from when the church had been a church. It was one thing Finley hadn't changed. Ivy's was the nicer of the two, but mine had the washer and dryer, which might sound like a detriment, but I'd always found it useful.

"I don't understand why you're helping me," Getty said as I elbowed the light switch on and back-kicked the door shut. "Most lunkers want to put you in a cage or squish you. Jenks said . . ." Her voice cut off and she flushed.

"Towel?" I asked, raising my hand so she could step onto the rack when she nodded. "Jenks is a really nice guy," I said as she arranged herself. I took a sip of iced tea, then downed half of it in one go. "You're going to be fine," I added when I came up for air.

"I shouldn't have hit that car." Getty studied the bathroom for possible threats as I got the water started. "One moment I'm flying above the trees, and then I'm in the road, my hat gone and smacking into a window. Something blew me into it."

A story I would doubt if pixies weren't honest to a fault. Glass still in hand, I looked in the mirror, near horror bubbling up at my hair. *Not enough charms in the world* . . . "Ah, Stef feels really bad about that. Don't worry about paying Jenks back. Stef will take care of it with some heavy lifting in the garden. Jenks will make sure you stay fed."

"I don't know how," she muttered, attention on the small stained-glass window. "I have yet to see him in the garden."

I set the glass down with a sharp tap, my brow furrowed. I could teach a 400-level class on turning insecurity into bitchiness, but she was badmouthing the man who had saved my life more times than I had shoes. "A man's worth is found in who he loves and who loves him," I said stiffly.

"I wouldn't know," she said bitterly, wings drooping as a steamy warmth rolled out of the shower.

My shoulders slumped. I wanted to say more, but I didn't have a clue as to what would help. "He's not going to kill you. Unless you try to kill me," I joked. "Do you need anything before I get in? Hungry? Jenks has stashes in almost every room."

She shook her head, becoming busy with her tights as I began to strip. "Ah, about that demon. Hodin?" she said as I sighed at my skinned knee. "He was lying to you. I could see it in his aura."

My heart gave a pound, and I forced myself to keep moving. "About what?" I pulled a towel from the dryer to cover myself.

"That something went wrong," she said. "He wasn't lying about the bet being a sure thing, but his aura flared when he said something went wrong." She paused. "Maybe I shouldn't have said anything."

"I'm glad you did," I said, thinking if Hodin was lying to me, I was really up shit creek. I needed to talk to Stef. Alone. As soon as possible. She had to know what had gone into that smudge stick and quencher.

Which sort of begged the question as to why she hadn't told me already.

CHAPTER

12

STRETCHING, I SET THE OUTDATED TEXTBOOK ON THE stack before me, my attention going from the ice-filled, condensation-wet glass to the dark garden and the conspicuous gathering of pixy dust glowing in the shadows. Ivy had turned the air so low a pixy could skate on the kitchen counter, driving me out onto the open-air porch to do my research. The evening air was nice and the indoor/outdoor couch I was schlumped in was comfortable, even if my thoughts were not. Pulling the bowl of chips closer, I wondered if I'd ever get a straight answer out of Hodin.

But I had a class tomorrow—if I survived the night—and I *still* didn't know what I was going to talk about, much less what I was going to wear. *Something black,* I mused as I wound my blessedly clean and spelled-straight hair around a finger, but even the darkest shirt and pants wouldn't hide my new smut, and worry made my gut hurt. They'd see it.

"What are you all doing out there?" I whispered as I eyed the pixies gathered into a hovering knot over a distant tombstone. It wasn't unusual to see pixies at night. They were active through the dark hours except a few hours around midnight when everyone but the sentries slept. But Baribas and his kids weren't dancing, or laughing, or preparing food. They weren't moving at all. *Must be talking,* I thought. About Getty?

Concerned, I ate another chip, wiping the salt from my fingers before reaching for another book on the low table between me and the garden. Finley had put in rope lighting around the perimeter of the ceiling, and that with the citronella candle was enough to read by if I squinted, but it didn't matter—my discarded school texts were too simple and the demon books were too, ah, graphic.

"Why did I tell Vivian I'd do this?" I moaned as I snapped the book shut and dropped it with the rest. Pike's logos shifted in the draft, and I made an untidy stack of them, too. I was a runner, not a teacher. I had no idea what to talk about. Demon or not, I felt totally inadequate. Especially now that I was covered with enough smut to have been sent to Alcatraz in the late 1800s without trial. The shadow on my aura would garner mistrust. Lots of it.

"Freakin' fabulous," I muttered, turning to the kitchen's French doors as they squeaked open.

"What's fabulous?" Ivy said, her low voice tripping down my spine to make me shiver in spite of the heat.

Stifling it, I smiled at her narrow-waisted silhouette coming closer. Like magic, my unease dissolved and I relaxed when the last piece of the puzzle that was our church seemed to fall into place. "Me not having anything to talk about tomorrow," I said as I moved two books off the adjacent chair and dropped them on the table with a thump.

"Don't let them scare you." Ivy sat with a languid grace, her back to the kitchen and her eyes on Pike's logos. He had been badgering me to pick one, and I still couldn't decide. "Finnis's flight arrives in a few hours. I'm heading over to the Cincinnatian to make sure his quarters are adequate before I pick him up." Her long fingers pushed the napkins, receipts, and torn paper around, arranging them. "Get him settled before your dinner meeting. Pike is asleep on the couch. He'll be fine once the Brimstone works its way through, but taking him tonight to meet with Finnis probably won't give the impression you want."

I winced, remembering Pike's white bandages, scraped skin, and slumped, beaten form. He looked as if he'd lost the fight, not won it, but me showing up alone would give Finnis an even worse impression. "He's got to go," I said. "He's Constance's scion. Fortunately I'll have Trent and Jenks with me in case there's trouble. We'll keep him safe."

"I know you will." Ivy's brow furrowed in concern. "Dinner for five," she whispered, focus distant as she leaned over the logos.

She was markedly calm and relaxed for the trouble I was in. I'd like to say that it was because Nina had brought meaning and stability to her life, but her easygoing mood was probably because of her and Pike's, ah, extended quality time.

"Pike has an amazing skill set," she said, confirming my suspicions as she began to stack the books into two piles, one spell books, one demon tomes. I thought it cool she knew the difference.

"Yeah?" My gaze went to the garden and the pixies. I didn't think she meant Pike's charisma and ability to get things done. "Good to know."

She chuckled, and I stifled a shudder. "Nina has been encouraging me to share blood with someone other than her." Ivy pushed back, the logos stacked neatly once again. "Especially if that someone knows what scars are good for. I think she wants to bring some new techniques to our own bedroom."

"Don't need to hear this, okay?" I said, taking the top book from the stack and opening it up, hiding behind it, really. I wanted a chip, but not when she was talking about blood and sex. Ivy knew me eating crunchy things in front of her wasn't the usual invitation to bite me, but why tread on those instincts?

"He needed the blood." Ivy smiled, her sharp canines catching the candlelight and shining. "And I was curious if he could keep up with us." She took a slow, languorous breath as she eased deeper into the cushions, expression vacant. "He can."

"Ivy," I protested. "I have to work with the man. I don't want to know."

"Need and want are two sides to the same coin, and you're wasting a good opportunity to enjoy yourself. Trent won't mind if you keep it to blood only."

Trent *would* mind, and I eyed her sourly. "Still looking after me, huh?" I said, and her smile became fond.

"Life is short. I'll never understand why you don't take joy when it arrives on your doorstep." Her gaze went to the newly stacked spell books. "Searching for a spell for Finnis?"

I dropped the book on the stack with a thump. "That's what I *should* be doing. No, I'm trying to find something to talk about at that class I promised Vivian I'd teach. I think I'm going to call and cancel on her." But even as the words left my lips, I felt a surprising pang of loss.

"Why?" Ivy nudged the book I had just dropped, making it perfect with the rest. "You've got a lot to share."

"Yeah, about what not to do." Dismayed, I glanced down at myself. You couldn't see your own aura apart from its reflection in a protection circle or ley line spell, but everyone past a 100-level course would know how to use their second sight to see someone else's. "It doesn't matter what I say after they notice the smut I'm carrying. The administration is going to get calls. I'll be lucky if I don't get escorted off campus."

Silent, Ivy went through Pike's logos and pulled one aside. "You're teaching demonology, right? If you didn't have some smut, they wouldn't take you seriously. Relax, Rachel," she said as she swung her long hair around and began working it into a tight bun. "Own the smut. Have some fun with it. It gives you street cred. You could explain why no one can summon demons anymore, or why the new ever-after isn't a red-smeared hell, or the origin of the ley lines. I bet none of them know that the lines they're using are hardly over a year old."

My focus blurred as I thought about that.

"You have an enormous amount of information that you take for granted," Ivy said as she began playing with the citronella candle, pinching the flame and letting it go before it went out. "They might have book learning and lab hours, but you have practical knowledge that no one else has."

I looked across the tidied table at her, grateful she was here. "I suppose. But it doesn't matter if I can't get through tonight."

"Tonight is nothing." Ivy peered into the dark garden as the pixies' argument became loud. "You go. You arrange for a meeting with Constance. You leave. He wouldn't expect to see Constance tonight even if she was still running Cincinnati. That cold bloodsucker would make Finnis wait at least two days before granting him an audience. He's expecting to get into Cincinnati tonight, have a nice dinner, talk with Constance's scion to arrange a meeting, done. If he doesn't see her by the end of the week?" Ivy shrugged. "That's your window."

"A week? Great . . ." I exhaled, relief easing the band about my chest. If I couldn't do this in a week, then I didn't deserve to hold Cincinnati. Pike would be up and functional in a few days. Until then, I'd have Trent, Jenks, and even Ivy in a pinch.

"This porch is really nice," Ivy said as she studied the open beams, still bright and new. "And the kitchen," she added. "When Jenks told me you were rebuilding the back, I was worried it wouldn't feel the same. It does. Seeing you here with your books—"

Her voice broke, and I put my feet on the floor, my lips parting. *Is she crying?*

"I forgot how much I liked being here," she said, damp eyes meeting mine before darting away in embarrassment. "Of being a part of something I helped make. But mostly because it was here, in our church, that I learned I was worth loving. This was where I learned to love myself and quit trying to be what everyone wanted so they would love me."

She didn't wipe her eye, but let the tear roll down. "Thank you for never giving up on me."

This was more emotion than I'd seen in her over an entire year, and I smiled, reaching across the small space between us and giving her hand a tight squeeze. "You are my friend," I said softly. "I wouldn't have survived becoming who I am if not for you and Jenks."

She nodded, almost laughing at the dark memory of how chancy my life had been, how tenuous as I figured things out and my skills became commensurate with the tasks I needed to do to survive. "I love Nina," she said, her hand turning under mine until our fingers laced. "And I love everything she and I are doing together. But I miss hearing you and Jenks talking about nothing. Your passive-aggressive bitching when I used all the hot water. That you never gave me any grief about needing a plan for everything and let me overkill our runs." Her attention went to the garden. "Watching Jenks's kids grow up."

I gave her hand a tight squeeze. "Ivy . . ."

"DC is starting to feel like a trap," she continued, head down. "Though Nina has found an amazing amount of control among the undead." She chuckled and wiped the damp from her cheek, her love and pride for Nina easy to see. The woman had died after channeling one of the old undead, leaving her with all the hunger and none of the control. "Don't get me wrong," she added. "I don't want to live in the church. My life has changed too much. But I do miss . . . this."

I didn't know what to say, except that I missed it, too— even with the ugly, hard parts. Her hand slipped from mine, and she took a slow breath, her expression evening out. "This is the best of the lot, in my opinion," she said, tapping the diamond logo that she'd left on top.

I hesitated, wanting to tell her that we could find a way to reclaim everything we'd had, but we'd left it for a reason—and there was really no going back. *So we go forward using our shared past to define our present,* I thought.

"Pike told you about his logos?" I said as I settled my hand in my lap, and Ivy visibly relaxed, glad I hadn't said anything and let her unload.

She nodded, gaze on her tear-damp finger. "We had a long chat." Her smile went soft. "Anyway, I think he's right. You need something that confirms the actions you're both taking to protect the city. Word will get around and your position will be more stable."

"I never thought about it like that." I pulled the twined *M* and *W* closer, wondering if all anyone would see was a diamond bracketed by two parallel lines.

"Did you know he's in line to inherit his grandfather's entire estate?" Ivy asked.

I turned the logo sideways, squinting at it. *Looks like a stylized imperial fighter.* "He said something like that, yes."

"He's sort of a prince in waiting."

My head came up at the wistful lilt to her voice. "So are you."

Her expression had gone sultry. "Above-average street smarts. I bet he knows at least three disciplines of martial arts."

"Ivy Tamwood," I said, voice light. "I do believe you like the man." But my smile faltered at her pupil-black stare. "Ah, yeah," I added. "He's half the reason I'm able to keep Cincinnati intact. Piscary's lost children like him. They are his eyes and muscle. He knows what it's like to be orphaned and he has their loyalty, even if he's alive. I'm there as glue, I suppose."

Ivy, too, was one of Piscary's lost, and the rims of brown around her pupils grew in the memory of both hating and loving her twice-dead abuser. "That glue being the soul curse of yours currently waiting for FSCA approval," she said. "If the old ones get that struck down, Cincy will turn on you, Pike or no. Rachel, I have a bad feeling that Nina and I won't be allowed to come home to Cincinnati if Finnis confirms that you and Pike are managing the city, not Constance."

I pulled my feet under me, worried. "Can they do that? Can't your mom . . ."

The ice in my glass shifted and she twitched, the candle-light sharp on her defined cheekbones. "My mother doesn't have enough pull. Piscary might have, but he's gone. The old undead don't like that Nina and I are on equal footing because I hold her soul. The DC vamps believe it's the promise of your soul curse that is keeping the Cincy vampires in line, the living and undead both. If you withdraw your application, the master vampires might look the other way and Nina and I can come home, but they will send someone when you lose control of the city. And you will lose control."

I sank into the cushions, thoughts whirling. *God. What a choice.* "Ivy . . ."

"Or," Ivy said softly, "you keep pushing to get the curse through FSCA and hold on to the city, leaving Nina and me hostages to ensure you do what they tell you to do. I'm trying to decide how selfish I am. My happiness, or everyone else's."

"It's not like that," I protested, but my gut said she was right. "The curse only works on the newly undead. It would be a tiny fraction—"

"A fraction that would grow every day," Ivy interrupted, her gaze on the dark garden and the lights of Cincinnati across the river. "Every day, every week, every year until the old undead are utterly gone, or worse, simply no longer in control."

I slumped, worried. I felt as if I had been backed into a corner, and as I watched Ivy begin to give up on another hope, I vowed I'd find some other way. "Or there's curtain number three," I said, "where we convince Finnis that Constance is still in charge and I push the FSCA into registering my soul curse."

"Rachel . . ."

"No, this will work," I said, uncurling from the couch and putting my bare feet on the floor. "Hodin's fulfillment curse is crap, but I'll find a better spell." I shifted closer to the end of the couch, nearer to her. Trent had tons of books in his mother's library. There would be something there.

"I'll make sure Finnis leaves Cincinnati thinking that Constance is alive and calling the shots. If they send someone else to verify it, I'll do it again. I'll eventually get the soul curse pushed through, and until then, I don't see why *Constance* wouldn't ask for you and Nina to come down and help Pike bust some heads. If Constance says she needs you and Nina, then who are they to refuse?"

Jaw tight, Ivy took a shuddering breath. "Damn it, Rachel. Hope hurts."

I nodded, a quiver running through me when her eyes met mine. "I've got this. With Pike, and Trent, and Jenks, and you—it's possible. It's just one undead vampire, right?"

Ivy nodded. "I wouldn't mind seeing Pike reopen Piscary's old restaurant. Kisten—" Her voice cut off. "Kisten deserves to have someone breathe life into his legacy. But, Rachel, you need to wrap this up. Convince Finnis everything is as it should be so I can bring Nina home."

My brow furrowed at the flicker of fear in Ivy, the sour smell of frightened vamp lifting off her skin.

"Nina gets fretful if her soul is too far away for too long," Ivy whispered. "She becomes careless, less herself. It's the only reason I was allowed to come. They wanted to see what would happen."

God, I was making Ivy choose between who she loved and who she was in love with, and my gut hurt.

"Two days," Ivy said softly. "If you meet sooner than that, no one in DC will believe it."

"Two days," I echoed, but Ivy was scared. For Nina, not me, and I leaned forward and gave her a hug. My aura seemed to rise against hers, and I pulled the smut back, shoving it down before it tried to shift to her. *Good grief, is this stuff ever going to soak in?* "It's going to be okay," I whispered, breathing in the scent of her shampoo as her hands went about me, almost spasming as she made a shuddering exhale, completely devoid of any bloodlust.

At least, that's how it started, and I pushed away as a tendril of heat uncoiled in my belly. "Sorry."

Ivy held herself still, breath going in and out in a smooth sound. "I'm not."

And then her head snapped up, black eyes turning to the open door to the kitchen. I followed her line of sight, stiffening at Stef in the doorway, a bag of groceries in her arms.

"Sorry to disturb you," she said nervously. "I was looking for Getty. I bought her some pollen."

I shifted away from Ivy, and the living vampire smirked. "Ah, she's with Jenks in the belfry," I said. "He can watch everything better from up there."

The bag crackled as Stef retreated. "Sorry."

Ivy stood, stretching languorously to show her pierced belly button. "Good God. You witches really need to get over your hang-ups."

But her mood and confidence had been restored, and I felt better. "Stef, can I talk to you for a sec?" I said, and the woman flushed, clearly nervous.

"I gotta go," Ivy said as she leaned to give me a peck on the cheek. "See you tonight. Three a.m. I'll have a table at the restaurant."

"Sure." I almost rolled my eyes. The kiss good-bye was unusual. It could be because I said nothing when she had told me her fears and that was what Ivy needed. But I was guessing it was to tell Stef that I was still hers and to back off. Vampire logic was like that. Finding a compliment in there, I smiled.

Stef retreated a step as Ivy paced forward, as smooth and sure as a lioness after a kill. Ivy hesitated at the doorway, breathing deep before shooting her hand out with a living vampire's quickness to grab Stef's wrist and turn it up to show the two demon marks. "You should have Rachel look at that," Ivy said as Stef froze, her arm extended. "Before it kills you."

Giving a yank, Stef pulled away, her fear triggering Ivy's bloodlust. If Ivy hadn't only now satisfied it with Pike, Stef might be in trouble, but as it was, Ivy simply smiled, lips closed.

"You're bringing Jenks, right?" Ivy asked, waiting.

"That depends." My attention went to Stef. "Are you home, or do you have to go in to work?"

"I—I'm home." Stef stared at Ivy standing on the kitchen's threshold. "I can watch Getty. Is she doing okay? I bought some pollen from a health food store on the way home."

My lips pressed. "Are you sure that Hodin isn't going to make you spell for him?"

She flushed. "I'll watch Getty. I'm the one who hit her."

"Good." Ivy took her phone out and started scrolling. "See you later." Head down, she walked out, but the feel of her was still within the walls, and I settled deeper into the couch, my eyes on Stef.

"We need to talk. Got a minute?" I said, and Stef flushed deeper.

"Actually, do you mind if I check on Getty first?"

I stood as she turned to leave, feeling like the demon I was even if I had to brush chip crumbs off my camisole. *Thank you, Ivy, for reminding me who I am.* Ticked, I tried to decide what to open with: accusing her of slipping something into that curse Hodin had "taught" me, or how dangerous it was to let Hodin push her around in the name of a "relationship." If I was wrong, the first might alienate her. The second would piss her off. I went with piss her off.

"Did Hodin promise you something in return for becoming his slave in everything but name?" I said bluntly, and Stef jerked to a halt, her back to me as her shoulders hunched. "Because if he did, I want to know about it."

Stef spun, her bag of groceries held to herself. "That's my business, not yours," she said, trying to hide her fear in anger.

It was something I'd done a thousand times before, and my own anger vanished. "Stef, I can help," I said as I came forward. "I've been *exactly* where you are. I know how scary it is, but you can get yourself out. I can help."

"Out?" she said, red spots on her cheeks. "Out of what? I have this under control."

"I thought so, too," I said, holding up my own now-pristine wrist where I had worn my promise to Al. "Please. Tell me what's going on. I know you're skipping work. I'm pretty sure you're spelling for him." I hesitated as fear washed over her. "I had help. Let me help you."

But her jaw clenched and her chin lifted. "You aren't the only one who can have a relationship with a demon," she said with a misplaced anger. "Jealous?"

A laugh choked from me. "Are you serious? I don't know what you've heard, but I never had sex with a demon."

She flushed, telling me she had. "My God, Stef. Are you okay?" I said as I came forward, hands outstretched. "I've seen this before. Is Hodin—"

"Hurting me?" she interrupted, eyes narrowing. "You already asked that."

"No," I blurted, though that was what I had been going to say. "I wanted to know if Hodin is using sex to stretch your ability to hold line energy. That's how they used to make sentient familiars more useful. I'm not saying he's trying to make you his familiar, because it's illegal, but if he is stretching your ability, you should ask him why."

She stared at me, then stammered, "That's none of your business."

"It is when you have two demon marks."

Stef took a step back, afraid, and I leaned forward. "Do you know what it means to be a demon's familiar?"

"Sure. You prep the curses."

I shook my head. "Three marks means he owns your soul, and with that, you have no will unless he allows it. You could be prepping curses twenty-four/seven because he might cause you to forget how to sleep. At best, he'll use sex to expand how much line energy you can hold to make you more useful. At the very least, he will dump on you all the smut he generates, and, Stef, it can be a lot. The further a curse changes reality, the more smut is created, and you will be holding his smut until you die, paying for his magic after your death."

Which couldn't be proven, of course, but the demons went to great pains to get rid of their smut. There was a reason, even if it couldn't be proved.

"Tell me, Rachel Morgan," she added, voice trembling. "Are you saying I shouldn't trust Hodin because of who he is? Because he's a demon? I thought you were all about innocent until proven guilty. That you can't judge a demon bad simply because he's a demon. Or maybe you are trying to ruin my relationship so everyone thinks it's only Rachel Morgan who is smart or powerful enough to survive a demon boyfriend."

My lips parted. Were they her words, or someone else's giving her a way to justify a really bad decision? "Stef, if I'm right about what is happening, you aren't safe, and it's not because Hodin is a demon, but because you are not. There's a huge gap of knowledge and ability that you aren't considering."

She stiffened in a flash of fear, and then the anger returned. "Hodin likes me for who I am. He doesn't care that I don't know a lot of magic. Excuse me. I need to check on Getty so you and Jenks can go to your *big meeting* with that vampire." Shoulders stiff, she walked away.

Crap on toast, I'd made things worse. There was no way now that she would tell me what, if anything, had been in that quencher and smudge stick that I didn't know about. "Stef?"

I heard a yelp from the hallway, but it was just Stef running into Pike, and the two did an awkward dance around each other with the grocery bag between them until Stef stormed past him.

"Sorry," Pike called after her, a plate of fried chicken in his hand smelling wonderful and reminding me I hadn't eaten anything but chips. "Didn't mean to scare you."

"You didn't scare me!" she shouted, and then she was gone.

Pike smirked, his dark eyes wide, leaning slightly to keep the weight off one foot. "Is Ivy gone? Damn, I can't believe she left me like that. Not even a note."

A flicker of amusement rose and fell. I wanted to chase after Stef, but if she was looking for Getty, she'd also find Jenks. I couldn't count the number of times the pixy had talked sense into me. Or tried.

"It's her way," I said softly. "She's got prescription-grade commitment issues."

Pike sighed as he sat at the high eat-at counter and stared out onto the garden. "That's not all she has," he said as he began picking a thigh apart.

I pushed the door to the porch closed, enjoying the cool, dry air of the kitchen in my hair. "Ah, is there more of that?" I asked hesitantly, and he extended the plate. "I'm eating because I'm hungry," I added as I reached for the tiny thigh piece, and he chuckled.

"Not because you want to share blood. I got it, ice queen," he said, and my bite faltered.

"You seem better," I said, then gave up, stifling a moan as I sank my teeth into the fat and protein. It was cold, but that was how I liked it.

"Yeah. Better." He licked his fingers, and I hitched my hip up onto the stool beside him, elbows on the long counter. "But I'm starving. How long until we have to leave?"

"For the meeting?" I chewed and swallowed. "Late dinner at three. I'd say we leave here around two. I'd rather be early than late. Will you be okay? You're there for show. Trent and Jenks will back me up if it gets ugly."

"I'll be fine." He set the plate down and, still licking his fingers, he went to the fridge. "How long did you and Ivy live together?" he asked, and then his smile fell, his gaze going to the ceiling.

"What . . ." I started, then shut up, hearing it, too. Stef was screaming.

"Shit," I muttered, spinning to the garden. The pixies were gone. "Jenks!" I shouted as I bolted for the hallway. "Getty is under fire!"

Pike should have been faster, but I was closer and he was still hurt. I tore down the hallway, hardly registering the rumpled blankets on the couch in the sanctuary as I dove for the foyer, yanking open the door to the cramped stairway. Breath fast, I raced up the stairs, pulling in line energy to make the tips of my still-damp hair float.

Jenks, I thought both in relief and fear as I heard him cry out in anger. He was already there. Stef's voice rose, Latin spilling from her as I shoved open the door.

"Stef! No!" Jenks shouted, and then I was blown backward and down into the dark stairwell as her burst of raw ley line power hit me.

The bell in the belfry tolled. My arms pinwheeled and I tried to grab the banister, failing. My feet slipped out from under me . . . and then Pike caught me, shoving me upright and into the room.

I blinked, reorienting myself. I was not careening backward down the stairs. I was standing in my room, hazed with pixy dust. Stef had a hand to her forehead, gasping, down on one knee. The scent of ozone was heavy and I looked for Jenks. A brilliant glow under the fainting couch pulled me to my knees, and I peered under it, sighing in relief.

It was Jenks and Getty. Both pixies were upright, Jenks clearly angry, with his sword sheened with blood. Getty was scared, a long tear in her dress as she brandished her dagger.

"Getty?" Stef said, pain etching her face as she rose, frantically scanning the room. "Oh, God. Getty! Where are you?"

"Tink's diaphragm, woman!" Jenks said angrily as he stalked out from under the couch, and Stef spun. "You could have smashed us into the wall!"

"I'm sorry. I'm so sorry!" Stef dropped, oblivious that her own aura was still visible from the energy that she'd pushed through it, slow to fade. "They were trying to kill her. It shouldn't have rebounded like that. I didn't use that much energy."

Thanks, Hodin, I thought, seeing as I hadn't taught her how to explode air like that. "Mistakes happen when you're scared," I said. My nose wrinkled as the night air sifted in and the pixy dust evaporated. One of the windows was cracked, but the rest had been open, and papers were slowly falling from the screens and where the blast had stuck them. How many times had I overreacted? *God help us. She's going to make all my mistakes in one night.*

"Getty, are you okay?" I asked as Stef cupped her hands protectively about the pixy.

"I'm fine," the small woman protested. "I fell over is all. Stef, I'm fine!"

"She's unhurt." Jenks hovered beside me, a glittering stream of sparkles falling from him. His jaw was set, and there was a tear in his shirt. A small scrape showed past it, and blood spotted his face. "You got this? I have to take care of something."

"Jenks, wait," I said as he eyed the night past the windows, but he had already darted out, cutting the screen in one swipe. He was not dusting at all, and a chill took me.

Pike inched in, shifting to the side so he wasn't blocking the stairway. It made the room slightly less claustrophobic, which I appreciated.

"Baribas." Stef stood, Getty in her palm. "Jenks was on his way down to talk to you, and Baribas . . ." She looked at the windows, expression riven. "He was waiting, with all of them. He wanted to *kill* her," she exclaimed. "What's wrong with them?"

What is wrong, indeed, I thought as I went to the window, a hand going to my mouth as I watched a brilliant light go out. Another followed, this time with a cry of warning. Jenks was tidying his garden. It was horrifying, but I had lived with pixies long enough to understand the cold logic. It was Jenks's garden. He had taken in Getty, and by attacking her, Baribas had tried to claim it. A third light vanished, and the rest rose up, a veritable flow of them flying over the high wall, fleeing one sword held by one very pissed pixy who was utterly comfortable with who he was.

"They tried to kill her," Stef said again, soft this time as if trying to understand, and Getty's wings shifted, sifting the barest amount of silver dust. Her tiny features eased, and I wondered if she finally felt safe.

The rasping of Jenks's wings was loud as he landed in the open window, and Getty flushed, tugging her skirt to cover a tear.

"They're gone," he said, sword sheathed but his hand hovering over it. "They might be back. I let Baribas live so his children would have a chance to survive. He might be desperate enough to try again despite my kindness."

And it was a kindness, for when one parent died, the other died of heartache, the children scattering in grief whether they could survive on their own or not.

"This is *my* garden," Jenks said, voice hard, and I swear I heard Getty sigh.

"You tore your shirt," the dark pixy said, and Jenks started, spinning comically in the air to find the rip.

His wings were glittering when he halted, a hand clamped firmly to hide it. "I've got another shirt," he said, chin high.

Getty's wings began to glitter, a dark, mysterious gray with black sparkles. "I can fix it," she said, voice hesitant. "If you'll let me. I might need some thread and a needle, though. Mine are on the other side of the city."

Jenks froze, his wide eyes looking both horrified and grief-stricken. "I . . . I have some," he croaked out, and my shoulders slumped in understanding. In the highly structured society of pixies, it was the wife who mended her husband's clothes. Jenks had bent the rules enough to accept clothing made by Belle, but the fairy had been so distant from his beloved Matâlina that he probably saw it as a slightly questionable rent payment, nothing more.

Getty, though, was not a fairy. He had vowed to protect her. He had seen that she had food. He had mended her wing. And as I watched Jenks's dust shift from silver to blue to red to silver again, I felt my heart go out to him. The memory of his wife tore at him, staining the possibility of finding something with Getty that would leave them both . . . happy? I was half a step away from crying, and

Pike and Stef stared at me, clearly oblivious that more than a shirt was being mended.

"I've some thread downstairs," he said again, then rose to hover before Stef. "Keep her safe, okay?" he said, and Stef nodded. "I'll be right back," he finished softly, this time to Getty.

"Jenks, hold up." I pushed into motion to follow him, but he was gone and I almost fell on the stair trying to catch him, my feet were moving so fast. There was no way that Jenks was coming with me tonight. He needed to be here until he was sure Baribas wouldn't try again. I could make do with Trent and Pike. Ivy would be there as well. We were only saying hello and making arrangements for another meeting. What could go wrong?

"Jenks, wait!" I called as I hit the sanctuary, and he drew to a halt, hovering over the newly inlaid floor, his dust a pale gray. My pulse was fast as I came forward, and my heart hurt at the tormented guilt and pain in his face: memories of Matalina, his anger at Baribas, his need to care for someone. Getty.

"You're not coming with me tonight," I said. "She needs you more than I do. Tell me I'm wrong, and I will shrink down and smack you. Stef can't keep her safe. You can."

He took a breath to protest, then looked at his hands, shaking and covered in someone else's blood. "Thank you," he whispered in relief, his wing hum lowering in pitch.

I gave him a weepy smile, wishing I was small or he was big so one of us could hug the other. He had needed to hear me say it was okay.

And by God, it was.

CHAPTER

13

"THANK YOU," I SAID AS I HANDED TRENT'S KEYS TO THE AT-
tendant outside the Cincinnatian, giving the Were a smile
before looking up the façade of the old building. I'd driven,
since Trent had been on the phone trying to put out yet
another fire with his quick money move. The nearby lights
from Fountain Square lit the underside of the clouds, making it seem like a cloudy day instead of two thirty in the
morning. I tugged the strap of my dress up as I stifled a
yawn. Two a.m. wasn't unusual for a witch, but Trent and I
had been trying to keep to a schedule that we both could
handle, and I was tired.

"We are so early," Pike grumped as we stood and waited
for Trent to finish talking to the attendant. "Why are we
early?"

"Things happen." I felt nice in my sleek black dress, and
I swayed to feel it brush about my calves. Car traffic was
sparse, but the pedestrians made up for it as Inderlanders
took over the city, enjoying the few hours before the sun

rose and it got sweltering again. "We can wait in the bar if you want."

He shook his head, his battered hands hidden in black driving gloves. We'd stopped at Piscary's on the way so he could change, and he looked better in a clean suit—even if he was still limping and smelling of Brimstone strongly enough to send the I.S.'s drug dogs into a loving frenzy. "Is being early some kind of witch thing to have the high ground?" he said, shoulders shifting uncomfortably. "There is no high ground when you're dealing with the long undead. There is only surviving."

"I disagree." The noise of the city was soothing, and I relaxed as I lovingly watched Trent. He had also changed into a lightweight suit and tie, his white-blond hair slicked back and a sprig of lilac that was probably a charm tucked into his lapel. He seemed to be wrapping it up, handing the young man a folded bill as they talked.

"Mmmm. Overdone tip," Pike said, then winced, clearly wanting to sit down.

"Perhaps, but I bet our car will show up ninety seconds after we hit the curb." I turned to Pike, recognizing his fatigue through the Brimstone boost. "Jealous?"

The scarred living vampire started. "No. At least, I don't think so." He grinned, showing me his small but sharp canines. "I'll let you know, Rachel Morgan."

His widening pupils caught and held my attention, sending a soft quiver of promise through me. "You should not be hungry," I said. "Stop flirting."

His smile widened, a hand rubbing his stubble as he found a compliment in my words. "You never did tell me how long you and Ivy lived together," he asked.

"You mean me on one side of the hallway, her on the other?" I smiled at Trent as he clapped the attendant on the shoulder and headed our way. "Long enough to miss her, and short enough to be able to do the same."

"Mmmm."

Yes, it had been cryptic, but he knew exactly what I was

saying. The longer you associated with a living vampire, the less likely you were to leave their presence. They tended to become your world through their pheromones, trapping even the curious who lingered too long. It was evolution's way to find them willing blood sources after their first death, and it was highly effective.

Trent came to a rolling halt, gesturing to the revolving door. "Shall we?"

I nodded, my mismatched shoulder bag held tight to my middle as I went in. The small elevators were to the left, the modest reception desk to the right, and the expansive bar straight ahead. A four-star restaurant was tucked around behind the reception desk, its few windows facing the adjacent street. It was somewhat open to the bar, but nowhere near enough that the TVs tuned to the sports channels intruded.

"Pike?" I said, hesitating to read the news ticker as Trent and Pike jostled before the host stand, waiting for someone to notice them. "Is that your . . ."

"Brother," Pike finished tightly as he turned to look. "Why is Brad still at the airport?"

Trent's arm looped possessively in mine as he read the scrolling banner. "They're asking if anyone knows who he is." His brow furrowed. "That doesn't sound like fulfillment."

I frowned at Brad's confused, angry attitude as the airport police detained him. "No, it doesn't," I murmured, an unsettled feeling beginning to grow. "I should have listened to my gut. I'm like eighty-plus percent sure that there was something in that curse that Hodin erased from the recipe. Either Stef doesn't know or Hodin is keeping her from talking." Grimacing, I watched the newscaster ask for help identifying Brad. "Are you going to claim him?" I asked Pike, and he chuckled bitterly.

"Hell no," Pike said, spinning from the TV to the restaurant.

Trent leaned close, making my entire side tingle as our

auras rubbed. "Jenks told me the university library wants you to come out to inspect their security on their ancient book locker." His lips quirked mischievously. "I'm still trying to find my demon books, but they might have a copy of the curse. Nothing to stop you from looking while you're there."

"Oh, my God! You're a genius." Pleased, I bumped his shoulder, wanting to call Lenny that very moment. "That would make this a lot easier. Trying to pin Hodin down is like trying to catch a greased pixy."

Beaming, Trent tugged me into him. But then the vibration of his phone intruded. Groaning, he reached to answer it, my arm slipping from his, leaving me feeling alone.

Pike made a rude sound, a knowing smirk on his face. "Does he have his phone on every time you go out?"

Shrugging, I looped my arm in Pike's instead. "Absolutely. And so do I." But my smile faded at Trent's sudden concern, and I pulled away from Pike, not caring that the host had finally shown up and was now stiffly waiting.

"Is it the girls? Are they okay?" I blurted when Trent closed his phone down.

"Yes," he said, brow furrowed. "I mean, I don't know. That wasn't Ellasbeth." He smiled at the host. "Three for Finnis's table?"

But I dug my heels into the low carpet, refusing to move when the host walked off. Trent moved three steps and stopped. Pike sighed and rocked to a halt as well.

"What is it?" I asked Trent. "Is it that business deal you've been working on?"

Trent took a breath as if to deny it, then relented. "Apparently they need me to visually confirm something. I'll do it in the morning." He smiled thinly at Pike. "Lawyers. Can't live with them, can't kill them. Not even during the Turn."

I glanced at the host waiting for us, then back to Trent. "Do you need to take care of it?"

"No," he said immediately, and my eyes narrowed.

"I don't need a pixy to tell when you're lying," I said, and from the corner of my sight, I saw Pike rub his temples in frustration.

"You want me to go ahead?" Pike asked, ignored by both Trent and myself.

"It can wait." Trent drew me forward with a hard yank when I refused to move. "We're meeting with Finnis."

I shook my head, knowing that if he didn't take care of it now, the entire deal might fall through. Not to mention he'd be thinking about it and not the current situation. That he was willing to risk his business meant the world to me, but I didn't want me to be the reason something failed. I might have lost Jenks, and now Trent, but I still had Pike. "Go do what you need to do." I arranged his lapels and smiled, meaning it. "Pike and I will be fine."

He grimaced. "I can always find another property."

"For one point two million dollars?" I guessed, and he winced. "Go. I'll order for you. You'll be downtown, right? If you don't take care of it, you'll be thinking about it from hors d'oeuvres to dessert."

Trent's grip on me eased, but his brow was furrowed. "Are you trying to get rid of me because Finnis is a vampire?"

Pike groaned as the host got tired of waiting and left, and I went up on my toes to give Trent a kiss. "No. Go do what you need to do. Pike and I got this."

Pike sighed, looked at his watch. "I see now what you mean about being early. He does slow you down. First with his shoes. Then the leaf under the car's wiper. Now this . . ."

Trent's attention flicked to Pike. He might be right before me holding my elbows, but his mind was already somewhere else. "Thank you," he said softly. "I really want this to happen. I don't know why they are being such sticklers. I'll be back."

He gave me another kiss, then paced quickly to the door. Pike eased up beside me, shoulder to shoulder, both of us watching. The spicy scent of annoyed vampire tickled my nose, and I breathed it in, enjoying it. "I never would have left you," he said.

"Which is why we will never date, Pike." Concerned, I scanned the restaurant, but the host had vanished. Pike sighed, hands in his pants pockets as we returned to the host stand.

I felt oddly undressed as I stood beside Pike. No Jenks. No Trent. Ivy wasn't down here, either. The place was top-shelf, but a little too froufrou for my tastes, heavy on the gold brocade and velvet. A few too many glasses and forks.

A young couple huddled in a corner, their heads so close I could almost see a proposal in the making. A couple of businessmen having their separate dinners, enough space between them to prevent any easy conversation but not so much that they would feel alone. Two elegant women in high-powered suits chatted over coffee and glowing tablets. Everyone in here was an Inderlander: vamps, Weres, witches. *Elf?* I wondered, studying the blond man by himself, reading his tablet and enjoying a cup of coffee.

No, he's a vampire, I decided, thinking the hair wasn't quite right even if the suit appeared as pricy as one of Trent's best. His shoes, too, were kind of . . . blah. It was hard to know without seeing his eyes. Elves generally had green eyes, but not always.

"Are we down to two now?" the host said pleasantly, and I started.

"We're joining Mr. Finnis," I said, and the host nodded, seeing as Trent had already said as much.

"Yes, ma'am. This way, please."

I went first when Pike gallantly gestured for me to step out, but my mood soured when it became obvious that there would be no wall for my back to be against. We were in the front window. I sighed, not appreciating the "best seat in the house" and feeling as if I was on display. Even with all the delays, Finnis wasn't here yet, and I had my choice of seats. Pike took the one across from me, and the host gathered the extra setting before the window.

"Ah, I'll have a chocolate malt," Pike said when it became obvious the host was waiting for our drink order.

"Coffee, black. Wait, no. Tea and one of those little

honey sticks," I said, changing my mind. I didn't particularly like tea, but Jenks loved honey and I could take it home to him. Sort of an I-missed-you thing. The host nodded and walked away.

"Chocolate malt?" I questioned, and Pike grinned to show his teeth.

"I'm hungry . . ."

And looking good enough to eat, even with the bandages, I mused as I sat up, then slouched, trying not to get nervous. There was a deathday party going on in the bar, and I tracked a high-heeled, scantily clad, lace-necked floozy going past them, looking for a date.

And then, as if from nowhere, a tall, blond vampire in an overdone suit, vest, and tie came to a ghostly halt before the host station. He was old, he was undead, and he was smiling with long, sharp canines, his expressive voice like butter and cream. "Pike, is Finnis blond?" I asked, feeling a little breathless at the vampire's domineering presence.

"I don't know." His attention followed mine, and he made a soft grunt. "Constance never talked about him."

I sat up, my ankles crossing. "Yep, that's him," I said as the host turned and they both studied us. "Where's Ivy?"

Pike stood as the two of them wove through the mostly empty tables, the almost-sour scent of nervous vamp rising. "I'm sure she'll be along. I can't imagine him going out without an entourage to make him feel important."

I found my feet as the vampire in his gray suit and tie waved the host off, one hand extended as he approached. "Good evening," he said, and I stifled a shiver at the pull of just that. "Mr. Welroe?" The undead man's lips were closed in a careful smile as he and Pike shook hands. I squinted, not liking that Ivy wasn't here.

"Mr. Finnis. It's a pleasure to have you in Cincinnati." Pike smiled at me. "This is Ms. Rachel Morgan. She's Constance's enforcer in nonvampiric issues. Constance thought you would appreciate meeting her as well."

"Ms. Morgan." Finnis's black eyes found mine, making my pulse quicken. "Ivy has told me so much about you."

I balked at his pale, somewhat malnourished hand, deciding I didn't want to touch it. The hairs on the back of my neck pricked, and I glanced behind me. No one was there except that guy with his coffee and tablet. His attention wasn't on me, but he was watching, nevertheless. Suspicious, I leaned to see Mr. Finnis's shoes.

"Excuse me," I said as I edged past him and walked away.

"Rachel!" Pike all but hissed, but Ivy was not here, and I didn't have time to explain.

Pulse fast, I wove between the tables, stopping before that lone vampire with the thousand-dollar, blah shoes. "Mr. Finnis" was wearing Men's Store specials. I breathed deep as the vampire looked up from his tablet, pulling the scent of his domineering strength through me, tingling me alive. Running through it all was a hint of what the other guy was missing. Ivy.

"Can I help you?" the vampire said, and I locked my knees at the pull in his voice.

Yep. Found him, I thought as I extended my hand. "Mr. Finnis. It's a pleasure. I'm Rachel Morgan."

From across the restaurant, Pike swore softly.

The real Mr. Finnis set down his tablet and shifted to face me square on. A delighted, demented smile was on his face, his long, pointed canines shining and his pupils holding at a soft dilation. I froze, scrambling to yank back that smut as he took my hand, turned it, and breathed in over the top, scenting me. "How did you know?"

I was glad he let go, because I wasn't sure I'd be able to pull away from him. *Damn, this one is old!* "The other guy doesn't smell like Ivy. You do," I said, glancing at the pretend Mr. Finnis. "And your shoes. His shoes aren't right. But mostly Ivy."

Finnis leaned to look at his shoes, then nodded at his doppelganger. Clearly peeved, the undead vampire left, taking a bottle of champagne from a bucket of ice in passing. No one said anything, and I smirked when that vampire floozy linked her arm in his and they vanished into the bar.

"My first scion," Finnis said. "He's a good man. I never thought about the shoes . . ." Finnis's eyes flicked to mine and I locked my knees. "Please. Join me."

Fingers fumbling for a chair, I sat down. My back was to the restaurant, but I could move fast if I had to. Pike sat as well, and no one said anything as our drinks arrived.

"I would think a cosmopolitan plate for the table would be pleasant," Finnis said to the waiter, and then to us, "Are you sure you wouldn't enjoy a bottle of wine? Spirits?"

"We won't be here long," I said when Pike remained silent. He seemed to be having some difficulty. Not awe, or fear, just . . . shut down. "Pike?"

"None for me, thanks," he said, voice strained. "Thank you."

Still smiling, Finnis laced his long, pale fingers over his tie. There were little skulls and crossbones on it. I'd never seen an undead with a sense of humor before. "You're looking well, Master Pike," he said as if Pike was eight and finally allowed to sit at the grown-up table. "I see your brother is at the airport. Has Constance been keeping you so busy you have forgotten to pick him up?"

Pike's eye twitched, and he seemed to find himself. "No," he said shortly, a flush coloring his neck. "It's a pleasure to meet you. Please tell me if you need something the hotel can't supply. Constance will be happy to oblige you."

I sipped at my tea, holding the fragile cup in case I had to throw it at him for an instant of distraction. "I thought Ivy would be joining us."

"She'll be along presently," Finnis said with a careless wave of a hand.

My pulse quickened, and I kept my breathing shallow. He had to know how he was hitting me, but he wouldn't react if I didn't. "Is she okay?"

Finnis's attention flicked to me and lingered. "I don't see why not."

My eyes narrowed on his. "Are you responsible for Trent being called away?"

He blinked, genuinely surprised. "No."

Head tilted, I carefully set my teacup down. "You don't talk much for a long undead."

Pike nudged my foot under the table, and I shot him a dark look. Finnis noticed, making a soft sigh of regret. "I think we're done here," he said, motioning for the host to escort us out.

"Whoa, whoa, whoa. Excuse me, Finnis, but as Constance's enforcer, I need to know—"

"You need to know what?" Finnis said, and then I was standing, my back to a pillar as the undead man rose, his pupils wide and his teeth bared. "You need nothing," he intoned, his words seeming to flow around me and push from behind, a heavy, dark presence of equal parts hunger and threat.

"Sir?" Pike rose slowly, so very slowly, his face pale.

"Be still, Welroe," Finnis all but growled. I could hear people leaving as I stood there, pulse hammering. I held my breath, refusing to breathe him in as Finnis studied me, lingering on my perfect skin hiding a deep, abiding bite. He knew it was there, and I closed my eyes, knowing what it would feel like if he played upon it. *Oh, God. Please don't. Please don't. . . .*

"Ivy told me you were a demon. Do something."

He was right in front of me, confident that I was helpless. My eyes opened, and I scrambled to shove my fear away. Yes, I was a demon. I wasn't helpless—if I could remember to react. He was so damn close.

I took a breath, then another. Pike hadn't left, but this was my fight, not his. "Mmmm, no," I said, and a flicker of pleasure brought Finnis's lips up into a smile.

"No?" he echoed.

I found a deeper strength in his surprise, and I dared to meet his gaze. "No," I said again, louder, as I worked my way through the pheromones of desire, fear, and submission he was kicking out. "I'm not a windup toy. I'm here to keep Pike safe while you two arrange a time to meet Constance. Can we do that? Or should we come back when you're not so bored."

Finnis chuckled, the brown rims around his pupils growing. My shoulders eased, and I pushed from the pillar when Finnis eyed me, interested in me again. Talking to the old undead was about balance. If you were boring, they bled you. If you were interesting . . . well, they bled you for that, too, but for a different reason. But find that sweet spot, and you could talk to them and walk away. Usually.

I exchanged a quick look at Pike and felt behind me for my chair. I wasn't surprised to see that the restaurant had emptied. No one even watched from behind the kitchen's door as instrumental Beach Boys played on the hidden speakers.

"Keep Pike safe?" Finnis mocked as he sat and replaced his napkin. "You aren't doing very well. He's a mess."

"I'm alive," Pike said, and Finnis nodded.

"As are his brother and the three assassins he sent," I said as I cautiously sat down. "Do you know how hard it is to put down three assassins and a bad case of sibling rivalry without killing someone?"

Finnis laughed long and hard, startling me. I gave him a thin smile, but the tension had been broken and Pike took his seat when Finnis gestured for him to do so. "Where's my cosmopolitan plate?" the undead vampire shouted, and then reached across the table to top off my teacup from the nearby pot. "Gods, I'm glad there's something to do in this armpit of a city. I thought tonight would be an utter waste of time."

"Sir," Pike started, voice cutting off at Finnis's sharp motion.

"You are not in control. You will be silent," Finnis said.

"Pike—" I started.

"Is not in control," Finnis insisted. "Oh, he might wish he is, but he isn't. And if he was *honest* with himself, he will admit that he likes it that way. Most living vampires do." He put one arm on the table and leaned over it, looking for all the world like a harmless, very wealthy, somewhat odd man whose eyebrows needed a trim. Only the really old ones could pull off appearing truly alive and interested in who was around them. That's how they got that old. Piscary had been like that. Constance . . . not so much.

"Ah, here is our plate," Finnis said as he arranged his silverware. "Pike, another malt? Rachel, a fresh pot?"

"I'm fine," I said, and Pike had barely touched his. *Damn it, this guy might be more than I can handle,* I thought, fingers shaking as I sipped my tea and eyed the cheese and fruit plate. If they can't scare you, they lull you by making you feel special.

"I'm sure Constance will be able to work you into her schedule," Pike said, and Finnis scoffed.

"Stop. Constance is not even alive."

"She is," I said, breath catching when Finnis turned to me. "Pike is keeping her healthy and well," I added. "Enjoying all that Cincinnati has to offer. I'm willing to submit to any truth amulet you want. So is he."

"Which means doing so would be worthless." Finnis filled a small plate from the one at the center of the table. He wasn't hungry, at least, not for overpriced goat cheese and out-of-season fruit. It was an act. A very convincing act, but I'd seen the monster. We all had.

"We will play your game," he added as he motioned for the water attendant to top off his coffee. "Because the alternative is to rip out your throat here and now, and I don't want to lose my damage deposit. Not to mention you are more fun than a basket of kittens, Ms. Morgan," he added with a gut-punch of a wink. "If there is anything the undead crave more than blood, it is distraction. No, Constance is dead, and if you don't produce her by"—his gaze went to Pike—"say, Tuesday night, Wednesday morning? I will begin inquiries."

Inquiries didn't sound bad, except they would be in person and probably involve large, unwanted transfers of blood. Sighing, I put three pieces of cheese and a kiwi slice on my plate.

"Constance was my friend," Finnis said in an overdone show of sadness. "I'm not happy that she's twice dead."

Friend? I thought. More like a plaything, with the amount of mental baggage the undead woman had.

"Finnis," Pike said, blanching when the undead master squinted at him. "Sir, what do you want to simply walk away?"

Finnis's hand hit the table and I jumped, my sudden intake of line energy flashing my hair into a static pop. "There it is!" the undead vampire said triumphantly as I frantically shoved the energy back into the line. "Admit she is twice dead so I can go home, and I will petition that your trial be fast and your jail cell pleasant."

"Damn it, Pike." Lips pressed, I ran a hand over my hair to try to smooth it. "Finnis, she's not twice dead. She's occupied in a new hobby and doesn't want to be disturbed."

But Finnis was ignoring me, focused on Pike. "I will walk away," he said, and Pike's lips curled up in success. "Yes, I will walk away, but only when Rachel Morgan pulls her soul charm from FSCA consideration."

Grimacing, I stifled the urge to smack Pike right then and there. If I pulled my soul charm, I'd lose control of the city, but that's not why I wasn't going to do it. I owed it to the living vampires who had supported me in the past. What Ivy and Nina had was not wrong, and I would fight for it.

"That's not an option," I said. "It's not an option!" I said again, louder and glaring at Pike until he sullenly reached for his malt, sucking a third of it down in one angry go.

"Mmmm." Finnis considered me, his companionable show over, his threats hidden. "Then I need to see Constance. If she is dead and you survive my grief, you will be jailed for wrongful undead termination and a new vampire will be sent to hold your . . . city."

"You?" I said sarcastically, and a wicked grin spread across his face.

"Perhaps. My overwhelming sorrow will need much soothing."

Pike set his malt down with a thump. "I'll arrange a meeting. It might take a while. She's hard to pin down."

"The undead usually are." Finnis's attention returned to his tablet when it dinged. "Tuesday night, Wednesday morning. Before sunup."

His hard, black eyes found mine, but I didn't move despite the obvious dismissal. *Why are my choices always ones I don't like?*

"Rachel?" Pike stood, waiting, and still I sat, frowning at Finnis, who had dropped us from his thoughts like a two-year-old forgets shoes. At least, until I reached across the table and took a crumble of cheese right off his small plate.

"She is alive," I said as I stood, and Finnis tracked my motion. I think he'd stopped pretending to breathe, and it gave me the creeps. "And you will leave here with nothing but a pleasant week of distraction."

My heart hammered as I spun and walked off. Pike's fingers found my elbow, and I jumped, startled at a flash of heat.

"God, woman. Why don't you just piss in his drink?" he muttered, and a sultry sway crept into my hips as we passed the frightened people beginning to filter back. I was randy from the pheromones. My smutty aura made me feel badass. Pike's touch was sending delicious tendrils of promise through me—even if I felt vulnerable without Jenks. Exposed.

"You really like flirting with death, don't you," Pike added, and I took a deep, clean breath, snapping the last tendril of need that Finnis had instilled.

"We walked away, didn't we?" I said, embarrassed. "We know what he looks like now. Neither of us got our skin broken."

"Yeah." He sounded disappointed, and I took a sharp left before the door, aiming for the reception desk. "Ah, what are you doing? We need to leave before he changes his mind."

I pressed into the counter impatiently, and the tidy Were working the desk glanced up, a bland, professional smile on her face. "Ivy Tamwood. What room is she in?" Damn it, if Jenks had been here, he could have sniffed her out.

The woman tapped a few buttons on her keyboard, then frowned. "I'm sorry. She's asked to not be disturbed."

My lips pressed. "I didn't ask for you to call her. I asked what room she's in. Tell me. Now. Or I will blow your entire computer system." Finnis was making her a hostage. I knew it. Crap on toast, I hated dealing with the long undead.

Pike leaned casually on the high counter, sideways to me. "Ah, Rachel?"

"I cannot—I *will not*—allow my friends to be hostages," I said loudly . . . and then I jerked as a familiar tang of vampire incense drifted through me. *Ivy?*

I turned, my expression blanking as she came out of the elevator, seeming relaxed and smart in a jacket and short skirt, tall heels clicking on the inlaid floor.

"Wow, Ivy wasn't kidding," Pike said as he pushed off from the counter and gave the desk attendant a nod that we were done.

"Kidding about what?" I was almost breathless in relief, waving like a fool to get her attention. There was only twenty feet between us. Ivy saw and changed direction.

Pike rocked into motion as I headed forward. "How did you know she was there?"

"I just did," I said, not caring that he hadn't answered my question.

Beaming, Pike leaned into Ivy and gave her a business-like kiss on an offered cheek. "Damn, girl," he said appreciably. "You make flunky-to-the-undead look good."

Her perfect eyebrows rose, and then she turned to me, her smile fading at my lingering worry. "Are you ready? I thought Trent was coming."

"His business intruded." I drew her to a halt before she could move. "And we already talked to Finnis. Are you okay? I thought he'd made you a hostage." I took my hand back before she could feel it shake, but I figured she knew how upset I was. The meeting hadn't gone badly, but it could have been better. I'd forgotten how seductive the old ones were. Ivy had experience saying no, but sometimes she didn't want to, even when she knew she'd regret it later.

Frowning, she faced the restaurant. "Yes. I mean no, I'm not a hostage. Yes, I'm okay." Her gaze came to me. "He told me the wrong time is all. I should have expected that. He's exceptionally bored, which makes him exceptionally dangerous." She drew us aside to a cluster of lobby chairs. "Trent left? You met with him alone? Where's Jenks? Recon?"

"Jenks stayed home with Getty. Trent was called away," I said, wondering again if I depended on my friends too much.

Pike made a soft huff. "She wasn't alone. I was there."

Ivy flicked a glance at him. "You met with him *alone*?" she asked again.

"Pike was with me," I said, and the man beside me scrubbed his stubble, feeling the hit. "Ivy, you're not staying here. I don't care if Finnis has a cow, you're spending the night at the church. We have room."

Ivy pulled from my grip, an odd smile on her face. "Thanks, but I'd rather stay at Piscary's. I want to go over Pike's reopening plans." She shifted to face Pike, her tongue slipping provocatively between her teeth. "You *are* returning to Piscary's, yes?" She eyed him up and down. "You're not sleeping on Rachel's couch."

Pike's breath came in slow and came out even slower. "I was planning on going home."

I cocked my hip, waving my hand as if I could disperse the happy-vampire come-hither pheromones they were kicking out. "Guys . . ."

"Good." Ivy tightened Pike's tie, making him blink in surprise. "I want to see Constance. Erica says she's a hoot. Maybe I can talk some sense into her."

I took a step away, trying to keep my breathing shallow. "I doubt it," I muttered, shrugging when the two vamps coming in noticed the flush of incense and grinned. But an entire night under Ivy's tender care would do Pike good. Or kill him. "Do you need a ride?" I said, then faltered. Trent would need his car.

"We can take a cab," Pike said. "Ah, I'm not leaving you here to wait for Trent. We'll drop you off at the church."

I sighed, not relishing having to listen to their foreplay for the ten-minute ride across the river and home. "Okay, but I want one of those big cabs. You both sit in the back," I said, and Ivy laughed, the sound striking through me like icy fire.

"Wait here, ladies," Pike said gallantly, then went through the revolving door to talk to the door attendant.

"Please don't kill him by accident," I said, head down over my bag as I hunted for my phone to text Trent. I was not going to use Hodin's wand again, but seeing as it was one of Newt's curses, Dali might be able to tell me what I'd done to Brad—especially if I returned his books. If nothing else, he'd love to rub my face in some told-you-so Hodin crap.

"Meeting done. Everything okay. Taking a cab home. Coffee tomorrow before my class at one?" I texted Trent, the light from my phone bathing my face.

"Rachel?"

I looked up, phone in hand, as Ivy sidled close, her eyes on Pike through the plate-glass walls but her hand curving possessively about my waist.

"You will always be my favorite coulda woulda," she whispered, and then she smiled at Pike as he waved at us, a van cab waiting at the curb. Her hand slipped from me, leaving tingles in its wake. Grimacing, I slowly followed her out, shoving my libido down deep. *Damn vamp pheromones.*

"TRENT, IT'S FINE," I SAID AS I SLOWLY DROVE MY LITTLE MINI through the library's parking lot hunting for a spot. As expected, Lenny had been overjoyed to get my call, re-arranging his day to meet me this morning at the side entrance for a quick on-site assessment well before my class. I had no idea if I could figure out who took their books, but I'd be a fool to turn down the chance to find a copy of Newt's curse and perhaps something I could use in place of it. You needed special permission to even look at the university's ancient book locker, and I was going to use this to the utmost. "I got a ride from Pike and Ivy."

"I didn't expect it to take that long." Trent's voice was tight in frustration. "It should have been fifteen minutes."

"Don't worry about it." It was only ten, and the heat coming up from the pavement was already oppressive. "I'll be at the library for about an hour, maybe an hour and a half. You want to meet at Junior's? I'm going to need coffee before I walk into that classroom."

Not to mention return Dali's books, currently stuffed into my bag.

"Ahh . . ."

I slumped, breathing in the humid air and hoping I got home and into my shorts before I melted. After ransacking my closet, I'd finally settled on my old interview suit. It looked okay, but it was not conducive to staying cool. "Don't worry about it," I said, knowing I'd be getting my coffee alone. Hands on the wheel, I crept slowly forward, following a woman coming out of the library with a satchel of books. *Lavender,* I thought, tugging at the cuff of my suit. *What had I been thinking?*

"I swear, I'm ready to walk away from this," Trent said. "Their lawyers are asking that I redo everything I did last night to acknowledge a grandfather clause that just surfaced. It shouldn't even be an issue. If I didn't know better, I'd swear they're stalling in the hopes that someone else offers more and they can jerk it out from under me. I'm not signing until everything is in writing, because if I can't utilize the space the way I want, it's of no use to me."

The woman pointed her fob to make a blue SUV chirp, and I halted well back to give her room to leave, flicking my turn signal on to claim the spot. "Trent, it's okay." *He's buying space? Like, building space?*

"It's not okay," he said, and my eyebrows rose at the hint of his considerable temper. I didn't see it often, but when it showed, it tended to be frigid and over-the-top. "This should have been signed, sealed, and filed yesterday. And now I'm stuck in some tiny office staring out the window at a wall instead of sitting across from you having coffee on your big day."

"It's just a day," I said, spinning my pearl pinky ring on my finger as the woman got into her car.

"You're teaching a class. It's important. I wanted to be there," he said, and I knew he was mad because he was missing time with me, not because some lawyer was jerking him around.

"You will be." My pinky ring was glowing, and I smiled. "In spirit."

"If they don't have the paperwork finished by the time your class is over, I'm walking out. We will have a late lunch at Carew Tower, where I'll hear all about it and talk over whatever curse you find at the library to replace the one Hodin gave you."

A warm love suffused me. "That sounds good, except for the walking-out part. It's okay, Trent. Do what you need to do."

"I am," he said, voice hard. "And I will see you after class. Love you."

"I love you, too. Desperately," I whispered, and then the call ended.

The woman leaving gave me a little wave as she pulled away, and I returned it before taking her spot. Putting my MINI into park, I slumped, pulling my bag to me and dropping my phone in. "Figures," I muttered, disappointed about Trent.

Dali's books were awkward, and I wondered if I should leave them under the seat. But the demon would kill me if I lost them, and so I slung my book-heavy bag over my shoulder and got out. A man in slacks and a tie was hovering nervously outside the small side entrance. I'd put my panties on eBay if it wasn't Lenny.

My unusually high heels made me feel vulnerable, pinching as I click-clacked to him. Lenny was about my height, short dark hair, mid-forties, probably a witch if he had a key to the ancient book locker. He had some chair weight on him, but he carried it well, squinting at me in the bright sun as I approached. "Ms. Morgan?" he called, and I tried to find a professional mien.

"That's me. You must be Lenny," I said, feeling a tingle of stored ley line energy as I shook his hand. "Please call me Rachel."

"Rachel," he echoed, and I jerked my hand away when that damned smut rolled up from my chi, wanting to jump to him. "Thank you for coming out," he added as he keyed the door open. Clearly it was a one-way exit unless you had the code. "I'll take you down," he said, his expression one of worry as he held the door for me. "I appreciate you using the back entrance. We're trying to keep this quiet." He was pointing down an empty corridor, and I paused as he waited for the click of the lock before starting forward, his rolling pace fast.

"We haven't even filed a report with the I.S.," he said, clearly flustered. "We're not really sure how long they have been missing."

"Hopefully I can answer that," I said, patting my book-heavy bag, and his eyes went to it, his interest rising as he saw Dali's books.

"Those are old," he said, his curiosity obvious, and I swung my bag around to show him. I had one horrible instant of fear that he'd say they were the ones missing, but his smile widened, his appreciation for the rare and arcane obvious.

"I'm hoping to use them to trace who took the books," I lied, and he nodded, his steps slowing as we turned into a corridor and the chatter of phone conversations became obvious. "Has anyone looked at the security footage?"

"It was the first thing I did," he said as I followed him. "I went back two weeks. Melody was still here then, and I'm sure she would have noticed if they were gone."

"Melody?" I slowed at a passcode gate while he scanned his ID.

"She was in charge of restoration," he said as the gate hummed and he pushed it open.

Was, I thought as I followed him into the open office floor. People at homey desks were noticing us. A whisper began to rise, and I doubted it was because I was in head-to-toe lavender. *But then again . . .* "You fired her because three books were stolen?" I asked, appalled.

"No!" he exclaimed. "She retired to help her daughter with her kids." Lenny frowned. "She left me in kind of a spot, really. But she seemed happy when she came back last Friday to clear out her desk."

"Friday, eh?" I wondered if this was going to be one of my easy jobs. "Isn't that when you noticed the books missing?"

Lenny winced. "I know what you're thinking, but Melody is a really nice lady. She's been here longer than I have. I know for a fact that she hadn't been in the ancient book locker for about a month previous. I remember it because we had a professor from the university down there. No one goes downstairs without my knowledge. Her included."

I kind of doubted that. If Nick had known about the key stashed in the ceiling supports, then others had, too, Melody included. "Was the professor's name by chance Sikes?" I asked, and Lenny started.

"I think that was his name." His expression became alarmed. "Why?"

"Because I'm teaching his class this afternoon," I said softly. "He's gone missing." Sure, there was a chance that Sikes had stolen the books and skipped town, but I was betting that a demon was involved, probably one named Dali, and I tugged my bag with his books closer. It was starting to make sense, and it was pissing me off.

"I'm going to have a hard time replacing her," Lenny said, oblivious to my mood. "You don't know anyone skilled in ley line restoration with a degree in library science, do you?"

"Sorry, no." Crap on toast. If Dali was ignoring society's rules, they all would.

"Worth a try." Lenny pointed to the nondescript fire door set to the side, but I already knew that was where we were going. "Melody could restore a book with a spell. I'll never be able to replace her."

"She sounds skilled. What's the possibility that she took them?"

Lenny's brow furrowed. "I really hope not. Melody had been with us for forty years. She knew where the really expensive books were, and they are untouched. The ones missing were in bad shape. Demon tomes can't be restored like most everything else."

"No, they can't," I said, thinking.

Lenny nervously touched a pocket before punching in the door code. The lock on the fire door had been a simple one when Nick and I had snuck into the ancient book section, but you tend to up your security when you find a quart of blood on the floor and a smashed book cabinet.

"Sorry about the cramped stairway," he said as he opened the door and flicked on the light. "Apart from the freight elevator, this is the only other way down here."

I balked, reluctant to go down. "What about the entrance in the employees' break room?"

Lenny's eyes widened. "How do you know about that?"

I tried to keep from flushing, a hand on the doorframe. "I dated someone who worked here," I said, remembering that Nick *had* done a stint as a janitor, unless he had lied to me about that, too.

"No, we walled that up when . . . ah, we walled that up," he finished. "After you."

"Thanks." The dry scent of old books was wafting up the tight stairway, and whereas I usually would breathe it in like ambrosia, this one held the taint of burnt amber. Grimacing, I stepped down, my lavender heels making a soft and certain click. The railing was as filthy as I remembered, the lights as dim. Cement walls and bare stairs made an ugly passage. I wasn't claustrophobic, but memories of terror and betrayal were thick in my mind, and I nearly balked.

"I can't tell you how much I appreciate this," Lenny said from behind me, and I stifled a shudder when I heard the door thump shut and the light dimmed. "The missing books have been in our possession for over two hundred years. I've tried to contact Melody, but she hasn't called me back," he added, his words nervously fast. Apparently Lenny didn't like the cramped stairway, either.

"I'm going to need her number," I said, but I was beginning to suspect that either Melody wasn't such a nice lady or she'd been abducted along with the books. Dali wouldn't just steal books when he could get the librarian, too. Crap on toast, if the demons were abducting whatever and whoever they wanted, I was really up a creek.

The stairway ended at the expected wide hallway. Cinder blocks on one side, wire mesh on the other, it reminded me of the library at Alcatraz minus the scent of salt water. But as I stepped forward, my foot hit a hidden ward and I jerked away, ankle cramping.

"Oh, sorry." Lenny edged around me and muttered a word of Latin. Immediately the warning tingle vanished as the ward fell with a distinctive pop and a glimmering sheet of color. "We had additional security put in about four years ago along with the cameras. Our current security footage goes back two weeks, but it shows nothing."

I nodded, waiting for him to lead the way as if I'd never been down here before. Pixies could fix most cameras to make it seem as if no one was there. There'd be a hint of pixy dust before it went to loop, but most people didn't know to look for it. "I'd like to see the footage, if that's okay," I said, not yet ready to let go of the hope that it was a witch or elf who had stolen the books. *Please, anyone but a demon . . .*

"Sure." Lenny's expression was pinched as he glanced at the racks of books as we passed them, safe behind their chain-link fence. "Pixy dust and crackers, it's creepy down here."

I knew what he meant, and I followed Lenny down the corridor, the scent of old magic seeping past the chain-link feeling like a seductive caress. Tingles rose and fell, accented by the nearby ley line. I'd snuck down here with Nick to find a spell to help me bring Trent in as a genetic engineer. I'd left with my neck torn open by a demon. I wasn't sure what it said that both Al and Trent were now counted as my teacher and lover respectively. Smarter, maybe? Less innocent?

It was here that I had met Al, sent by Ivy's master vampire to kill me. He would have, too, if he hadn't tasted my blood and found something familiar. I still wondered if Al had allowed Nick to circle him so as to rub out the bargain the demon had made to end my life. Al had saved me in the hopes of possessing me, and I had worn his mark until I won my freedom. All of which made me wonder if I was Stef's Nick, leading her into a place she could not get herself free of. I, though, would not abandon her as Nick had abandoned me.

"Here it is," Lenny said nervously, and I scuffed to a halt as he fiddled with the mundane lock and the skeleton key he took from a pocket. "It might take a second. These old keys are finicky."

"Take your time," I whispered, staring at the racks of books behind the chain-link fence. I knew they hid a small room, unless they had changed that, too, and I stifled a shudder when the gate creaked open.

"Ah, the books missing were from the interior," Lenny said as he strode in. Frowning, I took a book from a shelf and set it in the doorframe. Lenny hesitated at the sliding sound, then smiled and nodded. I would not be locked in here. Not with my memories. *Why am I doing this again?* I asked myself, hoping I wasn't being as stupid as the first time.

"I don't blame you," Lenny said. "About four years ago, we found a gallon of blood on the floor and two books missing. We still don't know what happened."

"Imagine that," I mused, stifling a shudder as we came out from the informal aisleway and into a small room, its walls made entirely of books. My attention went to the pristine cement floor, then to where the wooden cabinet had once stood. It had been replaced by a glass-fronted metal one, but the worn table and three crappy chairs were still here.

God, I had been stupid, I thought, one hand covering my wrist where a demon mark once lay. It had been a promise to repay Al for saving my life after he had nearly ended it. Jenks said it was Nick's fault, but Nick had been the one to circle Al and end the attack, too.

The dented trash can was overflowing with takeout cups

from Junior's, a flowery *Melody* written on them. A half-melted scented candle sat on the table beside a printout, and I squinted at the acidic prickling in my nose.

Burnt amber? I mused, senses reaching as I breathed deep to bring the tingling sensation of the demons' calling card deep into me. I could smell burnt amber, more than what could come from the books themselves, and my gaze returned to the candle trying to cover it up. A soft tingle began in my fingertips, itching as it rose to cramp my arms. Burnt amber meant demons. Busy demons. It was the scent of power, and the more they practiced, the more they reeked of it.

"They were shelved in the cabinet," Lenny said, pulling me from my slack-focused alarm. "I had Melody make a list of what was missing."

He was fingering the printout, nothing more than a list of three library identification numbers, really.

"Melody?" I asked as I reached for it. "I thought you said they were taken after she left."

"I asked her to come down and look," he admitted somewhat sheepishly. "No one knows them better than her. We had a retirement party for her."

"Down here?" I questioned, and he shook his head, rightly horrified.

"God, no. But it got her out of the office long enough to get the cake ready and everyone in from the floor. In hindsight, I should have thought of something else. She was very upset about the missing books."

"No doubt." Lip between my teeth, I read the list. Slowly my smile faded. Yep. He was right. They were all demon, each identification starting with *ARC* for *arcane*. "Ah, thank you. This is helpful," I said, flushed, as I set my bag with a thump on the table. "It's going to take some time to set up the tracing charm," I lied, eyes down in embarrassment as I took Dali's books out of my bag as if I was going to use them. "You said I could see the security tapes?"

"Yes. I'll arrange it on your way out." Lenny rolled one of the dilapidated chairs closer, clearly intending to stay.

"Mmmm, the spell I want to use works by auras. If you're down here, it's going to mess up the auratic reading."

"Oh!" Lenny let go of the chair as if it was hot. "Sure. The room is yours."

"Thanks. Hey, if you have any recent photos of Melody, it might be helpful. I could use her contact information, too."

"Sure." Lenny rocked forward, then back, his hand going to his phone. "I took one of the party. You want it now?"

What I wanted was him out of the room, but I nodded, taking my own phone and waiting for him to airdrop it to me.

"I was going to put it in the newsletter," Lenny said as my phone dinged. "You don't think Melody stole them, do you? The books, I mean?"

"I'll know better in about an hour, but I hope not," I said as I accepted the picture. Immediately my brow furrowed. It was obvious who was Melody, the narrow, older woman standing behind a retirement cake and surrounded by smiling coworkers. She was mid-seventies maybe, and a witch, judging by the protection charms about her neck. But nothing could protect her from the demon mark peeping from behind her cuff. Two slashes, just like Stef.

Crap on toast, they are stealing what they want, again. This was not what I needed. Not when I had an undead vampire to entertain and befuddle. "Thank you. This is very helpful," I said, hearing my voice as if outside of my head. "Can you give me about an hour?"

"Sure." He turned to leave, clearly hesitant. "There are hundreds of more expensive books that Melody could have stolen. It couldn't have been her."

"I hope not," I said, and his expression eased. "She sounds like a nice lady."

But the truth was, Melody had a demon mark. Chances were good that Melody had been abducted along with the books. And Sikes. *Son of a mother pus bucket. Why do demons always pick the worst time to stretch their cosmic powers?*

"Come on up and have someone page me when you're done!" he called, lost somewhere between the stacks, and I shuddered at the sound of his fading steps.

Immediately my eyes went to the clean floor, my memory coating it in my own blood. The sensation of being alone stole around my heart and squeezed. "Buck up, Rachel," I whispered as I tucked Dali's books back in my bag. "No one has ditched you. Everyone is busy. You have things to do. They have things to do. Don't be such a wuss."

Even so, I couldn't bring myself to sit down in one of the chairs. Uneasy, I went to the old books, running a finger down the spines to feel which ones were simply bad, and which ones were really ugly. I'd discovered that Newt's books always had the same sensation: a disorienting disconnection laced with a hint of freakish power that made my gut cramp. The need to find a new curse to befuddle Finnis was high on my list, but I needed to find out what Hodin had left out of the recipe even more. If I was lucky, I could solve both problems with one tome.

The thought to beat it out of the tall, sallow-faced demon if I struck out here was starting to hold some merit. I hadn't seen Hodin or Stef at all last night after Ivy and Pike dropped me off. I hadn't seen either one this morning, either. They were avoiding me. *Maybe I shouldn't have opened my big mouth.*

"Ta na shay, bluequel," I whispered, letting a sliver of stored energy fuel the elven charm to facilitate a quick search. Unlike most elven magic, the spoken plea worked solely at the discretion of the Goddess. Seeing as I was looking for one of Newt's charms—and there was probably more mischief to be had if I found it than if I didn't—the mystics would probably help. Trent had taught me the charm after I couldn't find my car keys. That they'd been right where I'd left them at his poolside had seemed to support his claim that it worked best when the mystics would be amused at the result. The tiny motes of living magic fueled much of the elven magic—and demon, too, if they'd let it.

The faint, static prickling through my hair told me the mystics had heard, gathering to not only tweak reality for me, but to relate all to the Goddess. And whereas once I would have been terrified, I knew they didn't recognize me anymore. "Please, please, please let there be a copy," I muttered as I began to search, my fingers lightly tracing the demon tomes, lingering here, faster there, searching the tingling power imbued in them for a taste of the truly insane—until my hand sprang away at a sudden prick of midnight and stars. It was one of Newt's.

"*Ta na shay*, thank you . . ." I whispered, truly grateful as I drew the book from the shelf, sensing a lingering pull and snap as it left its spot. The uncomfortable sensation eased as I took it to the table even as my hair became more wild. The mystics weren't leaving. *Swell.*

Annoyed, I tucked a strand of hair behind an ear and gently set the book down. It was practically falling apart, and, breath held, I carefully shifted the cover open. There would be no index. There never was. I'd have to search through it curse by curse.

Maybe Newt took the books? I mused, trying not to read the curses as I flipped through the pages. But what would the Goddess want with charms and curses? She only had to ask her mystics to change reality.

"'Reverse Growth to Diminish Threat,'" I read aloud, frowning. The curse wasn't to restore youth but would send a person's mind backward in age, destroying their memory in the process. It sounded right, but the glyphs and ingredients were wrong, so I kept looking.

The next three curses were to remove sight, sensation, and hearing to lock a person into a state of sensory deprivation. Still not right, but everything so far was about manipulating the mind, and Newt tended to lump similarly acting curses together.

"That's it!" I whispered when I turned the page, my fingertips tingling as a familiar pentagram caught my eye. It was the spell Hodin had given me, but it was called *Damnatio Memoriae*, or the damnation of memory, not fulfillment.

Excited, I scanned the curse, my brow furrowing. Hodin *had* miscopied it, giving me no chance of being able to duplicate it myself. The bone Jenks had seen Stef buy was at the core of the smudge stick, and that vial of black and silvery dust was probably cremation dust, easy to slip into the quencher without me knowing.

"Mother pus bucket," I muttered, waving a glittering haze of mystics away as I studied the curse. The bone had to be harvested from a murdered woman or man, broken in the act of their death, and the dust was ash from a witch pyre, as in a witch burned at the stake—nearly impossible to find now. Either would get the curse labeled dark, and I felt ill.

"Hodin, our deal to keep your ass safe is so off," I whispered, horrified as I read the curse's application. It wasn't just a memory curse. It was a memory curse on steroids, not only clouding any new memories, but also working backward from the hour it was invoked to the day of birth, erasing everything day by day until there was nothing left. Worse, it was passed down from parent to child, like the curse that made vampires or Weres, becoming active only later in life, when it would kill a person's identity so slowly that it would take decades.

"Who would do this to a person?" I whispered, but they were called curses for a reason. Sick at heart, I fumbled for my phone to take a picture. I had to twist a cure before Pike's brother engendered a child.

Please, please, please, I thought as I turned the page, my breath escaping me in a sigh when I saw the counter-curse. "Oh, thank God," I said as I took a picture of that, too, but my relief soured as I read it. "Atlantis? Are you kidding?" I exclaimed. "Where am I going to get a reflecting telescope from the city of Atlantis?"

"From Atlantis, obviously, Rachel Mariana Morgan," intoned a deep, familiar voice, and I spun, shocked.

CHAPTER

15

"AL!" I EXCLAIMED AS I SAW THE DEMON STANDING BEFORE the books in his familiar crushed green velvet and lace, his red, goat-slitted eyes narrowed as he looked at me over his blue-tinted glasses. During the course of our association, I had seen Al appear as a jackal-headed Egyptian god in sandals and beads, a bear-size slavering dog ready to rip out my throat, and even Ivy, right here in this very room, ready to kill me with what I most feared. I'd seen him as a slick businessman, and even me in tight leather and wild hair. Always, though, I had known it was him. Now, he was still him, but I'd never seen him this angry.

His shoulders filled the space, his posture stiff and his hands in fists at his sides. He was hardly containing his rage. Panic raced through me, and I took a step back with Newt's book pulled to my chest. His surprise that I was here had been a quick flash, short-lived as he clenched his hands to make his knuckles crack. Then again, the last time we had talked, he'd thrown me into Alcatraz for not kicking Hodin to the curb.

"What," he said as he took a step in and I retreated two more, "are you doing here?"

His gaze went from my interview suit to my hair, still staticky from the lingering mystics. "Working," I said, a hundred thoughts fighting in me to be voiced. *I'm sorry. I need help. You were right. Hodin is an ass.* But all I did was hold Newt's book closer and add, "You?"

Al took his top hat off, dropping it onto the marred table with an accusing flip of his wrist. His gloves were next, the fine linen pulling from him in a soft hush, first one, then the other. "Melody told Dali how to get around the alarm so he could recover his books," he said as he dropped them into his hat. Hands bare, he went to a shelf, fingers hovering until he chose two raggedy-spined books and set them on the table. "I'm here doing the same." His eyes rose to find mine. "Or do you have a problem with me taking what was stolen from me—Rachel Mariana Morgan?"

He was using all three of my names. It meant he thought I was less than dirt, something to be bought and sold. But he was talking, and I took a step forward to drag my heavy bag off the table before he could see Dali's books inside. "No," I said, my arm jerking at the sudden weight. "But I'm sure if you went to the university and asked—"

"That is Newt's," he interrupted, his derisive stare going to the book in my grip. Slowly his lips curled up in an ugly leer. "Are you stealing Newt's books for Hodin?"

"No," I said shortly. The book was sending uncomfortable jabs of demand into me, but I held it closer, afraid he'd take it.

Al's smile widened to show his flat teeth and bad mood. "We're all taking our books back," he said, pulling another from the shelves and leafing through it before letting it drop with the rest in a foul puff of dust and bound power. "You'll probably be blamed for it, seeing as you are the one down here."

"Take them," I said, chin rising to indicate his growing pile, and he blinked, surprised. "If they're your books, you should have them. I never agreed with museums and libraries

holding the artifacts they stole for the betterment of their
bottom dollar in the name of cultural understanding. Stealing is stealing, especially if you're taking from those who
don't fit your narrow idea of civilized."

Again he looked me up and down, gaze lingering on my
interview suit as if trying to decide why I was wearing it.
"There is hope for you yet," he said distantly, then turned
his back on me to run his hand over the books' spines
again.

"Al, I need to talk to you." I rushed my words, jumping
when another book hit the stack, the ancient tome sending
up a puff of sparkling dust, choking in the low-ceilinged
room. "Please," I added at his low growl. "I am in so much
trouble," I whispered. "Hodin—"

Al spun to me. His focus blurred, and I warmed, knowing he was seeing my smutty aura. His vision sharpened,
his lip curling at my interview suit. "Is a backstabbing, lying excuse for flesh who would sell his own child for a crust
of bread and a pair of slippers. Actually, rumor has it he
did. Is he making you wear that? It's appropriately hid-
eous."

"It's for a class," I said quickly. "I'm teaching today."

"In that?" he blurted. And then he blinked. "You are . . .
teaching?"

"At the university," I said, his horrified shock making
me feel grossly inadequate. "Until Professor Sikes returns."
I hesitated. "Ah, have you seen him, by chance?"

Al faced me, the book in his hand forgotten. "You're
filling in for a *professor*? Teaching what?"

"Demonology?" I offered apologetically, and Al's eye
twitched. "It's, ah, not a full-time gig. One day, maybe two
until they find Sikes. Um, Dali doesn't have him, does he?"

My voice had risen to nearly a squeak. Sighing, Al set
the book atop the rest. "Hence Dali quitting his minimum-
wage pursuit," he muttered. "Or maybe he was fired. I've
never *seen* anyone so fixated on napkins."

"Dali has Professor Sikes?" I said, that same sick feeling
rising up around my heart. How long had Dali been com-

plaining about needing a couple of high-end magic users to get his restaurant going? And now he had one. Two if you counted Melody, though she seemed less waitstaff and more staff. "The Turn take it, I did not nearly kill myself making a place for you in reality so you could all blow it to hell because Dali needs waitstaff!" I exclaimed.

Hand waving expressively, Al spun to the shelves, coattails furling.

"You all agreed no more sentient familiars. We had a deal," I complained. "Where's Melody? Did Dali take her, too?"

His back to me, Al made a rude snort. "If you can't force your will on someone, you shouldn't make promises for their behavior. Dali required a host with enough skill to manage the multiple shifts and costumes required of his restaurant. With the return of his books, he needed a librarian. You don't expect him to put an ad in the paper, do you? I'm no longer in the trade of providing skilled familiars with enough ley line carrying capacity to survive channeling what a demon requires. I'm sure the contracts were properly notarized and witnessed." Al smirked at me from over his shoulder. "As legal as death."

Son of a fairy-farting whore. I didn't have time for this!

"We had a deal," I said again, stiffening when he dropped another book on his stack. "You follow the rules, and you can hang out in reality. Stealing a librarian and professor is not following the rules."

"Good-bye, Rachel Mariana Morgan." Al scooped up his books, clearly ready to leave.

"Wait!" I exclaimed, my reach for his sleeve hesitating when that damned smut tried to jump to him. My hair was crackling with mystics, probably lingering because I was so damned entertaining. *I'm never going to invoke the Goddess's help again.*

"Al, I know you gave me the crickets, not Hodin," I rushed, and he halted. "Please." Embarrassed, I set Newt's book down to run a hand over my snarled hair. The lights were dimming and brightening from the mystics, making me nervous. "Hodin tricked me. I need you to look at this and tell me how deep in the crapper I am."

"Tricked you?" he said, voice dripping with sarcasm. But curiosity kept him from leaving, and emboldened, I spun the book so he could see it right side up. Al pulled it closer. Studied it. "You got this to work? It's written in chicken scratch."

Worry was spiraling up around my chest, but he was listening, and it gave me hope. "It makes a wand," I said softly. "Six curses." I rubbed my fingers together, remembering the oily feel, remembering how I had to force the smut to stay with me. *Smut that didn't soak in* . . . "I think it's one of Newt's memory curses. The person I used it on began forgetting things, working from the present backward."

He made a small sound of understanding. "The vampire at the airport? Damnation of memory, indeed." His red, goat-slitted eyes fastened on me, a flicker of amusement quirking his lips. "Congratulations, Rachel. You are truly one of us."

My face went cold. "He said it was white."

"And you believed him. Perhaps you aren't one of us. Perhaps you are just stupid."

My knees felt like noodles, and my stomach felt light. "I was going to use it on Finnis. . . ." If I had, there would have been inquiries. It would have been traced to me. I might get some leeway with Brad because it was in self-defense and in conjunction with an assassination attempt, but damn. I had to fix this.

"It is a worthy idea." Al pushed from the book and snapped it closed, sending the faintest scent of burnt amber to tickle my nose. "If you are willing to pay the cost. You are erasing him, one memory at a time." Smirking, he inclined his head. "Enjoy your class. I'm sure they'll understand about the smut."

"He lied to me," I whispered, embarrassed not that I had believed Hodin, but that I hadn't trusted Al. There was a difference.

Al sniffed as he ran a finger over the closed book, sneering as the lingering mystics made the heavy cover glow. "Oh, did the foolish and naïve Rachel Morgan twist dark magic? You are in the crapper. There's no help for you as long as my *little brother* is under your protection." He touched his stack of books, and they vanished. "Good-bye," he added as he elegantly twirled his hat and jammed it atop his head.

"Wait!" I licked my lips, pulse quickening as he hesitated, standing as unmoving as the books surrounding us—and just as dangerous. "Hodin—" I said, blanching at his clenched jaw. "He's not teaching me," I protested, and I swear, a rising hum came from the shelves—the latent power of the mystics resonating in them. "I thought it was a gift."

I froze as the words left my mouth. *When a demon gives you something for free, you missed something.*

Anger pinched his ruddy features. "There are no gifts from Hodin," Al said bitterly. "Only curses. If he *gave* it to you, it was for his own benefit, not yours."

My eyes widened as he strode forward, forcing me to retreat until my back hit the cabinet. "If you want my help, listen to me," he intoned, a faint scent of burnt amber lifting from him. "You have allowed Hodin to infiltrate your church. It's his now. Accept this and abandon it before he brings you down without you ever seeing the knife."

I hadn't given Hodin anything but a room for six months, and angry, I pushed Al away. "I know you gave me the crickets to practice on." *I know you still care,* I thought, but I couldn't say it lest he say aloud that he didn't. "I need your help," I said, blinking fast.

"I *am* helping you, but you aren't *listening*!" he shouted, and a little pop of energy burst from one of the books, glowing as it drifted like ball lightning until it went out. "Hodin is a backstabbing trickster! If he gave you a curse without any payment, then you have paid too much. What did you give him for it?"

I stared blankly, my pulse hammering.

"A promise?" Al barked, and I gasped when the smut tried to jump to him when he grabbed my hand and turned it over to show my pristine wrist.

"No." My voice sounded small even to me. "Nothing." I reclaimed my hand, scared. "I thought he was trying to be helpful. To fit in. Make friends. Friends help each other for nothing." But my thoughts went over the last few days, and embarrassment filled me. God help me, I really was a fool.

Al's eyebrows rose as he saw me finally figure it out. Yes, I was a fool, but it was that same trusting foolhardiness that had kept Al from killing me the day we met—here, in the university library's basement.

"I thought he was trying to be a friend," I said, but it sounded weak even to me. "Stef . . ." My words faltered.

"You gave him your friend?" Al said, and my lips parted in horror.

"No!" I exclaimed, but now I wasn't so sure. "I didn't want to think he was untrustworthy simply because he was a demon," I added, beginning to get angry. "I didn't think you were!"

"Then you really are a fool and you will not survive," he said, and I froze as he ran his finger an inch over my shoulder as if feeling my aura. A shudder rippled over me as I felt the smut lift, yearning to go to him before it sank back down into me. "Tell me, Rachel. How is Jenks?"

I looked up, surprised at the shift. "Fine," I said, resigned that he wouldn't help me, but at least he hadn't tossed me into Alcatraz. "He's home tending a pixy. Stef hit her with her car."

Al made a mocking, confused sound. "Stef is not tending her?"

I shook my head. "Another pixy, Baribas, is trying to kill her, and Jenks is the only one who can keep her alive until her wing heals."

"How *curious*!" Al said, his sarcasm gathering my scattered thoughts into a sharp point. "Why is *Baribas*, another *pixy*, trying to kill her?" He took his glasses from his nose, snapping his fingers to make a cloth appear in them. "Did

she do something *wrong*?" he said as he needlessly pol-
ished the lenses.

My lips pressed, and I frowned at his mockery. "No. She
has black hair," I said, still angry about it. Leaving dark
newlings to die of exposure was a pixy tradition Jenks had
abandoned long before he met me, the beginning of it all, I
think. "Jenks likes her," I said softly.

"Mmmm. A dark-haired pixy." Al's voice nearly dripped
with scorn, but it was clearly aimed at me, not Jenks. "How
unusual. You lost your backup to the one thing Jenks would
abandon you for. A kindred spirit his own size."

"He didn't abandon me," I said, affronted. But I had
missed his steadfast presence.

"And your roommate, Stephanie?" he practically cooed,
his glasses again on his nose. "You say she and Hodin are
enjoying a friendship. Is she well?"

I stared at him, not liking what he was insinuating. "What
does that have to do—"

"Is she *well*, Rachel?" he thundered, making me jump.
"It's a simple question."

"She's . . . okay," I said, not understanding. He didn't
care about Stef. I was missing something. "She's mad at me
at the moment."

"Oh, that's a shame. And Pike?" Anger defined his voice,
his motion rough as he flipped Newt's book closed. "How
odd that his brother shows up the *very hour* that he finds
himself owing the exact amount that your Kalamack elf
had liquidated to buy property in Cincinnati."

"How did you . . ." I said, voice faltering. I was fairly
sure that Hodin had given the assassins a curse to make
their abduction of Pike easier. I'd force the answer out of
him if he ever showed his face again.

Al pushed up from the table, squinting at me. "Four
stones from one crow. All eliminated from your side: Jenks,
Stephanie, Pike, and Trent."

"Crow?" I echoed, getting the meaning from his twisted
metaphor. "You mean Hodin?" Son of a bastard. Getty said
Hodin had lied about Pike. The demon had overheard Trent

working on his business deal, too—before it had suddenly
gone wrong. Getty claimed something had blown her into
Stef's car, and I *knew* Hodin had given Stef a pain curse for
Getty when I'd left the room, earning her another demon
mark. I'd felt his magic in the stairway, and Stef had been
nearly in tears despite, no, because of Getty's quick recov-
ery. *Oh no . . .*

"How *kind* of Hodin to give you a curse to help you
convince a master vampire to leave," Al said bitterly as my
face went cold. "Yes, you're right. I owe you an apology.
You're not stupid at all."

I stared at him as understanding fell on me. Son of a
fairy-farting troll. Hodin had systematically taken away
everyone I relied on. And I had let him do it. "Why?" I said
as I looked up to find Al's mocking expression. "Why
would he take my friends away? He needs me. I'm protecting him from you all, and he knows it." But Al was right,
and my confusion barely overpowered my anger.

"You are protecting him." Al tugged the lace at his
cuffs. He only did it when I was being especially stupid,
and my face warmed. "Tell me, Rachel. What do you have
that he can't get for himself? What does he covet? What
does he see every day that you have and he can't get?"

"Nothing." I tried to find the flaw in his logic, something
that I could use to prove he was seeing everything through
glasses that twisted events to support his hatred of Hodin.
"All I have is my church, my friends. If not for them, I'd
never be able to hold on to the subrosa position."

My eyes flicked up to his. *Mother pus bucket catching
hailstones.* "He's trying to take my subrosa position."

Al smiled, and for the first time in a long time, it scared
me. "And here you are, sullied and stinking of dark magic
you twisted." He ran a finger an inch from my skin, nose
wrinkling in disgust as he rubbed his finger and thumb together as if gauging it. "You earned this."

I could almost hear him think, *spell whore*, and I
slumped where I stood, wondering how I was going to fix
this. *At least he's talking to me again.* "I am so sorry," I

said, and he made a bitter bark of laughter. "I should have listened to you about Hodin, but I didn't want to live in a world where demons were bad simply because they were demons."

"And?" he said, the single syllable holding bloodied thorns.

I took a breath, feeling raw and vulnerable. Hope that he might forgive me was painful. "Our kin aren't bad because they are demons," I said, picking my next words carefully because if I tried to take the teeth from them, I had no doubt they'd spend the next thousand years proving their godlike power. "They are bad because that was what they needed to be to survive. But you don't anymore. You proved that."

"A baseless argument that will not stand." Al's lips twisted. "And I am not . . . *nice*."

The word iced into me, carried by a malice born in a hatred of things gone before, and I scrambled to bring his thoughts back to the now.

"No, you're not nice," I said as I came closer. He was angry at himself, not me. "But you have compassion," I added, and he snarled, his frustrated gaze heavy on me. "I made a mistake that could have killed me," I said, standing now at the table. "I know you put that protection spell over the belfry. You kept me alive until I figured it out. I made a mistake. I'm trying to fix it."

"You are amazing in your ignorance," he said, and I took a careful breath, stifling my hope lest he see it and find offense there somewhere. "You might not end up in a bottle, but Alcatraz looks promising."

"I . . ." I swallowed hard, biting my lower lip. "I promised to protect him if you tried to put him in a bottle for mixing elf and demon magic. I never told him I wouldn't stuff him in a bottle for lying to me. And he lied to me. Gave me a dark curse. Told me it was white. I'm done."

Al froze, his red eyes meeting mine and widening in a sudden thought. "You left yourself a loophole? A good behavior clause? You may survive yet."

He lurched forward and I jumped, snatching that damned smut back when his thick hand hit my shoulder. "You can't teach such guile. You are born with it, or you die without it. Where are your spelling robes, Rachel Mariana Morgan?"

He was still using all three of my names, but now . . . it was in pride, and I felt my heart lift. "I have more important things to do than worry about what I'm wearing to talk to a room of wannabe demonologists," I said, wondering at the sudden shift.

"You *wish* to wear lavender?" he questioned, voice louder, more demanding. More himself. "You are a *demon*. You will play the *part*." He squinted evilly at me. "Unless you believe robes make you appear silly? Beneath you, perhaps? Tell me where you keep your robes and I'll fetch one for you."

I wasn't past redemption, and I almost cried in relief. "That's not it at all. I'd rather you look at this. I found a countercurse, but some of the ingredients—"

"Where are your robes!" he thundered.

"Hanging up in the belfry!" I shouted, yelping when the accumulated mystic energy in the room discharged in a sudden pop. The mystics were still here, and I winced, knowing Al thought of them as elven excrement.

But Al was grinning, his eyebrows high from the unexpected sound. "Oh!" I said, getting it, and Al's smile became downright evil.

"Shall I fetch one for you?" he practically oozed.

He was going after Hodin. "Yes, but don't—" I started, but he was gone in a swirl of sparkling black and red. "Damage the church," I finished, whispering it as the basement's silence soaked in, heavier now for Al having been here.

Mood bad, I picked my book-heavy bag up off the floor and dropped it on the table. Hodin had played me. Son of a bastard, he had played me, and I hadn't listened to Al, so concerned that I wasn't following popular cultural bias that I blinded myself—I ignored my gut instinct and let myself be taken advantage of. I might lose Cincinnati over it.

"Swell," I muttered, wondering if I should call Jenks and warn him. Head down, I shuffled past Dali's books to find my phone, scrolling for his number as it joined the library's Wi-Fi. But even as I searched, my phone hummed. It was Jenks, and my pulse pounded as I hit connect. "Jenks, are you okay?"

"Yeah, we're fine," he said, his voice unusually loud through the tiny speaker. "But something with eight arms and a mouth just tried to eat Hodin. Naturally I thought of you. What's up?"

I exhaled, slumping into one of those nasty chairs. He was okay. "That was Al. We're talking again. How's the church?"

"The bell might be cracked. Hodin is gone." He hesitated. "He has Stef," he said softly.

Damn it to the Turn. . . . "We'll get her back." I touched Newt's book, wishing I could take it home. "He played me, Jenks," I said, feeling stupid. "Pike's bad bet, Getty being hit and needing your help, Trent's business troubles. Me getting covered in smut. He's trying to strip everyone from me so I lose control of Cincy and he can step in."

Jenks's laughter sounded like wind chimes. "That's going to be hard with Al chasing him. You want me to come with you to class? You got time to stop at the church. We can bring Getty. She needs to get out. She's driving me crazy. That woman doesn't like to sit still."

My first impulse was to say no, but I hesitated and really thought about it. I didn't think my life was in danger unless Hodin showed up, and in that case, Jenks wouldn't be much help, especially if Getty was there. "No," I said as I stood and reluctantly reshelved Newt's book. "Trent is going to meet me after class for a late lunch, and we'll probably end up at the church."

"Be pixy-careful," he said, sounding like my dad telling me to be home early. "Ah, sorry about Stef, but she made her own decision."

"Based on my advice," I said softly. My fingers tingled as they left the book's spine, and I wondered if I could sneak it out of here. It wasn't as if anyone else could use it. Or even notice, probably. *I'll be back for you. Promise.* "Hey, I found out where Sikes is," I added sourly. "I'm going to have to scare the living daylights out of his class before Dali lures them into waiting tables, too. I should have guessed Dali was abducting people again when he quit Junior's." *Crap on toast. This is not what I need right now.*

"Dali, eh?" Jenks said. "Figures. You finally get a barista to make your coffee how you like it, and they quit to open their own place in another reality."

A faint hint of magic rippled over my aura, and I looked up—right as Al popped back in.

"Al!" I cried, and he spun, the ragged robe he now wore furling around his ankles. I'd never seen him in it before, a dirty red at the shoulders changing to almost black from filth at the torn hem. It clung tight to his waist and wrists, tapering to his heels to give his legs the freedom to move. His slippers were more like boots and leggings all in one, the silk rising in a precise woven zigzag pattern up to his knees. The scent of burnt amber rolled from him, stark and strong, almost repellent. He saw my surprise, and then he misted out, returning in his usual green velvet. A wad of dark green silk hung in his hands, and he dropped it on the table.

"Jenks. Gotta go," I said, and the phone went dark.

"Wear this," Al said, breathless but taut with tension, and I blinked, eyes watering.

"That's not my robe," I said as I held it up, and a pair of green slippers/boots matching his own fell from the black, bell-decked sash. "Did you find him?"

"Find him? Yes. Get him, no." Lips twisted, Al flexed his hand, now red with a soft burn. "I would have had him if not for that cursed elven bell giving away my presence."

He'd missed, and a sliver of fear spiked through me to leave only anger. "I, ah, set it up to know if he was spying on me." God, I felt stupid. Embarrassed. Angry. But mostly I was mad. Jaw clenched, I set the robe on the table, the green and black silk puddling like water.

"You will be pleased to know I restrained myself. Your pixies are fine and your church is intact." Al studied me in disgust. "Hodin has fled, but he will return." Coattails furling, Al spun, unhesitating as he plucked four widely spaced books from the shelves and shoved them at me. "These are yours. Take them. Newt willed them to you."

"She had a will?" I said, shocked as they tumbled into my arms. One was the book with the countercurse, and a thrill struck through me.

But before he could answer, Al stiffened, and we both turned to a soft scrape in the hall.

"Stop!" Lenny exclaimed, pale as he lurched out from where he'd been hiding in the stacks. "Those belong to the library."

I froze, four tingling books in my arms. I wanted them. Wanted them all. Telling Al he should take his books was one thing. This was another, and my words choked to nothing.

Smirking, Al looked at Lenny over his glasses. "They were stolen from Newt and I say they now belong to Rachel. Ta."

"Al?" I called as a swirl of gray and black rose up in the tiny room, and then he was gone, nothing to say he'd been there but eight empty spots on the shelf and a hint of burnt amber hanging in the stagnant air.

"They belong to the library," Lenny warbled, but Al had shaken him and his words lacked conviction.

The books in my grip were warm, wanting to be on my shelf. Faint in the back of my mind, an almost subliminal uproar was raging. Al had dropped into the collective and an impromptu, loud meeting was taking place. Clearly war had been declared on Hodin—and I wasn't going to do a damn thing to stop it.

"Um, I found out who took your books," I said, and Lenny stared, eyes wide, arms at his sides—helpless and knowing he was down eight more. "It's the demons," I added. "The good news is they're only taking the ones that belonged to them."

I couldn't look at him as I shoved the books into my bag with Dali's and dropped the silk robe on top. I didn't recognize the puddling fabric, but my initial thought that it had been Ceri's seemed unlikely. The slippers would have been too large for the petite late elf. Al had seldom dressed her in green, either. The cut, too, was odd, being tight about the waist and wrist. And the shoes? Couldn't really call them slippers. The bindings would go up to my knees. It wasn't the usual spelling robe, and I wondered what Al had given me.

Brow furrowed, Lenny made a soft sound of protest as I hoisted the heavy bag over my shoulder. "Those books have been in our collection for hundreds of years," he said, but the high-pitched whine in his voice told me it was all over but for the conference call with the library's trustees. "And before that, private collections."

"True." I stood before him, wanting to go, but he was blocking my way. "But they were written by demons who are still alive, not decedents. Stolen property goes back to the original owners."

Lenny gestured helplessly. "I can't tell my boss that the demons are taking their books."

"Why not?" I hoisted my shoulder bag higher, anxious to leave. "Look, doesn't the university have a protocol for returning illegally obtained artifacts? It's the same thing. I'm not saying you have to contact every demon to try to make reparations. Not many of them actually wrote anything down. And some of the books are so old and outdated that they probably don't want them anyway."

"I don't have the authority to release books. Not that old," he said, voice going soft as he slumped against one of the stacks, fingers pressing into his temples.

Pity rose, and I touched his shoulder, startling him. "Lenny, the missing books belong to them," I said softly, wondering if I should tell him my suspicions concerning Melody. "If they start taking things that don't belong to them, I can step in, but not until." I hesitated, thinking. "Maybe they will bring them back if you offer them a yearly stipend to store them here."

Lenny's breath caught. "Would you?"

Wincing at his hope, I shook my head. No. I would not. The second Al dropped the four books into my arms, they were mine, like a puppy. It was more than searching for another spell to use on Finnis. They *needed* me, and they were going on my shelf where I could take care of them. "Maybe you could call it a permanent loan."

Lenny's groan sent a flash of guilt through me, quickly quashed. It felt good to be moving, my hair shifting from my face as the last of the mystics were stripped away. My breath came in fast as I found the long hallway to the stairway, and my pace increased. "I'm sorry, Lenny," I said as I heard him following. "This was not my intention when I came over today. I'll try to get something on paper that shows they are mine, and maybe something from Dali and Al proving ownership of the ones they have. Until then, I'm taking them home."

Home, where they would sit on my shelf between my *Betty Bob's Cookbook for One* and my *Twenty-Five Easy Pentagrams for the Beginning Practitioner.*

"Um, about those books . . ." he tried again as he made a lurching step to catch up, and I kept walking, not envying his afternoon. *Hey, sorry, but the woman I brought in to find out who lifted our ancient books claims they were stolen and took some for herself.*

Newt's books tingled warm against me through the bag, and I touched them as if they were a nest of soft, helpless bunnies waiting to burst into flame and set the world on fire. Feeling for the first time as if I might be able to do this, I started up the stairs, sure now that I'd find a substitute for an Atlantean reflecting telescope. I'd get Pike's brother uncursed, and any smut I gained doing it was going to end up on Hodin. I had discovered his intentions before it was too late, and my friends were coming back, one by one.

But first, I had a class to teach.

CHAPTER
16

COFFEE IN ONE HAND, LAVENDER HEELS DANGLING FROM the other, I strode through the aboveground tunnel from the university's administration building to Kalamack Hall, where they did all the high-level magic labs. I'd taken the building connector instead of the sidewalk because I thought it would be air-conditioned, but no amount of cool forced air could touch the heat from the sun streaming in. My demon shoes made a soft hush on the sun-warmed tile. I wasn't late, but my quick stop at Junior's for a to-go coffee and to confirm that Dali had quit had robbed me of my chance to be early. Stopping at the bathroom to change into my robe had put me behind even more. The shoes had given me trouble. Oh, they were the right size, but it had taken me a good three goes to figure out how to lace the leggings so they wouldn't slip down when I walked.

Heads rose at the soft jingling of the bells on my black sash as I reached the end and blew into the main building. Jaw set, I tugged my seriously book-heavy, jacket-bulky bag higher up my shoulder. "Wear this," I mocked in a bad imitation of Al, but in all honesty, the interview suit had made me look like a student bucking for an A, and I tightened my jingling sash as I went up the stairs, a vision of billowing green and black silk, silver bells, and red hair. All I needed was the flat-topped, round hat.

Eyes were on me, and I grimaced at the click of a phone camera. *I am powerful,* I thought, channeling my inner Newt as I rose to the second floor and headed for room 273. *I am unique. I am forgetful and unbalanced.*

I did not want to be here, I needed to be home twisting curses when Hodin came to get his stuff. But I had promised Vivian, and seeing as Dali had snagged their instructor, maybe I could convince a handful of university students to pick a safer career. Like a dragon vet, maybe.

My pulse hammered as I stopped short at the door. Light conversation sounded behind it. Taking a slow breath, I opened the door, walked in, and shut it firmly behind me.

I didn't acknowledge them, my gaze fixed on the tech-rich podium and the long table beside it. The sun was bright, and there was a vid screen instead of a chalkboard.

"Oh, my God . . ." someone whispered as the multitude of conversations ebbed, and I stopped at the table to set my coffee, heels, and overflowing bag atop it. Somehow Newt's books had worked their way to the top, and I yanked my lavender jacket to cover them. *Not my first choice for show-and-tell, even if they are students of demonology.*

Only then did I look up, hiding my hands behind me as I took a moment to quietly panic. It was a small class. Twenty kids, maybe, and they were kids, some in shorts and tees, some in sundresses, their laptops open and surfing the web, earbuds mainlining music into their brains. Half stared at me in wonder, half were trying to decide if they should laugh.

Dead, I thought as my own sense of failure rose high in me. *You are all dead witches walking if you stay this course.* I cleared my throat, and the two students in the back broke from their shared video, blinking in surprise. "Good afternoon. I'm Rachel Morgan. I'm teaching your class today.

There's a reason your instructor is gone," I started, and the guy in the front row with the worn Howlers cap sniggered.

"You came to class in your pajamas?"

My eyebrows rose as I noted who laughed and if it was nervous or mean. "This is a spelling robe," I said as I took my hands from behind my back and posed for them, letting them see the stars and moons and how it gave me freedom of movement without sacrificing coverage. "It's a particularly rare silk woven into a glyph-based weave that incorporates charms to help isolate my aura and prevent it from contaminating a high-level curse or charm. The frequency the bells emit confuses mystics, who are attracted to strong draws on the lines, thereby helping prevent Goddess-based mischief. I'm wearing it in the hopes that some of you will realize how deep the water is and that you have been swimming in it without protective gear." I paused to let that sink in, taking the opportunity to sip my cooling coffee before setting it on the edge of the podium.

"Anyone else want to poke fun at my safety equipment? No? Good, because I didn't have time to prep a class and I'm going to have to wing it." Not wanting to hide behind a podium, I moved to stand before the table, leaning against it in what I hoped appeared to be confidence. Someone had done a search for me on the web, and they were whispering over my old I.S. ID photo—the one where I looked as if I had walked into a blowtorch.

"I recently found out that a demon I've allowed to live in my church is trying to screw me over. You want to talk about that?" I said bitterly. "Or we could talk about Professor Sikes, who has been tricked into signing a contract with the self-made leader of the demons. Either situation has a good chance of landing me in the ever-after with same said spoiled, ego-ridden, bored magic users if I don't do something about it, so let's use this afternoon productively, mmmm?"

They stared, but at least they weren't ignoring me. Even the guys in the last row.

"Does anyone have a syllabus?" I said after about three

heartbeats of silence, and a young woman in the second row began shuffling her papers. "Thank you," I said as she passed it forward, and I glanced over it as I slid up and back to sit on the table, bells jingling. My feet dangled, and I swung them to show off the lacing pattern on my leggings.

"How to summon a demon," I said, head down. "Wow. Right on day one. Protection against an escaped demon. That should have been first. Dark versus illegal: how to tell a curse from a white spell. Prevention of ley line abduction. How to choose, develop, and use a familiar to protect you. New laws protecting practitioners." I sighed as I dropped the paper. *Adsimulo calefacio,* I thought, tapping briefly into the demon collective for the stored curse, and the paper flamed, burning to ash before it hit the tiled floor. "This is useless," I said, grimacing at their lack of response.

"Week one." I slipped from the table and began pacing to make my bells ring. "Your instructor *should* have told you that demons can't be summoned now that the curse binding them to the ever-after has been broken, so don't try. Leave Grandma's ashes on the mantel." I spun at the windows and began my return trip. "And really, why would you piss one off by summoning him away from his dinner when you can go down to the waterfront and talk to one for the price of a coffee? Oh, wait a moment," I added sourly. "Dali just quit, seeing as he's given up his nine-to-five and abducted your instructor into abject slavery."

"She said his name," the woman said as she glanced up from her notes.

Good God. They're taking notes. "I said his common name," I corrected her. "Not his summoning name."

"Because he would show up?" the guy in the Howlers cap said, voice mocking.

"What's your name?" I said, and his foot twitched. *Yeah, it's a little harder when it's your anonymity I'm asking for.*

"Tony."

"Well, Tony. I'm not telling you Dali's summoning name because if I did, he might tell you mine, and even though you can't summon me with it anymore, it's my password into the demon collective. If you have that, you not only have access to their accumulated curses, but I'm the one who pays for anything you take out. Not happening."

A guy at the back raised his hand. "Then that is really a demon? Down at the coffee shop?"

I found my coffee, careful to keep my attention off my demon-book-laden bag. "With the goat-slitted, red eyes?" I nodded, took a sip, and warmed it with a thought. There wasn't even a glimmer of reaction from them. *Crap on toast. What does it take to impress them?*

"It was, but he quit," I added. "Now that demons don't reliably smell like burnt amber, the only way to tell if you're dealing with a demon is the eyes. They can change them, but they usually don't bother. Demons can be anything or anyone, but they love to be recognized even when they're trying to be someone else. It's an ego thing."

I waited while half the class wrote that down. *Gawwwd . . .* "Moving on. Weeks two and three. Protection against an escaped demon." I sighed, hoping Sikes hadn't gotten this far yet, filling their heads with duck and cover. "There is no protection against a demon other than to treat him with respect, but my advice is to steer clear and find what you need to know some other way. If you can't find it in the library, you don't need it. If a demon wants to teach you . . ." My words trailed off. Al *wanted* to teach me. Dali was teaching Keric for the pure joy of it. But nine times out of ten, they only taught you if they wanted to use you.

"If a demon wants to teach you, find out why," I said softly, conflicted. "Be very sure."

The same guy raised his hand again, and I nodded. "I heard that there's a demon teaching a baby," he said.

"Dali is teaching a Rosewood baby," I said, not wanting to divulge Keric's name. "Yes. Which is why he won't bother to teach any of you for anything other than service no matter how he couches his platitudes and lies." Okay, it was starting to sound bitter even to me, but it still stung. Dali had practically abducted Sikes and Melody, forcing me to react. "You might know more," I said as I drained my coffee. "But that baby? He's a demon and is going to live forever." I threw my cup away, surprised to find there were three others in there, all sporting Mark's logo. *Last week's trash.*

Tony snickered. "Sikes said a circle will protect—"

My eyes narrowed. "Make one," I said as I slid from the table, bells jingling. "Make a circle!" I shouted as I came at him, snapping the ley line through me so fast it hurt.

His lips parted and someone gasped. *"Septiens!"* he shouted as I made a hand gesture and a tidy ball of gold and red formed in my hand. He cowered in his chair as a solid circle sprang up around him, purple and green flaring through the predominately red glow.

I was standing right over him, feeling mean as I put a hand to his circle. He yelped as his bubble was suddenly awash in black smut. Panicked, I drew the smut back, shocked that it had tried to jump to him. Shoving it deep, I pressed my hand harder against the barrier, feeling his strength meet mine as his blue and green aura fought against my gold and red.

"Sloppy," I said as his hair began to rise as if from static. "Your circle isn't drawn. I'll be through it in half a tick and cover you in my smut like a wet blanket. What are you going to do?"

"You can't break my circle," Tony said, but he was scared. "It's a good one."

I pressed harder, my gold and red swamping him. "I am a demon!" I said, bells jingling as I stood over him. "And I'm pissed that you brought your petty wants to me as if it was my responsibility to wave my wand and make your life roses and hearts! Your circle isn't drawn, Tony." I leaned over him, energy crackling. "I can hold a hundred times the line energy you can. It will fall. It's vulnerable. Do something!"

"Tony!" someone shouted, and Tony scrambled in his pocket, his chair pressing into the interior of his bubble as he crouched and drew a line just inside his glowing circle. Half a heartbeat later, a second wave of energy rose between us, this time inside his first.

He looked up, finally afraid. *Now you might survive,* I thought, then drove a pulse of energy into the outer circle, easily breaking it. My hand hit his secondary barrier and I jerked at the flash of heat and burst of ozone-scented sparks.

"That's good," I said as I stood in the aisle, seeing who was still seated and who had gotten to their feet. "You're in a drawn circle. I can't easily break that." I smiled, and Tony paled. "Does anyone have Tony's number?"

They met me with silence. "His phone number?" I prompted.

"I do," someone said, and I glanced at the young man, pleased to see he was sitting with a wary stiffness, a stick of magnetic chalk in his hand. He'd drawn an uninvoked circle around himself. Maybe I'd gone too far.

"Call him," I said, and the guy stared at me. "Okay, the first person to call him gets an A on the next quiz."

"You aren't going to hurt him?" he asked, and I smiled even more.

"I am your teacher today," I said. "This is a demonstration."

"Damn it, Paul, don't!" Tony all but hissed, but Paul, apparently, began to scroll.

Gold, unharnessed magic dripped from my fingertips to hiss on the floor as I hummed the tune to *Jeopardy!* The rest of the class watched. Everyone knew what was going to happen. I jumped, feeling mean when Tony's phone rang, then punched through Tony's circle like tissue paper when the tiniest hole formed, created by a focused, pinpointed wave of Wi-Fi.

Tony gasped as his circle fell. I stiffened at the expected rush of energy, and I stopped, an inch from touching him. "Tag. You're dead," I said as he held his breath, staring at me. "Unless you're extremely unlucky and are now living in the ever-after as a demon's butler and bed warmer. Cats and dogs can't hold enough ley line energy to be of use as a demon's familiar, but you can. That is, after a few decades of hell where they painfully expand your abilities."

I turned and walked to the front of the class. "It's that fast, people," I said as I resettled myself atop the table. "There are very few circles that can't be broken. And if you go the other way and try to circle a demon to protect yourself, they will simply pop out now that the curse to summon them is broken. So don't think you can cage one and demand something in exchange for granting him freedom."

Tony resettled himself on his chair, shaken, stirred, and maybe a little smarter. "Making people familiars is illegal," he said breathily.

Not smarter. "Extradition from the ever-after is impossible. Who is to say you didn't fall off a bridge? But honestly, a demon will more likely ensnare you with a contract, not muscle. Contracts have the law behind them, and demons love using it to bring people down."

Heads were nodding, and I thought I might finally have gotten through. Everyone had returned to their seats. All eyes were on me. "Where are we. Week four? How to tell a curse from a white spell." I took a slow breath. "I can tell you right now, anything you get from a demon is a curse. They are all curses."

I pulled my robe tighter, feeling ugly in my layer of smut. They had all seen it coating Tony's circle. "And if you're wondering about my fabulous patina, I made a mistake by trusting the wrong demon this week. Why do you think demons are so pissed off all the time?" I said bitterly. "They keep screwing each other over. Even their friends."

They were silent. Maybe I was sharing too much.

"Week five. Prevention of ley line abduction." My eye twitched. There was a video of me being dragged down a snowy street by Al as he tried to abduct me. Cincy's PBS station had incorporated it into one of their public service announcements.

"Can we skip that?" I muttered. "None of you will ever see the ever-after."

"You've been there?" Paul asked. "I heard it was destroyed. That's why the demons are in our reality."

"It was, but they have a new one." I crossed my ankles, wondering if I should mention that it had been Bis and I who had made it. *Nah. They'd never believe me.* "It's smaller, but it was the only way to reinstate the ley lines. They're actually bands of force that connect the demons' reality to ours, so the next time you use a line to do a charm, you can thank a demon."

Not that the demons did it for the greater good.

Their faces twisted up in disbelief, and feeling the sting, I added, "Ley lines aren't just ribbons of energy, they are doorways, and if you know how to shift your aura, you can step from reality to the ever-after like stepping from room to room." Sure, it sounded amazing, but unlike the demons' highly sophisticated ability to pop from place to place, shifting realities by stepping into a ley line was considered lowbrow and subskilled. But that's where I was without Bis.

Even that didn't impress them. All my efforts were going to be for naught. They thought they knew everything. *Nothing changes.*

"Anyone can go to the ever-after?" the woman who had given me her syllabus asked.

We were in dangerous territory, but I didn't know how to back up. "You need to modify your aura to match the line's resonance to slip into and out of it, but yes. For place-to-place movement?" I shook my head. "Only a demon has the skill to do that."

"So . . ." Tony sat up, his smart-ass attitude once more in place. "If you were abducted and taken to the ever-after you could escape by finding a ley line and thinking happy thoughts."

I slumped, seeing the last twenty minutes as an utter waste of time. "If you know how to match your aura to the ley line's resonance. But that only works if the demon in question can't travel to reality and take you again, and we've been over that. Not to mention that the first thing a demon would do would be to solidify your aura so you couldn't modify it. Or even simpler, snap a bracelet of charmed silver about your wrist. It's not hard to be made vulnerable." *It happens to me all the time.*

I was losing them, and I felt a surge of anger. "Week six. How to choose, develop, and use a familiar to protect you."

I ran my fingers in a quick staccato against the top of the table. "If you want your kitty to take the brunt of your stupidity, you need to leave the room. Now.

"Weeks seven and eight. New laws to protect us from day-walking demons. Huh." I eyed them, seeing who was still taking notes. "Two whole weeks on laws, and only one on how to summon them. People, if you can walk out of here with only one thing wedged between the folds of your brain, make it this. Yes, there are laws: no human familiars, no dealing in dark magic, no sloughing smut onto anyone who doesn't specifically ask for it. But demons can and will trick you into an agreement that will have the same result."

I put a hand to my chest, and in a high falsetto said, "Ooh, come work with me. I'll teach you things they cannot teach you up in college!" I put my hand down. "Unlike what Mr. Sting says, you won't be able to wrap him around your finger."

I wondered if Stef had thought she could, then dismissed it. Stef was too up-front and honest. Yes, Hodin was teaching her, but our conversation at Findlay Market convinced me she was after a real relationship, not trying to seduce him into teaching her the arcane. I'd backed off on telling her how dangerous it was because I wanted to live in a world where Hodin wasn't a traitorous, conniving . . . demon. *Crap on toast. I'm right where I started from.*

But they all stared at me as if I was dispensing wisdom that would make them safe.

Maybe I should have worn my working leathers. . . . "Look," I said. "I know you won't listen to anything I'm saying because you think you're special and it will be different with you, but demons have not been made helpless. If anything, they are more dangerous now. They're *not* your friendly neighborhood magic user doling out coffee and beauty charms." *Damn you, Dali. . . .* "Demons, like everyone else, make a conscious decision to follow or break the laws. Don't give them a reason to want to break them. There's no one policing them except maybe for me, and I'm too busy to save your ass."

I began to pace again. "Every single one of them has been around for at least five thousand years. Every single one has been a slave. All but one has been a warrior, having charms and curses at his fingertips that can turn you inside out or shoot you to the moon without an air pack. You are a distraction or a means to an end. Don't fool yourself that they care." I hesitated, thinking of Al. "They have thousands of years of experience in luring, tricking, enslaving," I said, distracted by my thoughts. "That there are laws now only makes it easier to fool you," I finished, bitter and jaded.

They said nothing, waiting for something they could use to make a big mistake with. "Okay." I sighed heavily and glanced at my phone. "Maybe it's time for some questions."

They shifted as if reluctant to say anything. I wished I hadn't finished my coffee so I could hide behind it, but as I gazed at my cup in the trash beside the others, I frowned. If Sikes had been getting his coffee at Junior's, there might be enough DNA residue on the cup to make a finding charm. I could *prove* Dali had him—and then what?

I slid from the table, a risky idea trickling through me. I was going to have to take care of Hodin. Hodin's incarceration would be one hell of a lever. Maybe large enough to bribe them into behaving, or at least letting Melody and Sikes go. Warming, I pulled the trash bag with its accumulated cups from the can. "Fine," I said as they stared at me as if I was nuts. "If you don't have any questions for me, I have one for you. Do you know if Professor Sikes gets his coffee down by the waterfront?" No one said anything, and I set the liner bag with its accumulated trash on the table, the bells on my sash jingling. "Are these Sikes's?" I asked, giving it a little shake.

"Mmmm," I said when they remained silent. "I can't teach you to survive a demon when you are hell-bent on ignoring my advice." I froze as the words left me, thinking that was exactly what I had done with Al. "But maybe if I can get Sikes back, he can," I continued, an ugly reality overwhelming my annoyance. "I'm pretty sure I know where your professor is, but I have to prove it if I'm going to have any chance to cut a deal for his release. And for that, I need to know if these are Sikes's cups or not."

"Those are his," Tony said, his curiosity apparently getting the better of him. "But you just said not to make a deal with a demon."

The trash clattered as I pulled the bag closer, worry a dull wash through me. "You, no. Me? I am a demon. Even so, I'm going to need every trick in the book, and some that I make up. Getting demons to adhere to arbitrary rules is like training a dragon. You can't make them do anything they don't want to do. But you can move a mountain if you find the right lever." *And Hodin is going to be my lever,* I thought, because I could not allow Dali to think he could trick university personnel into serving as his staff with impunity. And right after I introduced him to Keric, too.

"You're going to rescue him?" one of the guys said, and I sighed.

"Maybe. If I can fit it in my schedule. Class dismissed." I picked up my bag, and then the trash liner with the coffee cups in it. Bells ringing, I walked out, bag over my shoulder, trash in hand.

God, I miss Jenks.

I WAS TICKED, ANGRY IN A WAY THAT I HADN'T BEEN SINCE I was at camp and Trent stole my best friend, luring her into liking boys and leaving me behind. The bells on my sash jingled as I went up the church's front stairs, my book-laden, suit-bulky bag heavy over my shoulder and my lavender heels in hand. My stomping lost a lot of impact seeing as I was still wearing those scrumptiously silent demon shoes, but the bells made up for it.

"Rachel?" Trent called from behind me, the sound of his car door slamming loud as I pulled heavily on the nearest line to bring in enough raw energy to fry the sun in case Hodin was stupid enough to be here. As promised, Trent had met me after class, but I'd been in no mood for a late lunch and we'd driven to the church in our separate cars. After I made some charms, I was going to confront Dali. Unless Hodin was here. That might shift my kicking-ass schedule.

"Hey! Hodin!" I shouted as I opened the door and strode in. My hands ached with power as I tossed my heels into a corner by the stairs and scanned the dusky foyer. Frustrated, I yanked my wadded-up suit out and added it to the pile. It had been a bad idea and I was going to donate it. I was not that person anymore, and I never would be again. "Hodin! I want to talk to you!".

The light dulled as Trent closed the door behind me. He reached for me and I pulled from his grip, walking into the sanctuary bright with late-afternoon sun. "Ah, Rachel?" he said as he hustled to keep up with me. "Is yelling the best course here?"

"I'm from the Midwest. It's how we start." My hands began tingling, all the way to my toes. Hands on my hips, I scanned the rafters for a crow. "Ho-o-odin!"

I snapped my head around at the rasp of dragonfly wings, but it was just Jenks.

"Tink's titties, Rache," he said as he hovered before me. "He's not here. Stef either."

Lips pressed, I dropped the bag of trash on the couch. "Are you sure?"

He shrugged, and I eased off on the line. Beside me, Trent sighed, clearly appreciating the lessening of power crackling between the walls.

"If I'm making a finding charm for Sikes, I can make one for Hodin, too," I muttered. The son of a bastard had played me. Played me right from the start. I didn't know which bothered me more, that I let him, or that everyone told me he'd do it and I didn't listen. *Innocent until proven guilty is going to get me killed.*

Pissed, I strode to the hallway. There was probably something in his room to make a charm. With it, I'd at least know if he was skulking about in the church, spying on me.

"Rachel, no!" Jenks and Trent shouted as I reached for Hodin's door.

There was the barest hint of warning, and then I gasped as a static pop of stored energy jumped the gap, flinging me across the narrow hall to slam into Stef's closed door. Power crawled over me, pinching at my elbows and knees. It hurt to breathe, my chest spasming. Disoriented, I shoved the energy down into the earth, but my hair was still on end, and I blinked, trying to see. *Huh. I'm on the floor.*

"Ow . . ." I whispered as Trent's cool hand touched me, pulling the excess energy from my cells in a gentle wash. Again the smut coating me tried to jump to him, and I scrambled to hold it back, shoving it down and mentally sitting on it.

"Are you okay?"

He held my face in his hands, and I blinked to bring him into focus. "Yeah?" I said, actually seeing the excess power in my exhalation as if it was a warm breath on a cold day. It was hard to see past Jenks's sparkles. At least, I think they were his sparkles.

"Didn't you see the ward on it?" the pixy shrilled, furious with worry. "You think he walks away and leaves his door unlocked?"

I peered up at them as the room spun and settled. "Good thing I didn't touch it." Breath shallow, I looked at my hands, wondering why they weren't red. "Wow."

"Wow?" Trent cupped my elbow and hauled me upright. "That could have killed you."

If I had touched it, maybe, but I hadn't. Dizzy, I leaned against the wall, hand at my middle. Trent's eyes were pinched in worry, the expression mirrored in Jenks's face as the pixy hovered beside him. I felt as if my muscles were humming, and I squeezed another wad of energy from the spindle in my head, shoving it back into the line. A shudder shook me as the excess power lingering in my cells shifted into my neural net as if by osmosis, filling my spindle again. If I hadn't been my own familiar and been used to holding large amounts of energy, I probably would have fried myself. "Son of a fairy-farting whore," I lisped as I dumped that energy, too. "I think I'm okay. I need some water."

Gaze down, I wobbled to the kitchen, one hand on the wall, one on my middle. It was getting better—better enough that I was starting to feel stupid.

"Hey, ah, Rache?"

I waved listlessly at Jenks hovering at my ear. Trent was

behind me, ready to catch me if I fell. "Water," I mumbled. My mouth felt like sawdust, and I shuffled to the sink, turning on the tap and drinking straight from the steady stream of cool water.

Water splashed, and I slowed, starting to use my hands as a cup. I was spotting my robe, and I wondered if it and the insulating shoes had helped to save me.

"That's better," I said when I finally came up to find Trent and Jenks staring at me. Getty was there, too, sitting on a spool of red thread as she worked on a quiver of tiny arrows. "I am such an idiot," I muttered, and Jenks's wings clattered, a smile of relief finding him.

"She's okay now," he said, then darted to Getty.

I yanked a dish towel from the rod and dried my hands and chin. "I can't believe—" I started, then frowned at Trent. "Yes, I can. Al was right to put me in Alcatraz for uncommon stupidity. Hodin played me, and I let him."

Expression wry, Jenks looked at the ceiling. "Which he knows you know since Al tried to eat him," he said, and Trent winced.

"I've always found it easier to subdue a problem when he or she doesn't know he or she is a problem," Trent said. "I have a charm to push him into the open if he's lurking. And if he's not already here, the bell will ring if he does return."

I nodded, but in all honesty, if Hodin was lurking in the church, he'd be laughing his ass off at me for slamming myself into the wall. Listless, I looped the dish towel on the rod and went to sit at the eat-at counter, shifting the stool to face Trent before hiking myself up.

Clearly anxious, Trent rocked from foot to foot, gazing about the room to make sure nothing was too close. Stance firm, he pulled on the line, wisps of hair floating as he pooled a ball of energy in his hand, the raw red power shifting to gold as he gave it purpose. *"Ta na shay . . ."* he sang, low and pulling. *"Dondola persoma,"* he intoned, voice rising and falling as if he was a monk singing to God, and the ball in his hands expanded. *"Dondola . . ."* he sang, arms gesturing outward until the glowing sphere widened, flowing over Jenks and pushing his dust into little eddies as it passed him.

"Perso-o-oma," he crooned, and I reached to touch it as it neared me.

"Ta na sha-a-ay . . . Dondola," he continued, and I frowned as my hand didn't go through, but hit an invisible wall.

"Ah, Trent?"

But he didn't hear me, brow furrowed in concentration. *"Perso-o-oma, ta na shay . . ."*

The bubble in his hands expanded in a smooth wave, shoving me right off the stool.

"Hey!" I shouted, arms pinwheeling as I twisted to find the floor in a controlled fall. "Gosh darn it, Trent!" I shouted from the tile, my robe hiked up to show my knees.

Jenks hovered, laughing silver sparkles as Getty frowned at him from the edge of the counter. "Way to go, Cookie Man," Jenks said, and I got up, feeling even more stupid.

"Rachel, I'm so sorry." Trent lurched to help and I waved him off before he touched me and that smut tried to coat him. "I should have thought of that. Come here."

"Why? You want to shove me down twice?" I muttered as he stood the stool up instead.

Trent's smile went soft, and he pulled me into a resisting hug. This time, the smut stayed put, and I felt myself relax as he gentled me to him. "I forget sometimes that you are a demon," he said. "Turn around. Your back to my front."

Jenks sniggered, watching us. "You two want to be alone?"

"Shut up, Jenks," I muttered, and he laughed all the harder—until Getty gave him a look and he stopped.

"Let's try it together," Trent said, his chin all but resting on my shoulder. A quiver went through me as his arms wrapped around my waist and a trickle of energy spilled into me. It was from Trent, and my mood softened even more. "I sing," he whispered, his breath warm on my ear, "and you make the bubble. If we both have a part of its construction, it won't exclude you."

My eyebrows rose, and I settled into him more firmly. "Oh! Okay."

"*Ta na-a-a shay . . .*" he sang softly, and I let the energy from him flow through me, cupping my hands and letting it grow. "*Do-o-ondola. Persoma-a-a-a.*"

My pulse quickened as a strange sort of feeling grew between my palms. I wasn't doing anything, and yet, there was the spell in my hands, coated with his aura.

"*Dondo-o-ola,*" he whispered. "*Ta na shay.*"

Slowly the bubble widened until we were both inside. Beaming, I spread my arms and sent the bubble out, flowing over Jenks and Getty, taking in the kitchen, the porch, the front foyer, and even the belfry in one glorious swoop.

Trent's hold on me was tight and firm, pure and real. We both jumped as the bubble found the reach of the church's demon-alert circle and the energy landed there with a thumping sensation as if to say here, and no farther. Trent's singing slowly subsided, and I turned in his grip, my arms lacing about his neck. God, I loved it when he spelled. His entire being shifted, became dangerous, wild, and unpredictable.

"Thank you," I said, his hungry look warming me clear through.

"Ahem," Jenks said, clearing his throat. "I say again, should Getty and I go?"

I reluctantly stepped back, Trent's fingers making tingles as they slipped away.

"I'm leaving anyway," Getty said, her high voice sounding both new and right in the church as she stood, her newly outfitted quiver and bow in her hand.

"Leave?" Jenks spun in midair, his sparkles a disbelieving orange. "How you going to do that, Miss Snapped Wing?"

Expression smug, Getty shot a thread-tied arrow to the door, fastened the free end neatly on the spigot fixture, and zip-lined down to the handle.

"Don't go out there!" Jenks rose up, dust a vivid silver. "I can't protect you out there!"

Getty eyed him from atop the door's handle. "Then get

your lily-white ass over here," she said. "Someone has to get those fairies to string sentry lines. You're not doing it."

Jenks's wings cut out and he dropped three inches before recovering. "You want to work with the fairies? Damn, girl," he swore, clearly pleased. "Alley-oop," he added, swooping over to her and scooping her up and flying her out in an assist. With a tiny hush of sound, the knot at the sink untied and the thread raced after them. Pulled into motion, the spool of thread spun and wobbled, falling to the floor until the thread ran out and was gone.

My fond smile faded as I went to pick up the empty spool and set it aside. Depressed, I sat with my elbows on the counter, my breath slow. I felt safer in Trent's spell, but that didn't change the fact that I had been dumb enough to trust Hodin.

"Do you know why pixies don't allow dark newlings to live?" I said. "Al once told me the tradition started because they were never sure if it might be Hodin. All demons can be what they want, but Hodin is the only one who takes it to such an extreme that you can't tell the real from the fake. I think he wants to be someone else, relishes it, while the rest would rather die than be someone they are not even for an hour—even when it would be to their benefit." I took a shuddering breath. "My head hurts," I whispered, pushing my fingers into my forehead when Trent's hand traced a silvery path across my shoulders as he went to the cupboards. "And I'm a fool three times over."

"For believing the best in a person?" he said, voice muffled as he rummaged under the counter. "That they are innocent until proven guilty? That's not being an idiot."

I looked up at the soft clang of a metal bowl hitting the counter. "It is when everyone tells you otherwise. Al was right. I didn't listen." Depressed, I turned to the wide windows and the bright garden. There were two shimmers of dust out there twining as one. *Give her a kiss, Jenks,* I thought. *Love her. She will love you. Matalina would want you to be happy.*

Grimacing, I put my head on the counter. "I have no idea

what I'm going to do," I said, feeling my words come back to me in a hot breath even as the air-conditioning shifted the hem of my robe and cooled my ankles. "Stef is in danger because I kept my mouth shut. Hodin is trying to take my subrosa position. I have *no* idea how to convince Finnis that Constance is still in charge. I can't use that wand. It's bad enough that I used it on Pike's brother. It's going to take a reflecting telescope from Atlantis to even hope to reverse it."

"Seriously?"

"Yes, I'm serious," I muttered, head still down. "Meanwhile, I'm coated with smut and have nothing but takeout cups to make a finding charm to prove that Dali tricked Sikes and some poor librarian into signing contracts." *And my birthday is tomorrow. Yayyyyyy!*

"Do you have any coconut?"

I pulled my head up to see that Trent had the flour, sugar, and a carton of eggs on the counter. No cookbook, though. "Are you even listening to me?"

Beaming, Trent leaned to give me a quick kiss. "No coconut? I'll make chocolate chip."

I slumped. "My life is falling apart, and you're making cookies?"

"Your life is not falling apart." Trent opened a drawer and took out the measuring cups. "Stef is not lost. She's surviving a hard life lesson. We will find her and help her. Yes, Hodin is trying for the subrosa position, but we know his goal and can act accordingly. Pike is no longer in jeopardy and is healing." He unwrapped a stick of butter and dropped it into the bowl, warming it with a thought until it sagged into just the right softness. "My lawyers have triggered the malicious intent to delay clause. I won't lose the property now even if it takes two years. Jenks . . ." Measuring cup in hand, he glanced into the garden.

My smile was both fond and full of heartache. "Jenks is taking a couple of sick days."

"He'll be back," Trent said as he added a cup of sugar, then spilled in a little more. "If you need him, Getty can stay with Jumoke. She'll be safe and Jumoke could use the help."

But his confidence wasn't catching, and I was depressed. "I look like a dark practitioner," I whispered.

"Your new smut?" Focused, Trent stirred the warmed butter and sugar into an even paste. "Actually, I'm surprised it took this long for the demons to renew their practice of tricking people into servitude. They simply need a re-minder it's more fun to play in our sandbox than lord over it. Bullies have no friends, and they have a charming, des-perate, hidden need to be accepted. You know Hodin's intent. We're here to help. What's step one?"

The scent of sweetened butter made my stomach rum-ble. "Find Hodin and yell at him," I said, but that wouldn't accomplish anything. Everything on Trent's list seemed insurmountable, and I dragged my bag closer, taking out Newt's and Dali's books to find my phone. Calling the I.S. about Professor Sikes and Melody was far from the top of my to-do list, but it was something I could easily cross off. "I'm calling the I.S."

"That's my badass runner." Trent glanced in admiration at the seven demon tomes stacked up beside me. I'd told him about Dali and Al recovering their books from the li-brary and that Newt had bequeathed hers to me, but he had yet to make the connection between that and his own miss-ing tomes. *I* wasn't going to bring it up.

"Al is talking to me again," I said as I looked for Doyle's number. I hadn't put him in as a contact, and finding him was going to be one long scroll. "I located the original ver-sion of the curse I put on Pike's brother—complete with countercurse." I realized I could still smile. "Walked right out of the library with it," I added, glancing lovingly at my four new books. "If I can find a reflecting telescope from Atlantis and break the magic, Brad might not press charges, seeing as he was trying to kill Pike at the time." You don't tell on me, and I won't tell on you. Oldest form of currency on the planet. Or maybe the second.

"New curse books. Good." Trent coughed at a puff of

flour, unaware that I was ogling his physique between thumb swipes up. "I still can't find mine." And then he hesitated, his eyes narrowing on my stack.

"Sorry," I said when he figured it out. "Now that Hodin and I are on the outs, I don't have a problem trading him for Sikes and Melody," I added, finally finding Doyle.

"And your smut?" Trent prompted sourly, but I wasn't sure if his mood was because his books were gone forever, or that Al and Dali had sidestepped his security procedures without his knowledge. *Welcome to my world, my love. . . .*

"I'm going to forcefully ask Hodin to take it, along with anything I get from the countercurse. He knew it was dark magic and hid it from me."

Trent smiled. "There you go."

I never thought I would ever call Doyle, and I listened to the phone ring with a feeling of nervousness. A woman answered, which didn't surprise me. "Hi, this is Rachel Morgan. Is Detective Doyle available? I have information about the missing university professor."

"Just a moment," the woman said, and then I heard distantly, "Sir? It's a Rashel Morgana. Something about a missing person."

"I don't know a Rashel Morgana." Doyle's voice came even softer. "Why is she calling me about a missing person? Transfer her upstairs."

Brow furrowed, I pulled the phone closer. "Rachel Morgan!" I shouted, hoping Doyle's vampiric hearing would catch my voice. "It's Rachel. I'm calling about Sikes. The missing university professor!"

"Morgan?" Doyle said, voice louder, and then a soft crackle of the phone shifting to his hand. "Yeah, I'll take that." There was a hesitation, and then, "Mor-r-r-r-gan," eased out of the phone's speaker like an oil slick. "I am both surprised and somehow not."

"Hi, Doyle. Hey, I've got some info on that missing ley line professor."

The man snorted. "I'm not your I.S. contact. I don't work for you. You don't pay me."

"Sure you are!" I said, remembering him serving me a warrant a few months ago. Twice. "And what are you complaining about. None of my flunkies get paid."

Doyle chuckled, and the gritty sound of the spoon against the bowl hesitated as Trent muttered, "Flunky?"

"I think Sikes signed a bad contract and is stuck in the ever-after," I said. "Has a report been filed?"

Doyle sighed, and then I heard the tapping of keys. "Yes. He's been missing since Friday. Mmmm. How did you know? It hasn't been released."

Doyle's low voice tripped down my spine to leave shivers. "I'm teaching his class. Temporarily," I added, deciding not to ask about Melody. "I have to verify it, but I'm pretty sure he's been taken by Dali, who coincidentally quit his barista job about the same time."

"Rachel, I am not in a position to—"

"I'm going into the ever-after to see if he's there after I whip up a finding charm," I blurted. "Unless the I.S. already has a runner going out?" I added sweetly. "If I find him, can you get me a warrant?"

"For a demon?" Doyle said, aghast, and I smiled at Trent.

"No, for Professor Sikes. A parking ticket? Failure to renew his witch license? Anything that I can use to legally yank his ass back across the lines."

"Mmmm." Doyle was silent as he did a little more clicking at the keyboard. "Are you aware that he's suspected of practicing dark magic?"

I slumped, not surprised. "No. Can I bring him in for that?"

Doyle chuckled, and not in a nice way. "No. If he's a dark practitioner he's a write-off."

"If," I said quickly. "You don't know that he is. Come on, Doyle. Wouldn't it be nice if I owed you a favor? It will take ten minutes for you to invent a reason for a warrant."

"And three days to get a judge to sign it," Doyle muttered. "What part of 'he's suspected of dark magic' don't you get? No one is going to do anything."

Trent's eyebrows rose, and I shrugged. This was where I was at, and if it got me what I wanted, then so be it.

"Besides," Doyle continued, voice sly. "Finding charms are illegal without permission or a court order. You have neither."

Yeah, they were technically illegal without permission, but no one had ever minded before. Resolute, I said nothing as Trent stirred in the chocolate chips until finally Doyle sighed. "I'll see what I can do," he said, and I beamed.

"Thanks, Doyle. You're a prince."

"Good God," Doyle muttered. "I'm working for the witch."

The connection ended, and I set my phone down.

"The professor first. Interesting," Trent said as he searched about for the cookie tins. He wasn't anywhere close, and I slid from the chair to get them. This was not the lunch we had planned, but I was nothing if not spontaneous when it came to cookies.

"What would you have done first?" I asked, a flash of guilt for Stef wrapping around my heart. But Stef was either at work and would be home later or, more likely, she was with Hodin. In either case, she was fine for the moment. My life was in triage, and the professor was the easiest thing to start on until the real help arrived.

"Me? I would've begun searching my new curse books for something to befuddle Finnis with. But I don't have a potential in with a demon named Al."

I wasn't exactly sure how much sway I had, either, and I set the cookie sheets beside the bowl of dough before running a finger around the edge to pick up a wad. Trent made a feint with the spoon to drive me off and I fell away, feeling sassy with my stolen cookie dough. Hips swaying, I went to the oven.

"Doyle needs time to work," I said as I set it for 350. "Those cups I brought home should make a good finding charm for Sikes. If he's at Dalliance, they will ping on him. If I'm lucky, Melody will be waiting tables, too." I leaned against the counter, the sweet taste of cookie dough light in my mouth. "Maybe if I return Dali's books he'll tell me why this smut isn't soaking in. I'm tired of having to yank it back every time someone touches me."

"Oh," Trent said, as if only now realizing it.

"Honestly, Trent, it nearly jumped to one of my students when I took his circle. It wants to leave me. Have you ever heard of that?"

"No." His back to me, Trent pushed identical-size wads of dough off a spoon. "Sounds like a bad curse. I'm sorry your class didn't go well."

I touched my silky spelling robe, feeling myself warm. "I never said that."

"You never said anything, meaning it didn't go well."

Shrugging, I went to the silverware drawer for a spoon. "Sucky and good all at the same time." *Al, you were right about the robe.* "They are so naïve," I complained, and Trent chuckled. "They have no idea how deep the water is. I tried to scare them into becoming art majors, but I think it backfired."

For a moment, there was the scraping of metal on metal, and then Trent said softly, "Just because Hodin—"

"It's not only Hodin. They all suck," I interrupted sullenly. "Except maybe Al, and I'm not all that sure about him, either." Bothered, I scooped out another ball of dough and ate it. "All of them trying to be so clever that you can't trust them to hand you an umbrella in the rain."

He chuckled, and my lips pressed together. "It's not funny."

"I'm not laughing at you," he said, but it sure felt like it. "I'm delighted. You're not scared. You're exasperated with them. It's a healthy place to be. I'm glad Al is talking to you."

Relenting, I scooped a third wad of dough out, and Trent pointedly moved the bowl out of my easy reach. "Me too." I paused, my thoughts on a mad-dash spelling session followed by a swordplay of words with Dali for Sikes and Melody's return. "That curse Hodin tricked me into using is awful," I said as I shuffled through the stack, taking down and opening the book in question. "I can't use it again. It's stripping Pike's brother's entire memory, working from today backward. He can pass it on to his kids, too," I added, and Trent's lips parted in horror.

Standing at the counter in my spelling robe, I flipped to the proper page, feeling ugly. "I have to fix this," I said as I looked at Newt's hate and anger given devastating direction. "The impetus for the smut to leave its maker must be written into the curse, because I've never seen it act like this before."

Trent took two trays to the oven. "Maybe it's not demon," he said as he slid them in and set the timer. "It sounds elven."

I winced, recognizing Newt's handwriting, recognizing the feel of the power she'd used to inscribe the words. "No, it's Newt's," I said reluctantly. The anger Newt must have felt when she crafted this had to have been unreal. No wonder she had dosed herself into a half-mad, forgetful existence.

But I managed a smile when Trent came forward, handing me the last, dough-filled spoon. The pages glowed under his touch when he turned the book to himself, and I watched his brow crease. "It seems to me," he said, "as if you're using the mirror from the telescope as a scrying mirror. I'd bet that any high-quality mirror would do, and at the time this was written, Atlantis might have been the best place to get them."

"You think I can break the curse?" I said as I cleaned the sweet dough from the spoon.

"If we find Brad before he engenders a child with anyone and passes it on, yes."

Relieved, I tugged him closer, my dough-filled spoon carefully held away as our arms wrapped around each other. For a moment, we just stood there, taking strength in the certainty that I loved him and he loved me as the scent of chocolate chip cookies became obvious.

"That leaves the amulets to find Sikes," I said as I reluctantly pushed back, my contentment slowly fading. "And Melody, maybe. Dali might give me both if I give him Hodin in a bottle."

Trent's head bobbed as he took the bowl to the sink and filled it. "Have you given any thought to petitioning for access to the war-curse vault? Hodin wouldn't know anything that's in there. You'd have the advantage."

"The demons' war-curse vault?" I echoed, uncomfortable as I sat on a stool and worked the cookie dough from between my teeth. "That's right. He was a captive and wouldn't know those curses."

The war with the elves that he not only sat out but worked against his own kin during, if Al and the rest were to be believed. Silent, I thought it over as Trent washed the bowl. If the demon collective was like a library, then the vault was the restricted book section needing both a password and an access code to get into. Unlike the demon collective with its stored curses, spells, and charms, I didn't have access to the vault. Just as well, seeing as, like everything else the demons made, the ancient prepped and stored curses were not free, and I stifled a shudder at the imagined smut even one curse from the vault would level on me.

"I don't know," I said as I slipped from the stool to drop the spoon into the sink. "The curses in the vault are like magic on steroids. They store them there for a reason. Al says the smut they created is what turned the original ever-after into that red-smeared hell that Landon destroyed. They're really nasty."

Trent washed the spoon and rinsed it. "So is Hodin."

"True." I pulled the drying cloth from the rack and reached for the bowl. "Al will know what might work and what might not get me into trouble. He's got access."

Trent took the dried bowl from me and tucked it under the cupboard where it belonged. "But not today," he said as he drew the towel from me and tugged me unresisting into his arms. "After you make Sikes's finding amulet, we are going back to my house for a ride in the meadow followed by a late-night swim. We haven't been riding in ages. Red has settled down. It *is* your birthday tomorrow."

I stood leaning against him and soaked him in. "Leave Al and Dali for the morning?" I said, deciding everything could realistically wait. Doyle might even have a warrant for Sikes by then. Sighing, I let my head thump into his chest and we rocked, the bells on my sash jingling as we drew strength from each other and in the assurance that we would find a way through this. "I bet I could find something in Stef's room to make a finding amulet focused on her," I said softly. "If I find Stef, Hodin will probably be there, too."

"Yes, a midnight prebirthday ride." Trent's voice rumbled up like distant thunder. "You and me and a saddlebag of wine, cheese, crackers. Both Red and Tulpa need a good run."

I sighed, both of us knowing that it was only a wish. I had too much to do.

"I wanted your birthday to be so special," Trent whispered, tugging me into him until I couldn't tell where his aura ended and mine began. My eyes closed, and I wished my life was different, but this was the path that had brought him to me.

"Thank you for being here with me," I whispered, and as he sighed, I felt his strength wash through me, warming us both.

I could do this without Hodin's ugly curse wand. Pike was mending, Ivy was on standby. Jenks was starting to be useful again, and even better, Getty might stay as our new security specialist. All I needed to do was convince Finnis that Constance was running Cincinnati, break the curse on Pike's brother, slough my smut onto Hodin, and hammer said demon into a bottle so I could offer him to Dali in exchange for Sikes and Melody.

All before my birthday. Swell.

CHAPTER

18

THE PRICK FROM THE FINGER STICK WAS AN OLD PAIN, AND I squeezed three drops of blood into the prepared potion. Seven amulets, one of them pixy size, sat waiting to be inoculated, and I smiled when the fresh scent of redwood blossomed from the cup-size cauldron simmering over the Bunsen burner. I'd taken the time to change out of my teaching robe into shorts and a black camisole, but I was still barefoot, and the cool air in the kitchen made my toes cold.

"Thank the Goddess the university cuts down on the custodial team during the summer," I said, my gaze sliding to the cups with Sikes's initials scrawled on them.

"And that Mark insists on names," Trent added. "Band-Aid."

I'd already surreptitiously wiped my fingertip clean with my thumb, and I eyed him as he unwrapped a self-adhesive bandage I hadn't even known he'd had in his pocket. "I haven't been sick since your dad finished tweaking my mitochondria."

The sterile wrapping crackled as he smiled. "Do it for me, then."

Feeling loved, I held out my hand and he put the unicorn-emblazoned bandage on, carefully wrapping it not too tight, not too loose. He clearly had them for the girls. "You do know I'll have to prick my finger again when I invoke it," I said.

He gave my fingertips a kiss. "And then I will have another Band-Aid for you."

Jenks's wings rasped, drawing my attention to where he and Getty had been going over the leavings from my spell prep. The small woman had insisted there might be something she could eat among the garden waste, but even she eventually admitted defeat, her thriftiness turned to unease by the candle wax, magnetic chalk, and salt-stained mortar and pestle.

"Jumoke has winter quarters in the conservatory, but they're outside now," Jenks was saying as I carefully applied half a cc of completed potion to the waiting amulets. "The rose garden, right, Trent?" the pixy added, his voice decidedly strained. Getty clearly wasn't buying that he had a dark-haired son thriving outside the city.

"It was." Trent was rinsing my spelling equipment, stacking everything in the sink for later. "But after they cleared out the aphids, they moved across the garden to set up a summer residence in the overhang of my spelling hut. Seems I have a slight rodent problem, and they want to be above-ground until their newlings can fly." Looking good in his casual lightweight shirt and slacks, he dunked his hands into my de-spelling vat of salt water. "Rachel, do you want to grab something to eat before we leave? Give them a chance to dry?"

"Sounds good." I hid a smile at Getty's orange dust, a mix of disbelief and distrust. "I'm going to put Newt's book away. Get some of my more mundane books to find something less ugly to hit Finnis with over hot dogs and chips."

"Please, Getty?" Jenks begged, and the woman spun, standing on the counter with the hem of her gray dress shaking. "I'm not going to leave you here alone, but I need to be with Rachel for her meetings tomorrow with Dali and Finnis. I'll come out there with you. Introduce you. It's just for a day. I'm not ditching you. The garden will still be here when we get back."

Getty turned, her expression riven. "Can you excuse me a moment?" she said, and before Jenks could answer, she looped part of her sash over a zip line and rode it to the far counter, where she stood at the window and stared at the early evening dusk.

Frustrated, Jenks stilled his wings. "It's only for a day!" he exclaimed, and her shoulders hunched.

Trent cleared his throat, uncomfortable. "Hot dogs and chips sound great."

"Thanks." I hung the amulets to dry from the cupboard knobs, then dunked my hands in the vat of salt water. Trent loved to grill, but I knew it wouldn't be simply hot dogs and chips. There would be chili for the dogs and spicy mustard followed by gourmet macaroni salad and imported small-batch beer ordered in from the nearby restaurant. "Jenks, can I talk to you for a moment about tomorrow's security?" I said as I picked up Newt's book, and the small pixy grimaced.

"Sure." Wings clattering, he rose, his gaze on Getty for one long, telling moment before he flew close. "I don't get it," he said softly, landing on my big hoop earrings. "I'm not asking her to leave. You need me, Rachel. And if this is some Tink-blasted excuse to try to convince me you don't, I'm going to pix you where the sun don't ever shine."

I glanced over my shoulder at Trent as I hit the hallway to the sanctuary, and he gave me a knowing look. "I need you. I need you like the desert needs the rain," I whispered, and Jenks's wings lost their angry sound. "I want to talk to you about Getty."

Jenks made a rude sound. "Yeah? She's driving me nuts, but at least she's not trying to knife me anymore."

My faint smile vanished when I passed Hodin's door and the book in my arm flared with a warning of pinpricks. "I think she's overwhelmed is all."

"About the church?" Jenks's voice brightened. "She'll get used to it. It's not always this chaotic."

"No." My mood softened as I paced through the bright sanctuary. Boots's food bowl was untouched, and I spared a worried thought for Stef. Maybe she'd taken her cat, too. "It's not the church. It's you."

"Me!"

I nodded, the draft from his wings shifting my hair. "I don't think anyone has ever asked her to stay, and you're falling over yourself to make sure she's safe. It's probably hard to take, much less trust that it's real."

"Of course it's real," he said, sounding offended. "I'm not about to . . ." His words cut off. "Tink loves a duck," he whispered.

"If I were her, I'd be scared that you're trying to get rid of me in a way that doesn't hurt my feelings. Or she's scared that you mean it and she might be valued for the first time in her life. She likes you. I think."

"She can't like me." Jenks lifted from my shoulder as I bent to gather my wadded-up interview suit, leaving the heels by the door. "I'm married."

"Jenks. I'm so sorry," I whispered, glad the dark hid my face. "But you aren't."

He was silent, the draft from his wings shifting my hair. "I gotta go," he said, and then he was gone, humming up the stairs before me, his dust almost nonexistent as he slipped through the crack in the door and probably into the garden by way of an open window.

"I am so sorry," I whispered as I slumped against the tight walls. No, he wasn't married, but he had been. Pixies died of grief when their spouse left them. There was no precedent, no map, nothing but his heart to tell him what to do, and his heart had been so full of Matalina that I wasn't sure Getty could fill the cracks.

I put a hand on the wall to guide me now that Jenks's glow was gone, but my steps hesitated at the loud thumping on the front door.

"Stef?" I called, pulse quickening as I turned. She

wouldn't normally knock, but we'd locked the front door and it only opened from inside. "I got it!" I yelled when I found the foyer, and then flung the door open.

"Vivian!" I exclaimed, hesitating at her severe frown. *My new smut,* I thought, but she wouldn't notice it unless she was using her second sight—and why would she bother? Regardless, something had set her off, and she was more angry than a wet pixy as she stood before me in the sun, looking uncomfortable in a pair of casual slacks and a light-weight top. Her diamond-encrusted coven Möbius pin gleamed, and she flicked her blond hair back, jaw set and her eyes lost behind a pair of trendy sunglasses. "Uh, hi. You want to come in?"

"Did you have a bad morning? Forget your coffee, perhaps?" she said, her high voice carrying down the street to where some kids were lolling in the shade with Popsicles.

"Uhhhh . . ." I stammered, surreptitiously hiding Newt's book behind me.

"I'm trying to figure out why you'd unload your shit-fest of a life on an entire room of students."

I felt myself warm, the cool draft from the nearby vent cold on my calves. "Oh."

"Oh?" she questioned. "*Oh?* Did you really tell them that Dali abducted Professor Sikes into abject slavery?"

"Ah, I might have?" I said, voice squeaky. "Do you want to come in . . ."

She took a step forward, but it was only to poke a finger in my general direction. "I thought you of all people would be able to handle this class in a bias-free environment," she said, and I cringed, feeling like a hypocrite. "That's why I asked you to teach it!"

"Well, maybe last week, but Dali—"

Vivian took another step forward, pushing me off the threshold and into the church. "I'm getting complaints!" she exclaimed from the stoop, and the kids began paying attention. "Were you *trying* to scare them?"

She had a point, but I didn't like being yelled at, and I

clenched my jaw. "As a matter of fact, I was. Did you notice how inexperienced they are?" I said, and her scowl deepened. "They need to be scared. And they aren't. I'm *trying* to save their lives."

"We don't teach philosophy. We teach how to recognize and avoid dark, illegal magic." Lips pursing, she leaned, trying to see what I was hiding behind my back. "You need to fix this."

"You want me to lie to them?"

She hesitated in her bluster and glanced at the curb where her car sat. "Detective Dalyn Doyle called me this afternoon for information about Professor Sikes. He says you're going into the ever-after to see if he's been illegally detained. Are you?"

Gee, thanks, Doyle. "Yes," I said as I put a hand on the doorframe to block her from coming in. "Tomorrow morning. If I'm lucky, Doyle will have a warrant for Sikes and I can haul him back across the lines. If Dali tricked him into signing a contract, I can contest it."

"Tomorrow?" Vivian touched the Möbius strip on her lapel as if it was a lodestone. "I'm going with you. Me, and anyone else from your class that I can convince between now and then."

"Are you crazy? I'm not taking twenty students into Dalliance," I said hotly.

"You are." Vivian's chin lifted. "You're going to show them that demons aren't monsters."

"I never called them monsters," I said. "I called them dangerous. And I am *not* taking them into the ever-after. I'm going to verify that Dali tricked Sikes and some poor librarian into signing something they shouldn't have. That's it."

But Vivian pushed closer, forcing me to retreat. She'd been trained since birth to lead, coming into her own when she'd taken the top position of the coven of moral and ethical standards. "If Sikes is there and they see their professor forced to wear a thong and sling drinks, then fine, dealing with demons is a bad idea. You're justified in your teaching method. If Sikes is not there, then you're wrong and you agree that demons are not the above-the-law force everyone thinks they are."

Great, either I look justified and the demons are a threat, or I look like a fool for overreacting.

"I can't believe you forcibly took that student's circle," she accused.

"I probably saved his life!" I exclaimed. Not to mention he said I was in my pajamas and he had ticked me off. "Okay." I put up a hand when her face reddened. "Vivian, I see your intent, but everything aside, taking high-level, clueless magic users curious about demons into the ever-after is a bad idea. It's like carting little piggies to market. They don't come back."

Vivian ran a hand over her head to slick her hair. "This will happen," she said, voice soft but no less demanding. "If you're afraid of repercussions, I will write up a letter of intent taking all responsibility."

Somehow I managed to swallow my sharp retort. I liked Vivian, but she was probably the only witch who might best me on her own, and her trying to force her will on me . . . rankled. "I'm not afraid, Vivian. This is a bad idea," I said, and she took a fast breath. "I'm not taking them!" I exclaimed. "I don't care if you hand me a get-out-of-jail-free card or not."

"There are laws," she said, her eyes lost behind her dark glasses.

"Laws they choose to follow because it's fun. Vivian—" I began.

"There are laws!" she interrupted.

"Which history shows they follow only when convenient or made to do so," I countered, and she seemed to back down, exhaling as she regrouped.

"Frankly, I'm surprised you aren't more amenable to this," she said, taking another tack. "Fostering a better understanding between two diverse cultures is your thing."

My jaw had clenched and I forced it to relax. I hated it when people used my own words against me. "This is completely different," I said as Trent eased up beside me and Vivian gave him a sharp nod. "I didn't make the ever-after as a field trip destination. I made it so the demons would have a place to be without being bombarded with all the crap in our lives. Somewhere without so much temptation as we muddle along in our pathetic lives looking for the easy way out of our problems. And you want to descend on them? Unannounced?" If the students *ever* saw Dali in his grease-stained robe making roast lamb, they'd never give him the respect he deserved.

"I don't think you see the balance everything is in," I continued when her frown deepened. "I hear what you're saying about fostering a new understanding, but the only reason demons agreed to follow the law is because it added a new dimension of difficulty to the games they play. Put too much temptation before them, and they will begin to test the waters. Don't you *dare* make me the enforcer of laws they follow out of convenience."

My pulse was fast, but I'd said what I wanted—what needed to be said. If the demons returned to their old ways of tricking people into servitude, my life would be nothing but one long battle. That wasn't what I wanted for me. More importantly, that wasn't what I wanted for them.

Vivian nodded, but my elation that she understood vanished when she said, "Tomorrow morning. Eden Park. Eight thirty."

"Eight thirty?" I echoed. The Turn take it, I wasn't even up then. "For little green apples, Vivian. You really don't get this, do you," I said as she spun on a heel and walked down the steps. "I am not going to be there, but I'll tell you what. If you want to come with me to see for yourself, I will take you to Dalliance right now."

"Now?" She jerked to a halt, her trendy sandals grinding on the cracked sidewalk.

"Now." I felt a wash of satisfaction at her sudden alarm. "Or are you afraid to go out there without twenty low-hanging fruits to distract them?" I added tartly, and her lips pressed.

"You are ready to go now?" She frowned as she looked at my shorts and light top in disbelief, and I nodded, backing up into Trent. He'd picked up my heels, forgotten by the door, and was holding them as if they were precious, not years out of date and too tight for my feet.

"Sikes's finding charms are almost dry," I said. "You want to come in and wait?"

Her eyes narrowed. "You should put on a spelling robe if you want them to take you seriously. I'll meet you at Eden Park."

You do that, I thought as I shut the door, my bluster dying when I met Trent's worried gaze. "Please tell me I didn't just invite the leading member of the coven of moral and ethical standards to a demon pajama party," I whispered, and he sighed, tugging me into a quick, earnest hug.

MY SHOULDER THUMPED INTO THE CAR DOOR AS TRENT took a corner fast and I looked up to see we were almost to the park. "Thanks for driving," I said as I hoisted my bag, still heavy with Dali's books, back onto my lap. I was hoping that returning them might get us around the rule that you had to dress appropriately for Dalliance or leave—not a problem if someone had put, say . . . that upscale New York bar into the jukebox. Lately, though, it had been all Mesopotamia and Greece; I didn't have any homespun robes or hemp sandals. The strict attire policy was the reason Dali needed his waitstaff to be high-level ley line practitioners capable of learning how to craft from nothing the hundreds of costumes needed, right down to authentic perfumes and hairstyles. That, and the demons got a kick out of ordering around magic elitists.

Trent smiled, his free hand giving mine a squeeze as we headed for Eden Park. He'd left his suit coat behind, the muggy heat having finally gotten to him, and he looked nice in the casual dress slacks and button-down shirt. No tie, and just enough stubble to pique my interest. The car's air was on full force, and it shifted his wispy blond hair as if the top was down.

"You have a lot on your mind," Trent said, and I winced. Sikes was sucking up my time, time I needed to uncurse Brad and find something new with which to handle Finnis. Even if we got in and out of Dalliance fast, it was going to be a very long night of spelling. *But I knew there'd be no midnight ride and picnic,* I thought as we slowed, searching for a place to park near Vivian's white convertible. She'd found the only slice of shade, and seeing her expensive car, a feeling of inadequacy pricked at me.

"I shouldn't have goaded her into coming," I said as Trent eased in between a VW Beetle and a monster truck plastered with Were graffiti.

"You didn't goad her," Trent said as Jenks checked his garden sword and refolded his red bandana. "You tricked her into coming here to verify a dangerous situation alone instead of with twenty vulnerable students. Want me to chaperone her?"

What I wanted was both of them to stay on this side of the lines, but I nodded, head down as I invoked one of Sikes's finding amulets, then the smaller one for Jenks. We'd stopped at a charm shop on the way to pick up half a dozen ley line–powered circle amulets. Just pull the pin and they would set a circle even if you couldn't tap a line. Priceless if things got sticky.

"Jenks, could you do a perimeter?" I asked as I held the tiny amulet out for him, and Jenks took it, adjusting his red bandana before humming off in a foul mood. He and Getty had argued over him leaving her alone in the church, whereupon the pixy had hidden herself in a saucy challenge. After five minutes of fruitless search, Jenks had given up, sourly declaring if he couldn't find her, Baribas wouldn't be able to, either.

Vivian had noticed us, the small woman already waiting by the ley line. I gave her a wave that she probably didn't see before I looped my bag over my shoulder and got out.

"Dali won't give them up for nothing," I said as Trent joined me and his arm curved about my waist, tugging me into him as we stepped out together.

"But you knew that," Trent said with a sigh. "We're only verifying Sikes and Melody's location and conditions of, ah, employment."

"Employment. Right." Pace holding a confidence I didn't feel, I crossed the grass with Trent, heading for the foot-bridge. The wind was hot coming from the nearby city, and the sky was a washed-out blue. The cicadas were an annoying scream, filling me with a sense of unease, a feeling made worse as Vivian turned to us and smiled. The woman looked as perfect as an uncut wedding cake in her professional suit, perfectly styled hair, and five-hundred-dollar sunglasses perched on her nose. Sighing, I felt a twinge of impostor syndrome.

Knock it off, Rachel, I thought as I hiked my book-heavy bag higher and resisted the urge to take Trent's hand. I was still in my shorts and camisole, but I now had on a pair of sneakers I could run in. Butt-kicking boots and leather would have been too hot, and besides, I was dealing with demons, and no amount of leather would protect me.

But Vivian's smile went stiff as she saw Trent beside me. "I didn't know Kalamack was coming," she said as he and I closed the gap. "Your business is settled, then?"

"It is. Thank you."

"Mmmm. How fortunate for Rachel."

Something didn't feel right as I scanned the park. But it was only couples walking panting dogs and sweating joggers dodging them. "Vivian, I changed my mind," I said, and Trent *almost* stifled a sigh. "I want you to stay here. If Dali has Sikes I'll do what I can and let you know. I goaded you into coming and I'm sorry."

The small woman frowned, clearly not used to anyone telling her no. Trent had been like that. Still was, actually. "Demons are part of this world," she said, her eyes hidden behind her black sunglasses as the hot wind shifted her straight blond hair about her ears. "I'm not going to cower on one side of the lines because they're bullies. Those young men and women in your class are the beginning of a new understanding. They need their courage restored."

"Courage?" I felt my face warm. "Vivian, just because you have the right to go fishing on a frozen lake at midnight doesn't mean you should or that you're especially courageous by relying on your magic to keep you safe. It means you're an entitled snot holding the delusion that you can overcome nature, someone who selfishly gives no thought to the lives of the people who will be called to rescue you when you fall in."

Trent cleared his throat, a fist to his lips to hide a smirk. Vivian's frown deepened, but I was too angry to care, and I leaned into the small woman's space.

"I want to be clear," I continued, "that I am going into the ever-after with you now so you won't do something really stupid by trying to bring my class here on your own."

"Your class?" she said, and Jenks darted up with a rasping of wings. They weren't my class, but somewhere between burning the syllabus and taking Tony's circle I had begun to feel responsible for them.

"Until Sikes returns, my class," I said, cringing inside. "And I take *offense* that you would think to risk their lives to promote your idea of equality. Equality doesn't exist between the paranormal species. There is *balance*, and by forcing them and yourself into the demons' scrutiny, you are throwing it out of whack. I'm not your personal rescue team, and I can't believe that you are using me as such. Go fishing for equality on your own time, Vivian."

"That's not what's going on here, Morgan," she said stiffly, and Jenks landed on my big hoop earring in a show of solidarity, his wings making a cool draft on my neck.

"No? Then back off and let me do this alone with my team. Fine," I added when her lips pressed in refusal, and I swung my bag around, looking to find those ley line circle amulets. "A piece of advice from someone who has survived the level of stupidity of what you're about to do. If a demon is nice to you for no reason, there is a reason. If he looks harmless, there is a reason. If he does magic or refuses to, there is a reason. We are going uninvited into their *home*," I added, hammering on the word. "You wouldn't do this if it was an undead vampire; I don't know why you are doing it here. Take this." I held out a circle charm. "I'd suggest not making a circle apart from a last resort. Most demons indulge a foolish trust. It will work even if someone hits you with a joke spell and you lose contact with the ley lines."

"I'm not taking that," Vivian said, clearly insulted, and for one brief moment, I thought I'd broken through and she would stay. Until she pulled herself straight and exhaled. "Let's go."

I began to protest—and then she vanished into the ley line. My shoulders slumped and I handed the charm to Trent instead. He wisely pocketed it. I knew he wouldn't use it, either—unless he had no choice.

"Laying it on a little heavy, aren't you?" Trent said as we stepped into the ley line and I shivered at the tingling heat that enveloped me. My new coating of smut seemed to dive deeper into my chi, and I felt ill.

"No." The jolt of raw power flowing through me made me shudder, and I ran a hand over my head to try to get my hair to lie flat. "Ready, Jenks?"

"Yep," the pixy said from my earring. "It's nice to be on the smart side of things for once. Tell me again why we're doing this, though?"

"Because I want to live in a world where we don't have to be afraid of demons," I whispered, and at Trent's nod, I shifted my and Jenks's auras to match the resonance of the line. I knew Trent would follow. This was the easy part. Getting back was the hard.

In the time it takes for a molecule to spin, we were there.

"Whoa," Jenks said, my earring swinging as I pulled up sharp. The expected grassy field stretching to distant, white-capped mountains was gone. It was rock and hard sand to the distant horizon. Purples and oranges melted together like ancient rivers flowing through the rock face, broken only by the occasional sage and low cactus. The late-afternoon sun beat down on us and our feet kicked up a haze of dust.

"Why does the ever-after look like Arizona?" Trent said from my elbow, and Vivian turned from the low rise hiding Dalliance. Takata's "Black Coin" was faint in the rising wind, and I realized someone had put my tulpa of the Arizona desert into Dali's jukebox. Not only that, but had gone on to allow the restaurant to encompass a larger-than-usual amount of space.

Vivian's lips pressed in her confusion. "What happened to the grassland?"

"It's still here." I squinted in the bright light, wishing I'd worn my sunglasses. "This is the tulpa I made to prove I was a demon," I said, and her lips parted in surprise. "My mom's car is probably where Dalliance usually is." I pointed to the rise where the loud music was coming from, and she remembered how to shut her mouth.

"I don't like Arizona," Jenks said, and my earring swung as he took off. "The pixies are crazier than June bugs out here."

"You made this?" Vivian said in awe, and Trent nodded, clearly proud of me. "It's enormous."

"I might have overdone it." I tugged my bag up, eager to give Dali his books. "They were stuck underground at the time, the ever-after polluted to a red-smeared hell. I wanted them to remember the sun."

"Who pulled it from your thoughts?" Vivian asked, surprising me that she knew that bit of tulpa lore, but she *was* the head of the coven of moral and ethical standards.

"Al," I said shortly, glad she'd lost her elitist attitude, even if it was likely only temporary. Only a female demon had the mental stretchiness to create a detailed enough memory to make a tulpa, and only a male demon had the mental stamina to sift it from her mind, teasing the tulpa from her psyche and then harnessing the memory into a solid construct. The opportunity to maliciously manipulate someone's thoughts when sharing mental space that close was easy—which might be why Newt hadn't made many tulpas. Dali's jukebox was filled with the memories created by long-dead demons—and a few from me.

"It knocked me out for three entire days." My eyebrows rose. "And then I nearly died getting rid of Ku'Sox." *Remember?* I thought mockingly, but she said nothing, not even a hint of guilt or gratitude as she scanned the distant horizon, her sunglasses as dark as sin.

Trent's thoughts were clearly on something other than psychotic demons as his arm curved around my waist. "Best. Vacation. Ever," he said softly, and I rested my hand atop his. Leaning closer, he whispered, "Something feels off. Might Dali know you're coming?"

"Possibly," I said, my gaze following Jenks as he shot straight up to do a wide scan. He had that small finding amulet with him, and I gave Trent mine, wanting both my hands free.

Trent frowned as the amulet glowed and flickered in his grip, squinting in the bright Arizona sun as he cast about. Sikes was here, but the amulet wasn't working well.

Resigned to hashing it out with Dali, I hiked my bag higher and followed Vivian to the top of the rise. My feet scuffed to a halt, and there it was, a big, blue four-door Buick where Dalliance would be. A red-and-white-checkered tablecloth was spread on the dirt beside it with two glasses of red wine and a bucket of fried chicken with the word *Dalliance* scrawled across it.

Dali stood at the open trunk, looking like a slightly over-weight traveling salesman from the fifties in dusty slacks, plaid shirt, and thin tie. The thump of the trunk slamming shut reached us an instant after it closed, the sound echoing in the wide, shallow ravine. Fists going to his waist, he stared at us, our three silhouettes and the glitter of pixy dust obvious as we stood at the top of the ridge.

"You shouldn't be here," I said to Vivian, and she huffed.

"I don't see Sikes or that librarian," she said bluntly. "Unless they are in the trunk." Head high, she started down the low incline with mincing, confident steps.

Trent glanced at the amulet in my hand in interest. "That they are in the trunk actually has some merit. You didn't get even a flicker from the amulets on the other side of the lines."

Frowning, I watched Vivian pick her way down. My arms were about my middle, and my foot jiggled.

"Well?" Jenks said as he hovered beside Trent.

"Friggin' work ethic is going to kill me," I muttered, then pushed into an awkward jog down the incline after Vivian, arms waving to distract Dali from the coven member.

"Dali!" I shouted as I pushed past Vivian. "I've got your books."

The old demon frowned at me, and I gave him a stupid wave to wait before I took Vivian's elbow and pulled her to a stop at the bottom of the incline. The proud woman yanked from my grip with a tingle of line energy, but she was staring at the memory of my mom's car made real, right down to the dent in the fender where I backed into a pole when I was eighteen. "Morgan made this?" she whispered, still in awe.

"Okay, you're here," I said, and Vivian's attention flicked to me. "Stay away from Dali. Either he has Sikes and Melody or he doesn't, but either way, he'd love to have you, too. 'Kay?"

Not waiting for an answer, I knocked her shoulder as I strode forward. If anyone could stand up to Dali, it would be Vivian, but she knew that, and that's why I worried.

"Hi, Dali. I should have returned these sooner but I kept forgetting," I said as I swung my bag around and let it thump on top of the closed trunk. "You put in Arizona?" I added, babbling almost, as I withdrew his books and extended them. "I've always wondered, does it work even at night, or is it a day-only tulpa?"

Dali took the books without answering, not even looking at them as they vanished. "Thank you," he said as he turned his attention to Trent and Vivian.

"Sorry it took so long." I smiled nervously. "Hey, ah,

you didn't accidentally take a librarian when you recovered your books from the library, did you? Name's Melody?"

"I know why you are here." Dali's red, goat-slitted eyes fixed on Vivian as Trent diverted her to the car. "But why is *she* here?"

A nasty smile blossomed on his face, and I scuffed my sneakers on the dusty earth. "I've been asking myself that same question. I've got a lot to do today, Dali. I know you have Melody and Sikes. I want to see the contracts."

Dali squinted at the faultless blue of the sky, a meaty hand dramatically to his chin. "Sikes and Melody," he said, voice distant as if in thought. "A librarian, you say? The other tall, dark hair, good with ley lines? I don't see either of them. Sorry."

"Dali," I protested, and the demon huffed confidently.

"It's hard to find someone who likes their coffee black with a side of demon lore," Dali said, and I grimaced. Damn it to the Turn and back. He not only had them, but was confident enough in his "contract" to flaunt it.

"Do you still have them? Did you sell them?" I glanced at Trent, who shrugged and tucked the finding amulet in his pocket. "Damn it, Dali, you know selling people is illegal." But I drew away, an icy drop of self-preservation chilling me when Dali made a low rumble.

"Nothing is illegal with consent, Morgan," Dali said, and then he jerked, his brow furrowing when Trent opened a car door and leaned in to pop the trunk from inside.

"Hey!" Dali shouted, and both Trent and Vivian jerked free of the car. "Get out of there! If you don't have a coin, you can't change the radio." But then Dali hesitated, his beatific smile making me shudder. "Unless Madam Coven Member would like to buy a coin with which to change the station?" He snapped his fingers, and I felt a tweak on the line when a dull, dented coin appeared in them. "First one is free."

"Seriously?" I said, but Vivian had already drawn away. I had yet to see a jukebox tucked behind the cacti, making me think that Dali had put the stored tulpas in the radio instead.

"No? Then allow me," Dali said, his voice dropping into a lower register.

Trent jerked in surprise as the vision of the Arizona desert dulled. Takata's music cut off in midstanza, and the air cooled and grew dark. I shuffled my feet, not surprised to find I was now standing on old, scratched floorboards. A cobwebby ceiling blocked the sun, and my nose wrinkled at the sour scent of old beer and cheap, scratchy lace. I was betting Sikes and/or Melody had been in the trunk and Dali had shifted everything to keep them hidden.

"Lord loves a duck, the stripper bar?" I muttered, slumping when Jenks darted to the back to search. There were no windows, which might be why Dali had chosen it. That, and it was probably the only tulpa he had at the moment besides my mom's car that didn't smell like lamb.

"No one likes it, which will help keep our conversation private," Dali said. Smile wide, he confidently moved his bulk behind the bar, now looking appropriate in his new purple, gold, and red pimp suit. I felt so out of control.

"Well, we fit in," Trent said from my elbow, but Dali's choice was making me nervous. He hadn't done it to make my life easier.

"Drinks on the house," Dali said cheerfully as Vivian briefly opened the door to see a cracked parking lot in the middle of a field of grass.

Brow furrowed in concern, Trent went to join Vivian. His hand trailing from my back left me with a feeling of solitude. *No such thing as a free drink,* I mused as Dali decanted a glass of red wine and set it on the bar, his solicitous attitude telling me there was no way in either reality that I would walk out of here with Sikes or Melody. I'd be hard-pressed to leave with Vivian.

"Did Rachel make this as well?" Vivian asked as she studied the stage, and Trent shook his head.

"Where are they? Kitchen?" If I was lucky, Trent would keep Vivian out of my way.

"Only a fool vouches for the behavior of another without the skill to enforce it," Dali said, and I stopped short. He was right, but if I didn't, who would?

"Rache!"

I looked up, relieved when Jenks dropped down. "Amulet pinged," he said, giving Dali a wary glance. "I found Sikes with Melody in the kitchen, cataloging his cookbooks."

I beamed at Dali. "Excuse me." Bag over my shoulder, I started for the kitchen's double doors. Until I ran nose-to-chest into Dali.

"No."

Jenks's wings hummed a warning as I rocked back, my pulse racing. I hadn't even seen him move. "I want to talk to them," I said, and Dali pulled his lips into an ugly smile.

"They are mine." Goat-slitted eyes flicking past me to Vivian and Trent, Dali snapped his fingers and a black envelope appeared in them. "A copy of their work contracts as requested. Be a dove and file them for me in Cincinnati's work visa office, mmmm?"

Frustrated, I took it, shoving it in my bag to give to Trent. If there was a loophole, his lawyers would find it.

"Leave," Dali said again. "You and your prying pixy. The coven member can stay. I'm hosting an event tonight and I'm out of party favors."

Son of a bastard . . . "Don't do this, Dali," I said. "I worked too hard to get you all back into the sun."

"What is it you really care about? Us, or your reputation?" Dali asked.

"You," I said, but Dali's next words went unsaid when two demons popped in, their grimaces of disgust becoming delight when they saw Vivian. Immediately Trent shifted to get between them, tense in warning as Vivian retreated to the stage. My pulse quickened, but Trent met my gaze, wordlessly telling me he had this. *God help us all if you don't.*

"Excuse me. My newest employee needs some coaching on proper greeting etiquette." Calling out to the demons, Dali strode away, a hand raised in acknowledgment.

"Vivian is not your employee," I protested. "Dali!" I

shouted, and he jerked to a stop, holding himself unmoving for three—long—heartbeats until he turned, his eyes fixed on me with the hatred born in a millennium of slavery. *Crap on toast* . . . "Please," I whispered, feeling utterly alone. "You agreed to follow society's mores. Tricking people into serving as your waitstaff isn't it."

"Perhaps you don't know your society's mores as well as you think."

I took a breath to protest, but he had already spun away, eager as he gave the demons now dressed in bell-bottoms and polyester a hearty greeting. *Damn it all to the Turn and back.* "Jenks, I'll get Sikes and Melody. See what you can do," I said, and Jenks bobbed up and down.

"You got it, Rache, but don't take too long." His dust a faint silver, Jenks flew off.

"Vivian!" I called. "You've seen enough. We're leaving."

But she only managed a step before Dali shoved his bulk between her and Trent. Three more demons misted in, driving Trent farther from Vivian. She was clearly their focus, standing in a tight-lipped anger as questions were raised about everything from her dress to how much line energy she could hold. I could feel the power in the room growing, and it would only be a matter of time until someone touched her and set her off.

"Damn you, Dali. Why can't you play fair," I whispered, my drive to find Sikes and Melody hesitating when a wave of gray mist rose atop the nearby barstool, condensing into Al wearing a wide-lapel business suit. Relief spilled into me, short-lived as he glanced over his shoulder at Dali jovially fending off the demons before Vivian.

Slipping from the stool, Al reached over the bar for a bottle of something amber and gold. "I understand you returned the books I stole for you from Dali," he said as he helped himself to a glass and poured himself a drink. "You didn't find them useful?"

Suddenly unsure, I shifted so I could see Al and the stage both. "I did. But if he was collecting his books from Trent and the library, it was only a matter of time before he showed up in my belfry. Al—"

"Bringing a Kalamack and a coven member into Dalliance?" he said, interrupting. The gold and amber in his tumbler swirled without mixing as he took a sip, eyeing me over his blue-tinted, wire-rimmed glasses. "What *were* you thinking?"

"She thinks you've been made safe by society's laws." I gestured at the stage in frustration, tensing when Vivian refused Dali's offered drink. Not a glimmer of magic wreathed her, and I thought it was the smartest thing she'd done all week. "She was about to cause me more trouble than bringing her here would," I added, pressing into the bar as the number of demons continued to grow, all of them fixated on Vivian.

"Mmmm, well, her mistake. Or perhaps yours." Al's nose wrinkled as bad seventies music began thumping from hidden speakers. "This is a foul tulpa. I don't know why Dali keeps it, except that we got so few new tulpas from Newt that they all have some sort of value."

Where are you, Jenks? I thought as I scanned the rafters. Vivian was practically pinned to the stage, and as I watched, she scrambled up on top of it, not a hint of ley line energy showing as she held out a hand to keep the demons at bay. No one made the jump to join her there. It wasn't because they were afraid. She was on display, and I felt ill. "Will you excuse me. I need to get Vivian and Trent out of here before Dali steals them, too."

Al reached out, a surge of ley line energy washing from me to him as his fingers clamped on my elbow and our balances equalized. He let go, and I began to breathe again. "We don't talk nearly enough, itchy witch."

I froze, gut in knots. He didn't want me to intervene? Why? Was he in on this?

"Shall I pop you home, love?" Al added, and I stared at him in horror. Dali stealing people I might understand, but Al? Okay, it had once been his livelihood, but he had changed, hadn't he? "You will want to preserve your plausible deniability," he added, smiling.

"Rache!" Jenks called as he darted to me, bringing with him the scent of burnt toast. His wings were singed, but he seemed okay if a little frazzled as he beat a fizzling ash off his arms. "We have to get out of here," he said, his dust a worried green, and I nodded.

Al chuckled, the sound going to the pit of my soul, chilling me. "Rachel, yes. Kalamack, perhaps. Vivian Smith? No. Dali likes her. Apparently *Professor* Sikes can't keep up with some of the requirements and Madam Melody is only interested in cataloging his considerable library."

"Vivian knows better than to sign any dumb contract," Jenks said, but I was more than worried. Damn it all to hell. I could either fight for her and prove that demons were a certain and present danger, or abandon her and preserve the fragile and mistaken belief that demons were behaving themselves and the world was fair.

Vivian, I can't believe you did this to me, I thought, frustrated. She knew demons were dangerous, and sure, we both wanted society to accept them, but we both knew that you don't tease the tiger in the zoo with raw meat lest he follow his instincts and help himself. And because I was here, and a demon myself, I would be blamed for it—at the very worst time it could possibly happen.

The very worst time . . .

My head snapped up and I stiffened as the demons continued to shout music suggestions for Vivian to dance to. A faint, mocking smile was on the small woman's lips, not even a hint of defensive magic flitting about her fingers. She wasn't afraid, and my pulse hammered as a handful of thoughts coalesced into a new, really scary idea.

She hadn't crossed the church's threshold when she'd dropped that ultimatum on me to take her and the students into the ever-after at eight freaking thirty in the morning. What witch willingly gets up that early, coven member or not? Her colossally stupid plan to bring twenty students into the ever-after would get me blamed if they were abducted, her get-out-of-jail-free card or no. Not to mention her surprise that Trent had been free to accompany us—how had she known he was having business trouble to begin with? But her big tell was her attitude, standing there on the stage, not a hint of magic showing. She was overly confident. Even I had a light thought resting in the lines in case I had to do something fast.

Pulse fast, I turned to Al. He was staring at me, his eyes narrowed as he watched me figure something out. He didn't know. But it was obvious when you put it all together.

That wasn't Vivian. That was Hodin.

CHAPTER

20

CRAP ON TOAST. HOW MANY TIMES DO I HAVE TO MAKE THE *same mistake?*

"What is it, itchy witch?"

Al reached for me and I blinked, turning away lest he figure it out and I lose the element of surprise. It had to be Hodin. But I had to know for sure, and as the demons thumped the tables and demanded that Vivian strip, I silently walked to the other end of the bar.

As expected, Jenks hovered a moment, then followed me. "I need you to get a message to Trent," I whispered, feeling Al's attention on me. "He's not going to like it, but I need him to go to reality and call Vivian."

Jenks's pinched expression went to the stage, his dust shifting blue in confusion. "Her phone won't work here. I can get a message to her."

Glass shattered. I spun to see Vivian, tight-lipped as she dodged a thrown glass. The demons roared in delight at her scowl. There had to be at least thirty of them in here now, and I met Trent's worried frown from across the room. "I don't need to get a message to Vivian," I said as Jenks landed on my hand, wings shifting. "I need to know if Vivian is here or if she's still in reality."

Jenks spun to the stage, then me, his wings shifting into invisibility as understanding blossomed and his gold dust shifted to look like a living sunbeam. "Holy mother pus bucket!" he yelped, and then he dampened his dust, a mischievous slant quirking his lips. "It can't be Hodin. Her eyes aren't red. I can see past her glasses, and they are *not* goat eyes."

"He can change them if he wants. They all can. They don't because deep down they want to be recognized, especially when they are making trouble. Go," I said as a glass of beer hit the stage and Vivian's lip curled. "And keep your dust neutral. Once Trent is in reality, I want him to stay there. Got it? He sends you back to tell me if she answers her phone. That's it." I hesitated, meeting Trent's concerned gaze from across the room. He knew something was up. Hell, Al knew something was up, staring at me with his eyes like coals. "I'll be fine. Just hurry."

Jenks's wings sifted a conflicted blue and gold. "He won't like it. I know I don't."

"They aren't after me. Besides, Al is here. Go before someone touches her. Him. Whatever."

If he hadn't been inches away, Jenks never would have heard me. It had gotten loud. The demons were trying to get Vivian to do some magic, shouting to be heard over the raunchy striptease music. Finally Jenks nodded, his angular face creased as he flew a ceiling-high path to Trent. Breath held, I waited, watching Trent.

I knew the instant Jenks told him. The man jerked, his face pale and tight in refusal as he looked at me. My expression pinched, pleading with him. Half a bar away, Al got to his feet and started toward me. "Go," I whispered, and finally Trent began to edge to the door.

"What are you doing?" Al muttered at my elbow, and I jumped.

"You might want to put yourself in a circle," I said as I

scrambled up onto the bar. No one but Al noticed, and I gathered my strength, feeling ill as I pulled in the line until every demon in the place could feel it. A head turned to find me, then another.

"Mother pus bucket," Al whispered, and then he spun, suit coat furling as he scribed a circle on the floor with his toe.

"Dilatare!" I shouted, invoking a simple white charm.

The spell exploded outward, raising cries of annoyance and pulling every eye to me as they rocked back. My hair was a staticky halo. Line energy dripped from my fingers as I glared at them in the new silence. Even the music had cut off. Jenks and Trent were gone, but no one noticed. "You'd better know what you're doing," Al said as he dropped his circle and edged a few feet away from me.

Grimacing, I flicked a wad of unfocused energy at an incoming curse, bursting it before it got three feet from its maker. The second one found me, and black crawled over my hastily invoked protection circle until Dali yelled at them to knock it off before they damaged the bar. My knees were wobbly, and I didn't dare look at Vivian pinned down on the stage. They could shoot spells at me if they wanted, but they knew better than to really piss me off. *God, please. It has to be Hodin.*

"Vivian Smith is mine," Dali said as the last spell fizzled. Clearly pleased, he vaulted up onto the stage to leave a cautious eight feet between him and Vivian. Her lips were pressed in hatred, but her eyes were still hidden behind her glasses. "You have lost, Rachel Morgan. Even your elf has left you. Get off my bar. Go home. Warn them we are back and to be afraid of the sun as well as the night."

I was alone. My face was cold, and I locked my knees. *Trust me, Al,* I thought as I looked at him, trying to tell him I had a plan. Everyone was staring at me, waiting to see what I'd do. Al gestured for me to get on with it, and I took a slow breath.

"I'm not trying to tame you," I said softly, my gaze far from Vivian. I had to stall until Jenks returned. If I was wrong and that was really Vivian, they'd kill her thinking she was Hodin. "I'm trying to keep you in the game," I said, and several demons chuckled. "Every game has rules. You agreed to them. Don't screw this up."

Dali laughed, the bitter sound making me shudder. "Rules don't exist if you can't enforce them." He looked over the bar at me. "And you are outnumbered."

I fidgeted as a few low grumbles joined into a hum of background noise. They were not the frightened, powerless demons I had convinced last time. I had to give them an excuse to behave, one that would save their pride. Fortunately, some twisted logic might give me just that.

"You really want to turn the world against you over *her*?" I said, gesturing vaguely at the stage. "A single coven member?" I said, head shaking as if in disbelief. "No offense, guys, but wow. Right now you can walk anywhere, anytime, sun or moon. You can go shopping and drive the clerks mad with your endless questions they have to answer. You can get a driver's license and rack up points for bad behavior, and as long as you pay the fines they can't do anything because you belong to society and are following the rules.

"No, listen!" I said when several began to lose interest. "If you start a war with reality, you will win, and I'm sure you will all have fun proving your strength and punishing people who dare to stand up to you, but you're going to end up right where you were before, stuck in a magic-polluted hell, on the outside looking in. But can you imagine the news coverage you'll get when you misbehave and then willingly pay your dues? Or the frustration you will cause by finding legal loopholes to evade punishment? Doesn't that sound fun to you at all? That's what you are giving up if you start snatching people."

Most were shaking their heads, and Al sighed, thinking I'd lost my mind, but I needed to give them something to justify agreeing with me when I dropped the real kicker on them.

"Laws and rules are there to hobble true power," Dali said. "Why should we hold to your ideas of what is morally right and wrong?"

Because I'd given them a sun of their own and they'd already forgotten the night with no dawn. A low rumble of discontent began to rise, and I lifted a hand, acknowledging it. "I see your point," I said, glad I had a wall behind me even if it was mostly mirror and bottles. "I did accompany a highly valuable, very experienced magic user to the ever-after. It was stupid," I said, risking a glance at Vivian. "But if you let me walk out with her, I can give you something you all *really, really* want."

Al made a soft sound. It was the beginning of under-standing, no more, but it was enough. His weight shifted, and he began to look around, searching for a clue as to what I was doing, where I was going with this. All I knew for sure was that they were listening.

"What is it we *really, really* want?" Dali mocked as he stood beside Vivian, and I allowed myself a little smile.

"Hodin."

A smile curved over Al's face, and he leaned against the bar, shoving one of the encroaching demons away from be-tween us. It was a small move, but it was noticed.

Dali frowned, arms over his chest. "Hodin. Who you have vowed to protect even at the expense of losing your teacher." His gaze flicked to Al's new protective stance. "Perhaps we should address this arrangement you have with Hodin. Seeing as it's more than you and me here. With you gone, we could have a go at him. Take who and what we want. It's a big win-win—for us."

"Short-game, maybe." I walked down the top of the bar until I stood over Al, feeling like Newt all of a sudden. *I'm not alone, Jenks. I'm going to be okay—but hurry.* "Did Al tell you he drove Hodin from my church?"

Dali's eyes slid to Al, then me. "Are you breaking your word, Rachel Morgan?" he asked, the oily words practi-cally dripping threat. "To rescue a soul that isn't even yours? A demon's word is truly all he or she has. Disregard-ing it brings any number of penalties against you. Penalties you don't have enough to pay for." He smiled evilly at me, but I wasn't afraid. Breaking their word was exactly what they were doing, but in their minds, if there was no one to tell them different, it was permissible. That's how demon logic worked.

"My, oh my," I said lightly, and Dali's smile froze as Al chuckled. "I am in a hard spot, aren't I? All my allies out of commission or driven from me?" I fanned myself as the demons began whispering. "My subrosa position uncertain? If Vivian and I don't step from the ley line and back into Eden Park together, I'm sure to have the I.S. knocking at my door with a warrant for my arrest. And we *all* know how honest Rachel Morgan is. I'll go to jail. Oh, boo-hoo."

Dali squinted at Al. *I am not alone,* I thought again, hope welling up, not because Al was beside me, but because Al was beside me having no clue where I was going. He trusted me. And as I stood before all of them, I really, really needed that.

"She left herself an out," Al said, and the demons buzzed and whispered, vestiges of a past hatred blossoming anew on them. "She agreed to stand between us and Hodin concerning his decision to do elven magic. She never said she wouldn't put him in a bottle herself."

Dali shifted his bulk, head tilted. "And why would Morgan do that?" he prompted.

Al shrugged, but he hadn't joined me on the bar, and I knew his help was conditional on me actually having a plan. "He lied to her," he said simply. "As he lies to everyone. She outed his plot to rob her of her subrosa position."

"Before or after she lost it?" Dali asked as he scanned the crowded room. "Regardless, it doesn't follow that she is leaving with Vivian Smith, much less Sikes or my new librarian. We have a contract."

"Perhaps." I shrugged in a false nonchalance. "I propose a trade," I said, relief sagging through me when Jenks darted in, flashing me a bright green across the room in a pixy version of a thumbs-up. Al's eyes narrowed when he saw him, but the demon probably thought I was simply getting

Trent out of the line of fire. A quiver raced over my aura as Al began to ease power into himself, so slowly that no one else would likely sense it.

"You tear up Sikes's and Melody's contracts," I continued, forcing myself to not look at Hodin on the stage disguised as Vivian. "And I tell you where Hodin is."

Dali's attention shifted from me to Al. "It took us forever to pin him down. No deal. You put him in a bottle and we can talk."

My legs felt like water, and I locked my knees. I knew I should have eaten first. "Fine," I said, and someone guffawed. "If I'm to have a chance to put him in a bottle, I need access to the vault. I have to have something he doesn't, or I'll never catch him."

Dali made a low, evil chuckle. "You want access to a millennium of war curses, most crafted by our long dead, each holding enough hate and bile to destroy two realities? It would take an entire class of disposable flesh to buy access to our world-breaking curses."

My lips parted. Disposable flesh? He was talking about high-magic users. My students. He thought I'd give him my students to gain access to curses to catch Hodin so I could sell him to Dali to buy their promise to hold to our laws and not snatch people? What kind of backassward deal was that? Besides, I'd already gotten from them their promise to not steal people. I needed a way to enforce it. Like . . . say . . . the ability to put them in a bottle?

"What if I bring him before you?" I said, thoughts churning. If I put Hodin in a bottle, I'd have the clout to make them toe the line. Win-win. "If I do that, can I have Sikes, Melody, and your promise to cut this crap out? No more tricking people into servitude."

The demons were exchanging ugly glances. Al frowned as the call to take the deal rose up and was seconded, and in a wave of agreement, Dali put up a hand, silencing them. "They are mine, therefore it is my decision," Dali said, clearly thinking I'd never be able to bring Hodin before them. "No, Rachel. I will only give you Sikes and Melody for Hodin in a bottle. Until you do that, they stay here." His smile became ugly, reminding me of who he was. The friendly neighborhood barista had never been anything but an act. A means to this end, perhaps. An end that I was going to snip cleanly and leave no thread for them to pull.

"Fine. Let me hear it," I said as someone called for odds on a side bet and Al harrumphed, interested. "I need to hear that everyone agrees. If I bottle Hodin, you free Melody and Sikes, and no more luring people into servitude." I didn't dare look at Vivian, but Jenks was watching, and I knew the demon didn't have a clue I was onto him. *Where is Stef, you slimeball?*

Dali, though, squinted at me in distrust. I knew how he felt. If you think you're getting the better end of the deal, you aren't. "Not can, but *do* bottle him, Morgan, and yes, you have your deal," he finally said, and my held breath slipped out. "But you only get Sikes and Melody. You forgot to add Madam Coven Member to the deal. She is mine."

"I didn't forget," I said, smug as I turned to Hodin. "That's not Vivian. That's Hodin."

"What!" Dali exploded, and in a thundering clap of sound, the diminutive shape of Vivian vanished in a swirl of yellow and green.

An angry howl of a roar rose as the demons found their feet. In a wash of magic that set my hair on end, the room went suddenly silent as they vanished, chasing him.

"Damn my dame!" Dali exclaimed, and Jenks giggled, sounding like a soothing rain.

"Where are Melody and Sikes?" I said as I sat down on the bar and took Al's hand, allowing him to help me to the floor.

"No!" Dali spun, his face red. "This does not give you anyone. How long did you know that was Hodin?" he said, then softer, more angry, "You should have told me. I might have . . ."

"Caught him?" Jenks landed on my shoulder, a wash of dust spilling down my front.

I smiled, feeling both strong and vulnerable as Al

slipped in behind me. "Her idea to bring my class here to prove you were safe was really dumb. Vivian knows you are not tame and you never will be."

Dali pinched the bridge of his nose. "We will never catch him if he is doppelganging again."

"Why not?" Jenks asked, and Dali squinted at his four-inch-tall belligerence. "I've seen you guys change into everything from a dog to a vampire to a redheaded, pain-in-the-ass witch. Al pretended to be Hodin just this last spring. What's the diff?"

Dali jolted as if stung. Al cringed, then pulled himself upright under Dali's obvious disgust. "I was ascertaining if Morgan was taking instruction from him. That's all."

His frown heavy, Dali looked me up and down as if I was stupid, and wincing, I decided I probably had been. There had been differences I should have recognized: "Hodin's" ordered feathers, the way he talked, the casual feel of him. "Ah, I would think a finding charm would be enough to ferret him out from the real person," I offered, and Dali nodded, easing himself behind the bar as if needing something to do.

"It normally would be," he said, and each glass he touched sparkled as he charmed them to a shiny purity. "But when Hodin changes, he goes down to the DNA. It can be done, obviously, but why when surface appearance is sufficient?"

Al pulled his lips from his teeth in a wide smile of remembrance, and I stifled a shudder. The night we had met, when he had turned into what scared me, Al had become a vampire. Not just a vampire, but Ivy, filling me with vampiric enzymes and leaving me paralyzed. That demons didn't become another so fully all the time was a matter of convenience, apparently.

One by one, Dali lined up the glasses in a row under the counter. "The elves demanded purity in their entertainment," he said, his thoughts clearly in the past. "Hodin learned how to shape-shift beyond what is normal to survive. When he is a crow, he is a crow. When he is a pixy, he is a pixy. When he is the leader of the coven of moral and ethical standards, he is Vivian Smith in all but his thoughts. He is a true chameleon, and if he has chosen to hide as another, we will never catch him."

"We don't have to catch him," Al said. "Rachel does." His lip twitched, and I saw odd tension in his shoulders. "Your thinking is short-term, itchy witch. What you intend will last only as long as demon eyes remain closed. What we see, we covet, and we will be under no obligation if, say . . . people wander in? Finding is not luring."

"That's not how I saw this playing out," I said, and he shrugged, his predatory gleam growing. Worse, if there was one thing I knew about Cincinnatians, it was if you tell them something is illegal for their own good, they'll try it to find out why. If I could get Melody and Sikes back, their story *might* be enough to keep the curious at bay until Trent could get something on the books and close the ever-after borders—if only on paper.

Dali was still frowning, putting his glasses away one by one. "You should have told me it was Hodin. If I had taken him thinking he was a coven member, he could have killed me."

"Then maybe you need to rethink your practice of forcing people into signing contracts," I said, tired of it all. "Sweet hotcakes with syrup, why do you hate each other so much?" I said, not expecting an answer, but Al's head had snapped up, his gaze almost frightened as he looked at Dali. The old demon had gone deathly still.

"You believe you deserve to know?" Dali said, and Al moved, eerily fast, to take my elbow and draw me stumbling away.

"No, she does not," Al said, and I scowled, jerking from his tight grip.

But if Dali was angry, Al was scared to death—which made me more than a little curious. "Hey, if I'm going to put him in a bottle, I need a reason other than you don't like him," I said, dropping back when Al reached for my arm again. "He's a citizen, same as you. The I.S. will be on my case for wrongful incarceration if I slap him in a bottle without cause. You guys are always writing things down. You locked him up before the lines fell, right? You must have his original arrest warrant somewhere."

"Yeah," Jenks said, his wings rasping as he hovered by my ear. "You got anything to keep the I.S. off Rache's case?"

I doubted the I.S. would care one way or the other, but I wanted to know what Hodin had done that was so bad he deserved to be jailed for the rest of his life.

"We did not keep records of Hodin's indiscretions. We lived in their aftermath!" Dali thundered. "Get out of my restaurant!"

I gasped as I was suddenly shoved into a ley line. There was a moment of disconnection as I threw a bubble around Jenks and myself—and then Al's aura slipped over mine, shifting his aura to reality and taking me with it. *The park. My car is at the park!* I thought frantically before Al dropped me at my church—and then I was again in reality, my sneakers pressing into the beaten-down grass and the low sun shining on my face. Eden Park. "Trent?" I called, scanning the park benches.

"I'll get him," Jenks said as he flew up and away from my earring.

"The Goddess save you, Rachel. We do not remind Dali of his son. Ever." Al's face screwed up in distaste as an elaborate fan misted into existence. "It is bloody hell hot up here."

"Maybe you should put on a pair of shorts," I said, eyeing his overdone Victorian finery. "I didn't know Dali had a son." My thoughts went to Keric, the Rosewood baby he was teaching—for free. "What did Hodin do to him?"

Al studied the nearby buildings, hazy with humidity. "I don't wish to speak the words."

"Seriously, I ought to know what he's done if you want me to put Hodin in a bottle."

A bitter bark of laughter, cold and hard, came from him. His focus shifted to me, the hatred in him striking me cold. "*You* want to put Hodin in a bottle. We want him dead.

However, the agony of inescapable incarceration has a long-term satisfaction. Death is an empty revenge."

"What did he do?" I asked again, then spun at Trent's distant hail. "Trent," I whispered, relief bringing my shoulders down.

Beaming, Trent jogged to close the gap as I paced quickly to him. "I was giving you five more minutes," he said as we met and he gave me a relieved hug. The scent of warm cookies and the snap of magic felt like home, and my entire body relaxed. "Did they catch Hodin? Where's Sikes and Melody?"

I glanced at Al, the demon having changed into a billowy silk robe that wouldn't be out of place on the Sahara. We weren't done yet. "No on Hodin. Until I can catch him, Sikes and Melody stay with Dali." I'd brought up the warrant idea simply to get Dali talking, but the more I thought about it, the more I wanted one. I didn't care if it was hours old or eons.

Al sniffed, a decidedly supercilious expression on his ruddy face. "Too bad you committed him to Dali," he said as he made an overdone, sarcastic flourish to the joggers who noticed him. "I would've given a lot to have him on my shelf to torment."

Trent's relief paled as he flicked a glance at Al. "Don't ask me to do that again." Trent gave me another sideways hug, clearly reluctant to let me go. My hand found his, and I clasped it. If that hadn't been Hodin . . . But none of us would have been there if not for him.

"Thanks for making that call," I said as I turned us to the parking lot, and Jenks smirked.

"You should have heard Vivian." Jenks made annoying circles around Al until the demon swatted at him. "She's furious. Her convertible has been missing since this morning. She's on her way here right now to pick it up, and she wants to talk to you." Wings rasping, Jenks glanced at Trent and Al. "All of you."

"Cool." I scuffed to a halt in the shade, wondering at

Al's distant mood. His fists were clenched, and his eyes narrowed on the past.

Trent tugged me into another relieved hug, his lips brushing mine. "Seriously. Don't ask me to leave you like that again."

I slumped, not able to make that promise. "Hey, ah, I want to talk to you and Vivian about legally closing the ever-after off to demons and invites only," I said, glancing at her car. We were getting noticed, and I wasn't entirely comfortable. "Make the fine high enough that even you wouldn't chance it. Enough people know that the lines are gateways, and I don't want to have to rescue every idiot who thinks it's cool to picnic in another dimension." I glanced at Al, but he was still lost in his thoughts of Hodin. "Which reminds me."

Head down, I swung my bag around and dug out that black envelope. "Would you have your lawyers look at this and see if there's a way we can get Sikes and Melody back through the courts?" Al's derisive snort drew my attention, and I frowned at him as Trent took the envelope. "You got a problem with that?" I added, and Al leered at the passing people, all of them wisely giving us a large berth. "I'm serious about that warrant for Hodin. It would be just like the I.S. to harass me about missing paperwork. If you want him incarcerated, I need the documentation that says he belongs there."

"We twice made the mistake of letting him live," Al said bitterly. "Yes. Let's do it a third time."

I took a breath to protest, but Al vanished, leaving me with an unsettled feeling.

"Guess he doesn't want to talk to Vivian," Jenks said mockingly, and Trent tapped the envelope against his hand before tucking it into a pocket.

"That was a little dramatic, even for Al," Trent said as Jenks landed on his shoulder and the two of them watched me in expectation.

"Um, Dali had a son, and Hodin . . ." I shrugged. "Maybe he killed him?" I guessed, my concern growing. "I don't know. None of them are talking." I took a cleansing breath and tugged Trent closer. "I'll find out. In the meantime, you, me, dinner, and a couple of spell books. We still need a way to get Finnis to back off."

"Deal," Trent said, and I smiled, glad I didn't have to do this alone.

CHAPTER
21

IT HAD RAINED DURING DINNER, A HUGE DOWNPOUR THAT left the usual streets flooded until the sun went down. The air was cool and the garden still wet as I picked my way through the tombstones, heading for the cloche Hodin had made last spring. The demon had crafted it for Jenks in exchange for rent, the red and gold dome cutting the stench of a magically enhanced lily I'd used to drive Constance from Piscary's.

"It's still here!" Jenks called, and I angled to him, relieved. The resident fairies were sheltering, and there were no pixy kids to light the night. It was just Jenks and me, and my ley line–sourced light hanging in a mundane lantern making shifting shadows in the damp garden.

I'd been hoping that Hodin had forgotten the cloche, seeing as I couldn't get into his room and Stef's had contained nothing of his. I needed a non-DNA-specific focusing object to make that aura-solidifying curse, and the cloche was perfect. If it worked, Hodin wouldn't be able to travel via ley lines until he figured out how to break it.

"He didn't take it," I said, surprised as I found the heavy glass cloche half-hidden by a swath of uncut grass. The lily it had once covered was gone, but I could smell it in my imagination. "Thankfully we only need a piece of it," I added.

Jenks's dust was a dull gold in the dark as he hovered over it. "You want me to bust it?"

"I'll do it." Lips pressed, I cast about, finally deciding to use the butt of my ceremonial knife. I had it in case I found anything I wanted to gather, but it would work as a careful hammer, and I set my lantern down and eased the cloche onto its side.

The light glinted on the broken glass that Hodin had fused together, and after a moment's consideration, I spread my gathering scarf under the raised rim and made a sharp tap on a yellowish-green piece. It was the same color as Hodin's aura; it would help make a connection.

I winced at the obvious crack, wondering if I had felt a ripple of energy when three glass shards fell into the waiting scarf, as if whatever magic had been imbued into the glass construct had broken. Immediately I wadded the scarf into a ball and shoved it into a pocket as I stood the cloche up. I only needed the one piece, but I might use the others to try to make a few charms with which to positively ID Hodin so I didn't accidentally incarcerate, say, Trent.

"You can use it as a rain shelter," I said, and Jenks dropped down, wings carefully folded as he stood at the new opening and looked inside.

"Yeah."

The word was flat, and my brow furrowed. He'd been in a foul mood since dinner, the honey he'd gotten from my tea to give to Getty still on the porch table. "So . . ." I turned to the church and started slowly back. "Has Getty come out of hiding yet?"

"No." Jenks rose up and landed on my shoulder. "But she's around. Laughing at me."

I nodded, careful not to smile. I'd be worried that Getty might be Hodin in disguise, except that I'd seen the two of them together several times. "Jenks, she likes you, or she would have left. Busted wing or no."

"Yeah?" His wings made a cool draft on my neck. "She has a funny way of showing it. She's driving me nuts. She's got her zip lines all over the place so I know she's okay. The fairies know where she is, why not me? Matalina never . . ."

His words cut off, and I stepped carefully over the low wall separating the graveyard from the garden. *Getty wasn't Matalina.* "I have an idea," I said as I scuffed to a halt outside the porch's light. "Here." I crouched, fingers searching until I found a tiny, stunted acorn from last year. "Try this."

Jenks darted from my shoulder, his narrow face pinched in frustration. "What the Tink-blasted hell do you want me to do with that? Knock her on the head with it? We don't need another tree, and besides, it won't germinate. Even the squirrels don't want it."

"True." I nodded. "You want her to come out of hiding? Plant it." Jenks's frown deepened, and I added, "Make a big show. Measure the depth twice. Water it with gathered rainwater. Mark its location with a bright stone. Clear the encroaching leaves so it gets the right amount of sun. Then fall asleep guarding it."

Jenks's dust brightened, his wings humming as he darted down to my palm to take it. "She's going to want to know what it is. Not knowing is going to kill her."

"Or at least bring her out of hiding," I said, feeling good.

Jenks's wing hum rose in pitch. "I have something better than an acorn," he said, inking dust as he darted into the night.

"Jenks!" I shouted, and he looped back to me, clearly impatient. "Ah, do you still have that no-magic-zone amulet I asked you to store for me?"

"Yep. I'll be glad to get rid of it. The thing gives me a headache," he said, taking off in a different direction. I continued on to the porch, not surprised when his dust dampened and he seemed to vanish. I waited on the steps, breathing in the night. I could hear the kids playing in the dark: the yap of a Were pup, the hiss of bike wheels. It would've been a fabulous night for a midnight ride through Trent's forest and field, and my shoulders slumped at the massive amount of spelling I had to do between now and tomorrow night to contain Hodin and send Finnis packing.

It would have been easier if I had access to the vault, and Dali's comment of "not enough disposable flesh" hung sour in me. I was not going to give him my students in exchange for access in the hope that the vault contained something I could catch Hodin with. Besides, if there had been anything in there that would work, they would have used it already. The vault was a typical demon wish: something that looked like a godsend but only made things worse. I was on my own. Al's warning that they were too ugly didn't sit well with me, either. They were war curses, and the demons had been really pissed, willing to make morally bankrupt choices in the name of revenge.

I didn't have time to cook up a lot of new spells, but modifying existing ones was an acceptable shortcut. Constance's old no-magic-zone amulet was stuck in the open position, making it decidedly . . . lacking in versatility. If I could fashion a new pin for the NMZ amulet so I could turn it off and on at will, and maybe make up a charm to solidify Hodin's aura to prevent him from popping in and out, I might be able to hold Hodin long enough to cage him in something more permanent.

"Take it. Take it!" Jenks exclaimed as he wobbled from the dark, a heavy layer of dust spilling from under him. The light in my lantern was snuffed as he got close, and I held out my hand, feeling my connection to the ley line utterly vanish as the braided circle of charmed silver thumped into my palm.

"Thanks, Jenks," I said, but he was already gone, his path high and his dust cheerful. The ley line amulet felt odd against me, the usual prickling cramp of ley line energy utterly muted. But that's what the amulet did, and I turned it over to blow the flakes of herbs off the metal circle. The invocation pin was absent—lost when Constance threw it out the window of Cincy's Ferris wheel—but I could see the holes in the braided circlet where it would have run. Until we found a way to replace it, the amulet was stuck in the on position, annoying at best.

I left the unlit lantern on the porch steps, my smile soft as I looked at the brightly lit kitchen and saw Trent behind the counter arranging ley line pins between bites of cookie. He flushed when I pulled the French doors open, his hand drawing away from the open bag of Oreos.

"Find it?" he asked, starting when I got close and his connection to the ley line vanished.

"The cloche? Yup. I think Jenks is going to make it into a summer house." I set the NMZ amulet on the counter, followed by the gathering scarf, carefully opening it to show the chips of glass. "I don't mind doing this alone. You want to take a nap while I try the pins?" It would be a miracle if one of them worked, but not trying would be stupid.

"No," he said as he pushed the shards around with the tip of a pen. "I'm good. I think we might have a problem trying to retrofit a pin for this." Hunched over the counter, Trent put an elbow on the stainless steel and picked up the braided circle and tried a pin at random. "Pins can be replaced when you lose them, but it takes magic to re-pair them. And since the amulet negates all magic . . ."

"Catch-22." Bent beside him with our shoulders touching, I handed him another pin. Past the windows and porch, Jenks's light flitted over his dark, dripping garden. Trent fitted the pin, and I reached for a ley line, failing. *Nope. Not that one.* "You can't re-pair a pin without magic, and without the pin in place, you can't tap a line."

Trent exhaled, rising to his full height as he tried another pin. *Nope.* "That lead-lined bag is still an option," he said, and I stretched across the counter to pull a salt-spotted theme book closer.

"True, but I wouldn't be able to carry the amulet and reliably do magic both. All the bag does is shift the acting radius from twenty feet down to three. I should have spent five minutes on the floor of that gondola and found the pin before I turned myself in to the I.S."

Trent's smile widened as he fitted another pin to no effect. "I can't tell you how pleased I am that I'm not the only one in this relationship who has done time."

My eyebrows rose as I leaned against the counter and flipped through the theme book. It was mine, a messy collection of the charms and spells I had modified or invented over the last couple of years. Maybe someday I'd take a few weeks and organize them, but I doubted it. "You've never done time," I said as I found the page I wanted and pressed the theme book open on the counter with a cringeworthy spine snap. "You've had your picture taken and sat in a cell for twenty minutes until Quen posted your bail. The time-out cabin at camp doesn't count."

He laughed, his expression decidedly fond as he bumped into me and I let my head touch his. Together we silently looked at my cramped script. "I think I know how we can get that pin back," I said.

"It's been four months." Trent drew the cookies closer, giving me two for his one. "That pin is long gone."

"No argument there." I snapped through the cookie, the bitter chocolate waking my appetite as I pointed at the page. "I 'ot a 'urse 'hat I oozd to move that lily forward in time two seasons." I swallowed. "It's Newt's. Probably the same curse she used to shift a surface demon through a century in thirty seconds. But the curse can go backward as well as forward. If I send the amulet back in time past the point where Constance used it on me, it will have a pin in it. Maybe."

Trent's lips parted, the half-eaten cookie in his hand forgotten. "You can do that?"

His astonishment washed through me, leaving doubt. "I think so," I said as I pushed the book aside and used a silk cloth to remove any stray ions and crumbs from a section of counter. "The curse is in the collective. They don't like me using Newt's magic, but I can do it."

"Is it dangerous?"

"Obviously." Still, I smiled as I dropped the NMZ charm into its lead-lined bag and cinched it shut. It was still interfering with me tapping a line, so after I spilled a three-foot salt circle around it, I retreated until I could reach a ley line and energy filled me with a tingling presence, rubbing out my headache.

Watching, Trent leaned against the counter, hiding another cookie. I glanced at my theme book for the invocation phrase. *Rhombus,* I thought, to set a circle around the amulet and give the curse a place to act. The barrier sprang up covered with smut and I winced. I'd forgotten about it, but at least it wasn't trying to jump from me anymore, and I cleared my throat. *"Ab aeterno,"* I intoned, starting at the hiccup of incoming energy. More black skated across the surface of my circle as the spell began to send the amulet back in time, and I allowed a trickle more energy.

"Your aura is really dark," Trent said, his brow furrowed.

"It's temporary." *I hope,* I thought, gasping when the three-foot section of counter delineated by my circle suddenly . . . vanished, and a harsh clink of metal on metal came from the cabinet underneath.

"Stet!" I shouted to end the curse, leaning forward to peer into the hole in my brand-new, four-month-old counter.

Trent looked from me to the damaged counter in the sudden silence. "Ah, did you know that was going to happen?"

I shook my head, then laughed, my shoulders dropping as I figured it out. "It worked," I said as I strode forward, pleased when I never lost the ley line. The counter hadn't been here four months ago, and now it was missing. *Dang, it even took out a section of drawer.* "I should have twisted the curse on something that hadn't moved in the last four months, like the pool table." Sighing, I reached in to get the small lead-lined bag that had fallen into a nestled set of bowls. Trent came closer, and our foreheads touched as I shook the amulet into my hand, smiling at the lost pin once again in place, returned by pushing the amulet back into a time when it had had it.

"Goddess tears," Trent whispered. "This has tons of applications. Little bit of smut, though."

"I did push it four months into the past," I said, feeling

as if I was finally making progress. "Moving something alive two years forward was a lot harder. This will help cut Hodin's magic out from under him. Halfway there."

Trent took the amulet and dropped it back in the bag. "You're scary good at this, you know?"

Sighing, I looked at the counter. Jenks was going to have a hissy. "If I was that good, I wouldn't have a hole in my counter," I said as I moved the cutting board to hide it. "Hodin can still line jump with the NMZ amulet invoked. To keep him pinned down, we need to either cuff him with charmed silver—"

"Which would require physical contact," Trent interrupted, brow furrowed.

"Or solidify his aura," I finished. "It took me six hours to figure out how to break the joke curse when Al slapped it on me. It's not insurmountable, but it will buy us time to safely cuff him. Five seconds, maybe." I took up my gathering scarf with the glass shards, glancing at the huge clock Finley had put over the sink. "I've got everything to make it upstairs. Do you want to help me go through Newt's books to find something for Finnis and Hodin?" One spell to trap, the other to cow into submission. If I was lucky, it would be the same charm. Curse. Whatever.

Trent tucked the bag with the NMZ amulet into a pocket and gestured to the hall. "Absolutely. Upstairs it is."

Nodding, we headed for the sanctuary, my fingers finding Trent's as we walked through the quiet church. "How is Jenks doing?" he asked, his gaze on the empty rafters. "He seemed down when we got back from dinner."

"Fine?" I said, making it a question. "I think he's falling in love with Getty and it's killing him. I'd swear that she likes him, too, but she's been avoiding him since we went to the ever-after. I don't know why."

A faint, sad smile quirked Trent's lips. "Does she know Jenks can't engender children?"

I started, having forgotten that. Jenks was just . . . Jenks. "Probably not," I said as we entered the foyer and I fumbled in the dark for the door to the stairs. "Why?"

"You should tell her."

"Why?" I asked again, stifling a shiver when his hand curved suggestively about my waist and tugged me close.

"Tell her," he whispered.

"Next time I see her," I said, thinking it would be a really awkward conversation. *How do I even bring that kind of thing up?* "So, I've been giving Finnis some thought," I said as I rose up the stair, feeling the air grow more humid and stifling with each step. "I found a demon-based memory hiccup curse that's technically white since it doesn't permanently modify perception. If we combine that with an elven glamour or distraction charm, maybe we can get the same result as what Hodin's *fulfillment* curse was supposed to do. Sort of put Finnis's thoughts into a loop every time he thinks of Constance."

"That has possibilities."

His melodious voice was low as he followed me, and a tendril of heat curled about my chi, inviting his touch.

The door to the belfry creaked open to spill a soft light into the stairway. Three of the blinds were closed against the heat of the long-set sun, and as Trent looked over the small space, I flicked on the light and pulled the rest. The small room was decidedly stuffy, and I opened a couple of windows, seeing as it was still cooler outside even with the cool air being pumped up here. Rex sauntered out from behind a box with a little chirp, jumping onto the sill of an open window and stretching to pat the blinds.

"I haven't been up here since Hodin moved in," Trent said as he set the bagged NMZ amulet on the dresser.

"It's pretty tight, but I like the view." I put my wadded-up gathering scarf with the glass shards next to the amulet, the night air spilling about my ankles as I turned to my tiny bookshelf. The gaps where Dali's books had been now held the four I'd gotten from the library, and I wondered if I should take their shelving tags off as I hunted for the two books I wanted. *Where are you?* I thought, fingers spilling lightly over them until my hand cramped. *There's one.*

Trent's shifting feet went still. "I didn't give you those," he said, and I glanced up to see him focused on the string of pearls I had looped over one corner of the dresser mirror.

"Constance had them around Nash's neck. I don't know why I kept them, except that they remind me of him." *And here's the other*, I thought as I found the slim volume bound in black leather. Elven spell book and curse tome in hand, I went to sit on the low couch. "You want to see?" I said as I handed him the elven text. "The two magics might not be sympathetic."

"Sure."

Trent's weight as he sat pulled me closer, and he sighed in contentment as he began flipping through the pages. "Mmmm," he muttered, his legs awkwardly stretched because of the low couch. Rex jumped from the sill, tail crooked as he came to get a head rub. "The energy up here feels odd. Sharp, almost," Trent said as he obliged the orange cat.

"It's probably the protection charm Al put in." I shifted the old pages of my new book quickly, not entirely comfortable. If Vivian knew what was in my library, she might find reason to confiscate much of it.

Satisfied, Rex flopped down out of Trent's easy reach. "I don't remember letting you borrow this . . ." Trent said as he leafed to the front of his book to peek at the publication date.

"I do. Take a look at this," I said, and his attention shifted. *Circulus vitiosus*, I thought, my finger running through the premises behind the demon curse. Vicious circle. Yeah, that was about right. "If I understand it, the curse works by tying the targeted memory to an object, whereupon you forget it until you see the object again."

"As in not remembering why you went into the kitchen until you return to the living room?" Trent frowned. "Memory hiccup. I assumed all magic affecting memory was illegal."

Clearly concerned, he touched the pages of the book resting on my lap, and a tingle of shared line energy sparked through me. "It would be if we were erasing it," I said. "This is more of a joke curse."

"Mmmm." His low utterance was neutral, and I tucked a loose strand of hair behind an ear and scooted closer, liking the way he smelled, of green meadows and cool forests both.

"If I tie the memory of why he's here to something we can hide, he won't remember why he's here and go home—maybe."

Trent's eyes shifted to the book on his lap. "And the elven charm of distraction?"

"Is so he doesn't dwell on the fact that he doesn't know why he's here," I said, not sure we could combine the two charms, or that if we could, it would have the desired effect. "If nothing else, it will be a statement that I'm not going to accept their authority."

Trent, too, seemed less than confident as he dragged Rex closer, setting the cat on his lap and peering at me from between his ears. "Sounds a little gray to me," he said, wincing when Rex leapt off him, tail switching as he sauntered away.

"But not illegal," I said. "People forget things all the time. If nothing else, it will give me some breathing room. The memory hiccup curse isn't hard. It's in the collective." Just perform the gesture to call it up, pay the cost, and bam, instant magic.

Still clearly not convinced, Trent nodded, head down over the elven spell book. "Sort of a one-two punch. I can't pull curses from the demon collective. You'll have to do the memory hiccup curse."

"Yes, but I want to try to do them together, blend them into one stored spell with a single invocation." My fingers on the text were tingling, and I studied the curse's invocation gesture. *It's an Isa rune. Curious. Purification and forgetfulness found in ice.*

Our sides touched, and a trill of desire rose and fell. "The memory hiccup curse is invoked by a gesture, and the elven spell by an incantation," I added as I put my book half atop his so as to better compare them. "In theory, they could be invoked at the same time. After seeing how we made that demon-expulsion spell the other day, I think if you started the elven charm as a base, then held it as I layered the demon curse over it and invoked them together, that we would end up with one, ah, curse, I guess. I could store it in a ley line charm. All we have to do is hit Finnis with it, and we're done."

Trent exhaled, sounding tired. "Legal enough for government work," he said, and my entire side tingled as he strengthened his grip on the ley line and ran a long finger over the elven invocation phrase.

Ignoratio elenchi, I thought. *Ignorance of the issue. Makes sense.*

"Let's try it," Trent said as he stood, and I stared blankly at him. "We need to share space," he added as he set the open book on the dresser, his tall height looking scrumptious in my tiny turret room. "Unless you want to wait?"

"No. You're right. We should practice. If we can't blend the two magics, then I need to think of something else. I do *not* want to use that wand." I snapped the demon curse book closed, leaving it on the couch as I stood. The phrase to pull the memory hiccup curse into existence lingered in my mind, and I dropped a stray thought to the collective. Smiling, I settled in before Trent as I had downstairs, feeling a little nervous as his hands curved about me, finding mine and holding them in front of us. He smelled of cookies, and his lips next to my ear started a slow shiver. Jenks's claim that Trent and I couldn't spell together without ending up between the sheets flitted through me, and I smiled. The Isa rune was all about fire and ice, of passion and possibilities hidden below a purifying forgetfulness of cold. Sort of like Trent.

"Good thing you aren't in heels," he said, his breath raising goose bumps. "This won't work if we can't store the charm in a ley line amulet. I'm not doing this in front of Finnis."

"Agreed," I said, exhaling into another passion-born tingle. "Once we know if it works, we can make another spell for Finnis and I'll drop it in the collective in my private storage area."

His weight eased closer yet, and his hands holding mine tightened. "And we will know if it works how?" he whispered, lips about my ear.

"Um, Rex?" I suggested, distracted as I cast about to find the cat sitting on the sill cleaning his ears. "I wouldn't mind him forgetting he likes to claw the furniture."

Trent chuckled. "Okay, what do we link the memory to?"

"Mmmm." I reluctantly pulled from his grip, the two steps to the dresser feeling like a mile. "How about a pearl," I said as I carefully snapped Constance's necklace, and in a sudden rush and clatter, the pearls bounced everywhere.

"No-o-o-o!" I exclaimed, shoulders slumping, and Rex jumped to the floor, patting them into corners and pouncing on them. "That was not my intention," I said as I corralled one, and Trent grinned, beckoning me closer. He hadn't moved, and I took in his casual slacks and sock feet, wondering if I would ever see him in shorts. His shirt was undone a button more than usual, and that little extra skin was . . . tantalizing.

Smiling, I tucked in before him again, feeling our energies trying to mix as he cupped my hands holding the pearl. Rex rolled the pearls noisily about the floor, the sound seeming to mimic the feel of Trent's aura rubbing against mine in a delicious sensation. We were both connected to the same line, and I could feel his masculine energy in it, intoxicating.

"Simultaneously?" Trent said, and I hesitated, trying to bring my thoughts into focus.

"Not to start. You make the foundation bubble for the spell to work in," I said. "Then make and hold your spell just before invocation. I'll layer my spell in it, then invoke them both at the same time."

"It sounds too easy. How come no one else does this?" he asked, his arms about my waist taking on more of my weight until I was pressed against him.

"Probably because no one else has a demon for a girlfriend," I said, enjoying the sensation. The pearl was perfect and small in my palm, and a wash of desire flooded me as a tidy bubble of red and gold, aura-laced thought blossomed in my hand. The pearl was inside it, and I exhaled, totally at peace as his low voice shifted deeper, his magic carried by the sound of his voice.

"Ta na-a-a shay," he sang, and I felt a wash of power echo from me to him. The simple elven phrase both settled his thoughts and asked the Goddess to lend her strength. I thought it odd that the petitioning of help was the single difference between elf and demon magic, though neither of them would admit it. Apart from a few lingering elven phrases, they were the same.

Immediately the free strands of my hair began to float as Trent's energy flowed through both of us in a sparkling awareness. It wasn't a power pull, but it was close, and I quashed a rising feeling of unsettled need as a delicious desire took me when his intent-imbued energy filled my cupped hands.

It was unexpectedly . . . tantalizing, and as a lustful thought of power pulls began to dominate my mind, I sent a sliver of awareness into the demon collective. Immediately I lost the sensation of Trent's hands cupping mine as a multitude of conversations rose, whispering like a fading dream. They were not *my* thoughts, but in the span that I was here, I shared them.

Unfortunately the connection went both ways much as the party lines in my mother's youth, and I tried to keep my randy thoughts quiet as I heard the patter of Rex's paws and the musical rolling of a pearl. *Circulus vitiosus,* I whispered in my mind, elated as I felt the curse shift to me, settling in my chi until I could give it direction and proper intent with the gesture.

Pulse fast, I pushed the curse to my hands, turning Trent's bubble a more vivid gold, shading it with my new black patina of smut. "Oh, wow," I whispered, and Trent took a breath in surprise. It was still his bubble, but it held both his spell and my curse. We were doing it.

Sort of, I thought as I suddenly found myself scrambling to keep it there. Like the smut that wanted to leave me, the curse obediently filled Trent's bubble until I took my attention from it, whereupon it tried to sink into me like unresolved energy going back to ground, leaving tantalizing trills of magic in its wake.

"Hold it for a second more," I said as I wrestled the energy into my cupped hands, and Trent's breath shuddered on the inhale—not in pain, but in pleasure. The small sound hit me hard, and I scrambled to keep my breathing slow and my thoughts from straying as his very pulse seemed to have become erotic.

"Ta na-a-a shay-y-y, ignoratio elenchi . . ." he intoned, and I jumped when his spell washed through me in a wave, leaving me fighting to keep my curse in my cupped hands.

"Hold it," I rasped, heart fast as I layered my curse over his spell, both of us staring at our joined spell and the pearl, now an unreal black and gold. "Just a second more."

Trent's breath came in a pant. The rising sensation of our magics mixing was becoming increasingly hard to ignore, and I locked my knees, trying not to think about how delicious Trent felt behind me and focusing on Rex and that he was going to forget he liked to claw furniture.

Like a bell beginning to chime, my thoughts and the bubble of energy in our joined hands began to resonate with the idea. It was working, and my pulse quickened as the energy in my palms took on my intent, and then . . . as if reluctant, Trent's magic as well. I could hear the stress in his breathing. "You okay?"

"Hurry," he rasped, the sound diving to my core.

"Ignoratio elenchi," I whispered to invoke Trent's spell, moving my hands to make a three-dimensional expression of the Isa rune to invoke the curse simultaneously. Heat flashed through my palms, and I yelped as the two annealed magics shot at Rex.

The energy hit Rex square on his back and the cat jumped, yowling as his hair stood on end. My hands flashed apart. Trent's grip fastened tight about my waist, demanding. Surprised, I watched the pearl roll under the dresser as the angry cat hissed, tail twitching while the gold and red energy soaked in. Clearly disgusted, the cat slunk from the room.

Trent's arms tightened around me as I stepped to get the pearl. He yanked me to him, and I turned in his arms, worried it had been too much. "Are you okay?" I said, then blinked, startled when he leaned in and found my mouth with his with a sudden, obvious heat.

"Mmmmph . . . mmmm," I said, my surprise zinging into a hot desire. My hands laced behind his neck. His lips left mine, his breath fast as his hands explored, potent with need.

"Oh, yes, please . . ." I almost moaned, and then gasped when his lips found my breasts through my camisole. One hand clamped me to him, the other pulled my camisole free from my waistband, little trails of fire erupting as they brushed my bare skin.

"I like spelling with you," he said, his melodious voice rough with a fast desire. His lips had found my mouth again, and our energies mixed freely. "You pinned my magic down," he whispered. "Made it yours. I gave it to you, and you . . . God, Rachel."

My own need flooded me, all the stronger for having tried to deny it. My leg twined in his, pulling him closer. Focused, I pulled his shirt up and over his head in one possessive move. "We don't have time for this," I said, and his motion to shove my shorts down hesitated.

"You want me to stop?" he said, incredulous, and I stared at him, my own desire redoubling as I saw him there, his shirt off and hands tightly cupping my backside.

"God, no," I said, then yanked him to me, almost falling when my balance shifted.

The spell had been one long, drawn-out foreplay with our mixing energies and combined auras, and I reached for him, my lips hungrily on his as my fingers undid his slacks.

A half growl, half sigh rose between us, and then I gasped, startled when he pulled me to him, turning us at the last moment so my back hit the narrow wall between the windows.

But he had finally gotten my shorts down, and I wrapped

a leg around him, pulling him tight as my arms laced behind his neck, imprisoning him as he had imprisoned me.

I could hardly think—the need for this having come so fast. His soft sound of desire went to my core, igniting me to a more fevered pitch. Somewhere, a tiny rational thought intruded that this had happened really fast, that our usual pattern, while not spanning hours, was never this abrupt need. But I didn't care, and when Trent eased us down on the fainting couch to find my breasts with his lips, I groaned and reached to guide him in, demanding that he do more than dance around the edges of our passion.

He made a sound of relief, rising up and slipping into me at the same time.

Gasping, I clutched at him, overwhelmed at the sudden sensation. His breath was heavy in my ear, our motions coming in waves until, almost too soon, I climaxed, throwing my head back as I clutched him even closer.

Groaning, he followed me, his grip both imprisoning and gentle as waves of pleasure washed between us, slowly ebbing.

"Where the blue blazes did that come from?" Trent panted, wincing when I laughed.

"I'm sorry. I'm sorry," I said when his brow furrowed and he shifted his grip, hoisting me higher in the hopes that my internal muscles would let go—which they did, seeing as the entire incident had been as fast and as satisfying as a whipcrack. And then I gasped, all thoughts of his discomfort vanishing as I saw the walls behind him. They were glowing.

"Trent?" I said, and his ruefully fond expression vanished at the warning in my voice. "Are you seeing this?"

He reached for a blanket, handing it to me as he stood and hoisted his pants up with a serious quickness. My eyes followed the blue tracings of bound energy to the ceiling, seeing the lines arch to a close overhead. It was a cage, and my pulse hammered as I reached for a ley line, relieved to find that I could.

Not a cage, I thought, realizing it was that protection

grid I'd felt yesterday on the stairs. But then I blinked, lips parting when I followed Trent's attention to the floor. "Whoa," I said as I took in the room-size circle and the pentagon it held. Most of it was hidden under boxes and furniture, but it was obvious that it was bound by three exterior circles, three mid circles, and three central circles. Glowing glyphs were etched at the corners and almost every free space.

"Careful," I said, concerned when Trent touched a line and pulled a haze of blue away.

"It's a protection ward," he said. "We probably triggered it with all the . . . ah . . . energy we just released." His gaze met mine, his fingers rubbing the blue haze to nothing. "Al made this?"

I twined my blanket tighter about me, not worried, but discomfited. "I think so, but it didn't look like this before. I thought it was only a minor protection curse. Why would it show itself now?" I said, feeling uneasy. "We've been up here before." Granted, probably not with that intensity, but damn . . .

Brow furrowed, Trent touched an elaborate glyph, his sheen of sweat giving the blue haze something to glow against. "The demon-repellent ward I engaged earlier might have peeled off a don't-notice veneer. Al, huh?"

I nodded, shocked at the complexity. "Al," I echoed in a wash of guilt. He hadn't simply put up a protection ward. He had crafted an ironclad Hodin-free zone where I could sleep without risk, safe in my willful ignorance. "No wonder Hodin doesn't come up here," I said, amazed at the complexity of the fading lines. My bedroom had been Hodin-free for four months. I'd thought he had finally learned his boundaries, but it had been Al. Protecting me from him. Protecting me from myself.

Good demons, bad demons. How the hell am I supposed to tell the difference when they both lie so well? Guilt made my frustration sharp as I grabbed a new set of clothes to take down to the shower. Son of a fairy-farting troll. I didn't even know when Al had put it up. It looked like a three-day curse, minimum.

Throat closing, I slumped, my socks and undies in hand. Al had been protecting me even as I hurt him. I had spouted words like *compassion* and *forgiveness*, applying them to a traitorous demon slime when Al should have been the one I believed. He was my teacher, and I had walked away thinking the world would spin the way I wanted if I only saw it that way hard enough.

I need to talk to him, I thought as I glanced at my scrying mirror shelved with my books, then down at myself. Half naked. Sounded about right. *Maybe I should get dressed before I try talking to a worldly cosmic power.*

"Shower?" I said, distracted, and Trent nodded, shirt open and pants hardly zipped as he followed me downstairs, his brow furrowed in an unvoiced concern as we left the safety Al had given me.

CHAPTER
22

I STARED UP AT THE SHADOWED CEILING IN THE SANCTU-ary, my hands folded on my chest, a comforter smelling faintly of Pike pulled to my chin as I pretended to sleep on one of the couches. Trent's even, slow breaths from the chair beside me were soothing, and I watched the now-familiar pattern of the glow of a car's lights appear in the corner, flicker through the trees as it grew stronger, and then race from one end of the church to the other as the car went past. Sighing, I looked at Trent.

He'd fallen asleep about ten minutes ago in the chair beside me, the man going down fast from the lack of his afternoon nap. His slim, bare feet were on the low table, and he slouched in an undignified slump that made me love him all the more. His hand had held mine until a few minutes ago, and I thought it was sweet that he hadn't wanted to go home in case Hodin showed up. Sweet, but I'd be lying if I didn't admit I appreciated his presence. Trent's ward yesterday had only expunged any demon presence. It didn't stop them, and I only had the original warning on the bell to tell me if Hodin returned.

Trent shifted and I sat up to move the plate with its cookie crumbs and leftover takeout before his feet could shove it off the table. My elbows on my knees, I stared at Kisten's pool table in the corner, worry keeping me awake.

"Rachel?" Trent whispered, and I leaned to take his hand as he reached for me.

"Go back to sleep," I said as I stood, his hand slipping away as I pulled the afghan up and around my shoulders. "I'm going to get some air."

"Okay." He slumped down, never really having woken. Midnight wasn't late for a witch. If I kept to my personal schedule, I wouldn't go to sleep until two or three, getting up at a reasonable noon. And if I was awake, Al would be.

Glum, I sifted past Trent's architect magazines and my *Spell Monthly* to find my scrying mirror, sliding it out and padding through the church to my beautiful porch, where I could stew under humidity-hidden stars.

The church at night held an entirely different specter. The garden felt even more alive with bright gleams of light as the pixies darted about, but they were quieter somehow, tending to more work and less play—or at least they would be if Jenks hadn't evicted Baribas. The sounds of the city were muted under the frogs and crickets. The wind still blew and the trees still moved . . . but the entire space was centered, almost more mine without the distracting light, and I felt at peace as I passed through the now-tidy kitchen.

The click of the French doors brought a faint wing rasp, and I sighed as Jenks darted up to investigate, his bright red dust of warning shifting to a pleasant gold when he saw me.

"Oh, it's you," he said, and I lifted the scrying mirror in explanation.

"Sorry. Didn't mean to give you a start." I eased the door closed behind me and went to sit on the wide stairs leading down into the garden. The church felt massive behind me—holding my security and everyone most dear. Before me was the black garden trying to release the day's heat, and beyond that, Cincy herself, the lights and noise bouncing off the haze between us and the stars. I loved it here, sucky weather and all.

"I miss not being up this time of day," I said, knees to my chin as Jenks perched on the railing beside me, his glow fading as he tended a small tear in his wing.

"You're up because you miss sitting in a baking sauna in the dark?" he said, glancing pointedly at the mirror beside me.

"Okay. I'm worried," I admitted, and a smirk blossomed on his angular face.

"We got this, Rache," he said confidently. "I haven't seen Rex claw one thing since you picked up all those pearls. The memory hiccup spell works. Don't worry about tomorrow."

I stared out into the garden, missing the lights of pixy children. "I'm not worried about tomorrow," I said, my chin dropping to my knees. "I'm worried about yesterday."

Jenks's wings rasped as he fanned them, his feet unmoving from the rail as his gold dust flowed over us. "The past lives in the future, Rache," he said, and I turned to him, not understanding. "Yesterday is as alive and full of potential as tomorrow."

"You can't change what you've done," I said. "How is that alive?"

But Jenks shrugged, a faint smile born in memory. "The past is alive," he insisted. "I chose to keep my son Jumoke, to see something other than fear in his dark hair and eyes. He lives in my past, and because of it, Getty lives in my present."

I grimaced, looking at the empty black garden full of too many insects and not enough pixies. "I don't see how that makes the past alive."

"What we remember and choose to act on is not dead, not set in stone," he said, and my shoulders slumped. "There's no *I did this then, so that will happen now.* That question of what we choose makes the past as fluid as the future. Yeah, you made a mistake with Al and Hodin."

"Just one?" I muttered, and he grinned, his light brightening.

"But you're out here moping about it, so your bad choice is still alive. Change it."

"How did you get so smart? You're like four inches tall," I muttered, and he laughed, sounding like wind chimes in the dark.

"Pixy magic, baby!" he said as he rose up. "I've got to do a perimeter. I haven't seen a dusting of Baribas, but Hodin is still at large and he probably wants the stuff in his room. Getty will sing out if anything comes into the church."

"You found her?" I said, and he dipped and steadied, sparkles falling from him.

"She found me."

I nodded, hearing a potential lifetime in those three words. Smiling, I dropped my chin to my knees. "Jenks?" I called when he darted away.

His wings clattered in annoyance as he came back, clearly eager to be gone. "What?"

I took a breath, then let it go. "Getty did an amazing job organizing the fairies into a tight net of security when we were in the ever-after. I think we should ask her to stay." Jenks dropped an inch in altitude, and I shrugged. "The past lives in our future," I said, and his panic eased into confusion. Hesitating, he took a breath as if to say something, then changed his mind and flew off, his dust rimmed in blue.

My life was in tatters, but I had friends to help keep it together, and knowing that I could still help them convinced me to pull my scrying mirror onto my knees instead of throwing it into the dark garden like a fifty-cent Frisbee.

I needed Al to overcome Hodin, but he needed me, too, damn it.

The past is alive, I thought sourly, not sure I believed it. Afghan about my waist, I gazed into the inky black and red sheen between me and my reflection.

I'd lost count of how many scrying mirrors I'd made until I learned how to find and use the collective without one, but the mirror was etched with glyphs to ensure a more certain and private conversation. I think it was the first curse I'd ever made, the one that had convinced Ceri that I was a witch-born demon, not a once-sickly witch who had survived an elven-engendered genetic defect that should have killed me.

Peace settled deep as I put my hand atop the pentagram, fingers lightly touching the communication glyphs at the points. It was beautiful, really, and I closed my eyes, setting my thoughts on Al. He'd cracked the mirror the last time I had tried to talk to him through it, but it would still work. Jenks was right. I had to keep the past alive so it could impact my tomorrow the way *I* wanted it to.

Al? I whispered in my thoughts, hoping he was awake.

There was a breath of hesitation, and then, with a satisfying relief, my emotions seemed to double. Al's feelings of annoyance, frustration, and maybe a little relief slipped into me as if they were my own. *What do you want?* came his flat thought.

It wasn't the best greeting, but he *was* talking, and I pressed my hand deeper against the cool glass to strengthen our connection. Hodin had become a thorn in my mind. I needed to know what he had done, but after seeing Dali's grief turn to anger, I was afraid to dig. *Um,* I thought, and his irritation redoubled as he recognized my reticence and guessed what I wanted.

I will not talk about it, he thought, a sour sensation rising from not just his thoughts, but a hastily buried memory he didn't want to share.

That's okay, I immediately thought back, and his bitter amusement tinged my embarrassment. He could sense my disappointment. *I, ah, wanted to say thank you for the protection glyph encasing my bedroom.*

You found it? Al's attention seemed to sharpen, and I scrambled to hide from him exactly how the powerful lines had become visible, even if for only a moment.

Ah, Trent pushed a demon-expulsion ward through the church. I shoved the thought to my forebrain, hoping he wouldn't dig. *I was worried that Hodin was lurking. It stripped whatever don't-notice curse you had on it.*

Oh.

His presence went misty, leaving me feeling lacking. *So . . .* I thought, *thank you for keeping me safe from Hodin as I made my big mistake.*

Al huffed, and from the recesses of our connection, I felt a satisfaction born in a wash of heat and the faint image of sparks. A fleeting surprise lifted through me/us as my fingers found the smoothness of the steps instead of the rough-hewn log that Al was sitting on. He was tending a fire, I realized, and I relaxed even more in the hopes that he would sense the peace of my midnight garden. *Al, I have harbored him for months. I need to know what he has done. Please. Why do you hate him so much?* I thought, my own dissatisfaction twining with his. *It has nothing to do with him mixing elven and demon magic.*

It does, he shot back, and a heat of anger washed through us both, Al's born of the past, mine of the demons' stubborn resistance. *We have simply grown accustomed to your foul quirks and hope that you will outgrow them when you tire of your elven toy.*

Trent is not a toy, I thought, and Al's presence slipped into a haze of hidden memory. I got a glimpse of heartache and fury . . . and then it was gone, hidden. *Al, what did Hodin do?*

The smoothness of an egg seemed to fill my hand, my thoughts drifting to how hot the skillet over the fire was. I sensed a rising guilt and shame in him, and worried, I yanked my awareness away.

But Al sank a tendril of thought into me, and as I drew my thoughts back to my midnight garden lit by pixy glow and city glare, Al shifted his aura, slipping into a ley line as if it were a warm bath. My mind connected to his seemed to grow and expand. I felt the glory of the universe at his fingertips as he rode the lines, his body reduced to nothing but energy and thought as he fixed on my aura and, with an enviable demon skill, materialized beside me.

A faint bong from the steeple drifted over the humid night, announcing his arrival. My breath shook as I lifted my fingers from the scrying mirror. Our connection was broken, but I didn't need the mirror anymore. He was here beside me. The thought it might be Hodin came and went, but I had called Al. I had been in his mind, and there was no way to fake that.

"Once you agreed to protect him, your ignorance became your only protection," Al said, his eyes on the unbroken egg in his hand. Shoulders slumped, he sat beside me on the top step, breathing in the bound energy of the city and exhaling regret, his thoughts clearly on the past. "But even that is gone now."

"What did he do?" I said, pleading almost, and Al handed me the egg.

"Hodin's great betrayal was our failing," Al said, his gaze avoiding mine. "We let him do it, and he played upon our worst proclivities. He begged me to let him be captured so as to work from within to free our kin. It was his plan. And when it succeeded and he escaped with our captive children, he became a hero, trusted and loved."

Al turned to me, and I quailed at the old pain in him. "He brought our stolen, damaged children home," he said, voice even and without emotion. "And then he said nothing as they began to die. He'd cursed them himself, laying the blame on the elves so we would mount an attack on them in our grief."

"My God," I whispered, wanting to take his hand. The pain was thousands of years removed, but it was still fresh in him, still raw. Guilt rose up, guilt that I was too afraid to ask who he had lost. I didn't know if I could bring that pain to him. *Hodin cursed their children?* I thought, horror making my pulse grow fast. "Why didn't you tell me this before?" I said. "You let me defend him. You did nothing as I allowed him to live in my church."

"I told you not to!" Al bellowed, and I shrank away. But his pain and frustration vanished as fast as they had come, to leave a frightening emptiness. "Our trust in him is not a history we are especially proud of," he added. "And he never admitted if he cursed the children or simply looked the other way when the elves did. The result was the same."

How many atrocities are committed from one person turning a blind eye? I thought. Reaching out, I touched Al's shoulder, my grip on him tightening when he stiffened and then relaxed.

"Newt never trusted him." Al's sigh shifted his shoulders as he stared unseeing at my garden. "And still, we lost nearly half our number before she realized it was the children who were making us ill. Be gentle with us, Rachel. It is a cruel, cruel thing to force a people to watch their children choke on their own breath, unable to ease their passing knowing that to touch them meant they would die as well. That, I believe, is where we lost most, my kin choosing death over letting their children die alone. Those who survived still carry the guilt of seeing their own die without comfort, without touch."

"And so believing Hodin, we followed him when he promised a way into their stronghold to punish them in turn," Al said bitterly. "We would have our revenge upon those who hurt us so deep and with such disregard, but as you probably surmised, it was a planned betrayal. We went not to our revenge but to our captivity. He sold us all using the coin of vengeance. If not for Newt, he would have had us all." He turned, expression empty. "And you want a warrant?"

"You should have told me," I said, horrified, and Al slumped deeper into himself.

"Perhaps, but it is a hard thing to remember. I gambled that you would be safe from his worst impulses as long as you didn't know the truth and he believed he could manipulate you. Which he did. Now it will be harder. There's nothing elven you can use to best Hodin. He knows all their lore. More than any elf alive. The only hope you have of surviving him is what's in the vault. So I ask you now, what are you willing to give, itchy witch, to put an end to such a mind? What will you sacrifice to stop someone willing to do so much harm with such disregard for life?"

"You told me—"

"I know what I told you," Al said, his mood harsh. "But we fought Hodin for centuries, and the only curses able to overcome his elven wisdom were those he was not privy to. You need the curses in the vault, no matter the cost. The longer you wait, the more he will hurt you."

His words hung between us for a moment, the crickets and distant traffic holding the night until I figured out what he was saying and recoiled. "You want me to—I'm not going to sell my class to Dali for access to the vault," I said, horrified. "Not even for a day with the expectation that bottling Hodin would return them."

Al inclined his head, his empty gaze fixed on the egg still in my grip. "If you can't overcome Hodin, then he will kill you. You have heard his past, and even that thin protection is gone. But I understand your discretion. Perhaps if you simply help them find their way across the line? I'm sure Dali will enjoy entertaining them for a short span without commitment. A dress rehearsal, shall we say? If you don't pin Hodin in your first five minutes, you won't."

Angry and feeling the pinch of fear, I tossed the egg to him, and Al easily caught it. "I'm not selling my students for access to the vault. If you all hate him so much, I don't know why Dali won't simply let me in there."

Al scoffed, his attention going to the church looming behind us. "You should not have reminded him of his son," he said. "The thing about demons is that you get exactly what you expect. Meaning, if you assume they will keep to their word, they will, and if you anticipate they will break the laws, that is what they will do. What do you expect from us, Rachel Morgan?"

"I expect you to do whatever the hell you feel like, Al," I said, jumping when the kitchen light flicked on behind us, bathing the porch in a dusky glow.

Al predictably vanished and I slumped in a slow exhale. I'd never be able to jump the lines like that. Until Bis recovered, the only way I could get to the ever-after was by standing in a ley line. It was a piss-poor way for a demon to travel. "What the Turn kind of a demon am I, anyway," I whispered as Trent shuffled out with a bag of cookies in his grip.

"I heard the bell. Was that Al?" he asked, and I nodded as he sat down where Al had been, his bare toes hanging over the edge of the step. My gut hurt, and I took a cookie when he offered me the bag. My first thought to tell him Hodin's past rose and fell. It was an elven curse that had killed their children. No wonder the demons had cursed the entire elven species with a slow but certain cascading genetic failure.

"Ah, he thinks I need access to the vault to trap Hodin, and the only way they will let me in there is if I give them my students. I'm not going to do that, Trent. It's telling them what Dali is doing is okay, and it isn't."

Nodding, he sidled closer across the slightly damp step and tugged my forgotten afghan over both of us. Jenks was among the tombstones, his bright, cheerful glow a single light in the cricket-noisy garden. Squinting, I saw another, fainter, almost gray, but brightening when the two became one and he flew them inside. *Getty?*

"We will find another way," Trent whispered, and I slumped, my head falling to rest against him as he pulled me into a sideways hug to give me strength.

But remembering what Al had just told me, I wondered.

CHAPTER

23

SOMEONE WAS BANGING ON MY FRONT DOOR. IT REGIS-
tered in my sleep-addled brain on some level, but it wasn't
until the belfry bell rang that I woke up, the resonant bong
echoing into the sanctuary with the sound of demand.

"What the Turn . . ." I mumbled as I pried my eyes open
and looked toward the foyer. Bright afternoon sun shone in
to make puddles of color on the old oak floor, and I scrabbled for my phone on the low coffee table. Trent and I had
fallen asleep in each other's arms, but he was gone. And it
was after noon. And someone was still hammering on my
door as if the devil himself was after them.

"I'm coming!" I shouted as I sat up and listened to the
new silence. "Trent?" I called, but I didn't smell coffee,
which meant he was probably gone. Blinking, I squinted at
the folded note making a little tent on the table. It had my
name on it, and I dragged it closer.

"'Went to get charms for tonight's meeting with Finnis.
Sleep yourself out.'" I whispered as I read it. "'Happy
Birthday.'"

Tired, I set it down. Birthday. Right. He'd been gone since six fifteen. What a god-awful time to be up.

"I said, I'm coming!" I shouted again as the pounding renewed, and I stood, wobbling forward and feeling the stiffness the couch had put in me. Trent and I had worked all night on that memory hiccup curse, storing it into a looped bit of charmed silver. *Nothing like waiting until the last moment . . .* I thought, touching my jeans pocket where the ley line charm rested.

A rasp of pixy wings drew my attention, and I gave Jenks a wan smile when he darted in from the foyer. "Rache, we have a problem other than your hair."

I slumped to a halt, my gaze going to the door. "Who is it?"

"Detective Doyle." Jenks alighted on my raised hand since my unbound hair was everywhere. "And Pike, and three I.S. agents."

"Doyle? Good." I shuffled into the foyer and pushed the locking bar up. "I want to talk to him. Did he get me that warrant for Sikes?"

"Rache, wait!" Jenks exclaimed, but I'd already opened the door, blinking at the cluster of people on the front stoop. Doyle was there in a suit, his detective badge hanging about his neck. As Jenks had said, there were three stone-faced I.S. agents with him, all witches, judging by their insignia. Pike was a step down, his bruises from Sunday looking ugly in the sun. Behind them was a news crew setting up at the curb.

"And a news crew," Jenks added as he braved my hair to land on my shoulder.

Doyle's hand dropped from where he had been ready to hammer on my door again. Startled, he stared at my morning-wild hair, and then he grinned to show me his small but sharp canines in a confident bluster. "Rachel M. Morgan?" he practically crooned.

I touched my hair, wishing I had taken the time to grab a spell. "Last I checked," I said, suddenly conscious that my clothes were wrinkled from having slept in them. Doyle was taller than me in my sock feet, and I didn't like it. The witches, too, were already holding a ley line, and a bad feeling began to grow in the pit of my gut. "You're not here to sing me 'Happy Birthday,' are you."

"I'm here to escort you to the I.S.," Doyle said. "You're wanted for questioning on the presumed abduction of nineteen university students."

"Wait. What?" I jerked, startled when the witches pulled heavier on the line. "Pike?"

"He's got a warrant," Pike said. He didn't sound convinced, but rather tense and ready to act.

"Is it good?" Jenks asked, his tangled wings tugging at my hair.

"Just hold on," I said, but when I raised my hand, Doyle tried to slip a band of silver around it. "Hey!" I shouted, retreating to avoid it, and Doyle stepped forward, right into my church.

"I did not invite you in," I said, using my court-useful words. "Get out. All of you," I added when the three agents behind him pushed in as well.

Jenks took off and I tapped a line even as I backed into the sanctuary. I shook my head in warning at the agents behind Doyle, not liking their attitude. Doyle was too confident as he eased to a halt, eyes roving. I didn't like that, either. The light shifted as Pike closed the door, and a disappointed protest rose up from the media.

"I don't know anything about missing students," I said as the witches made inroads to try to circle me. "Are you talking about my students? I spent a good twenty minutes yesterday warning them to steer clear of demons. Ask Vivian. She reamed me out . . . about . . . scaring them." My words slowed. Actually, it hadn't been Vivian. It had been Hodin.

Son of a bastard. Hodin sold my students. I looked at Jenks, suddenly very much awake. The pixy just stared, not getting it.

Pike leaned against the archway between the sanctuary and the foyer, clean but bruised in his new suit, his pupils

showing only the barest hint of widening. "He's got witnesses saying they saw you at the park this morning with
your students."

"Shut it, Welroe!" Doyle shouted, and Pike pushed up
from the wall, peeved.

"I was sleeping," I said, forcing myself to stay unmoving
when every nerve of my body said to flee. "It wasn't me," I
added as the three witches studied the sanctuary. They
seemed disappointed it wasn't covered in demonic symbols.
"Do I *look* as if I was at the park this morning?" I gestured
to the rumpled blankets on the couch. "I've been sleeping
since three. If someone saw me taking my students into the
ever-after, it was probably Hodin pretending to be me."

Jenks chirped his wings in understanding and Pike sighed,
his brow pinching in thought.

Doyle's attention lingered on the blankets. "You were
alone?" he said as he picked up Trent's note.

"Jenks was here, and Trent," I said as he read it and let
it fall.

"Until six fifteen." Doyle motioned for the witches to
move, and my pulse quickened. "Anyone with you after that?"

"I was with her." Jenks hovered over my shoulder. "Both
me and Getty. It was Hodin who did it. He's trying to get
her in trouble."

Doyle made a little huff. "So, no credible witnesses?" he
said, and Jenks bristled.

"It wasn't me." I backed up until my calves found the
coffee table. "It was Hodin. He was here yesterday pretending to be Vivian. Call her. He stole her car, then tried to get
me to take my students into the ever-after to prove demons
weren't dangerous. Which I didn't. Please tell me he didn't
take everyone."

"Not everyone," Pike said, and Doyle glared at him to
shut up. "A guy named Tony stayed behind. A jogger said
she saw you and your students vanish into the ley line. She
said only you came out."

"You don't need to be here, Welroe. Get out," Doyle said,

and I tensed when he lifted the spelled-silver handcuffs again. "Put the silver on, Morgan."

I shook my head and Jenks rattled his wings. This could not be happening. "Call Vivian," I said as Doyle came forward. "She'll vouch for me."

"We tried. We can't get ahold of her," he said, halting three feet away. "The video footage from Eden Park security says it was you. The student who was smart enough to say no said you tried to convince him to go. You want to keep talking, that's fine with me, but one way or the other, you're coming in for questioning."

That was as close to the Miranda as I was going to get, and I felt my world spiral down to a hard certainty. If, over the course of a few days, Hodin could learn Vivian enough to fool me, then he could certainly learn enough of my mannerisms in the two months that he'd been living in my church to fool most everyone else.

"Do you have proof that the students are in trouble?" I said, and Doyle's grin vanished.

"That's not my department," Doyle said. "Cuffs on."

"No. I'll come in to answer your questions, but not in the back of a squad car." My eyes darted to the three witches. None of them seemed eager to press the issue, especially now that my hair was beginning to snarl from the ley line energy I was pulling in. "Let me grab my things. Put my hair in a braid. Change my clothes." My gaze went to Jenks. "Five minutes."

Five minutes would put me in butt-kicking boots. I could walk into the I.S. with my charms and spells. I would not go helpless. Not this time.

Doyle frowned and my aura prickled as the witches tensed. I could feel them pulling energy off the ley line, ready to give the raw power direction. I had just gotten my church back together, and now I was going to rip it apart because as sure as hell is hot, I wasn't going to allow this to happen.

"Sir?" The older agent rocking a silver Mohawk shifted

uneasily. "None of the witnesses saw Morgan get into a car and leave. She vanished. Morgan can't translocate unless she's in a ley line. Besides, her car is cold. I checked."

"Excuse me?!" Doyle barked, his eyes flashing pupil black as he practically pinned the I.S. officer to the floor with his stare. "Did I ask your opinion, Ustice? Did something give you the idea that we are a *team*? That we are working this together?"

"He's right," I said as Ustice clenched his jaw. "I can't line jump properly. And since you don't have anyone other than me willing to go into the ever-after and find out if they are okay, I suggest you stow the cuffs and let me put on some shoes so I can help you find out where they are, because last I checked, *we* are a team, Doyle. Whether you like it or not."

Doyle's lip curled to show a sharp canine. "I do not work for you."

"And I did not take those students into the ever-after," I countered. "You know it. But I might be the only one who can get them back without this devolving into a cross-dimension incident."

Jenks darted closer, his hand on the butt of his garden sword. Pike sidled up to me as well, his threat more obvious as he used a veritable pigsticker of a knife to clean under his nails. The scent of confident vampire began to tickle my latent scar, and I held my breath as a shiver of pheromone-based heat darted through me, right to my groin. "Let me get dressed," I said, voice low. "I will not be hauled out of here in cuffs when there is media on my doorstep."

I stepped from Pike as much to distance myself from the delicious scent of angsty vamp as to find my boots. "Jenks, I need you to make a couple of calls," I said, staring at Doyle. He was between me and the stairs. "Doyle, move. My clothes are upstairs."

"Ustice, go with her," he said shortly, pointing to the agent who had spoken up, and the tallish man paled. "If she runs, it's your job."

I looked Ustice up and down. "Right this way." It took

all my moral fiber to not knock Doyle's shoulder as I went past him, snagging my bag off the table in the process. "Pike, keep Doyle company, will you? Jenks, walk with me," I called over my shoulder, hips swaying as I sauntered into the foyer. Sure, I seemed confident, but I had to get out of the room before Doyle figured out how upset I was.

Hodin was pretending to be me. He had been there, pretending to be Vivian, when Dali had made his offer, and now Hodin had sold my students for access to the vault. Lucky for me, like the collective, his access would hinge on knowing my password, but the damage he could do—was doing—pretending to be me was unthinkable. I had a tiny window to act before I was hauled in, charmless. My meeting with Finnis wasn't until tonight, but I'd run out of time. It was now or never. Doyle would get me into the I.S., and from there, I'd find Finnis.

My steps on the narrow, dark stairs quickened. Behind me, Pike's soft voice rose as he began to educate Doyle on who was the most badass vampire in the room. Doyle had a badge, but Pike was a scion, the closest thing a living vampire could get to being undead without actually not needing to breathe. Ustice was unnervingly close. I didn't like it, even if he had spoken up for me. He'd have to be proficient at bringing in dark magic users if Doyle had asked for him, but even in my church, I was at a disadvantage. He had a license to do illegal magic to uphold the law. I didn't.

"You'll tell Trent where I am and why?" I said to Jenks as I felt my way up the dark staircase, and the pixy bobbed up and down, his dust lighting my path.

"Sure, but I'm coming with you," Jenks said, his eyes on Ustice, not me, and I cautiously nodded, not yet ready to fight that battle.

I shoved the door to my room open, grimacing at the mess. "Crap on toast, all my hair charms are downstairs," I said as I made a beeline to the dresser, dropping my bag on it and beginning to sort. This was going to be a sucky day. I could tell already.

"I got it," Jenks said as he darted behind me and the

familiar feel of him parting my hair tugged through me. "Damn, girl," he added as my chaperone came to a cautious halt on the threshold. "I'm never going to get this into a braid without dusting it. Getty? You any good at braiding lunkers' hair? I could use the help."

I peered up through Jenks's heavy, antistatic dust, following his gaze to Bis's shelf, where Getty was peering down at us, the bottle that held the gargoyle's soul beside her. "Braid that?" she said in horror. "That there needs more than dust. That needs product." She jumped, skirts billowing as she half fell to the dresser, that quiver of laced arrows with her.

Ustice was getting an eyeful of my life, and jaw set, I pointedly put my splat gun in my bag, then my extra shot. They'd be confiscated if Doyle took me in through the front, but until then, I could use them. Finnis was one smart move from taking over the city, and I had to do this now.

"Rache, stop moving," Jenks complained as he worked. "It's fighting back."

I tried to hold my head still as I took a couple of uninvoked pain amulets from a drawer and dropped them into my bag, making sure Ustice saw the medicinal code stenciled on them.

"Why would Hodin risk Dali maybe figuring out it was him?" Jenks asked, rising up until I could see his reflection expertly weaving the parted strands of my hair. "That's a lot of ifs for vault access, especially after you outed him once."

"He's going for broke," I said. "He gives Dali my students, gains access to the vault, and gets me hauled in to the I.S. for human trafficking. Win-win-win." *Should I bring that wand?*

"My God. You really did sell your students?" Ustice said, and I glanced up, making Jenks sigh as my hair pulled from him.

"I did not," I said, hurt that he thought I might, then returned to searching my bric-a-brac for something unique to tie a memory hiccup curse to. Trent wanted something rare, like a jewel, but I was tending to something more mundane. *Pencil stub, no. Broken earring, no. Pearls, definitely no.* Frowning, I dropped a love-worn She-Ra figurine into my bag. There might be, like . . . ten in the world now.

"Dali gave Hodin access to the vault?" Jenks said, and Getty frowned, hands on her hips as she watched him work. "How by Tink's little pink dildo are we supposed to beat him now?"

"Half access." I shoved the NMZ amulet into my pocket, where it made an uncomfortable bump. "He needs my password, too." One of Newt's books was sitting on the fainting couch, and I winced when I realized Ustice was staring at it, clearly knowing it was demon written.

Getty's wings shifted. "You're doing it wrong," she finally said, agitated. "The main strand needs to go this way first. It captures more strays and won't fall apart so easy."

"That's not the way Matalina did it," Jenks said tartly.

"Matalina didn't live in the walls of a salon for a winter eating Moon Pies," Getty snapped. "It goes the other way. You won't have so many escaped strands."

"That's why I'm dusting it," Jenks said, and I winced at his increasing tugs on my hair.

Getty looked positively ticked, and I shuffled around in my bag to make sure I still had those unused ley line circle charms. The need to get moving was growing, and I brushed a hand over my wrinkled clothes. They'd have to do. I wasn't going to change with Officer Ustice standing at the door.

Getty cleared her throat, an odd pink dust pooling at her feet. "You should have taken that strand that way," she said, pointing. "It allows for more flex, which would be safer if you're going into battle."

"That is not how Matalina did it!" Jenks shouted, and Getty turned her back on him. She could still see him via the mirror, but Jenks clearly felt the hit.

"Ah, Jenks? I need you to call Ivy, too," I said as I fingered that damned wand Hodin had tricked me into making. I wasn't planning on using it, but leaving it here seemed like a bad idea, Al's protective glyphs or not. "Tell her I need to talk to Finnis. Today."

Ustice visibly stiffened, and Jenks's wing hum rose in pitch.

"Now?" Jenks said, and I slipped the wand into my bag.

"Now," I repeated. "I can't retrieve the students if I'm in jail, and to stay out of jail, I need to take care of Finnis before he pushes Doyle into locking me up."

I eyed my chaperone through the mirror, seeing by his blush that I was right. No wonder Doyle was letting me walk in under my own power. He had an ambush waiting. Wanted for questioning, my lily-white ass.

"Trent is going to be pissed," Jenks said as he tugged and wove my mane into something manageable.

"Then he shouldn't have left," I muttered. "I want you to stay here, too."

Jenks rose, a curling strand of red in his grip. "You need me," he said, suddenly pale.

"Getty needs you more." Someone was coming up the staircase, and I spun, my hair slipping entirely from his grip. "See if you can verify that Vivian is okay," I added, worried. Jenks hadn't moved, hovering there with a terrified expression. *Phone,* I thought, then remembered I'd left it downstairs. I turned to the door only to pull up short. It had been Pike on the stairs, the man practically shoving the I.S. agent out of his way and into my room.

"I don't think Doyle wants you for questioning," he said, and Ustice paled.

"Me either."

"I'm going with you," Jenks said, his young face white as he followed me to the stairs.

Getty fidgeted, her grip on her skirts tight at her waist. "Puck's pucker, I don't need anyone to watch me."

"See? She's fine," Jenks said, tone almost bitter. "I used to leave Matalina all the time."

But it was Matalina's garden, I thought, unable to say it, my shoulders slumping.

"I will be fine!" Getty shouted, a bright gold dust exploding from her. "I can stay with the fairies again. They don't care what color my hair is."

"Neither do I!" Jenks exclaimed.

Clearly shocked, the tiny woman adjusted her quiver of arrows. "The Goddess help you, I've been taking care of myself since I was two," she finally muttered. "Go help Rachel." Getty shot an arrow to the bell rope, snaking up the line as if she was a spider. "Go!" she demanded, and I winced, embarrassed.

"Um, I'll be downstairs," Jenks said. Wings a low hum, he fled.

Sighing, I brought the ends of my hair around to my front and finished the braid. I'd feel better with Jenks along, but still . . . "If they don't admit they are falling in love, they're going to kill each other," I muttered as I pushed past Ustice and clumped down the stairs.

"Love?" Pike fell into place behind me, and suddenly the stairway seemed rather . . . tight. "They've only known each other for two days."

I nodded, setting my feet carefully on the dark boards. "It's that fast with pixies. They don't live long enough for it to be anything more than love at first sight." But when I found Doyle and his other two witches waiting impatiently for me at the base of the stairs, Jenks's love life became the least of my worries.

"Thanks for waiting," I said as I leaned against the wall to tug on my boots. I hadn't put them there; it must have been Trent. Or Doyle, maybe, trying to hurry things along. The small foyer felt crowded with Ustice lingering in the stairway as Pike handed me my phone.

Light and shouted questions spilled into the church as the door opened. Doyle was tight-lipped and mean looking. His conversation with Pike had clearly left him stymied but no less determined to bring me in. And yet he hadn't forced the issue of those charmed cuffs. But why would he if he had a trap waiting for me at the I.S.

"Pike, I'm riding with Doyle. Bring my car, will you?" I asked as I dug my keys out of my bag and tossed them to him. They hit Pike's raised hand with a familiar jingle, and Jenks's wing pitch increased. "Jenks, you're with Pike."

"Hey!" the pixy exclaimed, thinking he was being gotten rid of, and I pantomimed being on the phone, then pointed at him. He'd get the message. Ivy.

"Doyle and I need a little alone time," I added, and Jenks's grin widened.

"You are in so much trouble . . ." Jenks half sang, and Doyle grimaced, the scent of angry vampire growing.

"Out," the I.S. agent said, eye twitching as he gestured to the sunlit stoop.

Pike ducked his head, hiding a smile when Jenks landed on his shoulder and whispered something. "Ah, I'll lock up and be right out," Pike said when Doyle gave them both a sharp look, his vampiric hearing probably catching what I had missed.

The news crew had perked up when the door opened, giving the reporter plenty of time to get her mic ready. "Ms. Morgan!" she shouted, managing to stay professional in her monochrome suit despite her flush. "Have you been asked to make a statement at the I.S. in regards to the missing university students? Was that you at the Eden Park ley line this morning? Have you and Trent Kalamack set a date?"

I jerked at the last question, deciding to keep it to a friendly wave when the three agents Doyle had brought flowed down the steps and pushed the woman and her camera detail to the curb. The I.S. van was across the street, and I stood on the stoop and waited as the I.S. did their job, enjoying the complaints and shouted questions I didn't have to answer, glad someone else was going to fight the press for me if only this once. The afternoon sun was warm, but the humidity was gone. It was going to be a beautiful day. Too bad I was probably going to spend most of it underground with Finnis.

But my good mood faltered at the rasping certainty of the door lock sliding into place behind me. Doyle reached for my arm, and I shied away. "Touch me, and I will put an elbow in your gut," I said, lips barely moving as I continued to smile for the camera.

"Then move," he growled, squinting at the bright sun.

Tugging my bag higher over my shoulder, I thumped down the stairs to the cracked sidewalk. If he thought I was getting in the back of that van, he had another think coming.

"Detective Doyle!" the reporter shouted from behind the living wall. "Can you tell us if Rachel Morgan was at the Eden Park ley line this morning? Detective Doyle? Any comment? Come on. Give me something!"

Ignoring her, Doyle opened the van's rear door. "In," he demanded, his eyes pupil black. Somehow I squelched my desire to pat his cheek. Beaming, I flounced my way to the front passenger's door. It wasn't locked, and I waved to the news crew as I stood on the runner before getting in and yanking the door shut.

My smile vanished. I tugged my bag onto my lap, fumbling for my splat gun. The door to the back was still open, and I heard Doyle softly swear. I could down three agents and Doyle here and try to bull my way into the I.S. with my charms to find Finnis, or wait and hope I got deep enough into the I.S. with my charms before I had to insist on keeping them. The choice wasn't hard.

"Keep them on that side of the street!" Doyle shouted, and I jumped when the rear door slammed shut.

I had moments, maybe, and I shifted my splat gun to my lap, hiding it under my bag. I wanted to talk to Doyle, but I wasn't stupid. He was clearly angry as he got in. He put the key into the ignition but didn't start the van, his arm muscles bunching as he gripped the wheel and stared out the front window at nothing. The reporter was still trying to get a comment from the I.S. agents, but when Pike and Jenks came through the rear gate, she abandoned them, practically dragging her camera crew across the grass.

"All right. We're alone." Doyle's low voice was thick with a frustrated anger as he held the wheel with a white-knuckle intensity. "If you think I'm going to—"

"Thank you," I interrupted, and his focus shifted to me, an instant of shock showing before it vanished. "Thank you," I repeated, softer this time. "I would've had to do some serious damage to my church and reputation to avoid those cuffs."

His grip on the wheel eased, and his lips quirked as his gaze went to Pike flirting with the reporter in the middle of the street. "I didn't do it for you."

"No?"

Half-lidded, his eyes found mine. "I know you didn't sell those witches. You don't have it in you."

"I appreciate that," I said, and he laughed. It wasn't a nice sound.

"That wasn't a compliment." One hand fell from the wheel, and he half turned to me. "Finnis isn't at the I.S. He's at his hotel. If you want to talk to him, that's where he'll be."

"And you are telling me this why?"

He shook his head, his bad mood returning, but this time, I didn't think I was the reason. "Because I'm tired of these games," he said. "It's wreaking havoc with everything I know. But understand this, Morgan. Finnis is going to chew you up and swallow you down. I'm simply keeping myself in the game."

"Oh, really," I said, immediately wishing I hadn't, as it was about the lamest thing I'd said in a week.

"Really." Doyle's other hand dropped from the wheel to the ignition. My grip on my splat gun tightened, but we both hesitated when Jenks plastered himself on the front window like a highway casualty.

"Rache!" he shouted, muffled, but he didn't come in when I lowered my window. "Ivy says Finnis is at the Cincinnatian, not the I.S. She'll meet us in the lobby to get us to the executive floors. Trent is on his way, but it's going to take about an hour. What do you want to do about Doyle and his thugs?"

Doyle's lips twisted into an ugly smile. "Like I said. You will not survive, and things will go back to normal."

"Maybe." I twitched my finger, telling Jenks to hang close. "But I want to keep my I.S. contact safe in the meantime."

"Safe?" Doyle echoed, and smiling, I leaned across the van, giving his face a little pat to distract him with one hand as I shot him with a sleepy-time charm with the other. His eyes widened at the puff of air, recognizing it. His scowl of anger was like visual adrenaline, pure enjoyment pulsing through me as the little blue ball hit his chest and burst.

"Morgan!" Pissed, Doyle recoiled, a hand going to the sting of it. "I'm going to . . ."

And then my smile widened as his head dropped and he slumped. The potion hadn't been enough to get through his shirt, but he'd touched it with his hand, and that had done it.

"Slicker than snot on a doorknob," Jenks said through the window. "What about the witches?"

I exhaled, relieved. *For a moment there . . .* Gun in hand, I looked at the I.S. agents, oblivious as they kept the reporter at bay. Not that she was paying any attention to us at the moment, preoccupied with the sexy and oh-so-interestingly scarred Pike, who seemed utterly enamored of her. As I watched, his hand rose to touch her hair, artfully resisting at the last moment as he laughed, low and visceral.

"Ask Pike to bring them around to the back," I said as I reached across Doyle to get the keys. "Do you think the reporter might like a tour of the garden?"

"If you leave without me, I will pee in your coffee every day for a year." Jenks darted to Pike and the reporters, and I began to spindle ley line energy—slow, so no one would notice. It was a skill that I was becoming increasingly thankful for.

Jenks's dust brightened as he lured the reporter and her camera operator behind the six-foot wall. Pike plied his considerable charms on the three agents, all of them too wary of him to do more than glance at the front of the van as he led them to the back. The grinding squeak of it opening startled me, even as I was expecting it.

"Everyone in," Pike said when they balked, the same instinct that had pushed me to the front seat now telling them there was a problem.

"Doyle?" one said, and when the man didn't move, the witch yanked on the line hard enough to make my aura tingle. "Take her!"

"No!" Ustice shouted, jerking when Pike's vamp-fast strike hit the first square on the jaw. The witch fell, his dropped spell rolling into the gutter to fizz and go out.

"Stabils!" I exclaimed as the second agent threw a ball of unaltered energy. Our energies met in a shocking burst of light within the van. Half-blind, I scrunched into the seat, blinking furiously as Pike grunted and the van shook. "Pike! Down!" I shouted as I peppered the bright square that was the door with sleepy-time charms.

Another grunt of pain, then a yelp. Still firing, I wiped the tears away as Pike's foot slammed into an agent's gut. Huffing, the man dropped, downed from my spell coating his shoulder. Careful to keep out of it, Pike grabbed him and threw him into the van.

White-faced, Ustice put his hands in the air. "Peace!" the older agent exclaimed. "I'm not with them."

Pike gave him a dry look, then bent to pick up the other downed agent. "You couldn't wait to spell them before they got in the van, eh?" he complained as he tossed him on top of the first, and I hit him with another sleepy-time charm just in case.

"Seriously?" I complained as Pike manhandled Ustice close. "They're allowed to use lethal magic." I shimmied half out of my chair, my expression holding regret as I faced Ustice. "Ah, I'm going to have to shoot you," I said. "Otherwise you're going to lose your job."

"I'd appreciate that," Ustice said, surprising me as he pulled from Pike's grip. "My brother was on the bridge last year. When magic began to misfire? He could have suffocated, but you saved his life."

I lowered my splat gun as gratitude suddenly swamped me. I'd taken a lot of grief for the bridge incident, unjustly blamed for it when I'd actually saved the lives of everyone who had been caught up in the misfiring magic. To know that my efforts were not only understood but appreciated for a change was nice. "Thanks," I said softly. "I'll leave the keys on the front wheel. If you can, give us at least an hour before you find them."

"Good God, you want to kiss him, maybe?" Pike grumbled, but I couldn't stop smiling.

"Thank you," I whispered, and then I plugged him in the chest and his eyes closed.

Amused, Pike slammed one of the twin doors shut. "You are such a softie."

Maybe, but I felt good, renewed as I got out of the van to leave the keys on the wheel. Pike was already waiting, and as we headed for my car, I whistled for Jenks.

I did not have to contend with I.S. security to find Finnis. It was going to be a good day after all.

CHAPTER

24

ELEVATORS, I THOUGHT AS THE SILVER DOORS SHUT AND I eased to the rear of the tiny hotel elevator, trying to give Pike as much room as possible. The shaft was not air-conditioned, and I could smell the perfume and aftershave of everyone who had been in it over the past half hour. Even so, there was little that could cover the delicious scent of excited vampire as Pike and I descended to the lower, more exclusive levels of the Cincinnatian.

"You okay?" Pike eyed my tension, probably mistaking it for worry.

Nodding, I flipped my braid back and found a wan smile. "I don't like elevators," I said, though that wasn't exactly true. Jenks would have laughed his dust off, making me glad that he'd flown ahead to find Ivy and let her know we were on our way down. She hadn't been at the front desk, and I was worried. I would have called her, but I didn't know if her phone was being monitored. I was relying on pixy communication, which wouldn't give us or her much of a heads-up if we were walking into a bad situation.

"It is tight, isn't it." His hands clasped politely like a fig leaf, Pike studied the ceiling.

"Mmmm." I shifted my shoulders, uncomfortable when my connection to the ley line vanished. Doubt that I was doing the smart thing rose up, the kind that made you slow and question yourself, but honestly, this was where I needed to be and who I needed to be with. I couldn't do anything from an I.S. interrogation room, and that's where I had been headed.

Pike sighed as he continued to stare at the ceiling, trying to ignore that my pulse had quickened and my temperature had spiked. I could sense his bone-deep fatigue under the deepening bruises and mending lacerations. He was running on Brimstone and the blood of the undead, and when that ran out, he'd crash and burn like a blood drive during the Turn.

I was glad he was with me, though, and when he sensed my scrutiny and looked down, I gave him a little shrug. *No wonder Trent is jealous,* I thought as I ran my gaze over him, rather liking his tailored suit hiding his limp and gashed knee. And then my eyes dropped as a memory intruded of Kisten, and me, and an elevator. *My God. The man had known how to kiss.*

"Nothing to be nervous about," Pike said as the elevator halted briefly between floors and hotel security did a cursory check for sharp, metallic, pointy things before allowing us to continue to the executive levels. "I didn't think Rachel Morgan got nervous. No . . ." He ran a hand over his chin. "She gets even."

I chuckled, relaxing as the lift jostled into motion. "I'm not entirely comfortable forcing a conversation with Finnis when you are hurt," I admitted.

"I'm fine." Pike smacked his chest, then coughed. "Real good," he gasped as he caught his breath. "Never better." He hesitated, brow furrowed in concern. "Ivy's going to be there, right?"

I nodded. *In. Down to the executive suites. Curse Finnis, then out before they find Doyle in an I.S. van at my curb. Easy-peasy.*

But I was never that lucky, and I tugged my bag higher up my shoulder when the elevator dinged and the doors opened.

Pike strode forward, leaving me to blink at the heavy scent of the undead. Breath shallow, I inched out after him. Immediately my neck began tingling as I scanned the high-ceilinged lobby-like entry done in black and white. We were too deep to reach the ley lines, but I had a mess of energy spindled in my head and chi that would give me one, maybe two good pops. My splat gun and the memory hiccup curse Trent and I had made were in my bag, and I fingered one of the ley line circle charms I had originally picked up for Vivian. It would protect me if someone began using live ammunition.

The manned concierge desk was to the right, a modest fountain and moderately busy bar to the left. Vid screens on the walls gave the impression of being thirty stories up, not five stories down, and by the angle of the sun, I guessed it was a live feed.

A second bank of elevators went to the lower rooms, but it was the elaborate staircase going down where my attention lingered, all dark wood and white carpet. Finnis was there among the few long undead with enough money for city-hotel living. *Should have parked your undead ass in the I.S.,* I thought, glad he had underestimated me.

"Ah, Pike. The concierge is eyeing us," I said as I swung my bag around for my splat pistol, and Pike smiled.

"I've got this." Pike strode forward, leaning over the desk to hang up the phone and grip the living vampire's wrist. "Give us five minutes, and I will return your hand in the same shape I took it."

Uncowed, the scarred, well-dressed man began to protest.

Pike leaned in, his small but sharp teeth showing as he yanked the hapless clerk closer. "Give us ten minutes," he said, his low voice sultry with a bound heat. "And I will give you a night."

Holy crap, he's pulling an aura, I thought, pulse quickening as the wide-eyed clerk glanced from Pike to me, before returning to Pike. I mean, I knew he was capable of it. Most scions were. The number of times Ivy . . . And Kisten. Kisten had been able to bespell the willing. But Pike? Damn. He clearly knew what he was doing, and my breath caught when a spike of danger-driven desire dove to my groin and flashed through me.

I wasn't the only one. The clerk had fallen into a heavy, pupil-wide state as he licked his lower lip and nodded. "Sure," he rasped, shuddering as Pike let go of his wrist. Standing, the clerk put a BACK IN TEN sign on the desk and went to the bar.

Looking too smug to live, Pike straightened, his stance still holding the promise of dark sheets and high ecstasy. Seeing it there, heartache mixed with desire. I couldn't move as memories of Kisten plinked through me like diamonds: the passion he pulled through me with his touch, the danger that he would forget who he was, the thrill that I wanted him to.

"Oh. God. Sorry," Pike said, smile vanishing as he took several quick breaths to get his bloodlust under control.

"It's not you," I said, voice low. I missed Kisten, yes, but I would miss Trent more, and I forced my thoughts to the present.

We both turned as the elevator dinged. My hands were sweaty, and I dropped my splat gun into my bag where it belonged. It was all I had besides my charms. Well, that and my friends.

"Hey, Rache," Jenks sang out as he darted from the elevator, and I held my breath to force my pulse to slow even more. Ivy followed him out, smart in her short black skirt and professional jacket. Her white blouse was immaculate, and she'd wrapped her hair in a tight bun. I could feel Pike soak her in as if she was a long drink.

"Where is he?" I asked as she sauntered across the lobby. There were tunnels from here to just about everywhere in the city, left over from the Turn, and that he might be gone was a real worry.

"Finnis?" Ivy's placid gaze went from Pike to the concierge getting himself a stiff drink. Her eyebrows rose as she saw my flush, and I shrugged. "I suggest we take the stairs," she said as she gestured to them. "Rachel often has issues with closed spaces."

Jenks snorted as he tried to land on my shoulder. "Yeah, one time she and—"

"Stop," I interrupted him. "Or I'll have Getty tape your wings shut while you sleep."

"Ha!" Jenks barked, now flying backward before us. "You think she could—"

I raised my eyebrows as he thought about it.

"Never mind," he muttered, his dust becoming a dull blue as he settled on Ivy's shoulder.

Ivy's arms swung confidently as we took the stairs, our steps silent on the carpet. "Word is you sold your students to the demons this morning," she said.

"Hodin," I grumped as we passed the first landing and continued on. "He was pretending to be me. That's why I'm forcing our meeting with Finnis. It's that or an I.S. interrogation room."

She bobbed her head, glancing at Pike, who had slowed so he could watch her ass. "I figured," Ivy said, looking Pike up and down until he grinned at her. "No Trent?" she asked as we rounded the second landing.

"He made the mistake of going home," Jenks said as he flew from her shoulder. His expressive face twisted in distaste as he waved a hand as if to clear the air. We'd reached the lowest level, and the pheromones were making me jittery. "Tink's titties, Ivy. How can you stay down here without ripping everyone's clothes off?"

"You get used to it. Jenks, don't touch that," she added when he hovered over an objet d'art that was either two women passionately kissing or an ocean wave. The entire thing was crimson and gold, gaudy.

"Not there, either," I muttered when he tried to land on my shoulder, and the pixy went to Pike instead. Whispers were rising behind us. We were passing more living vampires than the undead, all of them service oriented, not clientele, all of them having a smug knowledge I wasn't comfortable with.

"What's going on that I'm not aware of?" I said.

"You're being recognized." Ivy made a sharp turn and pushed past two heavy double-swing doors. "He's at the pool."

My thought that the chlorine would help cut the vampiric incense vanished as I followed Ivy through another set of identical doors and the humidity jumped. It was a pool all right, much like any other hotel pool, with misty glass, bright lights, and sharp echoes. Individual tented cabanas lined one side, lounge chairs and low tables the other. A manned bar took up a third side, and changing rooms were against the last. There was no scent of chlorine, and I frowned when I realized it was a salt pool.

Finnis was lounging in the hot tub, bubbles hiding everything from the neck down. He was the only patron here, everyone else being staff.

"Hey, Rache? I think that there is a saltwater pool," Jenks said, and sighed.

"Smart," I said, pretty sure that the concentration would be high enough to keep my sleepy-time charms from invoking.

Ivy came to a wide-stance halt, her confidence vanishing as Finnis's gaze rose to us. "Rachel Morgan!" he said, loud voice echoing and long canines gleaming from the spray. "Welroe. And little pixy Jenks," he added insultingly. "I wasn't expecting you until tonight. How nice of you to break up my day."

"Little pixy Jenks?" Jenks muttered, and I spun a finger, telling him to loop the cameras.

"Finnis," I said as Jenks darted away, and Pike bobbed his head in greeting, settling in behind and a little to my left. It was the stance of a sentry, and I tensed even as I appreciated it.

"Ah, ah . . ." Finnis pointed cheerfully at us as if we were playing his game exactly as he wanted. "I had a feeling you'd show up unexpectedly. Relax. Enjoy my hospitality. Would

you care for something to eat? Drink? Allow me to call up
to the gift shop for swim attire. The water is to die for."

Good God. He didn't just say that. I glanced at the nearby
table holding his robe and room key. "No, thanks." The loss
of my splat gun was going to hurt. Fortunately ley line
amulets would still work—as would my new memory hiccup curse.

"Ivy, I will not need you until tonight," Finnis said as he
reached for his nearby drink of wine and took a sip. At
least, I was telling myself it was wine. Real blood would
have clotted. Unless they treated it. Which was not merely
possible but likely. *Stop it, Rachel.*

"I'll stay, thank you," Ivy said, her low heels planted on
the damp pool deck.

Finnis looked at us looking at him. His eyes flashed pupil black, and then he levered himself up, moving with an
exaggerated slowness to the stairs, bubbles reluctantly sliding from him like a lover's fingers. A tickling of vampire
incense began to unfurl deep within me: tendrils of danger
and ecstasy tugging at memories to make me lock my
knees and wish I was anywhere other than here.

From the corner of the room, a young woman I hadn't
noticed sprang forward with an insanely fluffy towel, drying him as he got out. His feet were thin and bony, and I
swear, probably the only part of him that wasn't scarred.
White lines detailing past atrocities covered him in a disturbing precision, as if whoever had marked him had been
making art. The parallel curves and spirals were everywhere, running under his baggy swim trunks to where my
imagination filled in the blanks.

"Word is Doyle was bringing you in for trafficking in
human familiars," Finnis said as he shrugged into the dark
robe the woman held for him, tying it smartly shut with a
firm yank. "Shame, that," he said, hesitating as he caught
me staring at his artful scars. "I mean, it happens, but
shame you got caught."

"That wasn't me." Anger burned, and my neck stopped
tingling. Disgust, perhaps, had driven even the vampiric-

pheromone-induced lust from me. The thought to curse him and get out of here rose and fell, but there was the chance I could convince him to leave, and he clearly wanted to chat.

Finnis didn't need to breathe other than when he wanted to talk, and yet, he exhaled as if tired as he settled himself at the round table. The long undead prided themselves on maintaining an illusion of life. It went hand in hand with convincing their children that they loved them, and therefore made them willing to sacrifice their blood, health, and often their lives.

Silent attendants brought him a new glass and combed his hair before melting back into the corners. The woman who had dried him knelt on a cushion at his feet and began to massage his toes. "It looked like you," Finnis said, low voice holding amusement as he twitched his robe to draw my eye to his calf and the swirl of scars hinting at the shape of an owl. "It sounded like you. I think it was you. More importantly, so does the I.S."

I yanked my shoulder bag higher, appreciating the comforting weight of my splat gun. He had dried off. I'd have to hit him right in the face or feet. Soaking his robe to reach his skin was a stretch. He might appear relaxed, but the eight feet between us could shrink to zero fast.

Finnis's attention went across the pool, and warning coursed through me when both Ivy and Pike stiffened. It was hotel security, their black uniforms detailed only with an elaborate *C*.

"I am fine!" Finnis bellowed as they filed in. "Get out!" But they didn't, arraying themselves along the wall like so many soldiers. Smiling, Finnis shrugged good-naturedly. "What can you do? If they neglected me, I would complain and demand a refund, yes?"

"You wanted to see Constance," I said, my thoughts on the memory hiccup ley line amulet. It would work, salt pool or no. "Soon as the sun goes down—"

"No need." Finnis took a sip from his glass. "We've been talking all afternoon."

"Wait. What?" Shocked, I sent my gaze to Ivy. She was clearly confused. Pike's eyes had dilated to a thin rim of brown as he held himself unmoving. My God. Had someone found her? Changed her back? It wasn't that hard.

"I'm surprised she's not out here by now." Finnis's focus sharpened on the changing rooms. "Constance?" he shouted. "Pike and Morgan are here!"

Pike stiffened, not in fear, but uncertainty. "Holy sweet mother of Jesus," he swore when the door to the ladies' changing room banged open and the small woman stepped out, her damaged body showcased in a white two-piece and her robe, twin to Finnis's, open to show her scar-ridden body and scads of jewelry.

"That can't be her," I whispered, and the spicy scent of Pike drifted to me, mixing with Ivy's in a tantalizing lure. "Pike, that can't be her."

"Why, because you killed her twice?" Finnis said, and I shook my head, too dumbfounded to explain.

"Pike, dar-r-r-ling," the woman crooned, her six-inch heels clicking as she crossed the damp pool deck. "Go put on a swimsuit. I insist. Rachel, you too."

I didn't move and she frowned, toying with her jewelry as she settled in behind Finnis, draping herself over him so her lips were by his ear. "I told you to stay in the pool, love. The salt will protect you."

Finnis chuckled as he played with a drooping ringlet of her dark hair. "You're afraid of Morgan?" he said, and Constance pulled from him, smiling to show her long canines.

"No, but you should be," she said.

And with that, I knew it wasn't Constance. It had to be Hodin. Crap on toast and burn Tink's panties, it was Hodin, a vampire's black eyes and all.

I glanced at Pike, seeing he knew it, too, and Ivy, by her angry expression. But the worst thing? I think that Finnis did as well. He knew and was going along with it. *Why?*

"We had a long chat, *Constance* and I," Finnis said as the small woman moved, driving the woman at his feet away with a well-placed kick before settling herself at the table beside him.

"That's not Constance," I said, worried that the real master vampire was dead. Twice dead.

Constance, or Hodin, rather, lifted Finnis's drink and took a sip. "Bravo," he said in Constance's high voice, his eyes shifting to their natural goat-slitted red and back again.

"Son of a bitch," Pike swore softly, and I scanned for Jenks's telltale dust, not seeing it. My mind was whirling as Hodin's plan unfurled within it. His shape-shifting was absolute. No one would believe that I hadn't sold my students to the demons, especially if Hodin went on national TV looking like me and boasting of it. No one would believe that he wasn't Constance if Finnis sanctioned it. I'd be in Alcatraz, and Hodin would rule Cincinnati after he killed Finnis and whoever else the DC vamps sent, probably blaming me for it.

Crap on toast, I had given Cincinnati to Hodin.

"That's not Constance," I said again, and Finnis snickered, his expression twisting even uglier as he snapped his fingers and pointed at his glass to prompt one of the bar attendants.

"I didn't come here for Constance," Finnis said as two new glasses were set on the table and the server retreated. "I came here to get that soul curse of yours taken out of FSCA consideration. Do that, and I will leave. Tell my colleagues that everything is fine in Cincinnati." His gaze slid to Hodin, taking in the treated blood in distaste. "You and Constance will be free to hash it out, may the best demon win. If you don't withdraw your curse from consideration, well . . . I sanction Constance's rule, whereupon your mole Doyle hauls you in and you go to jail for trafficking in human familiars."

Pike eased up to my right, Ivy to my left. I didn't know where Jenks was, but I knew he was okay. "This isn't going to work," I said, and Hodin chuckled, Constance's high voice sounding odd as it came from him.

"It already has," he said, maintaining his illusion of the small, dark woman. "You should leave before Doyle makes it past the front desk."

"He's here?" Pike glanced at the hotel security arrayed between us and the door.

Finnis sipped his drink, staining his lips red. "Of course he's here. Stuck in the elevator until I see fit for him to join us." Eyebrows high, he drew his phone closer and checked on something. "I'm an upright, honest citizen. I will not harbor a fugitive wanted for selling people to demons as familiars."

"Son of a bastard," I whispered as Ivy exchanged a long look with Pike, then turned her back on Finnis to stare down hotel security. Hodin's ugly past aside, I was beginning to understand why my demon kin all hated him. How could I trust anyone when it could be Hodin I was talking to? Hodin I was mad at? Hodin pulling my strings? If I didn't end this now, he would rule Cincinnati as an undead vampire. Forever.

Finnis took a sip of his drink and made a satisfied sigh. "Again, you are mistaken that I care. So. Morgan. Witch-born demon. Make your choice known. Agree to withdraw your spell from FSCA consideration, or I confirm that this is indeed Constance. Either way, you will ultimately lose the city, but one way, you are alive. The other . . . not so much." He shifted, his robe almost falling open. "Hodin tells me you're not a real demon. More of a witch with good contacts. Take away your friends, and you're easy to down. And you are down, Morgan."

Pike was beginning to fidget. On my other side, Ivy was frighteningly still. It was smelling like scared vamp in here, but it was coming from hotel security, not my team.

"It's my friends who keep me alive," I said, glancing at the men and women in black across the pool. It was their eight to Ivy and Pike's two, and the odds were not in hotel security's favor. Finnis, though, was clueless, and Hodin, obliviously, thought he was the pixy shits.

As a child, I had shuffled past too many closed hospital doors at the children's wing, knowing what heartache and agony passed beyond it. Children die. I was almost one of them. But to make them die alone . . . While their parents wept, unable to hold them as they breathed their last? *An eternity of captivity is too good for you, Hodin.*

"Well?" Finnis prompted smugly.

I forced my jaw to unclench and shook my hands out. Hodin's confident smile faltered at my knowing hatred, but it wasn't until I saw the faintest sifting of pixy dust from a potted palm that my resolve coalesced. "You're right," I said, and Pike turned to me, his expression blank with the worry I had given up. "No, he's right," I said again, twitching my eye in sort of a wink. Ivy cleared her throat, hands fisting, and Pike followed the slightest rasp of dragonfly wings to just over Finnis's shoulder. "I'm not exactly overflowing with demonic skills, but you've made a classic demon-practitioner mistake, Finnis. One I'm trying to impart to my students, who I will shortly bring back to reality along with their instructor and an overly inquisitive librarian."

Finnis's pupils began to shrink. "I made no mistake," he said flatly.

Thank God I brought everything, I thought, glancing over my shoulder at the eight nervous security guards. "It's when you think you got the better end of a deal that it usually bites you on the ass." I studied my nails as if bored. "That would be about now."

Hodin made a soft huff, drawing my attention. "You, Finnis," I said, taking a step closer, and from behind me, I felt hotel security stir, "made the mistake of hanging everything on Hodin, and he's a murdering, lying, self-serving, untrustworthy son of a bastard who will drop you as soon as he gets what he needs from you. Which is probably also now."

Still not believing, Finnis glanced at the image of Constance beside him. "And what does he need?" the undead vampire mocked as Hodin beamed and put a tiny dark hand on Finnis's.

I shrugged. I was too deep for a ley line, but I had a couple of good pops of magic in me. Ivy had braced herself, a wicked, anticipatory gleam in her eye. Seeing Pike almost oblivious, she nudged him and he mirrored her ready stance, clearly not knowing why. "A way to force me to act, I suppose," I said, mentally telling Jenks to stay put for three seconds more. "But if he doesn't have you, he's got nothing."

I took a breath, unwinding everything I had spindled in my head and chi. Power raced through my neural net, burning through old channels, spilling into new as it flowed to my hands. *"Celero dilatare!"*

Barely harnessed energy burst from me, rocking me back as a wave of force exploded from my hands. Ivy and Pike shifted with it, and then Ivy leapt clear over the swimming pool, her vampiric strength making it easy. Grinning, Pike followed. To a man, the eight figures in black had slammed into the glass walls, temporarily stunned.

Finnis sprang to his feet. Hodin, too, had stood, but the image of the small dark woman was gone and an annoyed demon in leather had taken her place.

"Finnis is mine, Hodin!" I shouted as I sprang for the vampire, simultaneously pulling the pin on the ley line circle amulet and throwing it at the alarmed undead.

Hodin retreated, clearly not having expected a frontal attack, much less a circle. The thought that I'd use someone else's magic probably never entered his mind. I grinned when the bubble swam up around Finnis, preventing Hodin from simply grabbing him and jumping out. *Divide to conquer. Yeah, I can do that, too.*

Ivy's shouts echoed in the hard space, punctuated by pained grunts and the splintering of redwood loungers. Cries came from the bar, and the massage woman fled to an overturned table.

"A circle?" Hodin said, clearly amused as he reassessed. "You are fine, Finnis. Relax. I'll have it down in a moment."

"I only need a moment," I said, then started when Jenks landed on my shoulder.

"This should be fun," the pixy said as I felt in my bag for my splat gun. "I haven't ass-kicked an undead since Piscary."

It was getting noisy behind me, but I didn't dare look as more pained shouts echoed. Someone went in the pool, and water splashed up. "Did you curse your kin's children yourself, or did you look the other way when your elven masters did it?" I said, splat gun in hand, my stance sure on the wet pool deck as I stood between Hodin and Finnis. "You foul little bootlicker!"

Expression twisted, Hodin drew a ring off his finger and threw it.

"Down!" I shouted, Jenks fleeing as I dodged the green and brown spell that blossomed between us. Hitting the pool deck, I rolled. A high-pitched scream drew my eye to the masseuse, but she was fine, cowering in a corner as the curse dissolved a table into a bubbling goo.

"Behind you!" Jenks shouted, and I raised my splat gun, dropping one of the security guards that had slipped past Ivy and Pike. Finnis cowered in his circle, yelling for security as spent energy rocked between the glass walls and made the pool water jump and crest.

I got to my feet, weapon unshaking in my grip. "Did you lure my class to the ever-after and sell them to Dali?" I asked. "Did Dali and Al think it was me?" I shouted, and Hodin's thin lips curved up in a Grinch-worthy smile of pleasure.

"Of course they did," he said, his entire hand glowing to his elbow with a coming curse. "They *want* to believe you are no better than them. It makes them happy," he mocked.

Angry, I shot at him. He vanished, the gray haze making an audible pop as it rushed in and was gone.

Instinct moved me, my splat gun firing into a flash of haze that might have been Hodin. The little blue balls hit the pool deck and broke, the charms inside made useless by the salt water.

"Rache!" Jenks shouted, and I turned, firing at Hodin before he could marshal a curse.

"You little canicula!" he swore, annoyed, then vanished again.

Pulse fast, I spun, looking for Hodin. Ivy was soaked,

her dark hair draped like ribbons as she continued to smack hotel security into the walls. Pike was right there with her, playing off her moves as if they had trained at the same dojo. Five men were down and not moving, one was floundering in the water. Hodin was MIA. Jenks hovered, blade pulled, as he scanned the pool.

"Is he gone?" I said, breathless, and when Jenks nodded, my focus sharpened on Finnis. The undead vampire had gotten to his feet, a dismissive sneer on his face. Eyes pupil black, he watched Ivy and Pike clearly enjoying themselves as they took out his remaining security. Hodin had broken the ley line circle spell at some point. Finnis was free, but that was okay. Now I could hit him.

"Hello," I said, and his dangerous gaze found mine. Lips parting, his expression promised equal levels of pain and pleasure until I died from it.

But I was so pissed, that didn't work on me anymore.

"You need to go home," I said, my aim on him never wavering as I sidestepped to where I'd dropped my bag.

"I am home," Finnis growled, hands crooked into claws.

And then he jerked, backpedaling when Jenks dropped down, his wings a harsh rasp and his sword slashing.

We are an effective team, I thought smugly as I fumbled for that memory hiccup amulet to curse Finnis into whatever state of bliss I wanted. Though, it might be hard to get him to believe that the chaos behind me was anything other than an attack on him.

"Hodin!" Jenks shrilled, and I gasped, using the last mote of energy in me to block an ugly incoming ball of green and brown. I hit the pool deck hard, the uninvoked memory hiccup curse pinging once before bouncing into the pool with a little *splooch*.

Three feet away, a potted palm tree burst into flame. I frowned at Hodin's disappointment as an annoying hooting began and the sprinklers over the bar engaged. New cries of panic rose, and more staff fled.

"You are such a *coward*! Leave or stay. Not both!" I shouted as I scrabbled to my feet and lunged at Hodin.

Shocked, the demon froze, his hand splayed to choose a ring. My foot slammed into his gut, and then he vanished, sending me stumbling to catch my balance against a pillar. *Got you, you little dimension-jumping bastard.*

"Ivy!" Pike shouted, and I turned, pulse fast, but it was only the two of them working to throw one of the hotel security into the hall by way of a window.

"You okay, Rache?" Jenks asked as the glass shattered, and I wiped the pain from the flat of my hand and looked for Finnis. The vampire was alone. At least, I thought he was Finnis. I'd have to down him to be sure. It could be Hodin. Maybe.

"I told you he'd cut you loose the first chance he got," I said, then shot him with a sleepy-time potion.

Finnis yelped at the sting, but he'd raised his arm and all I'd hit was robe. His eyes were darker than sin when they found mine, and I braced myself, seeing in their unholy depths his desire to rip my throat and pull every last ounce of blood into him.

"Try it," I mocked, and he sprang at me.

I squeezed the trigger, puffs of air jolting me as I unloaded the entire clip at him. Jenks was shrilling, and I retreated, squinting through Jenks's dust, my aim never wavering as I peppered the oncoming force of nature with little blue pellets that burst and blinded him into an unholy rage.

Yelping, I tripped on one of the dropped security. I went down, still firing. Three shots found the little triangle of scarred flesh below Finnis's chin and his howl of rage echoed, overwhelming Pike's shout and the crash of someone falling into the bottles behind the bar.

And then Finnis hit the deck. Out cold. Two feet from me.

Panting, I stayed where I was, my butt going damp from the wet pool deck, my empty gun pointed.

"Good shootin', Rache," Jenks said, wings rasping as he hovered over the barrel of my cherry-red splat gun.

"Yeah?" I spun at a sliding thud to see Ivy pull the last of the hotel security up, giving him a shake before tossing him into a pillar, where he hit and slid to the pavers. The waves in the pool were beginning to subside, and I sat there, feeling shaky with the vamp pheromones and adrenaline swirling in me. It was only the masseuse left, crying in the corner, but she seemed okay, and I exhaled in relief when Ivy flipped her wet hair back and sauntered over.

"Damn, Tamwood," Pike said in admiration as he fingered a new tear in his shirt. "Do you have any sisters?"

"Just one, and if you touch her, I'll skin you alive."

Pike grinned, stooping to pick up a lost shoe before limping forward. "Promises, promises. How about you and me, then. Friday night. I'm paying."

In more ways than you can guess, I thought as I rubbed my elbow to gauge the coming bruise. It was over—for the moment—and I nudged Finnis with my toe to be sure he was out. Little red pustules were beginning to rise where his skin showed. It wasn't my sleepy-time potion. Jenks had pixed him. Pixed him good.

Ivy extended a hand to haul me up. She was dripping wet, and I wondered if she had gone in the pool at some point. "You think you could keep up with me?" she said to Pike, but her eyes were on me until I nodded that I was okay. But I wasn't. I had a really big problem. Oblivious to it, she gave my shoulder a squeeze and went to check on Pike.

"It's definitely worth finding out." Pike groaned, his limp more pronounced as he scuffed to a halt. "You want to curse him here or in his room?" he asked as he felt his ribs, clearly pained.

Sighing, I stared at the bottom of the pool, where the circlet of twisted silver sat as if it was a demonic pool toy. "I need a hook," I said, glad that salt water didn't break ley line charms.

"I'll get it." Her breath catching, Ivy dove in to come up with it.

The hotel security people were beginning to stir, and Pike went to drag them into a pile where he could keep an eye on them, his vampiric strength making it seem easy.

"Jenks, sing out if Hodin shows," I said as I extended a hand to Ivy and helped her up onto the pool deck.

"On it," he said, dusting a cheerful silver as he buzzed to the bar.

Ivy handed me the amulet, her long fingers dripping as they met mine. A small smile flitted over her usually placid face as Pike manhandled the hotel security, coming across as both firm and understanding as they woke up. "He's good," she said as she wiped the water from her chin. "Not as good as me, but good enough to keep you alive."

I fingered the wet charm, wincing at Finnis covered in a painful-looking rash. At least I knew it was him. Hodin wouldn't have let his rage give me the chance to down him. "That was my thought, too," I said, worried as the hotel staff began to gather at the broken doors, afraid to come in but annoying all the same.

Hodin had bounced in and out of reality as if he had been stepping from room to room. How could I be the sub-rosa when I couldn't jump a line without Bis? If I knew how to skip realities, I could have followed Hodin. Finished this. As it was, Hodin was probably out somewhere pretending to be me, or Constance, or Finnis, or even Trent. *No wonder Al hates him,* I thought as I dried the amulet.

Clearly sore, Pike joined us. "That was fun," he said, worry settling into his brow as he noticed Finnis, out cold. "That's not catching, is it?" he asked as he squinted at the rash.

"No," I said, and reassured, Pike dragged Finnis to a support pole and propped him up.

"You going to curse him, or what?" he said, and I frowned, fingering the amulet in my hand, the twisted metal circlet utterly useless. Oh, the curse was still good, but using it wouldn't accomplish a damn thing. An entire night of spelling wasted. I could have gone to Trent's for that midnight ride for all the good my planning had done.

"This isn't going to work," I said, jaw tight as I put the curse into my bag, grimacing. The cloth purse was soaking wet.

Pike's eyes widened. "Why not?"

Jenks's wings rasped as he dropped down. "The cameras are on a loop. The only thing they got was us walking in and a few minutes talking." His gaze went to the hotel staff now beginning to inch their way in, their conversation loud and accusing as they saw the damage. "We're good, Rache. Do your thing."

"And after I curse him?" Peeved, I glanced at Ivy. "Hodin is still out there. I should have thought of this before, but I had no idea that Hodin would align himself with Finnis."

Ivy's lips parted. "Hodin can break the curse."

"Hodin can break the curse," I echoed, feeling stupid. "But even if he doesn't, Finnis is not here to see Constance. He said as much." I gestured to the unconscious vampire, wishing I could turn him into a mouse, too. "She's an excuse, a reason to give the media for his presence. He's here to quash the soul curse." My eyes met Ivy's, and she blanched. "Sending him home with happy thoughts about Constance won't accomplish anything."

Pike's face twisted, his weight going onto his good foot. "Because that's not what he's here for."

Ivy's hand trembled as she touched my shoulder. "Then that's what you should do," she said, her voice a pained whisper. "Withdraw the application. We can hold the city without it."

My chin lifted, and I pulled her into a quick hug. I felt her tense in surprise, and I tightened my grip, not letting her go as I felt her heartache. She knew holding Cincy without the promise of that curse would be impossible, and yet there she was, willing to sacrifice everything to keep me safe for one more day.

"I'm not taking the soul curse out of FSCA consideration," I said, finally pushing back so I could see her expression. "What you and Nina have is not wrong. The old undead want to quash it because they are afraid. There is love there, real love, and they know they can't match or overcome that. They're desperately clinging to their ways of domination through dependency. It's the only thing they have. They are afraid because they know their power will falter and die because of what you share."

"Rachel, I—" she managed, and then her eyes welled with emotion.

"It's okay," I said, giving her arm a squeeze.

Pike cleared his throat, but his gaze held a deep understanding, not embarrassment. "So what do we do?"

Jenks shrugged as I turned to Finnis. He looked utterly foul lying there, an unconscious spider of ego and id, his mouth open to show his long teeth and that great hole of a mouth that could never be filled or satisfied. "Nothing at the moment. Hodin is the greater threat." The Turn take it, I had so much to do. All of it revolved around Hodin.

"Nothing?" Ivy had collected herself, a fragile strength growing stronger.

"For the moment," I said again. "Okay." I brushed at my damp jeans. "Pike, I want you to stay here with Ivy. Help her with Finnis. I'll deal with him after I finish with Hodin."

"Sure." Mood content, Pike pulled Finnis's half-emptied wineglass closer. "As long as the minifridge stays stocked."

"I'm serious," I said as he emptied the glass. "I'll keep him spelled, but it will be up to you and Ivy to keep him away from Hodin. I'm going home with Jenks to change, meet up with Trent, and then the three of us will check on the real Constance. Get her somewhere safe before Hodin turns into me and squishes her on national TV."

Good God, the damage he could do was enormous. There was nothing on the law books about demons committing acts disguised as another, other than whoever contracted them to do it was to blame. Demons were too egotistical to allow a face other than their own to take credit for their actions as they wielded their enormous power. Hodin seemed to be the exception, and I didn't think it was a lack of ego. No, it was his lack of confidence. He had been denied the limitless power that lay in the collective, power that I, an adopted kin, had access to. Pretending to be someone else might be cowardly but, I had to admit, was extremely effective. Even worse, the I.S. would go along with it, glad to see me gone. And as I stood there, my hatred for Hodin trickled into something harder, more enduring.

"Babysit Finnis. Can do." Pike's gaze went to the unhappy woman now standing poolside, frowning at the damage with an eye to tacking it on someone's room bill. "Looks like it's all over but for the accountants."

I rocked from heel to toe, feeling my socks squish. "I have to catch Hodin," I said. "Maybe I can lure him into a trap by changing Constance back. He can't pretend to be her if she's on national TV."

Pike jerked. "You wouldn't."

"I might." I was damp and uncomfortable, and I didn't like that that woman with the clipboard was coming my way. "Hey, I gotta go. Ivy, you good?"

She nodded, her stance as she stood between hotel management and Finnis becoming sure.

"Text me if you need bail money," Pike said with a grin, and Jenks's laugh sounded like wind chimes.

Worried, I gave Pike's shoulder a squeeze, and his attention jumped to me in surprise. "Thanks. You do the same," I said before I walked away, taking the long way around the pool to avoid the tight-lipped woman and her clickety-clack heels.

Jenks's wings were a familiar hum as he flew beside me. "Don't worry about it, Rache," he said as I picked my way past the broken loungers. "I always said your best work is improv."

"Yeah?" The air in the hallway was cooler, and I stifled a shiver, feeling the damp in my clothes. "Maybe, but just once, I'd like a plan to go as I wanted."

Pixy on my shoulder, I took the stairs to the surface, confident that Jenks would warn me if anyone even thought to stop me. I should have been thinking about how I was going to rescue everyone, or what I could do instead of bringing Constance back from rodenthood to lure Hodin close enough to bottle. But as I found the surface lobby and asked the car attendant to bring my MINI around, I found all I could think about was Al.

Much as I didn't want to be that person, Hodin had to go, and me? Well, I was ready to stuff him into a little tiny universe of his own.

CHAPTER

25

HEAD DOWN OVER MY PHONE, I STEPPED OVER THE LOW stone wall separating the graveyard from my witch's garden behind the church. Doyle had a man at my front curb, but either he failed to remember that the property ran all the way to the next street and I could simply come in the back door—or he didn't care. Jenks was at my shoulder, his worried yellow dust telling me he wanted to fly ahead and check on Getty.

"Trent is at Piscary's," I said as I read Trent's text. "Constance is fine. He lured her into her traveling cage with a diamond cuff link he had in his glove box, and he'll bring her over as soon as it gets dark."

Jenks's wings rasped against my neck, cool and familiar. "The garden is clear, Rache. I'm going to check out the church." He rose up, his dust heavy as he flew to the porch door. "Getty? I'm here! You still alive?"

I felt good, sure that Getty was going to become a permanent fixture in the church whether Jenks liked it or not.

My knee hurt as I took the low stairs up onto the porch, but not bad for having downed a master vampire and scaring off a demon. I was still damp, too, and I was tired of being uncomfortable. "Jenks?" I called as I went into the kitchen. "I'm going to take a quick shower."

Jenks flew in from the front of the church. "The fairies don't know where Getty is," he said, clearly worried.

My gaze went to the quiet garden. "Baribas," I whispered as I dropped my shoulder bag onto the counter, and Jenks's hand touched the hilt of his sword.

"What did you do to Getty!" he shouted, looking over my shoulder and clearly not talking to me.

I spun, eyes widening. Hodin was standing in the hall leading to the sanctuary.

Gasping, I dropped back, yanking the power from the ley line into me as Jenks dove at the demon to give me a few precious seconds. Silent, Hodin raised his hand to ward him off, tiny bells on his spelling robe's sash ringing a surreal warning.

"Where is Getty!" Jenks shrilled, slashing at the demon's wrist before darting at his face.

He was here. In my kitchen. I was not fettered by charmed silver or so deep underground I had no power. Energy roared through me, burning as it flowed over much-used channels to my fingers. There was no time, and I flung my hand out, the words to blast him to hell on my lips.

"Rache! No!" Jenks shrilled, his dust a warning red as he rose up from Hodin, his sword bloodred. "It's Stef! It's Stef!"

Stef? The words to harness the energy died unsaid. I fisted my hands, agony burning my palms as energy dripped to the floor without direction. Hunched in pain, I met Hodin's red, goat-slitted, terrified eyes. They were not Stef's eyes, but the fear in them was not Hodin's, either, and I hauled the power in my hands back, burning as it scraped over my synapses and I shoved it down into the earth. I groaned, hands jerking as they found the counter even as I scanned the corners of the room for Hodin.

Crap on toast. I could have killed her!

"Stef?" I croaked as the last of the energy left me in a sensation of agonizing sparkles.

Hodin began to cry, heavy tears falling as his lips moved, trying to speak but failing. I looked at Jenks hovering between us. "Are you sure?"

He nodded, and I crossed the room, still searching the corners for Hodin. "Hodin never would have let me score on him. Besides, see her wrist?"

Three slashes, I thought as Hodin frantically held up his wrist, tears spilling from him as he thrust his arm forward in guilt and desperation. The circle with three slashes might have just saved her life, but it might mean it was forfeit, too. "Stef, is that you?" Which was admittedly a dumb thing to say, but she bobbed her head in relief, dropping her arm and clearly unable to talk. It was weird, seeing Hodin's dark hair and long, tear-streaked face. But it was her, and I jumped as Stef grabbed my arm and pulled me toward the porch.

"Where's Hodin?" I said, thinking that this was the most ugly thing I'd seen Hodin do yet and exactly why I had to bottle this nutcase. I could have *killed* her.

Silent, she frantically pushed me to the French doors. "Stef, where is Hodin?"

"Interesting. That would have worked if your skills were up to basic demon standards," Hodin said from the hall, and all three of us spun.

Again, I yanked on the line, pulling its energy in like a warm blanket. Stef yelped, her grip on me falling away. Pissed, I stepped in front of her, Jenks beside me. "I'm beginning to understand why your brother wants you dead," I said.

Lips quirking, Hodin confidently tightened his sash. He was dressed identically to Stef, and my jaw clenched when he held a finger up for me to wait before he tapped one of his rings and Stef shifted, thankfully regaining her own appearance. Her robe was now a bland black, though. No bells at all.

"Stephanie Ann McNorse, get my things," he said, and when the woman moved, I reached out, stopping her.

"I could have killed her," I said, and he smiled.

"That was the idea."

"You would have let me—" I started, not believing this. He moved.

Jenks darted up. I pushed Stef behind me, simultaneously shoving a ball of unfocused energy at Hodin's thrown ball of green and red. They met in the middle of my kitchen in a sodden thump of sound that rattled the pans and sent a shower of sparks to dance at the ceiling and floor.

"Stay clear, Jenks!" I shouted, squinting through the glare.

"Ta na shay, palurm!" Hodin shouted exuberantly.

Elven magic? Ohhhh, you did it now, I thought as I braced myself, confidently shoving an equal amount of raw energy at his curse. They met, color shifting wildly as the combined energy bounced back at him. The Goddess *liked* me. Asking her to help was *not* a good idea.

Yelping, Hodin scrambled to smack the misfiring spell with a hastily raised force, and the addled curse hit the fireplace. The heavy stones cracked with a startling pop, pissing me off.

"You think the Goddess is going to help you?" I shouted, breath catching when Jenks darted into the fray. "Jenks, no!" I exclaimed, but it was too late, and Hodin flicked a wad of energy at him to send the pixy flying across the room. He hit the wall and slid down, dust going dim.

"Jenks!" Getty cried, and my lips parted when her head lifted from the top of a cupboard. Arrow flying, she zip-lined down to him.

She had him, and I hesitated for one agonizing heartbeat before I focused on Hodin, ley line energy crawling down my arms to drip from my fingers. "I've had enough of you," I whispered. Sure, he was a demon with more practical knowledge at his disposal, but I could hold more raw energy than him, and as Hodin's gaze flicked from me to Stef, I think he remembered that.

I took a breath, the words to curse him catching in my

throat as he shrank, black feathers fountaining up as he turned into a crow.

"That's not going to help," I said, then threw the curse at him.

Squawking, he jumped to evade it, loose feathers vanishing into dust as he dissolved into a dark-haired pixy.

"Neither is that," I snarled. I strode forward, ticked, as I imagined a circle around him. If he was that size, I could fry him in a light charm. *"Lenio cinis!"* I exclaimed, and he darted away, becoming a sable hummingbird even as my bubble caught him.

Gotcha, I thought as the charm enveloped him . . . until he coated the inside of my bubble with his own, taking it.

Yelping, I dropped my circle as the energy rebounded in a threatening burn. If I was singed too deeply, it wouldn't matter how much energy I could manipulate.

Clearly shaken, the black hummingbird hit the floor. Dark, coarse hair bubbled up, mounding into a flowing, monstrous size. A deep growl thundered out, and then I gasped, stunned as a Kodiak bear filled the room, roaring at me. A rank musk filled my nose. Teeth bared, he roared again, spittle dripping from his teeth.

"Holy shit!" I backpedaled as he lunged. I wasn't fast enough, and a clawed hand the size of a garbage can slammed onto my chest. Suddenly I was on the floor, unable to think as his weight crushed me, one claw to the right of my face, one nearly on it.

"Get. Off!" I gasped, flooding him with raw energy.

Bellowing, he pushed from me.

I rolled, hand to my bruised ribs. He was a crow again, lurching in flight for the hall. *Coward,* I thought as I scrabbled across the floor for my purse and threw it at him.

The soggy bag hit him square on and he went down with a startled squawk, wings spread as he spun on the tile. Again feathers fountained, but I was waiting for him as he returned to his stoic, pissed-off self.

Energy dripped from my fingers. Stef was safe behind me, and Getty had Jenks.

I shook my head. The hall might be just behind him—but he would not make it.

"Humueuneric, de soulum," he intoned, and suddenly I was gripping my throat, gasping as I fought to make my lungs work.

Crap on toast, why did I wait? I thought as I neutralized the curse. My hand filled with energy, the spell to bring him down in my thoughts—

And then I stopped, shocked to find he'd circled me.

"Seriously?" I said as I looked from his smug satisfaction to Jenks, still on the floor and trying to focus, safe under Getty's tearful, determined stance. Stef was crying silent tears, once more at Hodin's side. The haze of his aura over me colored everything a faint blue and green as his bubble of force defined by his circle separated me from the rest of the world. I was trapped in a three-dimensional circle, but not for long. "You do know I can take this down, right?"

"Try," he mocked, and I put a hand to it, feeling a sensory burn start to bubble and sizz. "You're good, but not that good." Hodin shook out his robe to make his sash bells ring.

"You have no idea how good I am," I practically snarled, furious that he'd circled me in the instant I'd been distracted. If I had had Bis, I could have jumped out. But I didn't, and I had to burn my way free. I pressed my hand into the bubble again, feeling it give a little as I forced my energy into his circle curse. If I flooded it with my own energy, surpassing his, I could break it. But it was going to hurt like hell until I did and took control of it.

"Finish packing my things," he said, and Stef ran from the room, crying. "We could have ruled Cincinnati together," Hodin mocked as I pulled my hand away to let my neural net cool.

Ticked, I shook my head. "No. We could not."

"Consider it again," Hodin said. "As I said before, you are an apt student."

"Student?" I barked, and he colored, eye twitching.

"Then, I'd be willing to work with you," he amended

with a false graciousness. "You understand elven magic. You're willing to look beyond our limits."

A small knot of worry began to ease as I heard Jenks tell Getty he was fine and to quit fussing. "You would have let me kill Stef."

Again he shrugged. "Perhaps you shouldn't have tried to kill me."

I put my hand to his circle again, the pain in my mind growing as I hunted for a way out: a hole I could wedge my own aura into and take control of the bubble, a gas pipe, a strand of spiderweb, a ping from my phone. But my bag was on the other side of the room on the floor and would be of no help even if someone called me.

"I wouldn't mind sharing. I've been alone a long time."

"Big surprise," I said, gasping as I pulled my hand away from the circle, my thoughts seared from our energies fighting for supremacy. "You would have let me kill Stef. No, you wanted me to. No wonder Al . . ." My words faltered as I started to figure out Dali's words. *We will never catch him if he is doppelganging again.* "Hates you," I finished, staring at Hodin.

He stared back, his jaw set as he saw understanding crash over me.

"Is that what you did to Al?" I said, inching close to the bubble of force but not touching it. Waves of warning cramped my gut, and I reached out, accepting the pain, seeking it. Only through pain would I best his circle and break out of here. "Is that what you did to Al?" I shouted, my hand pressed to the inside of his circle. "Who did he kill by mistake? My God, did you trick him into killing Celfnnah thinking it was you?"

Hodin's lips twitched. "Stef!" he shouted, and I put both hands against his circle, head bowing as the pain redoubled.

It's not real. My hands are not burning, I thought, but the damage to my synapses was real enough, and it hurt. "They never should have put you in a bottle," I gasped. "They should have killed you!" Groaning, I jerked my hands free, gasping at the cold shock pinching my thoughts in the absence of his fire.

Hodin stood tall, an ugly expression on his face. "Leave me alone and I will leave you alone. That's the best you're going to get. Everyone else understands. Why don't you?"

Funny. That was exactly what I wanted Finnis to do, but unlike me, Hodin would be making mischief in his solitude. And so I stood in his circle, hunched in pain, ready to endure more. I just needed . . . a second. "I'm not an old, entitled demon, I guess," I said, pained sparkles cramping my arm as I tried to open and close my hands. "I have to fight for everything. Why should this be any different?"

"Mmmm." Hodin looked down the hallway to the rest of the church. "You should take me seriously and walk away."

"Yeah?" I inched closer to the barrier, so close that it hummed a warning and sent my hair into staticky knots. "I was going to say the same thing to you."

Anger flooded him. "Stephanie Ann McNorse!" he bellowed. "Get out here!"

The frightened woman inched forward into the light, a small bag in her hand. It probably contained everything that Hodin wanted out of Ivy's old room. Sort of a TARDIS kind of a thing.

"Stef stays here," I said as Hodin took possession of it. "She doesn't belong to you."

Hodin chuckled and the painful hope that had flooded Stef vanished. "Wrong again."

Stef's wet eyes lifted to mine. "It's my fault, Rachel. I should have listened."

"It's not your fault." Teeth clenched, I let my hand hover over the barrier of his circle. My outer synapses were burned to char, unable to feel the pain, but it wasn't getting any easier. "I should have sat on you until you did." *This circle is mine,* I thought. He wasn't a student I could easily overpower, but I could do it, and I put a second hand beside the first. *Mine,* I thought again, beginning to pant in the agony.

Hodin laughed as he tugged Stef to him. "Even if you break my circle, you have lost. I have everything that is you. I have peeled your support from you to leave nothing."

I held my breath as the burn began to sink deeper, but a faint hint of my aura was growing between my hands and his circle, and I poured more energy into it.

"I started with Al," Hodin mocked, leaning to put his face in close to mine, the wavering energy distorting him. "Then got Welroe out of the way. Distracted your pixy with the oldest lure in existence, and Kalamack with the second. I even stole your familiar out from under you."

"Stef is not my familiar," I rasped, pulse hammering. "She is my friend."

He laughed, but his smile vanished as he noticed the drop of gold between my hands, staining his perfect circle. "Your own mole is at the curb to bring you in for selling your students to a demon, and soon for detaining Constance against her will. You will be in jail by the end of the night, Alcatraz by the end of the week, and that is even without Constance pushing for it. Oh, how you have fallen, Rachel Morgan. You are done. And I am gone. Stephanie? I'm going to show you how easy it is to catch a demon. Rachel makes everything so difficult."

"No!" Stef twisted her arm until his grip broke. Expression ugly, Hodin yanked her back.

"I have a third option, Hodin," I rasped, and he turned, his mocking confidence cracking as my hands shook against his bubble and my soul seemed to burn. "I don't need help to put you in a freaking bottle. I will do it myself."

Groaning, I pushed everything I had into my hands, my throat going raw as I fought for control of his circle. Energy funneled through me until it went from fire to ice, and then, with a startling ping, I had it. His circle was mine.

Hodin's brow lifted as his circle flashed a brilliant gold of my aura. "Fool just like the rest," he muttered.

I had an instant of question, and then my smug satisfaction vanished as the energy in his circle rebounded. The line refused to take it, and it all came flooding to me, three-fold.

"No!" I shrieked as I dropped the line, but it only made it worse. He had hidden a spell in his circle. I couldn't let go of the line fast enough to escape it. My outer synapses were singed, preventing a quick dump, and I spindled it like mad, pulling the energy deeper instead of trying to force it out, desperate to give the energy somewhere to go. I sensed it crest . . . lapping at my extremes . . . and then I had it. I had it all.

Groaning, I dropped to the cool tile, my eyes closing as the line energy peaked in me, then reversed, flowing over my burn and back into the line through long-established channels. Finally I was empty. The overwhelming power was gone, and I lay where I was, helpless.

"Rachel!" Jenks cried out. His dust was warm, but I was cold without the heat of the line, and I exhaled, in no hurry to inhale again. It felt good to not move. *At least I'm out of his damned circle.*

"Touch her, and I'll kill you," Jenks threatened, and I took a slow breath when the draft from his wings pushed the hair from my face. Stef was crying, but I couldn't even lift my head.

"Let me go!" Stef exclaimed. "Let go! Rachel, I'm so sorry!"

Hodin's confident harrumph shook me. "One too many bad decisions," he said, but I couldn't even groan when he wedged a foot under my ribs and rolled me over. "At least you would have been alive if you had joined with me," he said, and then Stef's crying vanished.

They were gone.

"Ow," I whispered. I tensed to sit up, then decided not to as the world tilted.

"Rachel?" I heard close to my ear, and then I pried my eyelids apart when something poked my nose. "She's okay!" Jenks exclaimed, and I struggled to focus, his shape blurry from a thick silver dust. "Getty, she's okay!"

I took a deeper breath, afraid to see what I'd done to my synapses. "I don't feel so good," I said as I rolled over to put my face on the cool, cool floor. "Jenks. Call Ivy and Pike. Hodin might try to take the city with Finnis. I gotta 'ake a nap," I slurred as I closed my eyes.

Everything else could wait.

CHAPTER

26

I WAS WARM AND SOMEWHAT . . . DAMP. THE UNHURRIED sound of Trent's breathing was familiar, and I stretched, a cool draft hitting the small of my back when the blanket slipped. But it wasn't until the faint scent of vampire incense intruded that my eyes flew open to see the dark timbers of Piscary's front room.

"Trent?" I whispered as I sat up, pulse fast. My hair was still damp as I tucked it behind an ear, and it smelled like pool water. The room was lit with a soft electric glow, the unused fireplace a black hole as I swung my feet to the oak floor. Someone had put me on the overstuffed couch. Trent, presumably, since he was slumped on the chair beside me.

"I'm here," Trent said, his feet hitting the floor as he started awake. Blinking, he reached for my hand. "You're safe."

"Why are we at Piscary's?" I asked, scanning the rafters for pixy dust. "Constance . . ."

"Is fine," he said as he drew a small cage from beside his chair and set it on the coffee table between us.

I leaned closer, my damp clothes catching. Glints of jewelry glittered from around the neck of the little gray mouse. It was Constance, but where had she found such a tiny necklace?

"Ivy and Pike?" I said as the mouse squeaked and flipped me off. "Hodin needs Finnis if he is going to take the city."

Trent stretched where he sat, a contented groan slipping from him. "First, they are okay. Second, Jenks's message was about thirty seconds too late. Hodin has him." He collapsed in on himself and sighed. "Popped in, grabbed him, and popped out. Sorry about that, but at least Ivy and Pike are unhurt. Do you want some coffee?"

"God, yes. Thank you." Frowning, I eased into the cushions and plucked at my damp shirt, wondering if I'd ever get a change of clothes. My bag was close, and I leaned to get it and find my phone. *Eleven thirty? Crap on a cracker, the sun is down. The world could have ended while I was sleeping.*

Trent stood, yawning before he headed for the bar and the state-of-the-art coffee maker. Coffee would be great, but what I really wanted to know was how I got here.

Is it okay that I still miss you, Kisten? I thought as I tucked my phone away and looked over the quiet, lamplit space. Pike had nearly returned it to the original restaurant, and I gazed at the elaborate bar, melancholy rising high. Someone had painted Pike's diamond logo on the long mirror to give the entire room a feeling of protection. The tables were empty and bare, and two high-back chairs sat before the unlit fire as a place of importance. The old register at the end of the bar was gone, and I eyed the host stand with its built-in tablet with mistrust.

The room felt odd, an air of waiting hanging over the empty tables and stocked bar shelves. I finally found the mixed-population license over the fireplace, and I fought the desire to move it to where it had always hung behind the bar.

And with that, memories of Kisten swam up, blurring my vision as the sound of laughter and the crack of pool balls echoed in my thoughts. I had found acceptance here among Cincinnati's forgotten children. Piscary's being up and running would be a good thing, even if the reminder hurt. Pike was right.

Until an even more pressing thought brought me up cold and my focus darted from the locked front door to Trent. It was Trent, wasn't it? Hodin would have simply killed me, right? "Ah, what am I doing at Piscary's?" I asked.

"Hiding from the I.S." The sound of coffee chattering into two mugs was loud, and I tugged the blanket up over me. "You were out cold on your kitchen floor. I've only been that scared once before. I don't know what . . ." He hesitated, his shoulders hunched. "Jenks told me what happened," he continued. "Doyle showed up while I was trying to wake you. Jenks diverted Doyle upstairs while I snuck you out the front. Brought you here," he added as he crossed the room and handed me a black coffee mug full of blessedly hot brew. "Are you sure you're okay?"

I took a sip, the smooth, nutty flavor almost tasteless as I studied him. *Hodin, if this is you, I swear, I'll part your head from your neck and make your skull into a birdhouse.* "Where are Ivy and Pike?"

He sat beside me, and I moved when our weight slid us together. "Out searching for Finnis." His hand brushed my hair from my face, and he forced me to look at him. "Are you sure you're okay? Jenks said you collapsed after breaking Hodin's circle."

And Jenks was nowhere to be seen. Pulse fast, I inched farther away, my expression carefully empty as I saw the question in him. If it *was* Hodin, I was in trouble. I doubted I could work the ley lines at the moment, burned from taking down his circle. "Trent, what's the name of Newt's horse?"

His lips parted. "The Goddess help me. You think I'm Hodin?"

I stood, afraid to tap a line. Afraid I wouldn't be able to. "What's his name?"

Trent put up a hand. "Her. And it's Red. Rachel, it's me."

My shoulders slumped and I sat down, feeling silly as his arm went around me and he gave me a heartfelt hug. "It's me," he whispered. "God, this is going to be hard."

I nodded, starting to understand why Al wanted Hodin dead. How do you deal with a demon who pretends he's someone else in order to bring you down? *Coward.* "So, I'm hiding from Doyle, eh?" I said.

"Yes, but if you can prove that it was Hodin who took your students to the ever-after . . ." I shook my head, and he sighed. "We'll figure something out," he said, leaning in to give me a kiss. My arms went around him and I breathed him in, reluctant to let go. "Hungry?" he asked, and I nodded, my cheek pressed against his chest. "Sandwiches for your birthday dinner was not my intention."

I managed a slight smile as my arms eased their grip. "Sounds good, though. I'm starving." Together we stood, and I shook out the blanket as he went to the bar and slipped behind it with a slight frown. Hesitating briefly, he began to rummage about in the tiny fridge. "I, ah, singed myself breaking Hodin's circle," I said, and Trent winced in sympathy. "He had a secondary charm nestled in it, and after I seared my upper thoughts breaking his circle, I wasn't able to shunt the excess energy back to the line the way I should have. It was stuck. If I hadn't been able to spindle the entirety of it to break the bottleneck, I probably wouldn't be standing here now."

Trent set a tiny jar of small-batch mustard and an enormous bottle of mayo on the counter, followed by a plate of cold cuts and sliced cheese. "How badly are you burned?"

"I haven't looked yet, but my head doesn't hurt, so that's a good sign. Where's Jenks?"

"Doing a security check. Ah, I'd feel better if I knew you could at least set a circle."

Nodding, I steadied myself before slipping a tentative thought to the nearest line. Energy raked uncomfortably across my senses. I winced as it bubbled and frothed, filling my chi with a new warmth. It was rough going but possible. "I can spell," I said, and he nodded as he began layering meat and cheese on four slices of bread. One for me, one for him.

"He's got Stef," I said softly, and his smile faded. "Three slashes on her wrist." It used to be a mark of slavery, and unless I did something about it, it would be again.

"Jenks told me. She should be okay for a while."

I finished folding the blanket and dropped it on the couch. "I almost killed her. I thought she was Hodin. Trent, I have to put this guy away, and not simply to stop him from taking over Cincinnati. I'm going to go nuts if I don't know if I'm talking to you or Hodin." I carefully picked up Constance and moved her to the bar, and the vampire mouse hissed at me, long fangs bared. *Nice . . .*

"My reactions won't be fast enough if I'm questioning if it's him or he's disguised as someone I love." I hesitated, using my finger to doodle nothing on the mahogany bar.

Silent, Trent used a huge knife to cut the sandwiches, making two long rectangles out of his, and two triangles from mine.

"I'm just glad my first impulse isn't to kill what's irritating me," I muttered as I pulled the plate with the triangles in front of me. "Or Stef would be dead now."

But my first bite hesitated at the sound of pixy wings. "Face it, Rache," Jenks said as he flew in, looking no worse for wear. "If you killed what irritated you, half the I.S. agents and all of Cincy's bus drivers would be dead by now."

"Not all of them," I said around my full mouth. Mmmm, he'd put marmalade on it, and the bittersweet flavor was perfect with the cheese and roast beef.

"But you didn't, and she isn't." Trent frowned at one of the below-bar monitors. "Is that a news van?" he asked, and Jenks nodded, landing on the open jar of marmalade to use his chopsticks to help himself to a chunk of sweetened orange peel.

"Yeah, but we got at least fifteen minutes until they figure out why they can't reach a communication tower." He chuckled. "Hey, any honey back there?"

"No," I said flatly, and Trent pulled his reach back. "Jenks, how many pixy names does it take to make a good demon password?"

The pixy blinked, then smirked. "Four," he said, convincing me that it really was Jenks. "Ain't no one able to be me but me, Rache. You should know that."

"I do." I fiddled with my sandwich. "Are you sure you're okay? You hit that wall hard."

Jenks darted to the cheese, sword flashing to cut off a wedge. Poking the tip of his sword into it, he extended it through the bars to the grasping mouse. "Getty . . ." he said, and I glanced up as his voice broke. "Ah, Getty fixed me up," he finished softly. "I gotta check on something." And then he was gone, his wings humming a dull note and his dust a somber blue as he flew out.

Trent looked up from where he'd been fiddling with the camera angle, clearly surprised. "Is there something here I'm not getting?"

Uncomfortable, I fed Constance another chunk of cheese. "Where's Getty?"

"The church." He leaned an elbow on the bar, expression wary. "She's got the fairies organized and guarding the place. She cried when I took you out, embarrassed that she hid from Hodin and didn't tell you he was there." His gaze went to Jenks's fading dust. "Is that why he's upset?"

I took a big bite, needing to think about how to answer. "In pixy culture, it's the wife's task to keep her husband flying," I said after I swallowed. "Once he left his mother, Matti was the only person to care for him other than Belle. I think he could look past Belle cutting his hair and fixing his scrapes because she was a fairy, but Getty?" I met Trent's eyes. "He likes her, and I think he's worried that's a betrayal of everything he shared with Matalina."

Trent sighed heavily. "Oh."

"How much time before the media knocks on the door,

you think?" I said as I stood and leaned over the counter to try to see the monitors. "I can't believe how stupid I was." Flexing my sore hand, I dropped back down on my stool, and my focus blurred as I thought about Bis. If he hadn't been comatose, no circle on earth could hold me. "I've got to make some changes," I whispered.

The soft gurgle of Trent refilling his coffee mug drew my attention. "Why don't the other demons go for him now? Seeing as you rescinded your promise to protect him," he said as he gave me a new mug.

"I haven't. Not exactly." Constance was extending an arm past the bars for some coffee, and I let a drop fall into her cupped hands. "I never said I wouldn't put him in a bottle, but I still have to protect him against their actions or lose every ounce of credibility I have with the demons for the rest of my life." Pausing, I took a sip. "They can't help me. Besides, if I can't do this without them, I have no teeth to demand that Dali stop making people into familiars and release those he tricked into it. I should have been expecting this. They have been free for just over a year. They are bored to tears."

But boredom didn't give them the right to break the laws they agreed to abide by. That was the funny thing about demons. Their word was absolute, but they only followed the rules that you could enforce. I was not going to break mine by asking them to help me take care of Hodin.

"The past four months with Hodin have been one long setup," I grumped, and Constance delicately belched and held her hand out for more coffee. "I alienated Al," I said as I gave the vampire another drop from my finger. "Put Pike in a bad spot."

Trent smiled as he took my crumb-laced plate and set it in the bar sink. "You're talking with Al again. Pike put himself in a bad spot, not you."

"Sure, by listening to Hodin. I ruined your business effort."

"No, you didn't," he said, surprising me with his good mood.

"What was it, anyway?" I asked, and his expression became positively smug.

Elbow on the bar, he took a sip of his coffee. "You are looking at the new owner of Carew Tower."

"What?" I sat straighter, lips parting in surprise. Constance, too, seemed taken aback if her shaking the bars of her cage meant anything. "The entire building? I thought you were buying a couple of floors." Clearly the sum he'd given them was earnest money, not the purchase price. *Damn . . .*

"Everything but the restaurant," he said. "So do your best not to get banned from it. You were right about not moving in with me because it was too far out in the country."

"Oh," I said, my excitement suddenly falling flat.

"Working outside the city might have worked for my father—seeing as most of his endeavors were illegal—but it's not working for me. I need a downtown office, complete with an apartment so the disruption to the girls' lives is minimal."

"Ah." Crap on toast, my face-saving excuse for not moving in with him was disintegrating before me.

"Unfortunately you are too expensive for my insurance to cover," he said, and I blinked, unable to tell if he was serious or not. "So you can't move in with me."

"Oh, really . . ."

Beaming, he leaned across the bar and gave me a long, languorous kiss that went right to my middle. "Really," he said as our lips parted.

I laughed, feeling loved, and his smile widened. "That's better," he said in satisfaction. "Okay. What are we going to do about Hodin?"

I really liked the word *we.* Our heads were almost touching, the bar between us, and I lingered, reluctant to move. "Catch Hodin," I said, not knowing how yet. "Put him in a bottle. Force him to admit he was the one who sold the students to Dali. Rescue them. Eat some cake. It's my birthday." I slumped, remembering what time it was. "For the next thirty minutes, anyway. There should be cake."

Rising up on two legs, Constance wobbled into her hut, clearly disgusted as Trent's arm went around me and our foreheads touched. For one long moment we didn't move, him behind the bar, me in front of it, feeling each other's presence and gaining strength from it.

Until pixy wings rasped and we slumped apart.

"Guys! Guys!" Jenks shrilled as he came in, jerking to a dust-laden halt when he saw us in our private moment. "Tink's little pink dildo. You guys sifting dust again?"

"Not yet," I said as I tucked Trent's hair behind a pointy ear. "Come back in five minutes."

Jenks flew up and down the long bar, looking for something. "It's going to have to wait," he said as he arrowed down and stomped on the TV remote. "We've got a problem."

Trent frowned at the monitors behind the bar. "They're still setting up."

"It's not us," Jenks said as he toggled the channel and I turned to the wide-screen TV at the far end of the room.

"That's Fountain Square," I said, recognizing the lights playing on the downtown buildings. "On national TV." *Son of a bastard . . . Now what?*

Sighing, Trent came out from behind the bar to sit beside me. It was Fountain Square, full of people and lights. Finnis was on the music stage, Constance's diminutive, undeniable shape beside him in a white power dress and scads of jewelry. My gaze went to the mouse cage. *Hodin . . .*

A small crowd was growing, but no one but Finnis and Constance seemed happy. Uniformed I.S. and FIB personnel were keeping the crowd and the news crews distant. There was a podium, and I was suddenly reminded of the time I'd crashed one of Trent's press conferences.

"That's Pike. There by the planter," Trent said, pointing, and my lips parted. It *was* Pike, grim faced as he stood unmoving despite the jostling. I didn't see Ivy, and I turned to get my phone.

"I need to call Ivy," I said, my attention flicking to Constance. The vampire mouse was at the bars of her cage, screeching so loud it was hard to hear the newscaster explaining what was going on.

"Shut up, tiny blood bag!" Jenks shouted as he ran his sword over the barred ceiling, and she sank down, sullen and bad-tempered.

"—working closely with the I.S. to find the missing citizens," the announcer said as Trent turned it up. "We go now to Fountain Square in Cincinnati to the news story in progress."

"Ivy is not answering her phone," I said as the picture shifted and Finnis and Constance filled the frame.

"Finnis knows that's not Constance," Trent said, expression cross. "Why is he going along with it?"

"Probably because Hodin promised he'd put me in jail or kill me," I said as I hit Pike's icon next. "Either way, that soul curse gets stuck in FSCA purgatory."

My phone clicked, and I started, holding it to my ear instead of putting it on speaker as I usually did. "Pike? Are you at Fountain Square? Where's Ivy? What's going on?"

"We're here," he said, and Trent toggled the volume down and the captions on. "Please tell me that's Hodin up there, not Constance."

"Constance is here," I said, glancing at her as she renewed her screeching. "I'm guessing Hodin thinks he can take Cincy as her. Finnis is probably going along with it to get me and that soul curse out of the picture. What's the mood?" But what I really wanted to know was if anyone was believing the tripe that was now spilling across the bottom of the screen.

"Shut up!" Jenks shouted at Constance, and for a moment, I couldn't hear anything but her shrill mouse fury until she settled down, her thin tail switching.

"Ugly," Pike said, and I could hear it in the crowd around him, see it on the faces on TV. "David still has control of the Weres, but the vampire and witch factions who follow you are beginning to fracture. Not surprising since *Constance* is telling everyone you're dead."

"Dead!" I shouted, and Jenks snickered. "I'm not dead."

His green eyes thoughtful, Trent ran a hand under his chin. "Why would he tell everyone you're dead? He can't pretend to be you, then." His focus cleared as he looked at me. "Unless he thinks that last curse killed you."

"It wasn't that bad," I said, but it could have been if I hadn't been used to spindling excess line energy. Sure, I had a gargoyle to act as my familiar when it came to line energy, but Bis hadn't always been there, and I had learned to compensate by cultivating the ability to spindle an insane amount in my head. *Enough to survive Hodin, apparently.* "I bet he thinks he killed me." My pulse quickened. "Pike, I need to call my mom. If this is on the national news . . ."

"Go," Pike said, and I caught sight of him on the screen, his lips at odds with what he was saying. "Ivy and I will stay here to watch Finnis."

"No." I fidgeted, wanting to call my mom but having to finish here first. "I need you both with me. I'm at Piscary's."

"Be there in fifteen," Pike said, then ended the call.

Immediately Trent unmuted the TV as "Constance" promised Cincinnati that she would do everything she could to get the students back from the ever-after. Finnis was pledging the support of the DC vampires, saying that demons could not be allowed sway within the political system because they were corrupt to the core and could not be trusted.

"And you aren't?" I said as I texted my mom that I was alive and would explain later, and to please not plan my funeral again.

From the TV, a beaming Finnis vowed a return to the upright and honest balance of power that only vampires could provide. The I.S. would again be able to protect them, human and Inderland both.

I sighed as my mom's response popped up. It was an icon of a laughing tiger and a heart.

"I have been distracted," Constance was saying as the

real Constance shrilled at the TV, hurting my ears. "Betrayed by my trust in the demon Morgan. She misled me and my scion. But I have broken the curse she put me and Pike under, and things will return to normal."

Together, Constance and Finnis turned to leave, ignoring the shouted questions from the reporters. The I.S. closed in, and a wall of living and dead flesh ushered them away until it was only Cincy's newscasters struggling to fill their abrupt absence.

"A welcome appearance and more assurances from Cincinnati's master vampire that everything is under control despite an increased unrest at the city center. We are still trying to verify the claim of Morgan's death. A midnight vigil is planned tonight outside Morgan's residence—"

"Turn it off," I said, and Jenks obligingly stomped on the button.

"You look good for a dead witch," the pixy said, and I frowned at Constance. She would not shut up, and I couldn't think with the noise.

"Hey!" I shouted, and Constance dropped down on her haunches, whiskers trembling and black eyes glaring at me. "I never would've spelled you into a mouse if you hadn't been so nutso!"

Finally she was silent. I leaned over the bar, the flat of my arms on its smooth surface. As Constance, Hodin had control of the I.S. He also had the blessing of DC's long undead, who clearly didn't care who he was and were willing to work with him as long as that soul curse was effectively dead. The DC vampires' beef with me wasn't that I was a demon. It was that damned soul curse.

"This is tricky," Trent said as he settled himself on the stool beside mine.

Jenks's wings rasped. "It's March all over again, and I don't think you can lure Hodin onto the SkyStar and curse him into a mouse."

I resettled myself on the barstool, thinking. Should I use Hodin's belief that I was dead to my advantage? Or should I be alive and put the fear of doubt in him?

Doubt was good. Hodin was already not that confident in himself. Otherwise, why would he keep trying to be other people? But staying dead would prevent him from pretending to be me. "Suggestions?" I asked, starting at Constance's smug expectation. *Smug? She's smug?* I couldn't turn her back into a vampire to expose Hodin's subterfuge. I wouldn't.

"We kick some vampire and demon ass for your birthday instead of dinner and a nice ride in the ever-after," Trent said. "What do you need from us?"

Us. There it was again, and I smiled at Trent. Jenks was on his shoulder. Hodin's gamble hinged on me not having my friends to help me. The way I saw it, he'd already lost.

I needed to show everyone that I was alive. Not only that, but that I was the subrosa, the guardian of the city. I needed to prove that I was capable of it, either by outing Hodin as an impostor or returning the students, but preferably both. And for that, I had to talk to Dali. He had the students; he had the access code for the weapons vault. I had to have something he wanted. Newt's spell books, maybe, or that wand I was never going to use again.

Stifling a shudder, I looked at my phone for the time. *Almost midnight.* "I need to get to the church."

Jenks darted up, his dust a brilliant gold. "Shotgun!"

I nodded, opening my texts. "Jenks, I'm going to need you to get past the vigil. Trent—"

His shoulders slumped. "I'll stay with Constance," he volunteered.

"No, I want you with me, too," I said, head down over my phone as I texted first Pike, then Ivy, that we were moving to the church. "We have to come up with something Dali wants bad enough to let me in the vault." I turned to Constance. "If you promise to behave, you can come with us."

The little gray mouse stood in the center of her cage, eyeing me in anger, her fangs glistening. "Squeak," she said, and Jenks shrugged.

"That sounded like a yes to me," the pixy said, and Trent lifted her cage off the counter.

It was risky taking her with us, but leaving her here for Hodin to snatch was even worse.

"Okay. Let's go out the back to avoid the press," I said, and Trent grinned.

CHAPTER

27

IT WAS THE SECOND TIME IN LESS THAN TWENTY-FOUR hours that I had needed to sneak in through my garden, giving me flashbacks of trying to evade Mrs. Talbu when I didn't have the rent. The feat had required copious amounts of dog treats for Mr. Dinky, and even so, the obnoxious Chihuahua gave me away as often as not.

Trent's car was parked a few streets off, and between Jenks running vanguard and the general quietness of the street behind my church, we hadn't yet been noticed. The heat of the day was still radiating from the sidewalk, and it felt nice walking beside Trent, quiet homes on one side, the graveyard's six-foot stone wall on the other, the moon a little past full and nearly right overhead. I could almost pretend we were normal people with normal problems. *Almost*.

"Sorry about your birthday," Trent said, and I found his free hand and gave it a squeeze. Constance's cage was in his other, the vampiric mouse surprisingly quiet as she soaked in the night.

"It's just a day." I swung our joined hands in time with

our steps, slowing as I began to study the wall. "I've got a few toeholds around here somewhere. Up and over, easy-peasy."

"It's not just a day," he grumped. "I had things planned."

I loved that he seemed put out. "Me too," I said, brightening when my questing fingers found a patch of rough rock. "Got it. I'll go first. You can hand me Constance when I get to the top."

But a rasp of dragonfly wings cut through the crickets and I turned from the wall, my faint smile faltering. It was Jenks, but he wasn't dusting. Something was wrong.

"Doyle," the pixy simply said, and I slumped. "He's parked at the back car gate, busy with a six-inch sub sandwich and a supersize Brimstone shake, but if you break the horizon at the top of the wall, he'll notice."

I leaned against the wall, arms over my chest. We couldn't go in through the front. There were like thirty people out there with tiki torches and candles. "Seriously?" I complained. "Doesn't he ever give up?"

Trent's green eyes were almost black in the moonlight. "I'd take it as a compliment. He thinks you're alive."

Jenks touched the hilt of his garden sword. "Give me fifteen minutes, and I'll have him itching so bad he won't notice the sun exploding."

Trent, though, was studying the moon as if it was important. "Waning," he whispered. "Full would have been foolproof, but this is close enough for government work."

"What is?" I said as Trent's smirk became positively devious. "Your glamour charm?"

"Better," he said as he pulled me from the wall. *"Ta na shay, auren sy auren lumon."*

I shivered as Trent's aura rose to envelop mine, little sparkles of magic carrying his intent prickling along my synapses in a delicious sensation.

"Where did you go? Where are you?" Jenks said, eyes wide as he hovered.

"Wow," I said, impressed, and the pixy began to laugh,

doubled over and flying himself backward as a cheerful gold dust spilled from him.

"You thought you went invisible," the pixy choked out, his altitude falling as he laughed. "You need a refund on that charm, Cookie Man. I can still see you."

"The charm is fine." Trent frowned at Jenks. "I included you in it."

"Me?" Jenks's eyes widened. "I don't need no charm to be invisible. Take it off."

"Suck it up, pixy buck." Trent put his free hand on my shoulder and turned me to the wall. "It breaks when the moon sets, and it's not infallible. You do have to *try* to be unnoticed. Up you go, Rachel."

I appreciated that he wasn't going to insist that he went first, and beaming, I handed him my bag before I stretched for the first handhold and pulled. Another quick reach and pull and I was levering my leg atop the flat wall. Turning, I lay flat along it to reach down for first my bag and then Constance. The vampiric mouse was quiet as I set her cage beside me, her gaze fixed on the shadows as if she was seeing an old lover.

"Jenks is right," I said as I awkwardly shifted to make room for Trent. "Doyle's car is at the gate." Chuckling, I scanned the rest of the garden, not liking the light and noise coming from the front of the church. We'd have to be quiet while inside, but if we didn't turn on any lights, no one would know we were there. Probably.

In a breath of movement and the softest sound of grinding stone, Trent was before me on the wall, looking like a feral king as he crouched for a moment to take in the night before lightly jumping to the ground. His face was pale in the shadows as he reached for Constance. Seeing him there, the moonlight in his hair and deviltry in his eyes, something plinked through me, soft and sure, and abiding.

Damn, how lucky can a girl be? I thought as I lowered the cage to him. I had a boyfriend who not only knew how to jump a wall, but enjoyed doing it. Loving him, I scrambled down, my feet finding the earth in a thump more felt than heard.

Trent's hand went about my waist as if to reassure himself that I was there. His fingers trailed to leave goose bumps, and I knocked into him on purpose. It was delightful here in my garden in the cricket-filled dark, and I wished it wasn't my own church we were sneaking into, but maybe something more fun, like the museum for an artifact we needed to borrow, or the I.S. to shred our files. *I can work with Trent without fearing for his life,* I thought, tugging him closer to steal a quick kiss.

"Oh, for little wormy apples," the pixy complained. "Sift dust later. We got stuff to do."

Trent reluctantly rocked back, but our fingers remained twined as we picked our way to the path. The *cor mors* flowers on Nash's grave were blooming, and the sweet scent filled the space as we moved through the old stones. "So where did you get a charm that only works when the moon is full?" I asked, and Trent's mood softened.

"My mom. She gave it to me after I came home from camp scraped up from falling out a window. I was trying to sneak into the camp's kitchen for something. She said if I was going to be stealthy, I should have the right tools."

My lips quirked. "It was half of a three-layered cake."

Trent started, lips parting. "You remember?"

I grinned, letting go of his hand so I could better keep my balance stepping over the low wall separating the graveyard from my more cultivated garden. "Yep. Cherry with chocolate frosting. Lee knocked my share into the dirt. You broke his nose, and he threw you into a tree. That's where you scraped your arm."

"Lee threw me into a . . ." Trent's gaze went distant, his brow furrowed. There were memory blockers in the camp's water, but most things tended to come back with enough prompting. "He told me I scraped it falling out the window."

"Hence us tipping him into that abandoned well a week later." We had three glorious Lee-free days. And then they kicked me out of camp because I wasn't dying anymore.

Trent laughed, and a warm feeling suffused me. "With friends like that—"

"Who needs enemies," I finished, having often wondered about Trent and Lee's friendship, half a punch from an all-out war. The porch light was on, and I scuffed to a halt outside the warm glow, waiting for Jenks to finish his recon before we went in. Anxious, I peered at the wooden fence between us and the street. They were singing something low and mournful, kind of retro-melancholy. "Is that . . ."

Jenks darted up, his dust a strong gold. It was his garden, and he wouldn't sneak around in it. "Yep," the pixy said. "'Thursday's Child' by David Bowie."

"Mmmm." Lips quirking, Trent gave my fingers a squeeze before letting go to shift Constance to his other hand.

"Don't laugh. That's a great song," I said, and Jenks snickered.

"Sure, but they're singing it in memory of you."

"Hey," I whispered loudly, distracted when Trent touched me, urging me forward.

"No one is laughing," Trent said, but Constance was eyeing me as if she wished she could. "I think it's a fitting tribute."

"Don't you have a garden to patrol?" I said, and Jenks rose up, saluting me before he flew off, low and weaving among the stones. "There is nothing wrong with that song," I said, but inside, I was cringing. "Thursday's child has far to go," the nursery rhyme said, and while some people claimed it meant "destined for great things," others felt it spoke to children with unfair obstacles to overcome, be they medical, emotional, or just bad luck. Either way, the song was mournful and easy to sing. That they saw me in it? That was a debatable compliment.

"It's a good song," I said again as I padded up the wide porch steps. The kitchen was dark, and Trent unhesitatingly followed me in as I opened the unlocked French doors. The entire church was silent apart from the noise from the street.

There were no pixies, no roommates, only empty silent counters and a humming fridge.

"My books are upstairs," I whispered. "Newt gave me all of hers, and though I've only got the four, Dali might have had his eye on one," I said as I made my way down the hall to the sanctuary, Trent trailing behind. "Do you think those pearls I kept from Nash might have some ley line importance? He was wearing them when Constance eviscerated him."

I had said the last rather bitingly, seeing as the vampire was in a cage in Trent's hand, but my attention snapped up when Trent yanked me back.

The warning in him struck me cold. Breath catching, I looked at the mismatched couches and chairs around the big slate coffee table. A dark shadow was sitting there, hunched as if in grief. At least, he had been. My voice had pulled his head up, and I quailed at his frustration, the anger in the slant of his lips as he dropped the flamboyant top hat in his hand onto the table and stared at me.

"Al?" I said, freezing at the sensation of a huge power pull off the nearest ley line. My heart made a heavy thump, fear tripping down my spine. Suspicion took root, and I tapped into the ley line as well. I had no idea why Al would be in my church, but it was him in an exquisite suit of black and gold silk, red lace at his cuffs and about his neck. I'd never seen it before, and I hesitated at the fury in his red, goat-slitted eyes. *It is Al, isn't it?*

"Ah, I'm glad you're here," I said, but the real question was why was he sitting in my living room with a stack of books and that empty cricket cage from the belfry.

Al didn't move, didn't say anything. But that nothing struck more fear in me than if he had been raving. *The Turn take it. What have I done now?*

I looked at the books, wondering if they were my new ones. "Um, I need something to buy my way into the vault. Dali liked my garden. You think he might give me the code to the vault for a year's access to it?"

"Rachel?" Trent whispered, suddenly at my elbow. "We need to leave."

"It's my church," I said, annoyed. But my next words faltered when Al stood, his coattails furling. A dark haze hung over him, and I stifled a shudder. "Um, are those my books?" I said, stumbling when Trent pulled me a step away.

"They are Rachel's books," Al intoned, his low voice scraping clear down to where the nightmares hid in my soul. "Not yours. You will not survive this, Odie."

"He thinks you're Hodin," Trent said, his gaze flicking to the stained-glass windows. Someone had a megaphone, and they were starting to bear witness.

"He thinks I'm dead," I said, then stepped between Trent and Al, my most Rachely smile in place. "I am so sorry. I should have called you after I texted my mother. Hodin knocked me out. I just woke up. I've been at Piscary's avoiding the press. But I need something to—"

"You putrid filth," Al snarled. "I come here in mourning to take solace in what little you have left me, and I find you wearing her *visage*?" He shouted the last, and I jerked to a halt, the blood draining from my face as I felt him pull heavily on the ley lines again.

"It's me!" I exclaimed, face warming. I would not make a circle. I would not shut Al out. But as power dripped from Al's fisted hand, I felt I might have made a mistake.

"You might be surprised how often I think about the night I spared your life, brother," Al said—then he yelped, his gathered power fizzling when a tiny arrow struck his hand.

"Getty!" I tensed, breath held as the tiny woman zip-lined down the red thread to Al, dropping to the table before reaching him in a beautiful wash of silk and strength. She landed with her bow drawn, an arrow nocked and pointed at his eye. "Al, no! Don't hurt her!" I exclaimed, and Al brushed the arrow from his hand, snarling.

"I failed to warn Rachel once," Getty said, steadfast and unmoving. "I'll not fail again."

"Please. Don't hurt her," I begged, and Al paused, a hint of doubt swelling his heartache.

"Hey, Rache!" Jenks called cheerfully from the foyer,

his wings a growing hum. "Did you really pull some guy out of the tiger exhibit?" he said, then came to a shocked, dust-flowing halt.

"You killed Rachel," Al choked out, grief drawing his features into a tight knot. And then it was gone. "I won't make your death painless, but I will make it fast."

"Whoa, whoa, whoa!" Jenks darted to Getty, his hands outstretched as he hovered between Al and me. "Getty, stand down. They're just hashing it out. And don't you two dare bust my place up!" he added, looking from Trent to Al. "I only now got it fixed."

"It's me. I'm not dead," I said, freezing when Al's focus narrowed and he strode around the table. Little wisps of unharnessed energy trailed from him as he moved, and magic dripped from his fingers as he clenched his hands.

"You dare show up pretending to be her?" Al practically spat. "Asking for my *help*?"

"Kalamack, stand *down*!" Jenks shouted, his dust a brilliant silver. "He won't hurt her!"

But seeing Al's fury, I didn't share Jenks's optimism. Scared, I backed up until I found Ivy's baby grand. "I'm alive!" I got out, and then Al had me, his thick-fingered hand gripping my neck and yanking me forward. "You were right," I choked out. "About everythin-g-g-g . . ."

"No, don't!" Jenks shrilled, and my watering eyes went to the pixy glowing between Trent and me. The incensed elf held a glowing ball of something, and I think the only reason he hadn't thrown it was because it would hit both of us. Getty was with them, her bow still pulled and an arrow aimed. "He won't hurt her!" Jenks added, and Trent's lips parted in disbelief.

"He's choking her!" Trent exclaimed, his expression pale as I waved him off.

My chest was beginning to burn, and I was starting to wonder if I maybe should do something. "It's me . . ." I rasped, and finally my toes touched the floor.

I had leverage, and I swung my arms, breaking his hold. Gasping, I hit the piano, my stringy hair a curtain between me and the world as I held my throat and tried to cough my lungs from my body. "It's me," I choked out as I pulled myself up to find Al standing before me, his hands fisted at his sides, a glowing, promised death in them. "I'm not Hodin."

Jenks snickered, his dust a brilliant, happy gold. "See. Told you."

"Lie to me," Al said, shaking as he stood in his mourning suit of black silk and red lace. "Tell me you didn't kill her."

Constance began squeaking, the sound cutting off when Al sneered at her.

"He tried." My gut hurt, and my knees were wobbly. I looked at my bag on the floor, the cheerful red of my splat gun showing. Sure, I could have started slinging spells, but it was Al. I had given him my trust, and I would not take it away. Even if it killed me. "He circled me. Hid a charm in it. It singed me when I took his circle, but I'm okay."

Trent took a shaky breath. Unmoved, he stood where he was, arms loose and a wad of energy making his hair float. Beside him, Getty lowered her bow, and Jenks heaved a sigh.

Al's lip curled. "Even if it is you, *he* could be Hodin," he muttered. "The mother pus bucket can be anyone and anything." His red eyes narrowed on Jenks. "Anything."

Jenks's dust vanished. "Ah, that's not good."

My gut clenched as I felt Al yank on the nearest ley line. It shot through me: an electric warning. I wouldn't use magic to protect myself, but if he was going for Trent or Jenks . . .

"Don't you dare!" I shouted, pulling heavy on the line as well.

He felt it, turning in time to invoke a circle. My unfocused energy slammed into it, coating his bubble in a black patina of smut and gold. Hodin's aura was yellow and green. Surely he would believe it was me now.

"Not the windows!" Jenks said, darting to Trent, and the elf invoked his own protective circle. "For the love of Tink, not the windows!"

"Stop it, Al!" I shouted. "Neither one of them is Hodin. They've been with me the entire night since Hodin gave his lame little speech at Fountain Square."

Jaw tight, Al dropped his circle. "I will not be fooled," he growled, clenched hands glowing. "If she's dead, then there's nothing to stop me from killing you, little brother."

"Damn it, Al. It's me!" I shouted as he threw an unfocused ball of energy. *"Pacta sunt servanda!"* I exclaimed, wincing as my synapses burned, but Al's energy went spinning into the walls instead of hitting me. A flame licked up the wall . . . then went out.

"Please, not the windows. Anything but the windows . . ." Jenks begged from the rafters, Getty now safe beside him.

Hands fisted at his sides, Al came at me in slow, monstrous steps. I kept backing up, willing Jenks and Trent to stay out of this. "Morgan was all I had left that I could point to and say I had done some good in this world, and you even corrupted that when you convinced her to sell her students to Dali. You *ruined* her. You are dying. Right here. Right now."

My breath caught and I froze. *I'm all he has left?* "That was Hodin," I said, voice soft. "You know I wouldn't sell my students to Dali. Not for anything. There's always another way."

Inches before me, Al hesitated. Behind him, Trent stood ready with something ugly in his hands. I loved Trent so much at that moment, I could hardly breathe. He was there, trusting that I knew what I was doing. *God, please let me know what I'm doing.*

"Dali said it was just the next bad decision in a long list of them. You haven't been very smart lately. If that is indeed you—Rachel."

He'd only used one of my names, not all three, but he had filled it with so much venom that it scared me. "I don't care if you believe me or not about the students," I said. "I know what I did or didn't do. But I need to talk to Dali about giving me the keys to the vault so I can bring Hodin in." My shoulders slumped. "Alone," I whispered. "Like always."

The heat of magic in Al's hand vanished. His expression twisted, and I jumped when the demon howled, a bolt of liquid fire shooting from his hand to crash into Kisten's pool table. With a dull snap, the solid piece of slate cracked. "I'm not going to do this!" he exclaimed as Trent rose from an instinctive crouch. "I will not do this again!"

"Keep out of it, Kalamack!" Jenks shrilled as Al focused on me, and I stood there, shaking.

"I won't allow you to fool me again!" Al shouted, finger shaking as he pointed at me. "I don't care if you really are Rachel, you aren't getting access to the vault, and not through me!"

My breath was fast as I stood before Al with the lightest thought in the line. "I'm not Hodin," I said, tears starting to threaten to blur my sight. "Damn it to the Turn and back. Do you really think Hodin would show up trying to be me still damp from the Cincinnatian's pool? Look at my hair!" I shouted, and Jenks snickered. "It's a god-awful mess. Do you know how much detangler it's going to take to part this thing out? There isn't a charm or curse that will even touch it! And another thing. I never should have promised to protect him from you. You're all being total asses about it."

Al's attention flicked to my hair, and I felt myself warm. "No," he said flatly, his gaze shifting to Jenks hovering behind me. "You shouldn't have." Slumping, he abruptly sat in one of the chairs before the empty cricket cage with his head bowed. "Kill me, Hodin. I don't care."

I exchanged a glance with Trent to try to tell him to stay where he was. The worst was over—maybe. "Um, I know your summoning name. Is that enough to prove it's me?"

Al's sneer was ugly. "Everyone knows my summoning name."

"Your *other* summoning name," I said, which no one but me, Ivy, Trent, Jenks . . . okay, maybe there were a few people who knew, but Hodin certainly didn't.

It was starting to smell like burnt cinnamon, wine, and redwood in here, and I inched closer. "I'm not going to say what it is," I said, and Al huffed as if I was admitting I was

Hodin. "I mean, who's to say you aren't Hodin yourself?" My hand touched the couch, but I wouldn't sit on it just yet. "No wonder you all want to kill him. This is awful. How do you function like this? Not knowing who anyone is in truth?"

Al's gaze lifted from the floor, rising up my damp jeans and stringy hair. *There you are,* I thought as a flash of pain crossed him. Suddenly I was blinking at tears, a lump in my throat. It was Al. It had to be. And he knew it was me. Really me.

Al sourly eyed Jenks, then me. "Even if it was you, and you're alive, I can't help you. You're on your own."

I made a finger motion to Jenks, and he darted away to keep the mourners off the steps. "Yeah, well, I have a history of bad decisions when it comes to contracts with demons."

"That is the student's fault. Not the teacher's," he said, but I didn't know if this was good or not. Trent was coming forward with Constance, halting when Al glared at him.

I took a breath, not sure how far this new understanding went. "You're right. I deserve to be in Alcatraz. I gave Hodin sanctuary in my church for months while he drove a wedge between me and everyone I care about, including you. You told me, and I didn't listen."

Al sat there, silently waiting for more.

"He was playing me the entire time," I added. "He wants to take my power, put me in jail for doing dark magic and selling witches to Dali. He couldn't do it until he stripped me of my friends, and I let him. He distracted Jenks with the chance to find love . . ."

"Did not!" Jenks blurted, and Trent cleared his throat in a rebuke to stay quiet.

"He kept Trent occupied by playing on an old pattern of business first," I continued.

"Ah, that's not entirely true," Trent said, then shut his mouth when Jenks rasped his wings.

"He kept Ivy out of Cincinnati entirely," I added, my fingers gripping the couch as I began to feel sorry for myself.

"Misled Pike and got him in debt so deep he was sold to his brothers to pay off his mark. And he tricked Stef. While I was watching. I should have done something, but I wanted her to live in that world she believed in. One where demons weren't feared."

Throat thick, I looked at Al. "And he stole you from me."

Al was silent, his face utterly blank.

"Al, I almost killed Stef," I protested, sounding like a little whiny girl even to me. "He changed her into his image, and I almost killed her." I glanced over my shoulder as if I could see through the walls. "Right in my kitchen."

An old, silent pain crossed his face, drawing his expression in a knot. Immediately he steeled his features, but I'd seen, and I cautiously sat down, reaching over the table for his hand.

"Al," I whispered as he drew away. "I'm so sorry." *Please don't let it have been his wife.*

Al shuddered. "And you still expect me to believe it's not you, Hodin?" he whispered, a heavy pain in him. "Rachel Morgan never listens. Never learns. *That* sounded like an apology."

I inched to the front of the couch, my heart hurting. "You were right," I said softly. "I should have trusted you even when I didn't understand why. But I wanted to live in a world where demons weren't judged by their name or even their past. I let Hodin screw me over so I could pretend the world was what I wanted. I am a fool."

A heavy sigh shifted his shoulders, and I blinked fast when he looked up at me, forgiveness in him. "That is the teacher's fault, not yours."

"Then you believe it's me?" I squeaked out, my chest tight in heartache.

He made a huff of annoyance, a slim ribbon of his usual visage showing. "Hodin is not capable of apologizing like that," he said, his gaze touching on Trent and Jenks. "And no one reads a room better than a pixy. If Jenks is real, then you are real."

Elated, I leaned over the coffee table, fighting the urge

to take his hands in mine. He would only pull away again. "Will you help me? I can't do this alone. I need my friends."

A wry smile quirked his lips. "And have my student lose the only thing our kin respects?"

My word. Which was weird since they were all slippery liars.

"You say Hodin trapped you in a circle?" Al asked, his attention rising to the rafters. "I am surprised you survived at all."

"He was distracted. We both were. I was down to throwing my bag at him when he turned into a crow."

Al made a soft grunt of appreciation as he took his hat back in hand and spun it. "You got him to shape-shift? You scared him. Newt was the only one of us who could do that." His focus dulled into the distance. "But Newt scared all of us. I have to talk to Dali."

He stood as if to leave, and I rose as well, hope a bright flash as I glanced at Trent. "To recover my students, Sikes, and Melody?"

Al blinked as he realigned his thoughts, staring at me as if I was being stupid. "No. Even if it was Hodin who sold them, the deal was made. Besides, Dali needs them. The work contracts will soon be signed and filed in the I.S. You will have some explaining to do to the media, I'm sure," he said lightly. "Unless you can give Dali something better than a year in your garden and a string of pearls?"

I shook my head, arms about my middle as I glanced at Trent's frown.

"I'm not sure how this new workforce will last," Al said, hand gesturing grandly as his mourning frock vanished, leaving him in black slacks and an obsidian shirt under a flamboyant vest. "They're not very sturdy," he added as he inspected his sleeve and a silver embroidery folded into the fabric, the protective glyphs looking like stars and ivy leaves. "Especially Sikes. Perhaps if you could convince someone else to take their place?"

I wondered at the new, almost-contemporary finery, thinking it suited him. "You know I can't do that."

Al eyed me over his blue-tinted glasses, clearly ready to go as he picked up the empty cricket cage. "Where are my crickets?" he asked, tone accusing.

I started at the sudden topic shift. "Ah . . . they died when I was in jail. Al, about Sikes."

"You didn't feed them?" Al glanced at Trent and Jenks. "You must remember to feed those you are responsible for. Tsk, tsk. I'm sure Sikes will be fed at least."

"Sikes is not a cricket," I said, and Al made a noise of agreement.

"I'm curious," he said with a feigned lightness as he examined the empty cage. "Did you ever get the charm to work on more than one of them?"

"No."

"Pity. Newt could spell more than one person at a time with the same charm. I was hoping you might figure it out as well."

"I think it takes the Goddess," I said, and Trent shifted uneasily. Of all the demons, only Newt and myself had had close ties to her. And then Newt became her.

"Ah, well." Al sighed, and the cricket cage vanished. "You haven't done too badly, itchy witch. You are alive, which is shocking, having survived a curse that killed everyone else he used it on. Why is that?" he asked as he scooped up the books. They were the ones that I had just gotten from Newt, and I wondered why he had had them. *Oh yeah. He thought I was dead.*

"Probably because I wasn't relying on my gargoyle to boost my line intake," I muttered. I wasn't much of a demon without Bis, and I missed him all the more. But I had to admit that being forced to learn how to spindle that much line energy had stood me in good stead.

Again Al glanced at Trent and Jenks, still with Constance by the piano. "We need to fix that. Say good-bye. Time to go."

My pulse leapt. "You'll help me recover Bis?" I exclaimed, and Jenks darted forward, clearly excited as well.

"Not today. Today is for retreat and planning. Honestly,

Rachel," Al huffed, his usual superciliousness firmly in place. "Getting yourself stuck in a circle is intolerable. Anyone could bring you down. Even a vampire." Al's attention flicked to Constance as Trent came closer, the elf's expression wary. "Until we bring your gargoyle awake, fleeing to the ever-after to avoid persecution is an acceptable option. It would grant you the time to increase your studies. Say, a hundred years or so?"

"Ah . . . Rachel?" Trent murmured, and suddenly I understood why Al was holding my books. *He thinks I'm going to leave? With him?*

"I can't leave Cincy to Hodin," I said as I backed up to Trent.

Al frowned at us over his glasses. "I believe the word you want is *won't*, because you most certainly can," he said, lip curling as Trent's hand curved protectively about my waist.

"Can't. Won't. I'm not going," I said, and Al pinched the bridge of his nose as if in pain. Head shaking, I leaned deeper into Trent. "Especially if Hodin is pretending to be Constance. I need heavy-hitting charms that Hodin doesn't know. That means access to the vault."

Anxious, Jenks hovered over Constance, the pixy gesturing urgently at me. "But you think there's a way to recover Bis?" I asked, and the mouse sneezed, covered in pixy dust.

"Perhaps." Al shifted the books to his hip, and a not-nice smile widened his thick lips. "I've been giving it some thought. There's a chance that with enough smut, we can make a small, temporary reality. It won't last long without a ley line holding it to reality, but it would be enough to safely open the bottle, separate Bis from the baku, and then leave, allowing the reality to dissipate and take the baku with it. It might take a year to prep. You would need more smut than you currently have to create it, filthy as your aura is."

Trent's hold on me eased. "A year? You made the new ever-after in, what? Ten seconds?"

Al's gaze tightened on Trent, an old hatred smoldering.

"The baku is an elven abomination. If you are *sincere* in your frivolous quest to improve the relationship between our societies, you should do everything you can to destroy one of your most effective and heinous weapons."

"Why not do it now?" I said, thinking that "improving the relationship between our societies" was a far second to his goal of convincing me to flee to the ever-after. "It's not hard to make a new reality." No, the trick was to give it enough smut-based substance to get it to last long enough to make a ley line between it and reality to keep it from vanishing.

Again Al shifted the stack of books to his other arm, clearly annoyed. "Because if you don't survive the next twenty-four hours, it won't matter." And then he jerked, his eyes going sharp on mine. "Mmmm," he intoned, and my pulse quickened as the same thought struck me.

Could I trap Hodin in a collapsing, temporary world . . .
"Ah, Al?" I prompted, but the demon was already shaking his head.

"It will not work," Al said, and Jenks shrugged at Trent, both of them clearly not following our train of thought. "Hodin will simply jump out of any temporary reality."

"Not if I solidify his aura," I said, and Trent made a small sound in understanding. "He wasn't around when you were all tormenting each other with it. It will take him some time to break it."

Al looked at the books in his hand and frowned. "Hodin is clever. He'll figure it out."

"Before it collapses?" I asked, and Al huffed in impatience.

"I give him thirty seconds. Tops."

It was longer than the five seconds I'd given Hodin to figure it out, but my attention jerked to the front door when someone banged on it. Trent gave my shoulder a reassuring squeeze, setting Constance on the table before he and Jenks went to see who it was.

Deep in thought, I sank back down into my chair, making Al groan in impatience. Even if I could get Hodin stuck

in an alternate reality, that would leave my students and
Sikes in the ever-after. Unless . . . My breath caught as a
new idea flooded me.

"It won't work, whatever it is," Al said.

"What about a tulpa!"

Al frowned as Trent and Jenks went onto the stoop.
"You can't buy nineteen students and a university professor
for a tulpa." Al dropped my books onto the table and, startled, Constance hissed at him. "Even untutored ones," he
muttered, poking a finger at her until she lunged, scoring
on him. "The librarian, perhaps . . ."

"What if it had Hodin in it?" I whispered.

His eyes flicked to mine, and Al made a low sound, interested again. "If I could convince Dali that Hodin couldn't
escape it, perhaps. But you can't incorporate a living person
into a tulpa. It's a memory made real, Rachel. Not a prison."

My gaze went to Jenks's stained-glass windows as a
large industrial light suddenly lit them, brighter than the
sun. A news crew was here. "I think it could be," I said
softly, excitement tingling down to my toes. "If I held Hodin in my thoughts while I made the tulpa, I mean, make it
when both Hodin and I are nothing but thought, I could
code him into the construct. Not only that, but I could fix
that aura-solidifying curse right into his DNA the same
way I cursed Ku'Sox to be trapped in the ever-after. He'd
never break it."

Al made a soft noise as he understood what I was saying. "You want to make a tulpa while in a ley line? With
Hodin in your mind? You are crazier than Newt."

I nodded, finding hope that he hadn't said it couldn't be
done. "I'd need your help, obviously. Someone will have to
shove me out of the line after I'm done. But if I can catch
him in midjump and hold him while I make the tulpa, I can
incorporate him in it. He'll be nothing but thought, so he
should be stuck there!"

Al stared at me as if I had told him we could walk on the
moon if we sang the right song.

"All we have to do is leave Hodin in the tulpa when you

pull it free of me," I whispered. "Dali gets a tulpa with Hodin stuck in it, and I trade that to Dali for everyone he tricked into signing a contract!" Not to mention if I could imprison Hodin, I could do the same to them if they dared to steal anyone else.

My pulse pounded three heavy beats as Al thought, a dangerous light in his eye. "It will take too much time," he said. "You will be burned if you stay in the line long enough to make a tulpa."

"I've been burned before," I said. "And I know how to use smut as an insulation now. We both do. Like we did when the Goddess tried to burn us. I wouldn't mind getting rid of what Hodin tricked me into taking."

Al nodded, his expression worried. "The damage he could bring about while you work. Rachel, he will rake your mind to shreds as you hold him. There will be nothing left."

"Isn't that how you make a tulpa? Please," I pleaded. "You can put me back together."

Al looked to the door as Trent and Jenks came in, a flush of excited noise with them. "No one will spend time in a tulpa with Hodin in it," Al said shortly. "Dali won't buy it."

"Really?" I said, thinking his excuse was an affirmation that it could be done. "Not one demon wants to spend an hour with Hodin? At all? It's not as if you can kill him. You can't hurt a memory." Yes, I was stretching my arrangement with Hodin to the utmost, but that was allowed. Encouraged, actually.

Al sighed, his touch light on the books upon the table. "Rachel, I do not rip your thoughts from the tulpa. I lift the tulpa free. Hodin will ravage your mind."

"Will I step from it intact?" I asked, and he reluctantly nodded. "Then it's only pain. I can handle pain. Please, Al. This is the choice I have. I can't do it without you," I added, elation and dread making my stomach cramp. The fear that the aura-solidifying curse wouldn't work long enough was real. Fear that I couldn't hold Hodin while I made the tulpa was real. Fear that the smut wasn't thick enough and I'd burn my mind to ash was real. But Al and I had practice, and if the tulpa was something I was familiar with, we could be in and out of the line in . . . minutes?

God, can I withstand that much pain?

But it was all I had, and I begged Al with my eyes to give me the chance to try.

"Hey, Rache?" Jenks said, interrupting, and Al turned before I knew if he would do it. "Pike and Ivy are here. You want to stand in the street at midnight and call Hodin out?"

Al gathered my books again, extending a hand to help me rise. "A demon does not sneak out the back door," he said confidently, and I felt my knees go watery. We were going to do it. Well, at least, we were going to try.

As Jenks dusted a cheerful gold, I took Al's hand, letting him draw me to stand beside him.

It felt like the right place to be.

"THIS'LL BE GREAT, RACHE," JENKS SAID FROM MY SHOULDER as I stepped from the church, forced to come to a quick halt outside the door. Al was a heavy presence behind me. Trent was to my right, the cage with Constance halfway behind him to protect her.

"Hodin in a tulpa," the pixy continued as the reporters fought Cincy's citizens for a front-row seat. "Tulpa buys everyone's freedom. You get rid of that smut. Cake at sunrise."

Except for what to do with Finnis, I thought as Al muttered a word of Latin and the crowd reacted when a wave of gold and red energy pushed them back three feet. Nervous laughter rolled up, and I glanced at Trent in worry. Giving up on the vampires' soul curse wasn't going to happen. I needed to find a lever to move the undead, and find it fast.

"These are your people," Al said, then sighed dramatically. "Are you sure you want to do this? For them?"

I took a breath to answer, yelping when a shiver raced through my aura. Jenks left my shoulder with a muffled curse, and a soft mental rebuke slapped me. It was Al, and I held myself still as his magic washed through me, vanishing to leave me dry, my hair in a tight braid, and my working leathers on. *Even the jacket and boots,* I mused as I looked at my vamp-made ass-kickers. "I thought you said the robe made a better impression," I said as I hiked my bag up my shoulder, and Al harrumphed, a heavy hand landing on me as he leaned forward.

"You're not teaching," he whispered in my ear, and sensation rippled through me. "You're working. Don't tell them anything you don't want Hodin to know." His grip tightened. "He's out there. It's unlikely he'll try anything in front of the cameras lest he make a martyr out of you. He'll want privacy to turn your flesh into a puddle of goo."

Swell. I faced the assembled cameras, now a polite three feet away behind the glowing line hovering at waist height. This was not my best birthday . . . but it wasn't my worst, either.

"Morgan!" came a shout, and I eagerly scanned the crowd for Pike. "Let me through. Rachel!"

There was a yelp, and I smiled when suddenly a way opened and Ivy sauntered forward, svelte and sexy in her dark slacks and top, her hair free and her hips swaying. Pike was behind her, his obvious excitement a stark contrast to Ivy's placid confidence.

"What was that?" Pike said as he caught up to her. "Sort of a half nerve pinch with an ankle-tuck punch? Nice."

"It opens doors," she said, her neutral expression softening in the barest hint of relief.

I stepped forward, frowning when Al yanked me back. "Could be Hodin," he whispered, and I shoved his hand off my shoulder.

Then Hodin is going to get one hell of a hug, I thought as I reached for Ivy and gave her a quick squeeze. She felt real to me, and I put her at arm's length, searching her pupil-black gaze. The faint hint of vamp pheromones lifted from her, familiar. She was overly stressed and blood-hungry, and my attention slid from her to Pike. He was hungry and stressed as well, but I could sense the beginnings of trust between them, and I wondered if there might be a threesome in their future. Not with me, but Nina.

"How did my little spell pot get that small dent?" I asked as Pike took a finger-can of gold spray paint from his pocket and painted an oversize logo on the sidewalk before the steps.

"Your what?" Ivy said, confused. I stared at her until understanding seemed to blossom. "Oh. You'd have to ask Jenks," she added, and Jenks flew off, muttering about doing a security sweep.

It was the right answer, and I pulled her into another hug. She didn't know how the dent had gotten there. Or at least, she never admitted to knowing. "You're okay?" I asked, and she nodded, shifting to include Pike, now gazing in satisfaction at his logo. Al, too, was studying it, or rather, he was noting the soft stir it had made in the crowd. Pike had been right. It was a sign of solidarity, a promise almost, that someone would hold the line.

"Hodin has Finnis," Ivy said as Pike tossed the mini can into his car and came to stand beside her. "It was . . . too fast."

"He downed me, too," I said, surprised when Al inched closer, the demon clearly wanting to be included in the new logo-induced camaraderie as the reporters began to make statements for later broadcasts.

"Hodin is here." Al's lip curled. "We will not do this with your usual brainless flair, itchy witch. Make a statement so we can leave and properly plan Hodin's capture."

Trent chuckled as he handed Constance's cage to Pike. "Like Rachel's ideas ever work to plan? Give me a second and I'll prep the press for you."

Pike beamed at Constance as the mouse hissed at him, his mood good even if he was sporting a new bandage on his wrist. "I'm getting reports of a few protests, but no riots. Everyone is waiting to see what you're going to do."

Pike. Right, I thought, turning to him. "Pike, what color is my I.S. file?"

Al sighed in impatience as Pike grinned. "That would be red."

It was him. Feeling better with everyone around me, I tugged my leather jacket down and faced the news crews. Trent was keeping them busy, but they kept looking at me, and it was obvious I was their target.

"What's with Al?" Ivy asked, and my motion to join Trent hesitated. "I thought he couldn't help."

"He's not helping. He's just standing there," I said, and Al snickered, the evil sound of it drawing the attention of the closest people.

"Astonishing." Al studied the crowd, touching first on Trent prepping the reporters, then Pike's logo giving strength to my coming words, rising to Jenks maintaining a watch from the roofline, and finally to Ivy beside me keeping everyone at a polite distance. "You're managing everything without magic, but it's taking an entire village to do it."

I bobbed my head, then faced Ivy. "Al and I are going to trade Hodin for everyone's release," I said, lips barely moving so the news crews couldn't guess at my words. "Finnis could not care less who is in charge of Cincinnati. He wants the soul curse out of FSCA consideration, and I'm hoping that with Hodin out of the picture, he might back off, knowing if I can trap Hodin, I can do the same to him and anyone else they send."

Lips pressed, Ivy sent her gaze sidelong to Pike and Constance, clearly not sure. But Ivy was all about one step at a time, and she finally nodded.

Trent turned, a hand extended. "Rachel, would you like to make a statement?"

Al's hand clamped on my shoulder. "Too late. He's here. I can feel him."

I looked at Al's hand, then listened to the shouted questions of the crowd. "You know that everything-without-magic thing? Give me a second."

Al's hand fell away, and I moved forward to stand on the last step before Pike's logo, ignoring the mic being shoved over Al's magical don't-cross line. "Thanks for this," I said to Trent as I gave him my bag to hold.

"Say what you want," Trent said, giving Al's impatience a sidelong glance. "If you want to take questions, talk to the woman with the red heels or the guy with the orange-and-gold-striped tie. They're forward thinkers. Avoid the guy with the white mustache."

"Got it. Thanks." Feeling nervous but confident, I stepped out, my smile going thin when they began yelling questions. Jenks's dust sifted down unnoticed by all but me. At least, I hoped it was Jenks's dust. I wasn't exactly ignoring Al's advice, but unlike most demons, I had to lay the groundwork so I didn't end up in jail when this was over. A little heads-up with the media went a long way.

But they wouldn't be quiet.

"Shut it!" Al shouted, and took a slow breath as silence fell.

"Ah, I'm alive," I said, and someone snickered as a whispered "No shit, Sherlock" rose from the outskirts.

"Mmmm, I understand that Constance is accusing me of some ugly things," I continued, thankful that Al had worked a brush-and-wash curse on me. "I can't deny most of them," I added, and the demon practically growled in annoyance. "If you care to look, my aura is smutty. I was unaware that a curse I did to protect Constance's scion was illegal. That's no excuse, and I'm working to make amends as soon as I can find the assassins I accidentally cursed."

"You cursed an assassin?" the woman with the red shoes said. "Doesn't that fall under self-defense?"

"No, she's still liable," the man with the mustache said, and Al grumped about killing all lawyers. "What about the students you sold into slavery? And Professor Sikes?"

I thought it interesting that Melody's fate still remained unrecognized, and I tensed when Al leaned low to whisper, "Fifteen seconds, and I am jumping you out."

He was scanning the crowd even as I felt the energy

from the ley line he was tapping begin to coalesce in his aura. But I wasn't done yet. "Professor Sikes is chaperoning a select group of his students on a five-day demon immersion course for extra credit," I said, and I felt Al's magic hesitate.

"Well done. You may have twenty seconds," he murmured, and I inched away from him, the ties of his magic humming between us.

"That is a lie!" came a shout, and heads turned as the call went up that it was Finnis.

"No, wait," I muttered as pinpricks and tingles raced over my aura. Al was preparing to jump us out, but I was not done.

Again the crowd parted, half the mics extended now to Finnis. Ivy inched closer to my one side, Trent on the other. Jenks dropped down, his dust warming my cheek as his wings hummed.

Eyes pupil black, Finnis strode forward. I.S. agents with nightsticks and wands filled in behind, pushing everyone back as they made a living wall. I didn't see Hodin, but he had proved himself to be a calculating coward and Al's expression was enough to kill. *Twenty seconds . . .* I could do a lot in twenty seconds.

"You want to confront him?" Al said, incredulous, his words tripping down my spine like ice. "He's an undead vampire. He has no real strength."

But no real strength or not, he had political power and I had to address it. Now. In front of the world.

"Perhaps we should take this inside," Trent suggested, and I shook my head as Finnis came to a bluster-filled halt eight feet away. Pike slowly retreated, not because he was afraid, but because Constance was shrieking like a bat, and I stifled a panic-based laugh when Jenks told her to shut up.

"Retreat into a church?" Finnis said as the I.S. agents pushed the reporters to the edges. "Hiding again, Kalamack?" the undead vampire said. "Isn't that what got you flirting with bankruptcy?"

The rims of Trent's pointy ears reddened. "Why does everyone think I'm broke?" he muttered.

"It was dating me that wiped Trent out, not hiding," I said, and the reporters predictably tittered. I didn't mind the laughter at my expense. It had the desired effect, and Finnis's bold approach had been ruined.

"Marvelous," Al muttered. "I give you until Hodin shows. Then we are gone."

"Yep," Jenks said as the reporters began to find their courage again. "You should see her when she makes an effort. Rachel can put a spin on a two-dimensional button."

I wasn't as confident as Jenks, but I could fake it well enough, and as I shifted my fingers to ask Jenks to keep a lookout, I fixed my gaze on the undead vampire. "Finnis," I said, liking that the step I was on put me eye to eye with the taller man. "I'm glad you're here. Now that you have met with Constance, I imagine you will be leaving tonight?"

Hip cocked, I sent my senses searching, my thoughts lightly in the nearest ley line.

Finnis predictably smiled to show his long teeth. "No," he said, his confidence absolute with the I.S. heavies around him. "*Constance* has informed me that you are not effective as her enforcer and should be removed even if your recent activities don't put you in jail, which they will." His attention shifted over my shoulder to Pike. "Welroe as well. Constance will choose a new scion from one of my own children this week. Both you and Pike will be held in I.S. custody until the accusations of illicit magic can be settled."

The reporters were silent, their mics' aim shifting to me.

"I already settled it," I said. "I made an honest mistake and I'm making amends. The person who taught me the magic did so with the intent to do me harm. I was a tool, and tools can't be prosecuted." Smiling, I leaned over Pike's logo. "Besides, you haven't talked to Constance yet."

A flicker of fear came and went in Finnis. He quit breathing, his eyes going utterly black.

"No, I'm afraid you have been misled by the same person who I trusted to teach me a white curse," I said coyly, giving Finnis a way out lest he try to make one through me. "The woman you met with today? That was not Constance."

My hair began to snarl, stray strands escaping my braid to spark with the ley line energy Al was pulling from the line. It hazed all of us as we stood before Pike's logo. "That," I said, pointing to the mouse, "is Constance."

The silence held for a heartbeat, and then the reporters began shouting, mics extended and crushing forward. Finnis stared at Constance as the mouse railed against the bars of her cage, her sparkly necklace catching the light and looking like a cheap prop. But it was her, and by Finnis's pale face, I knew he believed it.

"You turned her into a mouse?" the undead vampire gasped, and the I.S. personnel closed in around him, threatening violence as the gathered crowd surged forward.

I backed up, my shoulder finding not Trent, but Al. "Surely you've heard of the university's new unofficial mascot?" I said, my shouted words almost lost in the uproar. "A vampiric mouse? Who did you think it was?"

Finnis's lips moved, no words coming from him as the protective ring of I.S. personnel pushed him into the street.

"Constance is alive!" I shouted, sure that there was a camera trained on me somewhere. "And I don't like you, Finnis. I don't like you coming into Cincinnati thinking you have *any* say in how we handle ourselves. I didn't like it when Constance tried, and I don't like it when you're trying. You should leave before I do the same thing to Hodin, and you, and anyone else who gets between me and the well-being of Cincinnati!"

My words were tiny in the pandemonium, but I knew he could hear me even as he was being hustled to a car. "Why don't you catch a show, check out the pandas and the museum of elven exhibits, and go home in the same shape you arrived in! Everyone knows that Pike and I have been running Cincinnati for four months. And you are not welcome here, Finnis."

I jumped when Al's hand hit my shoulder. Wiggling out from under it, I took a step sideways to stand on Jenks's potted plants. "That soul curse will be approved!" I shouted, and Al pinched the bridge of his nose. "And if you halt it, I'll put it on the illicit market and you won't make a *dime* of taxes off it. I am a *demon*, and there's no extradition from the ever-after, bud-dy. I can work from there as easy as from my church!"

"Rache," Jenks said, clearly uncomfortable. His dust was a brilliant white from the loosed, undirected energy, and I tossed the hair from my shoulder so he'd have a place to alight.

Finnis fought off the agents between him and us, refusing to get in the car. "I will not be intimidated! I am a DC undead!" he shouted.

"Blah, blah, blah," I said, making the appropriate hand gestures, and the vampire turned a bright red. "You, Finnis, are an old undead. And your time to rule is done."

The crowd erupted, pushing into the space between us. Someone jostled me, and my foot slipped off the potted plant. Arms swinging, I lurched backward, gasping when a ball of green and yellow energy hit the news van and exploded.

"Crap on toast!" I shouted as I fell into someone's arms, then blinked when I found they were Al's. My attention jerked to Trent as he threw a charm at a crow and the crowd began to scatter. "Time's up," I said, and Al's gaze narrowed on the scraggly bird.

"Al!" I exclaimed as my skin tingled from his gathered energy. His eyes tracked Hodin to blast his younger brother. "Get us out of here! Keep to the plan!"

Al's face twisted, and with an ugly roar of hatred, he expanded his magic, racing through my aura and shifting. *All of us!* I shouted as I found myself in the ley lines. *Al, I need all of us!*

And then I was real again, still cradled in Al's arms where he had caught me.

"Out of the frying pan," I whispered, my pulse hammering

as I realized where I was by the bad seventies music, low
ceiling, long bar, and tiny tables. "Here?" I said as we were
noticed and the music cut out. "You brought us here?" I
complained, then stiffened. It was just Al and me. "I said to
bring everyone," I added, and then I shrieked as Al dropped
me and my butt hit the floor in a painful thump.

CHAPTER

29

"I CAN'T TELL IF YOU ARE ON SPEAKING TERMS AGAIN OR not," Dali said as he came out from behind the bar. "Leave. I'm not open. I'm training my new star on proper attire and attitude."

Still on the floor, I glared up at Al. "You left them?" I said, and Al's jaw clenched. "I said to bring them along."

"I'm not bringing them here," he huffed. "They're safer apart from you, itchy witch. I thought you knew that."

Ticked, I raised a hand to Al so he could help me up, but he ignored it, and I painfully levered myself to my feet. Trent had my bag, but it was unlikely I'd need it—though I wouldn't mind plugging Dali in the face with a few splat balls for fun.

I cautiously nodded at a sallow-faced man in a flamboyant, cheap-looking vest cowering behind the bar. It wasn't one of my students, and I figured it was Sikes. The place was otherwise empty, the ugly music loud against the low ceilings and flat tables. "Where are the students?" I whispered, but Al ignored me, focused on the demon behind the bar.

"Dali . . ." Al wheedled as he came deeper into the strip club. "We fit in. Be a pal and set us up a round while my student and I talk."

Sikes silently pleaded with me: hollowed eyes, pale face, rightly too afraid to speak. "Where are the rest?" I asked again as the thin man continued to clean the bloodred glasses arrayed before him.

"I loaned them out." Dali grinned, his expression holding an enormous satisfaction. "It takes dedication to bring a familiar up from scratch, and it's easier to do it in pairs, not dozens."

Son of a bastard, why did I ever think they would change? No wonder the place was empty. The demons were playing.

"You little bitch!" came from behind me, and I spun.

"Vivian?" I exclaimed as the small woman hopped off the stage, staggering on her six-inch heels. She was in a showgirl outfit, tiny, that was designed to do just that: show the girl. "Vivian, my God!" I said as I pushed past Al. "I've been trying to call you. How . . ."

"You demon whore!" the small blond woman shouted, pasties swinging. And then she shoved me with both hands.

Backpedaling, I hit a table.

"I trusted you!" she shrieked, and I stared at her, bewildered.

"Wha . . ." I stammered, then scrambled to put the table between us as she picked up a chair and swung it high. *"Rhombus!"* I barked out, and my circle snapped into existence as the cheap wooden chair splintered over it.

"Get out of that bubble and fight me like a woman!" Vivian shouted, standing before me with her tassels shaking and kohl eyeshadow running to show she'd been crying.

"Vivian, it wasn't me," I said, and the furious woman splintered another chair against my bubble. There was a band of charmed silver around her ankle, which was probably why she was hammering at my circle with a third chair and not her magic.

Dali stood beside the bar and frowned, arms over his chest. "If you damage Vivian Amber Smith you owe me restitution, Morgan," he said, then to Vivian, "I never told you to stop dancing. Get up on that stage."

Ignoring him, Vivian continued to hammer at my circle with a busted chair leg. "I trusted you!" she screamed. "Look at me! I'm a stripper in a demon strip joint!"

Al made a tiny huff of interest, then turned to the bar. "I do believe Madam Coven Member thinks you sold her to Dali."

"You think?" I said sarcastically as I broke my circle, then shifted to put a tiny round table between us. "Damn it, Vivian, it was Hodin," I said, steadily retreating to try to keep out of her reach.

Dali went white. "Hodin!" he bellowed, and Vivian slid to a halt, shaking. Sniffing, she wiped her face, smearing the kohl even more. I wanted to give her something to cover herself, but there was nothing in the bar and I finally took off my jacket.

Dali spun to Al, who was now leaning over the bar to help himself to a glass of something amber. "That was Hodin?" Dali said, his expression shifting from shock to anger, and Al saluted him with the bottle.

"That was Hodin," Al said flatly. "Which is why we are here." Annoyed, Al frowned at Vivian. The coven member had collapsed into a tiny ball, hiding as her shoulders shook. "Please tell me you didn't give Hodin access to the vault in exchange for *that*?"

Dali's eye twitched. "She can handle the tulpa shifts." Turning to the bar, he shouted, "Which is more than I can say for Emanual Jonas Sikes!"

"I didn't know about Vivian," I said as Vivian rocked herself, her fury spent. I wasn't sure I wanted to go over there yet. She had been really pissed.

"This is your fault," Dali barked, and my head snapped up. He was pointing at me.

"My fault?" I said, and Al growled under his breath, his grip on his glass tightening. "How is *you* not knowing Hodin was pretending to be *me* my fault?"

"You allowed him to look like you," Dali said, red-faced. "Act in your stead."

"I did nothing of the kind," I protested, then I fell back, yelping as Al's thrown magic hit Dali's sudden burst of energy. Vivian jumped as the combined power smashed into a corner, where it bubbled and frothed, eating a table in a snapping gurgle of dissociation.

Peering at Dali over his blue-smoked glasses, Al moved to stand beside me, his glass of ice and spirits clinking. "Hodin tricking you is not Morgan's fault. Did you give him access to the vault?"

Dali glanced at Vivian. "They are mine. Legally mine. All of them."

I winced at the disintegrated table, now a frothing puddle. "You don't own them. You can't own people."

Vivian was still shaking, and I sidled over to her and extended her my jacket, but all she did was ineffectively slap at me, trying to get me to go away as she cried.

"Touch that charmed silver on her, and I will kill you where you stand," Dali said. "It took me three hours to get it on her."

Vivian's chin lifted. "You don't own me!" she shouted, tear streaked and angry.

"But I do," Dali said, snapping his fingers at Sikes until the man resumed cleaning the glasses. "Even if it was Hodin who did the selling." His lips pressed into a frown as I draped my jacket over Vivian and she finally took it, fingers shaking. "I didn't tell you to stop dancing. Get up there!"

"Screw you, Dali," Vivian snarled, and then I yelped as she vanished, appearing on the stage with a thump. Shrieking, she threw the chair leg at him.

Dali was smiling when I turned to him. "Mine," he said again. "All nice and legal." He rubbed his fingers, and a black envelope appeared in them. "A copy of the work contract. Be a dove and file it for me at the Cincinnati office with the rest, will you?"

"I never signed that!" Vivian exclaimed. "That's not my signature."

Dali's smile became ugly with confidence. "It looks like your signature."

My gut tightened and I felt ill. I doubted anyone other than Sikes really signed anything. "File it yourself, Dali. I'm not your lackey."

Dali's expression went blank. "The world thinks you sold them to me, and even if you didn't, I'm not giving them back. A deal is a deal." His attention went to the stage. "You!" he shouted, pointing at Vivian. "Dance!"

Al's low laugh raked across my spine like evil itself. "And you bought his act. Again."

I hadn't thought it possible, but Dali's mood worsened. Jaw tight, the demon retreated behind the bar. "He has you down, Morgan," he said as he held one of Sikes's cleaned glasses to the light, inspecting it. "Your voice, your hair, even your missteps and stumbles. Your life is his now."

"He is not me," I muttered, sullen as Al came up beside me, his glass now holding only ice.

"And don't think you would have done any better, Gally," Dali said. "Hiding in your wagon in the woods so you wouldn't have to figure out who was real and who was Hodin."

Al sighed as he levered himself up onto a barstool and tapped the smooth counter for another drink. "Fortunately for us, Hodin can't enter the vault even with the access code."

"Because Hodin is not in the collective," I said, and Dali nodded. "He can't get in."

"At the moment," Dali affirmed as he set a drink before Al. "Until he breaks your elf's arm to make you give him your summoning name."

I slumped, my back to the bar as I looked over the strip club. Swell. The demon's password system had worked fine when they were stuck in the ever-after, but now? Maybe I could make this work to my advantage, though. Hodin would have to come to me to get it. And then, I'd put him in a tulpa.

"I told you to dance!" Dali shouted, and as the sleazy music began thumping from hidden speakers, Vivian walked off the stage. "Petulant little coven brat . . ." Dali swore, and I felt his hold on the line strengthen.

"Dali, I want them. All of them. Contracts or no," I said, and Dali sniggered.

"You will never have enough," he said, and Vivian's yelp sounded from behind the stage. "I need them. They are my key to rebuilding my wealth."

I shook my head, tired of his domineering satisfaction. I'd hoped that particular expression was gone. "Rebuild your wealth on the backs of a weaker workforce instead of your talents? How very like a demon. Cheap and shallow. No personal sense of worth at all."

But if I had been trying to shame him, it didn't work, as he leaned an elbow on the bar and mocked me. "It works." He sipped his drink. "Does it not, Gally?"

I took a breath, finger rising until Al yanked on my arm and spun me around.

"Allow me," he said, eyeing me over his blue-tinted glasses, and I nodded. Al was by far the better dealmaker. Which made me wonder how much better of a deal he could have gotten for Vivian, Sikes, and a handful of students.

"Oh, for the breaking of the two worlds," Dali complained as Al kicked the stool out from under himself and stood, gripping the edges of his vest in an overdone show of importance.

"Vivian," Al said, voice strong and clear. "Sikes, that librarian you sweet-talked, and every last student. Freed with no reprisals."

"For what?" Dali said bitterly. "Hodin's head on a platter? You can't help her. It will be centuries before she manages it on her own, and by that time, anyone who cared about a handful of abducted witches dabbling in the dark arts will be dead." He grinned at Sikes, and the tall man almost dropped the glass he was polishing. "You will still be alive, though."

"I can't help her with Hodin, true," Al said, and Dali's attention flicked to him, drawn by Al's nonchalance. "But assisting her in constructing a tulpa is a well-documented task. Nothing out of the ordinary there."

I frowned when Dali began to laugh. "You want me to trade my livelihood for a tulpa?"

Al leaned over the bar, whispering, "A tulpa with Hodin encoded in it. Yes."

Dali stopped laughing, his brow furrowed in sudden doubt as he looked from Al to me. "Encoding a living being into a tulpa creates a mirror image only. The real person remains at large." His eyes went to the empty stage. "Like the memory of a vampiric stripper, able to do one thing, and one thing only."

"How would you know?" Al pushed from the bar in disgust. "Have you ever made one? If it works, you will have a functioning tulpa where you can torment Hodin twice a day and three times on Sunday. If she fails, she's dead and with it her promise to protect him. All it will cost you is a measly handful of familiars." He drained his glass and set it on the bar. "Familiars who are utterly unskilled at mixing drinks." He turned to the stage. "And dancing."

"Screw you, Al!" Vivian shouted from backstage, having clearly heard him.

Dali, though, was thinking. My knees were wobbly and I held my breath. I didn't like making deals with my kin. They followed the letter of it, often taking it farther than it was meant, to my detriment. I was, though, going to have to incarcerate Hodin, regardless, and since no one was going to pay me for it, I might as well win a promise to free who I could. Besides. What would I do with a tulpa of Hodin?

"Or," Al said as he idly inspected his fingernails. "My student and I could keep the tulpa and make more money than Newt. I have been toying with the idea of opening a coffee bar." He smiled at Dali. "A little competition never hurt anyone. I can't be a procurer of fine familiars anymore. Must adapt or die."

I winced, imagining Al in an apron, slinging coffee.

Dali frowned. "You think you can do this?"

I nodded. "Yes, and if I can put Hodin in a tulpa, I can do the same for all of you." My pulse quickened. "I mean it, Dali. This is not acceptable. We had an agreement. No more sentient familiars. Ever. I don't care if they walk in and beg for it."

Dali's lip twitched. "You think she can do it?" he asked Al, and I stifled a shiver when his hand curved around my waist, the feeling utterly different from when Trent did it.

"I missed the sun," Al said. "I missed it more than I now miss the status, parties, and . . . earthy compensation. More than the anger and fear directed at me. More than seeing a once-proud person find out they are absolutely nothing."

Dali's jaw clenched. "You're in no place to demand my adherence to any code of conduct," he said, and Vivian peeked out from behind the stage.

"I think I am," I said boldly. "If what I try works, none of you are safe from me." Al cleared his throat, and I added, "Fortunately, I'm a benevolent, softhearted, naïve, foolish witch-born demon who believes the world is a good place and that demons deserve to live in it even when I have to drag them kicking and screaming like spoiled entitled brats." I hesitated, wondering if this was going to be my life now: forcing demons to behave. "You want to be all-powerful, be all-powerful—but no more tricking people into servitude. That's too easy. And I want free access to every tulpa I make from here on out. Whenever I want. Hodin's included."

"I beg your pardon?" Dali said, blinking. "Free?"

"And you will make a public statement in reality effectively stating that it was Hodin who sold the students to you, not me, and his intent was to impugn my reputation. Oh, and a warrant. I want the original paperwork stating that Hodin escaped lawful incarceration, and another giving me the legal right to put him back."

"I told you, we didn't have warrants then," Dali said, and I leaned in.

"Invent one," I said tersely, and Dali turned to Al as if in disbelief.

Al shrugged. "Perhaps you should agree before she adds any more addendums."

Thinking, Dali rubbed a hand over his balding head. His weight shifted, and I caught my breath when his gaze locked on mine. "I don't think you can do it."

Al was behind me. I trusted him. "Then you have nothing to lose," I said.

Dali chewed his lower lip, and my pulse jumped when he extended his hand. Beaming, I took it, yelping in surprise when he yanked me closer. Panic was a quick flash, driven out by the satisfaction that I was going to get Vivian and the rest free.

"You give me a functioning tulpa with Hodin trapped within it, and you can have your students, their teacher, and even my new librarian," Dali said. "But the coven member stays."

"That sounds fair," Al said, and I tried to yank my hand away, failing.

"Vivian as well, or I walk out of here," I said, meeting Dali's surge of line energy with my own, making my fingers throb and feel like sausages. "How hard can it be to run a restaurant?" I finished, smiling nastily. "Mark does it. Even with you stealing his napkins."

My threat was well-taken, and Dali's grip on me eased. "Fine," he said as I reclaimed my tingling hand. "I accept all your conditions including the coven member, but you get nothing until Hodin is in my jukebox and I know he can't escape."

I nodded, refusing to rub my fingers. "Deal," I said, and then I gasped as the ground gave way, and I fell, right into a glowing ley line.

I CAUGHT MY MENTAL BALANCE FAST, SNAPPING A BUBBLE of protection around my mind as the warmth of the line coursed through me as if it was a ribbon of living thought. It sang, almost. The sound of the universe ringing. Bis said each line had its own song much as each star vibrates to its unique chord. I, though, wasn't good enough to discern the difference—which was why I couldn't shift realities unless I was standing in one. Bis was the only one who could teach me.

I want to check on Trent and Ivy, I thought, having to sharply angle the mental query to get it through not only my protection bubble, but Al's as well.

They are fine, Al thought shortly, his apparent confidence with Dali belying a deeper concern he couldn't hide from me. Not when we were this close. *Hodin is with Finnis, and Finnis is no longer at your church.*

But I need to talk to Trent. He's got my bag, I thought, not wanting our last words to each other to be those spoken on my church's steps in front of a news crew. I felt Al shift my aura to push us out of the line, and I stumbled, my hope to at least be able to say good-bye crashing when I realized he had dropped us at Piscary's, the bar and kitchen to my left, the tables and black fireplace to my right.

Hodin is at Piscary's? But seeing as Finnis needed somewhere secure for the day, it was a logical choice outside of an I.S. safe house.

"I really could have used the charms in my bag," I whispered, my lips parting when I realized my butt-kicking leathers were gone. Al had dropped me into that same green and black silk robe with the lace-up slippers that I'd tried to impress my students with. *I have got to learn how to do this,* I thought as I tightened the sash and the tiny bells rang a faint, beautiful peal. It would protect me from Hodin's charms better than my leather would. *Good. I had it right,* I mused as I lifted the hem to see the crisscross pattern of the shoes' leggings.

But the breath I took to thank Al slipped from me in surprise. He had changed as well, his Victorian finery replaced by a matching, bloodred robe that I'd seen him in when he had driven Hodin from my church. But unlike my pristine robe, his was clearly used, clean but shading to a tattered black at the hem. His shoes had those same laced leggings, but again, they were stained and worn from use. The sash was nothing more than a frayed rope. "That's what you want to wear?" I said instead of "Thank you," and he frowned.

"It's highly effective," he said stiffly. "Even in its current state."

Straight ahead in the dim light were the stairs leading to the building-wide upper room that had been everything from an open apartment to a pool hall to private dining to a disco floor where living vampires line danced to try to forget the misery their lives were. But that's not where Al was looking, and I followed his squinting gaze to the swinging double doors to the kitchen.

"He's here," Al said, making no effort to lower his voice. "Hodin? Come out, you little dragon shit. My student wishes to put you in a bottle."

"Al!" I hissed, and then I started, yanking the ley line into me as the doors to the kitchen shifted open. It was Hodin. Teeth clenched, I threw a wad of unfocused energy at him.

Hodin flung out a hand with a muttered word, sending power to intercept my hastily thrown energy and ricochet them both into a corner, where they spun and sputtered into nothing.

"Hold!" Hodin shouted, and my next spell died on my lips as I saw Stef in his grip, her eyes wide and scared. Hodin's arm was wrapped around her neck as he dragged her forward, using her as a living shield.

"Stef," I whispered, doubts rising up to nearly swamp me. If it had been Finnis . . . Well, it wasn't, and my glowing hand dropped.

"Bottle me?" Hodin's attention flicked to Al, his grip tightening as Stef continued to struggle. He looked like a half-starved biker with his long hair free and his heavy leathers on. "Not likely," Hodin added as the kitchen door swung shut behind them. "But I'm glad to see you, nevertheless." He hesitated. "In all your finery. What's your password to the collective?"

Lips pressed, Al gestured for me to have at it, and I sighed, pulling deeper on the line until my gut began to ache and my hair to snarl. My thoughts went to Ivy, Jenks, Trent, and Pike. I had to get him to line jump, or I'd never catch him. "Where's Finnis?"

"Downstairs." Hodin jerked Stef to him, and I tensed. "Where the dead belong."

"You've made a mistake," I said. "You can still walk away from it." But he wouldn't listen. None of them ever did.

"Rachel, do-o-o-o stop monologuing and bottle the bastard," Al said lightly. "It is your birthday, and someone said there would be ice cream."

Still holding Stef before him, Hodin inched deeper into the room. "My only mistake was leaving you alive," he said. "How did you survive? No one else has. Was it your elf?"

My chin lifted. I never thought that Bis's absence would save my life, but that was what had happened. "Maybe I'm better than you," I said, and Hodin's lip twitched.

"I doubt that." Hodin let go of Stef long enough to smack her into yelping submission. "I need your password. Give it to me, and I'll let her go."

Stef stiffened, and my heart hurt when her eyes became wide in hope.

"What is it!" Hodin shouted, Stef crying out when Hodin's aura suddenly covered her, burning her with the spell it carried.

"Hey!" I shouted, the bells on my sash ringing, and the glowing haze vanished. Stef sagged in his grip, her breath coming in short pants.

Smug, Hodin glanced at Al, unmoving behind me. "Well?" he prompted, and Stef's eyes rose to find mine. They were damp with tears, but I could see her core of strength had been unbroken—so far.

"Rachel?" Al said cautiously, seeing my indecision.

I had no intention of giving Hodin access, but he had Stef, and I began to fidget. *This would be easier if I had my bag.*

"Summoning name." Hodin's voice was soft, but his ringed fingers gripping Stef's arm were so tight it became bloodless. "Or she dies and I start on someone else," he said, and a chill dropped down my spine. "It's very simple."

My lips parted, pulse hammering. Stef was in agony, but I knew she wouldn't beg for her freedom, convinced that she should pay for one bad decision with her life. "You should walk away," I said, pulling on the line until my hair frizzed and began to float. "You have failed. You've already lost Cincinnati. You simply don't know it yet."

"Get him to line jump, Rachel . . ." Al whispered, and I shoved the table out of my way to give myself room to work. "Don't give him your password," he said louder. "He cannot be allowed to have access, no matter the cost."

"Then get Stef from him," I said. Pulling everything I had into my palm, I threw it at Hodin.

Sneering, Hodin flung out a hand. Our energies met in a burst of quickly smothered sparks. Stef choked back a terrified yelp. I had been there. I knew her fear. And as I saw Hodin's smug satisfaction and felt Al's resignation to her coming death at Hodin's hand, something in me snapped. I was going to trap his ass, and I was going to do it in a Goddess-damned ley line. And for that, I was going to need one hell of a lot of smut to insulate me.

Hodin had the access code. I had the password that would make it work. Give him that, and he'd have all the cards and I none. But the vault was the only place to get enough smut fast enough to do me any good.

I didn't need the curses in the vault. I only needed the smut. I was going to give him my password. Hodin was going to try to kill me. And Al and I were going to use the darkest spells the vault had, not to capture Hodin, but to acquire the massive layer of smut we'd need to survive lingering in a ley line.

"Password!" Hodin shouted, and I jerked, my head coming up and my hands dripping raw power.

Forgive me, Trent. I wish I was better at this. "You want my subrosa position?" I said, my face cold in anger. "My password? My place in the collective? *My life!*" I shouted. "Fine." I settled my laced-legging shoes firmly on the old, black floor as Al cleared his throat, not knowing what I was doing. "I don't think you can handle my life. Let her go, and I'll give it to you, moss wipe."

"What are you doing?" Al shouted, and Hodin's lips split into an ugly grin as he thought he'd won.

"Have her," he said, and Stef cried out in fear as he shoved her at me.

"Dilatare!" I shouted, bells ringing as I yanked Stef to the floor as the white spell hit the old timbers with a thunderous boom. Bottles shattered against the bar mirror, and

dust sifted down. Al flung himself clear as Hodin staggered, somehow retaining his feet.

"Flagro!" Hodin exclaimed, and I cowered, holding Stef unmoving when the woman tried to run as liquid fire coated my bubble. Al bellowed in anger and the coating vanished.

Panting, I looked up. Al stood over me, his demonic fury terrible to see as ugly Latin spilled from him. Hodin flung out a hand, meeting Al's power with his own. Sparks flew, and the scent of ozone pinched my nose.

"Go!" I all but hissed, breaking my circle and shoving Stef to the door. "Get to the church. Help Getty. I'll see you in three days. If I'm not back by then, tell Trent I love him." *Desperately.*

"Rachel, I'm sorry," Stef began to babble, nose runny and eyes wet.

"Go!" I got to my feet, and the woman awkwardly scrabbled up and ran for the door, hitting it hard to stumble into the night. I saw a flash of dark parking lot as the door swung shut. Shaking, I turned to Hodin and Al.

"Hodin!" I shouted, and the demon spun, his hands dripping green and yellow. Al cut his next curse short, and the two of them stared at me, one in bloodstained red silk, the other in leather. There was a new burn-edged hole in the ceiling clear through to the upstairs floor, and I winced. *Sorry, Pike. Maybe you could put in a firepole.* "I believe the deal was Stef for my password?" Pulse hammering, I shoved another table away to make more room.

"Don't!" Al exclaimed, his brow furrowed, but the more smut he had, the better both our chances of surviving the next five minutes in the ley line. The only place to get it would be the vault. But that meant Al would need reason to fight Hodin. And for that, I had to give Hodin a chance.

"Jariathjackjunisjumoke!" I cried out as I shoved another table to the edges of the room. "Take it, you soul-sucking, traitorous, know-nothing hack!" I almost spit at him. "Take it, and you will lose. You hear me, Hodin? You will lose everything!"

Al's face was riven, his hands clenching into fists as Hodin stood before me, his brow furrowed quizzically. "What kind of a summoning name is that?" Hodin said.

My face burned. "It's mine," I said. "You are a worthless, cowardly—"

"Rachel!" Al shouted, his red robe billowing as he yanked me clear of Hodin's thrown ring. It hit the floor with a ping and burst, a bubble of energy rising up in green and yellow, burning everything within.

Pulse hammering, I pressed back into Al. "This is going to cost you everything, itchy witch," Al muttered, a wisp of smoke curling up from his already charred hem, smelling of burnt amber.

"It's going to give me everything," I said, and Al's grip on me tightened. "I—"

"Move!" Al shouted, and we sprang apart, him going one way, me the other as another ring hit the floor at our feet. A larger circle sprang up. It rolled after me, and I shoved a chair at it, horrified when the bubble enveloped it and the chair seemed to expand, then contracted, and then exploded. Yelping, I ducked below a table as shrapnel peppered the floor.

Hodin stood tall over me, an unfocused, breathless expression on his face. "You made your last mistake."

Oh, if only I was that lucky.

"Get out!" Al shouted, gesturing wildly. "He has access to the vault."

"I need—" I started, my words faltering when Hodin's gaze sharpened on me. *Oh . . . shit.* "Kill me, and there's nothing to stop them from putting you in a bottle," I said, and Hodin's smile became ugly.

"If I kill you, they won't dare try," he said, and I felt myself pale as his aura seemed to grow darker, shifting into the visible spectrum.

Al's jaw clenched. "He's in," he said as he inched closer to me. "We have lost."

"We have not!" I insisted. "I need him to—hey!" I gasped

as Al yanked me close, the tingle of his aura rubbing against mine like pinpricks as his protection circle snapped into place around us. I jumped at a heavy thump, my attention going up to see Hodin's curse snaking over our heads, trying to get through Al's bubble. A ring of floor around us was smoking, and my mouth went dry.

Al's lip curled as he looked at the floor. The curse was trying to eat its way in to us. It would, eventually. "You need him to what?" Al said, his voice oddly muffled. The air was stuffy, and I was sure I could smell burnt amber, though it might be the smoking floor. "Hurry, Rachel," he prompted. "There are curses in the vault to rip through the best protection circle, and he will find them. You need him to what?"

I pushed back and stared at him. He was listening to me?

My pulse hammered. "If I'm going to bind him into a tulpa created in a ley line, you need all the smut you can get to insulate us while I'm doing it. What you have right now isn't going to cut it."

Al's brow furrowed . . . then his eyes watching me from over his glasses widened in understanding. "You *want* the smut the vault curses levy . . ." he said, starting to laugh. "The vault . . . yes. There is no better place for dark magic and the smut they put on you. You need smut? I will get you smut, my itchy witch."

My knees felt like water. Above Al, Hodin's curse burned and coiled against Al's protective bubble. Al glanced at it, took a breath, and then carefully maneuvered himself to stand between me and Hodin.

"Get clear if you can. This is going to be messy," he said.

But my smile of victory faltered as his expression seemed to go vacant and a horrifying ugliness seeped into him, prickling like black ice against my skin. He had accessed the vault, opening his mind to the curses the demons had created thousands of years ago in their war with the elves. He knew where every last ugly magic waited with the same surety that I knew where the flowers I needed grew in my garden. And he knew well enough to perhaps save my ass.

"Capax infiniti!" Al shouted, and I jumped as a burst of energy exploded his protection bubble outward, taking Hodin's curse with it. Shadow curled up from his feet, wreathing Al in smoke and flame. His head grew heavy, and his eyes like pits. There was death in them, and anger, and bitter, bitter desire to cause pain. It wasn't Al. It was the echo of the soul of whoever had made that curse, now staining him.

"What have I asked you to do, Al?" I whispered, and Al turned to me, his lifted chin telling me to get behind him. I hadn't known that by using the stored curses he took on the pain their makers had felt.

"Coniunctis viribus!" Hodin shouted, and Al flung up a hand, easily absorbing the curse even as his hand grew dark with it. Al had fought the war that his brother had sat out, and the older demon laughed, long and hard, magic wreathing his fingers and Latin spilling from his lips. I shuddered as I felt a massive curse unroll in him, crashing into Hodin to send him reeling back. Sash furling, Al threw another, and Hodin barely got his countercurse between it and him, sending the combined forces to hit the wall. Black goo coated the wall, chairs, and tables, and then they shrank in on themselves and vanished with a terrifying crunch of wood and stone.

My lips parted as the entire wall vanished. Night air and the sound of distant traffic rolled in. My breath seemed to choke in me, and I dove for cover behind a fallen table.

"Ad utrumque paratus," Al intoned, his fisted hands at his middle parting. I felt myself pale as a sparking bar of energy formed between them, glowing red and gold with his aura, dripping with evil. My lips parted when the bar broke in two, leaving Al with a blue-flame sword in one hand, a black-flame dagger in the other. They were curses made solid, and my breath shook as I exhaled. *You can do that?*

"Please don't run, *little* brother." Al stepped forward,

shadows clinging to him like death itself. "My friends are thirsty after so long a nap. This one," he said as he lifted the glowing sword made of blue light, "is Duco. And this"—he held up the smaller, wickedly jagged dagger—"is Quaere. I haven't lived so long that I have forgotten how to wield them."

"Demon swords don't kill demons, they kill elves," Hodin said as he stood before us, his long face pale.

Al laughed, the low sound rumbling about the walls until it echoed into the empty parking lot. "Why would I harm you? I'm a distraction while my *student* puts you in a bottle."

"Hinc et inde!" Hodin exclaimed, a wash of shadow boiling out from nowhere as a bubble formed about me.

I looked up, hunching into myself at the sudden lack of light and noise. It was a death circle, and I was in it. "Al!" I shouted as it began to shrink, then yelped when a burst of gold exploded the black into a thousand shards. Free, I backpedaled, feet shuffling to avoid the pieces of the curse making holes in the floor as they shrank into nothing and vanished. Little patches of my robe smoked, and I used my sash to pat them out. *Son of a mother moss wipe . . .*

My attention flicked to Al as I extinguished the last, thankful even as he swung his sword to drive Hodin away with bellowed, gleeful shouts in time with his swings. If he hadn't broken the circle, I would be dead. Smut wreathed them both, making them into shadows. It clung to Al, spinning with him as he moved, turning his tattered robe into a veritable wash of haze and smoke.

"De morume, ta na shay!" Hodin gasped, and Al cried out, falling to a knee and writhing as his sword hit the oak floor and vanished.

"Hey!" I stood, yanking the line deep into me, and Hodin's head turned as if on a swivel. "You don't want to bring the Goddess into this," I said as I shoved a chair out from between us. "We're besties."

Hodin spit blood, breathing hard as he stared malevolently. Al had propped himself up on an elbow, brow lowered as his lungs heaved. His hand was a bloody mess, and he couldn't focus yet. Pissed, I paced forward until he was at my feet.

My knees shook. Al's new smut hadn't yet soaked in, eddying about him like an ill wind.

"I am in the vault. You have lost," Hodin said, and I pulled myself straighter.

"And you have made the mistake of thinking that means anything," I said, my thought to trap him in a tulpa-shaped bottle fading. *"Ta na shay—"*

"Alea iacta est!" Hodin shouted.

"Rachel," Al whispered, his head bowed as he reached out.

We had fought together as one before, and trusting him, my hand smacked into his. I gasped at the expected jolt of our strengths joining. Shaking, I pulled the ley line's energy into us, doubling the force we could wield. An unending torrent poured through both of us, ordering itself into a heinous action as Al gave it direction.

"In se magna ruunt!" I screamed for him, the vault's curse burning as it left me. My hand flamed, and my arm shook as the curse arced from me to Hodin, enveloping his hand, already glowing with power.

Hodin's curse exploded in his grip to send the demon flying across the room. The walls shook and the lights popped, overwhelmed. It was only the burning circle that lit the dark.

"You okay?" I said as I let go. My shoulders slumped as my strength seemed to halve, and Al nodded, slow as he got up. His right arm hung useless, but as he felt the dagger in his left, he smiled. I could feel the smut the curse had left on me, see it wreathing my hands, and I smiled back.

"You can't help her!" Hodin shouted, frustrated, and Al chuckled as he wiped the blood from his lip, rubbing his fingers together and turning the red smear into a ruby dust that fell glittering to the floor.

"I'm not helping her." Al looked at Quaere, his desire to use the dagger obvious. "She doesn't need me to capture you. I'm simply keeping her alive while she does it."

Jaw clenched, Hodin took a step away, not in fear, but calculation.

"You can't best us both, little brother," Al mocked, flipping Quaere into the air and catching it.

Run, I thought, needing Hodin to flee into a line. Only there could I catch him. *Run like the coward you are.*

And finally, Hodin did.

"Snag him!" Al shouted as Hodin vanished, and I staggered, feeling my body shift to thought as Al shoved me into the ley line after him.

I floundered for the breath of a molecule spin, the roar of the line harsh as it oriented on me within the screaming energy flow. It burned, and I let it, needing to find Hodin before I could circle my thoughts and shut out the harsh discord. But it was my smut that burned, not me.

There, Al thought, the scent of burnt amber choking my memory. Al was with me, and it gave me strength.

Together we found Hodin, his anger and frustration a bright beacon of black in the shimmering fire of time itself.

Circle him! Al thought as I felt Hodin begin to shift his aura to slip from the line.

But I was faster. *Gotcha,* I thought as I snapped a bubble around both of us and the harsh friction caused by the sensory burn eased. *Al!* I shouted, and he enveloped us in another bubble, as light as gray gossamer, a nightmare of a daydream that was hardly there. Unnoticed.

That is, until Hodin modulated his aura to step from the ley line and nothing happened. My aura ruled his, and my aura hadn't shifted. It wasn't that I couldn't do it, but the last time I had tried on my own, I had burned my synapses to a crisp, skidding through space as I forced my way out.

Fool! Hodin thought, and I shoved my satisfaction deep into hiding as Hodin dropped his protection circle and sent a blast of hate-powered line energy straight into my chi.

Hey! I yelped, soaking in the force like a reverse power pull, spindling it in my mind as fast as he poured it into me.

Ow! Knock it off! I exclaimed as he turned to burning my surface thoughts, singeing me.

You can't destroy me by holding me in a ley line, Hodin thought as he drew back and the ugly sensation of his hatred faded. *You will suffer more than me, and when you die, your synapses charred to a twisted, unusable chaos, I will survive.*

Duh, I thought smugly. *But that's not what I'm doing.*

Hodin's confidence faltered as he realized I was painlessly holding us in the line. Al was shielding me, the agony of it muted by his vault-heavy smut. With a new panic, Hodin lunged his barbed hatred at me, digging his thoughts deep and twisting.

Al! I thought, and his presence grew, grasping Hodin about his theoretical throat and pulling him from my soul with the sensation of raking claws.

Work fast, Al thought, and then he was gone, rolling Hodin's psyche in a deluge of ugly memories to confuse and bewilder him.

As you wish, brother! Hodin's awareness crashed into mine, and then he was gone again, distracted.

How am I going to do this? I thought to myself as I felt them tumble about in one of Al's memories, the three of us nothing more than thought, lost in a line as Al's smut burned.

But like most things, tulpas begin with emotion. I felt helpless, frustrated, angry, afraid that I was not enough for the task. The ugly slurry roiling in me was not unfamiliar. I'd felt this before. And with a ping that shook me to my core, the memory of me sitting at my mother's kitchen table rose up to become my world. My father had died; I felt helpless. No one would tell me why; I felt frustration. I had tried to save him and failed; I had not been enough.

I cried out as Hodin freed himself from Al long enough to fling a hate-filled thought at me, burning: I remembered crying. My thoughts made a little push, shrinking me down from Al and Hodin as if I was smaller than a hidden idea.

From somewhere, I felt Al chuckle even as the sensation of his synapses burning drifted to me.

A calm satisfaction rose from my core. I could sense Al fighting Hodin. Al could not hold him forever. I didn't need forever. I was Rachel Morgan, and I could do . . . anything here in my mindscape.

I dropped deeper into myself, pulling on the emotions that Hodin had instilled, feelings that had dogged me too long. Inadequacy. Guilt. Wanting to be strong enough to save those I loved. Pain when I had proved too weak. They were all old emotions. I'd felt them before, and I knew the strength found in surmounting them. I just needed to . . . remember how.

What? Hodin thought as suddenly the clear nothing of my thoughts shimmered, became bright, and then began to settle. In my mind, imagined walls became solid. A ceiling, a floor, a window, a door. Cupboards and chairs. A Formica table. The ticking of a shifty-eyed cat clock.

We're still in a line? Hodin thought, and then suddenly he was there as well, standing in my mother's kitchen as I remembered the dents in the table—and they appeared. *What is this?*

It's me, I thought as I found myself appearing in my memory. I was my teenage self, gawky and awkward in jeans and a green T-shirt, flip-flops on my bony feet. I sighed at my frizzy, short hair and the scars on my arms where the nurses had been careless. Turning, I smiled at the faded curtains, and the bluebell print appeared, complete with the splashes of tomato paste from when Robbie and I had argued over who was going to wash and who would dry. Water stains decorated the ceiling, and one of the cupboard doors hung askew. The walls were yellow and the linoleum was faded. The sink dripped into a rust stain, and the memory of pixy wings hummed at the open window, curtains shifting in the night breeze.

It was my mother's kitchen made real, and panicking, Hodin tried to flee, but my thoughts held his, and he could not.

No you don't, little brother, Al thought, his presence suddenly beside mine, his still-bleeding hand catching the image of Hodin by the shoulder and practically throwing him into one of the kitchen's metal chairs.

Let me out of the line, you filthy whelp! Hodin exclaimed, and bellowing, Al punched Hodin square in the face. The younger demon went tumbling, slamming into the wall before Al grabbed him by the throat and flung him into the outdated stove.

Yes, it was all in my thoughts, but that didn't make it any less real.

Finish it, Rachel! Al thought jubilantly, then he attacked Hodin, a black flame seeming to flicker about his robe's hem as he beat Hodin into a cowering ball with the scent of char and fire. It was a battle that both was and wasn't, and I stood in my mother's kitchen, adding the hum and click of the old refrigerator, the sound of the TV in the other room. I remembered a pot of tomato soup on the stove into existence, and Hodin threw it at Al. I put the scent of burning toast in the air, and Hodin set the bread on fire.

But there was nothing Hodin could do that I could not mend with a thought, and as Al distracted Hodin, I added a splotch of paint on the window frame, a dent in the wall, the spelling bowls my mother hid from me behind the flour. And finally, with a ping, I had it. It was real, as far as real ever was.

Al! I shouted, my higher, teenage voice sounding odd in my ears. Magic radiated from me, making me feel as powerful as Newt in the tiny, perfect mindscape I had constructed. Hodin was pressed against the wall where Al had pinned him, the dagger Quaere at his neck. Here, where reality and the mind mixed, I could see all the way to the bottom of Hodin's soul. He was in pain. Anger and bitterness were his world. A denied need and an abiding frustration lived where empathy should have been.

You can't be doing this, Hodin said, panting. *We are in a ley line.*

I am doing this, and you have failed. I turned to Al,

those same feelings of guilt and failure coursing through me. *Al?*

He nodded, fear at the back of his eyes, fear that he wouldn't be fast enough, that Hodin would do more damage than he could repair.

But my mother's kitchen was here, my mind holding it in stasis, born from my childhood emotions of fear, guilt, inadequacy. To make my mother's kitchen real, I had to let Al all the way into my soul so he could pluck my mind from my creation. It would leave Hodin free to rip through me like the torrent of ley line energy that was slowly eating away at Al.

And so I let them in. Both of them.

The figure of my thirteen-year-old self collapsed. Hodin cried out in shock as I yanked his mind entirely into my own. The sound echoed in me, and suddenly he was there, tearing great gouts of memory from me, paring me to nothing.

No! Al thought, trying to smother Hodin with his own presence, and I pulled them both closer, even as Hodin dug deeper, seeking my core.

I moaned at Hodin's glee as he tore a memory of my dad sitting at that very same table from me. *This is how you die!* Hodin thought, throwing it into the hissing black abyss with a joyous abandon. *I will rip everything that is you away. You will be nothing!*

No, Al choked, catching the memory before the ley line could burn it to ash, holding it close to himself.

I failed, I remembered, the thought of holding my dad's hand as he took his last breath almost crushing.

And then it was gone as Hodin took that from me, too. *Ivy will die, and her soul will be lost,* Hodin thought as Al struggled to find the memory Hodin had taken. *The soul curse will die with you!*

I heard myself sob as Hodin shredded everything, leaving me with my feelings of inadequacy. I had felt this before, sitting at this table, helpless and miserable.

And then Hodin ripped even that from me.

Al scooped it up. He took my love for Ivy, my love for

my mother. He carefully gathered the memory of me trying
not to cry while sitting in the kitchen as I mourned my father's death. I felt Al's silent tears as he searched the ley
line for the flakes of my soul that Hodin was ripping away.
He carefully gathered the love my mother felt, the resolve
she filled me with along with her tomato soup and toast. He
held my memories close as Hodin savaged them. I felt great
swaths of myself vanishing, and it hurt.

I will survive, I whispered into my thoughts, remembering my mother holding me, rocking me as I cried into my
soup, and Hodin's gleeful laugh hammered on my bare soul
as he took that from me, too, and it was gone.

You are nothing, Hodin thought, and I gasped at the cold
absence beneath my memories.

Al's gentle brush through me was like fire against the
rips Hodin had left. One by one, Al found the feelings of
worth that my mother had instilled. But even as I was becoming emotionless and empty, the image of my mother's
kitchen became more sure: the table with a bowl of soup,
the curtains and dripping faucet, the shifty-eyed cat, the
hidden spelling bowls.

Slowly the image of my mother's kitchen grew clearer,
and the heartache began to ebb. I was freed from it as Hodin destroyed the emotions of that day. The guilt that I
hadn't been enough to save my dad, the helplessness that I
was so small and others so powerful, the frustration of not
being enough: all gone.

And yet, I somehow still held tight to one last emotion.
Failure.

I had failed my dad. I had failed Stef and Vivian. Hodin
saw it, and as Al groaned in a shared pain, Hodin stripped
it from me with glee. I screamed into the void as it peeled
from me, leaving a bright nothing behind.

You have lost! Hodin thought. *You betrayed Stef by ignoring her plight, and even if you survive, you will rot in
Alcatraz for selling Vivian and the rest.*

Dizzy, I felt my mind spin, the hint of Al's agony coloring the image of my mother's kitchen on the day my father

died, now pure and dead of emotion. Even as the ley line burned him, Al sifted through the ashes of my soul strewn the length and breadth of our shared existence. His cry when he found another piece of me struck me to the core. I almost wished he would leave behind the heartache I'd felt as I had sat at the table, the bowl of tomato soup and toast before me. But Al put it with the rest, knowing the strength born in such pain.

Seeing Al's tender sorrow, Hodin became scornfully confident. My father's death had been laid bare before him, and he relished it. *You couldn't save your father. He died to pay for your life,* he mocked, sure he had won.

But as Hodin had peeled everything from me, my mind had become clear, and a cold certainty had blossomed. Everything I was lay safe in Al's steadfast care, leaving me . . . quiet and sure. There was nothing left but my mother's kitchen, a bowl of soup on the table and toast waiting to be buttered. The memory of its rich and acidic taste remained, but it didn't remind me of my father anymore, and I felt a vague sense of unease.

But Hodin's glee faltered when Al began to snigger. *Why didn't you stop me?* Hodin thought, his confusion the only emotion sullying the perfect replica of my mother's kitchen. Everything it had meant to me was safe in Al's mind.

Because that is how you make a tulpa, I said, my thoughts utterly clear. I had found the still point and balance. I was entirely whole, and entirely empty.

I think I got everything, Al thought, and I wondered at his anguish, because I felt nothing. *I am sorry. He's a butcher,* Al added, bitterness dripping from his thoughts.

But thorough, I mused, my gaze straying over the counters and adding a hint of dust in the corners. *Perfect.* It was a place now, not a memory—and that's what a tulpa was.

Smug, I focused on Hodin. I could sense the fear in him. There was nothing left for him to rend from me and I was still here. Stronger for it. *Here. Hold this for me,* I thought, satisfaction a heady wash as I layered the curse to solidify his aura into his thoughts, embedding it into his DNA as if he was a child in the womb. It could never be removed, and it could never be changed. He would be stuck in whatever reality he landed in. It was how demon mothers cursed their children with gifts before they were even born—and only I could do it.

I felt Hodin recoil as it soaked in. *What did you do?*

In my thoughts, I ran my hand over the counter, finding the dent where I'd dropped a canister of salt. *I made you a permanent part of my mom's kitchen,* I thought, exhaling as I let the last of the smut from that memory curse he lied to me about flow to him. *You can have that, too.*

Hodin shuddered as it layered over him, and I quashed my feelings of guilt. *No!* his thoughts shrilled, and I turned to Al.

Take us home, I thought, imagining that Al pulled me closer, his arm stinking of burnt amber protectively around me.

Memoranda, Al thought, to fix the tulpa into the collective, and Hodin gasped in fear, both him and the sound of it vanishing along with the memory of my mother's kitchen.

A ping shook me as the tulpa became real, peeling from me to leave me empty. It was fixed to the collective, encoded so anyone could access it.

Things that must be remembered, I mused as the heat of the line began to intrude. *Al?*

But his presence around me began to flake away, the harsh discord of the line beginning to pierce into the cocoon of safety he had wrapped me in.

Al! I shouted as his aura completely disintegrated, and we were suddenly floundering, burning in the ley line we had lingered in too long.

Al! I shrieked, finding a sliver of his thought and pulling him close. I had bubbled us, but the pinch of being nothing had become a vise around my heart. *Jump us out. Al, jump us out!*

I don't feel well.

His thoughts drifted through mine like the gray curlings of smoke left from a forest fire, and I panicked. He had kept

me safe while he burned. I had taken too long. I didn't
know how to shift our auras to jump us out.

But I had done it before, and knowing it was going to
hurt like hell, I steeled myself, thinking of my church, the
pixies in the garden, the shade of the oak tree, the scent of
the earth and cut grass. There was a feeling of peace there,
of home, of family. I had made it mine with hard suffering
and joyful celebration, and I knew it as I knew my soul. I
just had to make my aura sing the right song.

As I felt my synapses char, I remembered the colors that
Bis had tried to teach me, the shading of memory that en-
compassed not only the now, but the past and future, of
green and gold and all things good that were the church,
that were my home.

Holding Al's soul within my own, I gave a little shove.

Pain raked through me. I tried to scream, but I had no
breath. I had done it wrong and the line roared in. Agony
burned, and I shifted my aura to a deeper green of peace,
then a shade of contented gold. Nothing. Panicking, I added
a flash of prideful purple. Still nothing. Each change felt
worse than the last until I thought of Bis, steady and strong.
My mind an agony of pain, I layered a hazy gray of possibility through my aura—and with a soul-shattering ping,
my aura chimed in perfect resonance with the line and I fell
out into reality.

Gravity flashed into play. I sobbed, gasping as I realized
I had lungs again—until my cheek and hip hit the floor and
my breath huffed out. Clenched into a ball, I slid three feet
in the sound of silk on wood.

And then I stopped. My breath rattled as it came in.
Everything hurt. "Ow," I whispered into the utter silence,
surprised my voice didn't match my utterly agonizing state.
Coughing, I curled in on myself, only then realizing that
Al's arm was still about me, the red silk smoking.

"Al," I whispered. Frantic, I disentangled myself from
him, inching myself upright as I tried not to throw up. My
head felt like a hollow ball of burned-out fire. He wasn't
moving, and I patted his face, then smacked it until he took

a gasping breath. "You're alive!" I shouted, and he winced, his red eyes squinting as a shaky hand patted my shoulder to leave ash marks.

"Well done, itchy witch," he groaned, eyes closing. "Next time, try to use a line already in existence instead of scraping a new one."

"Line?" I echoed, gut hurting as I looked up. I exhaled, bringing my second sight into play. "Holy crap on toast," I whispered, seeing the narrow band of red energy running straight down the center of the sanctuary at chest height, coiling and hissing like a living thing.

That's going to have to be moved, I thought as I let my second sight drop. The scent of burnt amber was chokingly thick, but we were in my church. Hodin was gone. For good.

I turned at a familiar click from the foyer, disorientation bursting over me as the oak door opened and the light from the streetlight flowed in. Still curled around me, Al shuddered as it found him.

"Rachel?" Stef said, her bewilderment obvious on her tear-streaked face. "How did you get here before me?"

I took a breath only to collapse atop Al, the pain in my head bringing me down.

CHAPTER

31

I LOVED THE FEEL OF THE GRAVEYARD IN THE SPRING, WHEN the damp earth smelled of growth and green, speaking of new life. I loved the muffled quiet of it on a snowy night, when the swirling flakes lit by the nearby streetlight made silver tracings of the black tree branches. I loved it in the fall when the red and yellow leaves hissed against the stones and slowly turned brown as they returned to the earth. But by far, I loved the graveyard on a summer night the best, when pixy lights darted like errant fireflies and the calls of the children at play on the street filtered in over the wall as if audible joy.

The yarrow in my hand held a newly spun spiderweb for Brad's countercurse. I had offered to find it just so I could come out here, and I was loath to go back inside. I lingered, resting on the fallen marker beside Nash's grave, pulled to the scent of the *cor mors*. When the moon rose, the copper-red flowers would practically glow a pale pink, but now, in the hazy city moonlight, they were a dark, deep red presence speaking of fulfillment.

Crickets and tree frogs overwhelmed the hush of distant traffic. The twin dust tracings of Getty and Jenks gave me the feeling of distant companionship, but I couldn't help feeling a twinge of sadness at just the two of them. The garden wasn't empty, but it felt . . . lacking.

Sighing, I plucked a *cor mors* and breathed in the scent. The magic to break Brad's memory curse was all but twisted . . . providing that Trent's claim that any high-grade mirror would work was accurate. Quen had tracked down Pike's brother to a local memory care facility, and if Stef and I could finish the curse before Finnis came over tonight, we were going out together to uncurse Brad at dawn. The woman was devastated that she'd had a part in twisting the curse, and I was hoping that if she helped untwist it, she could find closure.

That is, if I could convince Trent that I was well enough to leave the church.

Fatigue still pulled at me despite my expected, three-day, tulpa-induced nap. I'd been terrified that I'd wake with a neural burn so deep that it wouldn't matter if Bis ever regained consciousness. Fortunately my neural net was clear with only the barest hint of damage, and that would heal in time.

Al, though . . .

Al had been there when I'd woken. And Trent. Jenks, of course. And even Etude. Actually, the huge gargoyle had yet to leave, as if he was trying to fill in for his son, and his craggy silhouette on top of the church looked both terrifying and comforting.

All in all, I was fine, if a little tired. It was Al that I was worried about, and I had a suspicion that the burn he had suffered while I had crafted Hodin's cage was worse than he wanted to admit. He'd left almost to the minute of me regaining consciousness, evading my questions as to the state of his neural net and worrying me when instead of just popping out like usual, he stepped into the ley line now running through the church to shift to the ever-after—as I had to do. He'd have a long walk to his wagon in the woods.

Taking chances was acceptable as long as I was the one who paid for them, and the thought that Al might have lost his ability to use ley line magic because of one of my hare-brained schemes did not sit well.

It wasn't all bad, though. All charges against me for the students' abduction had been dropped after both Dali and Vivian had verified that I hadn't been involved in their abduction. Even better, I had a suspicion that Vivian's lunch invite tomorrow was to try to corral me into finishing Sikes's class despite the professor and Melody being returned safely to reality. Trent had finally gotten a closing date on Carew Tower and Pike had mended enough to be chasing Ivy as if she was a gold ring on a carousel. All that was left was Finnis. If I got my way—and I would get my way—Ivy would return to DC only long enough to bring Nina home to Cincy.

Bowed over the five-petaled flower, I breathed deep, bringing the heady fragrance all the way to my core, where it eddied and swirled. "Thank you, Nash," I whispered, tears pricking at the reminder that I was loved—even if my life tended to spread chaos.

Blinking, I sent my gaze to the church, light spilling out into the night on all sides. Stef had probably finished scribing the glyphs on the mirror by now, and so I stood, picking my way through the tall grass. All we had left was adding the spiderweb clinging to the flower and invoking the curse. And the waiting. We wouldn't know for sure if it worked for a few days.

"Ms. Rachel?" came Getty's high, clear voice, and I scuffed to a halt before the low wall separating the graveyard from my formal garden. The beautifully dark-haired pixy hung before me like a dusky angel, a small traveling satchel tied to her front. I'd seen Matalina carry her youngest like that, and a pang took me. Her wings again hummed a melodious perfection; she was leaving.

"Hi, Getty," I said, not seeing Jenks's glow anywhere. "Your wing sounds wonderful."

"Yes, ma'am." She bobbed up and down, her dust a pale

silver. "That's why I'm here. I've said my good-byes to Jenks and Stef, but I wanted to say thank you before I left."

"You're welcome, but Getty . . ." I hesitated, hoping I wasn't sticking my nose somewhere it didn't belong. "I really wish you would stay. Jenks could use the help, and the fairies listen to you better than they ever did to him."

Hands brushing her patched dress smooth, the small woman glanced at the darkest corner of the graveyard, her features bunching in distress. "I can't."

"Sure you can," I said. "I know Jenks complains, but he likes you."

Getty blinked fast, her dust sparkling. "That's why I have to leave. I like him, too. And . . . I won't risk having children who look like me. I won't, Ms. Morgan."

"He didn't tell you?" I said, my smile fading. "I told him to tell you. He can't have kids."

The pixy's eyes widened. "Someone . . ." she whispered, clearly horrified. "He's been—"

"God, no!" I exclaimed, lips quirking as I cut her off. "He used a wish to become sterile. Matalina was despondent about having children who wouldn't survive her death, so he used a wish . . ." My words trailed off as Getty spun in the air, her wing pitch rising.

"Why didn't he tell me?" she said, focused on a patch of dark graveyard.

I pushed from the monolith, embarrassed. "He, ah, probably assumed you wanted kids and he can't give them to you. He thinks you are beautiful, Getty. That you deserve a full life with a buck who loves you."

"Oh . . ." It was a soft breath, almost a moan. "I have to go," she said, then darted away.

I stiffened, then relaxed as her dust arrowed not over the wall, but to that far corner of the graveyard. *Forgive me, Jenks, if this causes you heartache over Matalina, but Getty loves you.*

Yarrow in hand, I stepped over the low wall and into my backyard. I could see Stef through the porch windows, and a lingering hint of guilt struck me. The woman was doing okay, but Jenks said she was still having nightmares.

Constance was in her traveling cage on the counter, probably still sulking in the bejeweled mouse hut that Pike had made for her. Trent had his own ideas about how to handle Finnis, but I liked simple, and since we'd cut Finnis's crutch of Hodin out from under him, I wanted Finnis to take Constance to DC as both a warning and a promise. Even if Finnis turned her back, seeing one of their own as a mouse might earn me some respect. At least, that was *my* plan. Trent preferred hitting them where it hurt—the wallet.

"One freshly spun spiderweb," I said as I went in, and Stef looked up from the small mirror we were using as our "Atlantean reflecting telescope." She had already covered it with runes and reversed symbols.

"Great." Stef gave me a quick smile, her brow furrowed as her fingertips rested on Newt's countercurse. "All that's left is placing it on the mirror and invoking it."

I set the yarrow beside her, careful to not disturb the spiderweb. Constance was out of her hut, the long-fanged mouse pressed against the bars as she tried to reach a plate overflowing with cookies. There was another plate in the sanctuary. I'd found an entire bag of them in the freezer. Apparently Trent baked when he was nervous, and it had been a long three days.

"You want to place the web?" I asked. Constance was beginning to squeak in frustration, and finding pity, I broke a cookie in half and handed it to her. "You have a finer touch than me," I added as the mouse hissed even as she took it, sitting on her haunches and watching me with her big, black eyes.

"Sure."

It was another of Stef's one-word answers, but she seemed okay, and as I began to drop the dirty ley line paraphernalia into the sink, she used her ungodly expensive copper-tipped chopsticks to array the web over the scrying mirror. The tiny rings piercing the arch of her ear caught the light, and I wondered if they were the same ones she'd had when she first moved in. They looked . . . shiny now.

A shudder rose from me as Stef hunched over the mirror, her whispered incantation rippling over my aura. The tingle of dark magic wasn't unpleasant, and only now beginning to think we could pull this off, I gave in and took a celebratory cookie. It wasn't smart to mix food and spell prep, but Stef was the one doing the magic.

"It's working," I said needlessly, making a soft *mmmm* of appreciation at the sweet chocolate coming alive in my mouth. *Damn, that man can bake.* But my chewing slowed as I looked from Newt's open curse book to the mirror. "What's that?" I said around a mouthful of choco-choco chip, and Stef's whispered words cut off. "That's not in the book," I said, frowning as I pointed at a twisted, upside-down glyph. "Or that. Or that."

My cookie went tasteless, and as Stef straightened from her spell-whispering hunch, a spike of angst took me, and I quashed the thought that this was Hodin and that I'd accidentally put Stef in the tulpa.

"It's so I take the smut from the curse and no one else," Stef blurted, and my breath caught. "Hodin taught me. He said it was going to be a joke, and like an idiot I believed him."

"Ah . . ." I started, not even knowing you could preemptively direct smut, and her jaw clenched. "I didn't ask you to help so you could take the payment. And I got rid of the smut from the original curse."

"I'm taking the smut." Stef lifted her chin as if daring me to protest. "You never would have twisted the first one if I hadn't hidden from you what was in it."

"Stef—"

"I'm taking it!" she shouted, and we both turned as Jenks flew in, drawn by her raised voice. "It's the one thing that Hodin taught me how to do that I'm grateful for," she added, flushed as she glanced at Jenks. "It's my smut. I'm wearing it."

I winced, not sure how to handle this. It was going to

look really bad: her living here, twisting curses under my supervision, wearing the smut from them. Not to mention her three-strike demon mark. "You don't know what you're taking on," I said, a remembered shame rising in me. "People can see it. They're going to assume—"

"I know what they're going to think. It's mine. *Sic semper erat, et sic semper erit.*"

I reached to stop her, but with the final words, it was done. My shoulders slumped as I felt the rising magic sink back down into the mirror. For a moment, the spiderweb and all the glyphs glowed with a greenish-yellow light. Then it faded, vanishing into the mirror and taking the curse with it. Even the web was gone, a faint memory of it etched onto the glass.

Stef winced as the smut soaked in. I didn't dare use my second sight to see what she'd done to her aura. "Oh, Stef . . ." I touched her arm, and her head snapped up, her breath coming in fast.

"I did this. I pay for it," she said, her color high in rebellion.

Jenks's wings rasped, and he rose, motioning for me to stay as he flew out of the kitchen. Someone was banging on the front door. It was too soon for Finnis, and Trent would have simply walked in. If it was important, Jenks would tell me.

"Here." Stef's fingers were shaking as she drew the mirror from the counter. "All he has to do is look into it. I know I said I'd go out with you, but they might not let me into the facility . . . now."

Her voice had risen on the last word, and my eyes welled as she rubbed the three demon slashes on her wrist and sniffed back her tears. She'd wear them for life, unable to pay Hodin for whatever favors she'd bought with them.

"Um, I'll clean this up later. I have to check on something in my room," she said suddenly, almost panicked. "Excuse me."

"I'll do it," I said as she fled the kitchen. "Finnis won't be here until midnight."

"I said I'll clean it!" she shouted, and I winced when her door slammed shut.

"Well, okay then," I said sourly as I slid the mirror into my bag to take out to the facility. If Trent was too busy, Pike might come with me.

"She's going to be fine," Jenks said, the pixy having flown in as Stef had left. "You'll hardly be able to see it after it soaks in. It's going to scare the crap out of her next boyfriend."

Leaning against the counter, I took another cookie. "Or attract the wrong one."

"In which case, she'll straighten him out. Fast." Mood content, Jenks dropped down to the cookie plate, laboriously rising to airlift that second half to Constance. She had finished the first and clearly wanted more. Most vampires didn't eat much solid food, but I had a suspicion that Trent had laced them with Brimstone to up my metabolism and get me on my feet faster.

Lover, warrior prince, drug lord.

"Thanks for telling whoever was at the door to shove off. Who was it? That guy from the paper again?"

"Nope." Grinning, Jenks angled the cookie through the top of the bars and into the waiting arms of Constance. "Doyle and Finnis. I told them to cool their heels while you finished your spelling."

I jumped, pulse racing as I brushed the crumbs from my front. "Finnis? Now? What did he bring Doyle for?" Great. I wanted to put on something a little less . . . T-shirty before they got here. Not to mention Trent wanted to be present. Now he was going to badger me all night for a "he said, then I said" play-by-play.

Jenks rose from Constance's cage, dusting her with green sparkles until she sneezed. "Like I know?" Hands on his hips, he looked down. "You ready to go home, blood blister?"

Constance made an eerie, gurgling hiss, dropping the cookie and falling to all four feet for balance as I carefully lifted her cage. I tugged my T-shirt straight with my free hand as I made my way down the hall, wishing I could just pop upstairs for that green spelling robe. The burn marks made it fabulously dangerous, and the hint of burnt amber would have given me some street cred.

I could smell irate vampire from here, and I tapped the small ley line now running through the church, enjoying the welcome rush of power holding a hint of my aura. I'd eventually push the ley line into the garden, but for now, it was more than nice having it this close.

"I thought we had agreed on midnight," I said as I hesitated at the top of the hall, and the two men currently studying the open rafters turned to me. One was dead, one was alive, both held themselves as if they knew something that would make my life even more joy-joy. "Trent wanted to be here," I added when neither one said anything, my voice a curated balance of respect and annoyance. "But that's okay. I know what he wanted to say."

"Morgan." Finnis slowly turned from the stained-glass windows to me, his brown-rimmed eyes pupil black in the dim light. His dull suit made him seem outdated but classy, especially with Doyle beside him in his bland I.S. suit and his badge around his neck. "The windows are beautiful. Original?" he asked, gesturing at them.

I came closer, my grip on the line absolute. Almost I wished he'd try something so I could smack him. "Not to my church, no." I stopped a good eight feet back and set Constance on the coffee table, where Doyle stared at her in awe. "Reclaimed from the wastes."

Finnis smiled, his teeth hidden as he studiously ignored Constance screeching at him. "They remind me of my youth."

That's nice. "Thank you for coming out here. I appreciate it. Apparently the management at the Cincinnatian doesn't want me on the premises." Banned again. The story of my life.

Doyle took a breath, his fingers reaching to his jacket's inner pocket, but Finnis was faster, smoothly interrupting the I.S. agent. "What is it, Morgan? I have a plane waiting for me."

I sent my gaze to Doyle as the man shrugged, his hands falling to a fig-leaf clasp. Whatever he wanted to give me was still in that pocket. *Please, not another warrant.*

"Okay. Fair enough," I said as Jenks lit on the rafters, his heavy dust an unspoken threat. "Since you're going to DC with your findings, I would like you to stay there and lobby for my soul curse to be approved. It will move forward, or I will move it forward without you."

Finnis blinked, then began to laugh. I hadn't known a dead vampire could laugh apart from trying to convince the living that they still had a sense of humor, which they didn't, and I patiently waited until he realized I wasn't impressed or cowed.

"No," he said, his lip twitching as he shifted two steps to the right to get out of Jenks's dust. "I'm returning to DC to more efficiently take bids on Cincinnati. I'm selling your scrap of a pig-farming city to the highest bidder. Your soul charm, much as yourself, is dead."

It was about what I had thought he'd say, which was why I had agreed with Trent's plan. "Okay," I said, wishing he was here to implement it. Nothing is more impressive than an elf making barbed threats about money. "But before you begin making calls, I want to remind you of something. My boyfriend supplies your Brimstone."

Doyle stiffened. He took a breath, holding it when Finnis lifted a finger for him to be silent.

Smiling, I set a hand on Constance's cage to try to get her to shut up. "And whereas Trent would have no problem setting the world on fire to prove a point, I'm more inclined to bring this to your attention as a reminder that I have at my disposal the bribes, kickbacks, and, more importantly, a distribution network to get another illicit drug or procedure onto the market."

Doyle's breath eased out of him in a slow exhalation, but his obvious relief seemed to prick through Finnis like a thorn to bring his anger to a tight, black-eyed stare.

"Tax-free," I added, smiling to show my teeth since we were all baring them at each other.

"You will remove your curse from FSCA consideration or Ivy dies," Finnis intoned, deathly still as he stood in my church. Behind me, Constance began to shake the bars of her cage, her shrill shriek cutting right through Finnis's pheromone trap.

"No," I said, waving my hand insultingly as if that might get rid of the "obey me" pheromones. Okay, they felt kinda good, but I knew the lie they were, and I'd seen the monster he was—right down to his core.

Finnis went still, his lips pressing. *Don't hear that word very often, do you, you entitled snot,* I thought. "This will happen," I said as Doyle cleared his throat, a hand rising to hide a smirk. "You can either step forward to chaperone its release, or stand by and watch someone else gain the credit and money. I'm offering you a chance to prosper. Take it."

Will you shut up! I thought as I smacked Constance's cage, and the vampire mouse finally went quiet. "Someone is going to make a lot of money," I added into the welcome silence. "And as Trent says, if you're not making it, you're losing it."

Finnis's hands trembled. He had quit breathing a while ago, becoming unmoving as thoughts and calculations fell through his mind. I tightened my grip on the ley line until my hair began to snarl. He knew better than to attack me in my own church, but I could tell it was just about killing him twice. "Demon or no," he said, "you won't survive if we call for your death."

I bobbed my head. I'd heard that before—and every time it had cost me almost more than I was willing to give to survive it. "Okay." I took a step back, glad Constance had stopped shrieking. "Then how about you add this into your calculations. I put Hodin, the demon you assumed was going to off me for you, in a veritable hell of an existence. I have been caring for the master vampire you sent to kill me. Or did you send her here hoping I'd kill her?" I added, and Constance made that eerie gurgling hiss again. "In less than a week, I forced the demons to toe the line and stop stealing people. If they have learned to respect me, maybe you should, too. But I bet that's not enough, either. I've noticed the undead are thicker than zombies. Here."

Never shifting my eyes from Finnis, I handed him Constance's cage.

Finnis twitched, his entire body jerking when the bedding Constance threw at him scored on his chest. Smirking, I waited, unmoving, until Doyle took her.

"Seeing Constance as a mouse does not scare me," Finnis said.

"It should," I said shortly. "You can turn her back with a gallon of salt water, but I wouldn't. She hates you more than she hates me." I leaned in, breath held to avoid the stench of angry vampire. "Unspell her. I dare you," I whispered, because that was where my true strength lay. I had turned their weapon, Constance, against them. That, he could understand. I might have transformed her into a mouse, but Finnis had sent her here to die—and she knew it.

Finnis's gaze flicked from mine for a brief second, and with that, I knew I had won. He had doubt. He was afraid.

"Get my soul curse out of FSCA hell, Finnis," I said, but this time it was a demand—and this time . . . he was listening. "You can either prosper from it as its champion or find yourself on the sidelines. I don't care. It's all the same to me."

And then I jumped, ley line energy crackling through me when Doyle moved, his grip jerking from Constance's cage.

"Catch her!" Jenks shrilled from the rafters, but it was too late and Constance's cage hit the floor as Doyle held his bitten hand, a ruby of crimson blood showing.

"You pantywaist troll turd. You dropped her!" Jenks shouted, his wings a tight hum as I danced away. Clearly upset, Jenks flew to the busted cage, water and bedding everywhere.

My breath caught at a caramel-colored blur. "Rex! Jenks, look out!" I shouted as the cat pounced on the cage, breaking it enough that Constance could wiggle out. In a flash,

Rex was after her, Jenks in hot pursuit as Constance ran down the hall and vanished under Hodin's door.

My held breath escaped in relief, but yeah, this wasn't good.

Tail switching, Rex patted at the crack before crouching down to wait.

"Stupid cat!" Jenks shouted, his dust an annoyed green as he came back. Oh, he could fly under the door well enough, but he wouldn't leave me alone with two vampires. Mood bad, he made a swooping, short stop before Doyle, hands on his hips and a scowl on his face. "Good going, moss wipe."

I met Doyle's eyes as he cleaned his bitten finger on the hem of his blah jacket. "I guess you won't be taking her," I said, worried. *Constance doesn't want to return to DC? Curious.* "I hope you enjoyed your stay in Cincinnati," I added, wanting Finnis out of my church. "Would you like Ivy or Pike to accompany you to the airport?"

"No." Finnis inclined his head, brow furrowed as he looked at Hodin's door. "I am . . . fine. Do you think you can catch her?"

Oh, worried, are we? I shifted my weight, hands loose and free. "Ivy is staying," I said flatly, and Jenks's dust shifted to a bright, happy gold. "Nina will be joining her at the earliest convenience. Make sure of it. Get her on a plane tonight if possible."

Doyle winced as Finnis's jaw clenched. Jenks's wing hum rose in pitch, and for a moment, I thought I might have gone too far, but then the undead vampire nodded. "Nina and Ivy will be allowed to return to Cincinnati."

I stifled another jump when Finnis spun with the quickness of the undead. His back unbowed and his steps long, he paced to the door. Doyle grimaced, clearly torn, and I said loudly, "You have six months. If there's no forward movement on the curse, I'm putting it on the illicit market." Because that was Trent's idea, and it was a good one.

Finnis jerked to a halt, the darkness in the room seeming

to pool about him. Turning, he stared, finally grinding out, "I will be in touch."

I couldn't tell if that was a threat or promise, but he was leaving and Ivy was staying. For now, it was enough.

I gave him a nod, and the imposing vampire opened the door and walked out. "Doyle!" he exclaimed, and the living vampire's gaze came up from the tiny bejeweled house amid the spilled water and bedding.

"For you," Doyle said as he handed me an envelope from his jacket's inner pocket. "You have until the end of the month to pay it, and then it goes to small-claims court."

"Doyle!" Finnis's shout came from the curb this time, directive and angry.

I opened the envelope to find a bill for repairs at the airport's parking garage. "This isn't small claims," I said, shocked at the amount, and Doyle grinned, his dark eyes glinting.

Jenks whistled long and low, his dust sifting down onto the paper. Lips pressed, I refolded it and stuffed it into a pocket to give to Trent. He'd done the damage. He could pay to fix it. *See, I can delegate,* I thought.

"A reminder that I don't work for you," Doyle said smugly. "There's also the question of you incarcerating a demon without trial. I'm going to need you . . . to . . ."

Doyle's words tapered off as I raised a hand for him to wait, my steps confident as I crossed the sanctuary to Ivy's baby grand and the purple folder lying atop it. *My God, it feels good to be one step ahead.* "I've got Hodin's original incarceration orders here," I said as I flipped it open and took out the two filings that Dali had couriered over. One was a stark, bleached white, the other a dull yellow parchment magically aged to look over two thousand years old. "And Dali's court order explaining his escape and giving me jurisdiction to commit him behind bars again. Would you be a dear and file them for me?"

Beaming, I handed the two orders to Doyle.

"Son of a bitch," he said, but he was grinning as he took them before he turned and nearly jogged out of my church.

"Son of a bitch!" he said again on the steps, but it was in astonishment, not anger, and it made me feel good.

"Sweet," Jenks said as I slowly followed Doyle to shut the door. "Sorry about Constance," Jenks added as we watched Doyle slide in behind the wheel, all four windows going down even as he put the car into drive and sped off. "Doyle is a wuss. You gonna dump your salt vat so she can't change back?"

"Good idea," I said, glancing behind me toward the kitchen. *Great. Just great.* We had a vampiric mouse in the church. She had about four hours to dig herself down six feet or she'd be twice dead come sunup.

"Getty might be able to find her. She decided to stay," Jenks added, and I felt a smile.

"Good," I said as I looked the other way for Trent. "You need to kiss her often."

His tiny sigh was full of memories of Matalina. "I know."

Where are you, Trent? . . . I gave the street a final glance before I shut the door. The glow of my phone lit the foyer as I scrolled for Trent. "Trent's not going to be happy he missed Finnis," I said as I texted him to take his time and maybe pick up some ice cream. "You'd think him having downtown property would make it easier for him to juggle his time, not harder."

"He's not at Carew Tower," Jenks said as he flew into the sanctuary. "He's at Dalliance."

I jerked to a halt, phone in my pocket. "He's . . . Excuse me?"

CHAPTER

32

JENKS'S DUST FLASHED AN EMBARRASSED RED. "AH, CAN you pretend I didn't say that?"

He flew backward before me as I paced across the sanctuary, following him. "Why is Trent in the ever-after?"

"Please, Rache," he pleaded. "It's a surprise. For your birthday."

I scuffed to a halt, excitement bringing me to a standstill. "I'm surprised. Is it a party?" I turned to the ley line running through my church. It would put me into the ever-after a five-minute walk from Al's wagon, twenty from Dalliance. Alternatively, I could go out to Eden Park and cross there, but again, it would take me twenty minutes to make the drive.

"Rache, wait!" Jenks cried as I put a hand into the line, feeling it echo with my aura's signature. *Someday*, I thought. *Someday I will be able to use the lines properly.*

"Etude!" I called as I remembered he was lurking on my roof. "I need a lift!"

Wings rasping, Jenks hovered annoyingly close. "Rache . . ." he all but whined. "You're going to ruin the surprise."

"I told you, I'm already surprised," I said, jumping when the twin doors slammed open with a thunderous boom as Etude monkey-swung into the church, his enormous feet skidding to an exuberant halt three feet from me.

"Where?" the huge gargoyle rumbled, his red eyes bright and leathery wings held open.

"Dalliance," I said, and he held out an enormous, craggy hand for me to step up onto it and, from there, astride his shoulders as if he was a gigantic horse. Gargoyles could translocate using the lines, taking anyone they wished with them. They were the ones who had taught the demons.

Jenks bobbed up and down, clearly distressed. "You're going to get me into trouble," he said. "Don't tell Trent I blabbed. Wait!" he shouted as I settled myself, my head nearly in the rafters. "I want to come."

"But then he would know you told me," I said with a smirk.

"Rache," he whined, a purple-green dust sifting from him in distress.

Eyes closed, I felt myself relax into the ley line, letting it pour through me as I nudged my aura to match it. Etude did the same, and in the breadth of time it takes a molecule to spin, we vanished, Jenks's last cry echoing in our thoughts.

My lungs rebounded to pull in the rain-scrubbed night air of the ever-after. Crickets and grass frogs sang, and I opened my eyes, sending them up into the starry sky. "Wow," I whispered, breathless. There were no city lights to mar the beauty, no primitive fire to dull all but the brightest. *Bis clearly designed this,* I thought as the Milky Way spread from horizon to horizon, silver, amber, and blue as billions of stars glowed in a hazy, remembered beauty.

Etude made a low rumble of pleasure, and then I gasped as his wings made one leathery pulse down, and we rose, my stomach falling as my grip tightened and the wind beat at me.

"That way," I said, pointing, and his gray-tufted ear swiveled, knowing where I was looking by the sound of my voice. "Thank you. Trent's late. He might be in trouble."

"That is my thought as well," Etude said, his low words almost a feeling as they rumbled up through me.

"You know about the surprise?" I said, my gaze on the dark woods to find Al's fire as we flew over the trees—but there was nothing.

"I do."

"What is it?" I asked, then pulled myself straighter, squinting at the gray haze filling the depression where Dalliance was—or should be, rather. "What is that?" I said, but Etude was already spiraling down, aiming unerringly to the misty nothing.

"Etude?" I called, worried when he showed no signs of stopping, an eager excitement in his silence as he unflinchingly angled to the fog. I gasped as we were suddenly in it, cool and damp. *Tomato soup?* I thought as the acidic scent tickled a memory.

"Hold tight," Etude warned, and I shifted my weight as he landed, his great wings beating away the odd sliver of fog to show the back door to my mother's kitchen.

"Crap on toast, it's real," I said as I stared at it, fog to the right and left, the bright yellow paint dulling with dirt at the threshold. Shadows of movement showed beyond the curtained window over the sink, and I swear I could smell toast. *This is my surprise? What is Trent doing? Killing Hodin?*

"If I wanted Hodin dead, I would have done it myself," I whispered, worried as I slid from Etude. "No wonder Jenks let it slip."

Etude only rumbled, an odd stiffness in him as he settled into a crouch outside the door, his white-tufted ears pricked and lionlike tail twitching as he stared at the moving shadows.

Unnerved, I strode forward, but my reach for the knob hesitated. Trent was singing.

I dropped back, feeling my expression empty as his

voice lifted and fell, beautiful and deadly with the power of a curse within it. A spell-hazed memory rose up with his singsong words, rising and falling, luring. I knew this curse. It was the one he had used to pull my soul from me and put it in a bottle. He'd done it to save my life when my body had been too broken to hold it. If Trent had not held my soul while my body healed, I would have died.

Unfortunately, once called, a soul remained vulnerable to a summons again, and I felt myself begin to slip into a dull haze, drawn by his voice. Slowly, my eyes lidded as a promise of peace stole into my heart.

And then I jumped, snapping to a harsh alertness when someone pulled on the ley line. Hard.

"Hurry up, Kalamack!" Al shouted, his voice jerking me from Trent's charm.

"Al?" I whispered. Pulse fast, I shoved the door open. If his tracings were burned, he'd have nothing to protect himself from Hodin. Hodin might not be able to die because he was encoded into the tulpa. But Al could.

I stopped, stock-still, on the threshold as elven magic tugged at me. The inane urge to wipe my feet rose and fell. Trent stood before the upended Formica table, wreathed in a haze of sparkled power, the purple ribbon of his Sa'han status about his neck. A glowing spiral of magic glowed at his feet and a bottle rested in his hand—a bottle to hold a captured soul. *Hodin's?*

"Damn you back to the Turn, pixy!" Al snarled, jerking my attention to him. He was struggling with Hodin, and I put a hand to my mouth as my teacher glared at me in annoyance. Hodin was bound in strips of charmed silver, all but immobile, but still he fought, red eyes bloodshot and teeth bared. "I give you one job," Al said, flicking his hair out of his face as his thick fist thumped into Hodin's gut and the thinner demon bent double, gasping.

"What are you doing!" Horrified, I lurched in, only to be jerked back by Dali. My feet skipped on the worn linoleum, and I struggled to find my balance as the placid demon gripped my biceps.

"You couldn't have created a larger room for Hodin's prison?" he grumped as he pushed me into the cupboards behind him, holding me there as Al dropped Hodin onto the spiral's center.

They're taking Hodin's soul? Why?

"Let *go!*" I demanded, shooting a stab of energy into Dali, but the old demon seemed to appreciate it, grinning as if I'd goosed his butt.

"You can't do this!" Hodin screamed, utterly terrified as he lay at the circle's center. "It will eat me alive!"

I froze, suddenly realizing what was going on. Trent had a bottle. They weren't trying to take Hodin's soul. They were going to add to it. They were going to add the baku. It was going to be a punishment worse than death, and perhaps the only one fitting of his crimes. Hodin couldn't die, but the baku was going to eat his soul shell by shell until he was empty. Perhaps then, Hodin would be made safe.

"Let me go," I whispered, white-faced, and this time, Dali did.

Al shoved his brother back onto the spiral. "Luckily—or unluckily—you can't die," he said, clearly exhausted as he glanced wearily at me. It was obvious he wasn't happy I was here watching this. "The baku will feed on you forever, starving and ravenous. Peel you down until you are nothing but the emptiness that you left in all of us. But unlike us, you will just keep living the nightmare—Hodin."

"Trent," I breathed, knowing this was not who he wanted to be, and from behind me, Dali harrumphed.

"You can take the elf out of the war, but you can't take the warlord out of the elf," Dali said.

"No!" Hodin exclaimed, a terrifying counterpart to Trent's singing, his calm, soothing voice asking for the Goddess to attend and give her blessing. *And Dali approved of the elven magic?* "No! Please! I'll do anything! Anything!" Hodin babbled.

His pleas struck me to the core, but I didn't move, didn't raise a protest. I would not. Not for Hodin. I had agreed to stand between him and his ugly past, give him a chance to be something better, and he had willfully chosen to use my trust to betray me, hurt my friends, and take what was mine—but mostly hurt my friends. Perhaps this was the only justice that would make amends for his atrocities, both past and present. But as I remembered what Al had told me, I wasn't sure anything could pay for what he had done.

"You will do anything?" Al said, voice harsh as he shoved his brother back to the spiral's core again. "Then do this. Kalamack, now!"

And as Trent sang, he opened the soul bottle.

"No!" Hodin cried in anguish, his voice choking to nothing as a glittering silver rose from the bottle. "Please, no!" Hodin screamed, eyes fixed upon the glowing haze, knowing what it was.

Pity welled up. I turned to Trent but it was too late. The haze had touched the spiral, and with the quickness of a snapped whip, the glow raced through the glyph to the center, where it vanished.

Hodin spasmed, shaking in his bonds, choking.

And then I quailed as Hodin opened his eyes . . . and found mine. He was—the baku. And it remembered me.

"You are mine!" Hodin snarled, struggling anew against his bonds of spelled silver. "Mine!" he shouted, and Trent fell away, slumped to the floor against the cupboards, the basket of his spelling supplies in his arms.

"Son of a mother pus bucket, the Kalamack elf did it," Al whispered as Hodin wiggled himself off the spiral. The enormous glyph was dark and empty of power. It had done its task and was now nothing more than a chalk line on my mother's kitchen floor.

"You will be *mine*!" Hodin raged, staring at me through his matted hair.

But I knew I was safe. Hodin's aura was static, unable to change thanks to the curse I had laid in him. It had been to keep him from jumping out, but now it would keep the baku from escaping. It was in Hodin for all eternity.

Exhausted, Trent lifted his head, a heavy regret in him as he pulled his basket closer, fingers shaking as he looked inside.

"Okay!" Dali shouted as Al gave Hodin a vicious shove, and I danced back as the demon slid across the kitchen and into the cabinets with enough force to make the overhead light shake. "Gally, we are done," Dali added. "Wrap it up. I'm hungry."

Al wasn't finished yet, though, and with a gut-wrenching yell of satisfaction, he slammed his fist into Hodin's jaw. The baku-ridden demon collapsed, knocked out. Panting, Al slowly got to his feet, clearly pained as his knuckles bled. He was bleeding, unable to use a charm or curse to mend his torn skin, and I felt my heart break. What had he lost so that I might walk the path I wanted?

"Now we are done," Al rasped, and I watched, numb, as he shuffled to my mom's old fridge and opened it to show the familiar outlines of Dali's jukebox.

Hodin coughed, struggling to regain consciousness. Behind him, Trent got to his feet, his basket in his grip. "Don't leave me. Don't leave me!" Hodin cried out, reaching as Al punched a button on the jukebox.

"No-o-o-o—" Hodin's voice vanished. I yelped as suddenly the counter I was leaning against was gone and I fell to the sand, hitting it with an abrupt thump. The scent of toast and tomato soup became the sour, earthy smell of goats and camels. The ceiling hazed, then cleared to show the stars beyond the softly hissing fronds of tall palms. There was silence but for the sifting sand and the whisper of an established dung fire. Etude waited, his huge shape catching the light to make him look like Death's mount.

"Not being able to use that tulpa is going to ruin me," Dali complained as he sat on a sand-worn pillow by the edge of the bright fire. "It's got the baku in it. You made it worthless, elf."

I got up, half expecting to see my mom's kitchen behind me, but it was Al, and I took his swollen hand in mine, sure now that he was unable to use the lines properly. *Al, I am sorry. No one should pay for my choices but me.*

"Consider it a bonus," Al said, weary as he pulled his hand from mine, a devilish glint to his eyes. "If you deem the tulpa too dangerous to use, then Rachel will not be here, picking up any more elven lore." Mood saucy, he turned to Dali. "Unless you want her talking to Hodin?"

"No."

Al's smirk became a frown as he looked at Etude. "You knew we didn't want her here. What if it hadn't worked?"

"I wanted to be here whether it did or not," Etude said, his great hands clasped. "Did it?"

Did what work? I thought, and then a bright hope stabbed through me as it all came together. They had let the baku out of the bottle. That meant . . . Bis?

"Trent?" I whispered as I saw him with that basket, and he blinked fast, tears running unremarked from him as he pulled the silken cover from it and Bis opened his eyes, found mine—and smiled.

ACKNOWLEDGMENTS

I'd like to thank my editor, Anne Sowards, whose generous insight, excitement, and kindness helped rekindle the fire of the Hollows in me, and my agent, Jennifer Jackson, without whom the Hollows would have ended before it was truly done.

Rachel Morgan will learn
that the price of loyalty is blood in the
next Hollows novel from #1 *New York Times*
bestselling author Kim Harrison.

DEMONS OF GOOD AND EVIL

Rachel Morgan, witch-born demon, suspected that
protecting the paranormal citizens of Cincinnati as
the demon subrosa would be trouble. But it's rapidly
becoming way more trouble than even she could have
imagined.

While Rachel and her friends may have vanquished
the trickster demon Hodin, his mysterious associate
known only as "The Mage" is eager to finish what
Hodin started, beginning with taking down Rachel's
power structure piece by piece.

When he frames Rachel for the death of a powerful coven member and the vampire leaders in DC
threaten to send a new master vampire to take the
city in hand, Rachel's friends Ivy and Pike are forced
into hiding, and even her lover, Trent, finds himself
under fire. With her world falling apart, Rachel desperately needs help. But with all of her supporters
under attack, her only hope is to make a deal with the
unlikeliest of allies. . . .

Ready to find
your next great read?

Let us help.

Visit prh.com/nextread

Penguin
Random
House